"That was crazy," she gasped as soon as he ended the kiss.

"Not crazy," he corrected, "wonderful." Keaton framed her face with his fingers and held her still so he could look into her eyes. "If you cook like you kiss, I'm going to be in trouble."

"In trouble how?"

"I won't be able to stop myself from wanting more."

Color flooded her cheeks. Lark hooked her fingers around his hands and pulled them away from her face. "I don't think you'll have to worry on either account."

"What makes you say that?"

"Because you've never struck me as a man who does anything that isn't good for him."

"What about kissing you isn't good for me?"

She set her hands on her hips and regarded him incredulously.

"Have you forgotten the bad blood between our families? It already forced Skye and Jake out of town. Can you imagine how bad it would be if we were caught?"

"So what are we supposed to do with these feelings between us?"

"What feelings? It's just a simple case of proximity lust. Nothing more."

Keaton studied her, wondering if that was what she truly believed, or if it was a way to let him off the hook. "Is *proximity lust* a scientific term, or something you just made up?"

* * *

Because of the Baby...
is a Texas Cattleman's Club: After the Storm novel—
As a Texas town rebuilds, love heals all wounds...

BECAUSE OF
THE BABY…

BY
CAT SCHIELD

Published in Great Britain 2015
by Mills & Boon, an imprint of Harlequin (UK) Limited,
Eton House, 18-24 Paradise Road, Richmond, Surrey, TW9 1SR

© 2015 Harlequin Books S.A.

Special thanks and acknowledgement are given to Cat Schield for her contribution to the TEXAS CATTLEMAN'S CLUB: AFTER THE STORM series.

ISBN: 978-0-263-25244-6

51-0115

Harlequin (UK) Limited's policy is to use papers that are natural, renewable and recyclable products and made from wood grown in sustainable forests. The logging and manufacturing processes conform to the legal environmental regulations of the country of origin.

Printed and bound in Spain
by CPI, Barcelona

Cat Schield has been reading and writing romance since high school. Although she graduated from college with a BA in business, her idea of a perfect career was writing books for Mills & Boon. And now, after winning the Romance Writers of America 2010 Golden Heart Award for series contemporary romance, that dream has come true. Cat lives in Minnesota, USA with her daughter, Emily, and their Burmese cat. When she's not writing sexy, romantic stories for Mills & Boon® Desire™, she can be found sailing with friends on the St Croix River, or in more exotic locales, like the Caribbean and Europe. She loves to hear from readers. Find her at www.catschield.com. Follow her on Twitter, @catschield.

To Sunshine Grandahl
for sharing her preemie experiences,
and Sarah M. Anderson for being
such a fantastic collaborator.

One

Lark Taylor gathered a deep breath as the elevator doors opened. Plastering a pleasant expression on her face, she straightened her spine. Time to go to work. With a cake box balanced carefully in her hands, she strode down the short hallway to the nurses' station in front of the ICU. The three women behind the desk didn't notice her approach, or if they did, they ignored her.

"So I told him if he thinks he's going hunting two weekends in a row, he can find a new girlfriend." Marsha Todd, a forty-year-old divorced woman with no kids, was holding court as usual. With her bleached teeth, flawless makeup and manicured nails, she was the same sort of shallow individual who had tormented Lark in high school. "So naturally he's staying home. He might not be the brightest guy I've dated, but he's smart enough not to mess with all this."

Jessa and Chelsea, the two other nurses working the ICU today, laughed in appreciation. Taken separately, either woman was tolerable to work with. Jessa was a quiet single mom with a three-year-old son and Chelsea had an alcoholic husband who worked construction. With Marsha as their ringleader, however, they took on a pack mentality. Which meant, if they didn't want to be on the bottom of the pecking order, they'd better make sure someone else was. That person was Lark.

"You're early," Marsha remarked, her tone pitched in criticism as Lark set the cake box on the counter.

"I'm going to spend some time with Grace. I just wanted to drop this off first."

"What is it?" Jessa asked. The nicest of the trio, she had borne the brunt of Marsha's bullying until Lark transferred to the ICU three months ago.

"A cake for Marsha's birthday tomorrow."

"You bought me a cake?"

"Actually I made it."

Chelsea opened the cake box and peered in. "You made this? Really? Looks store bought."

"It's a hobby of mine."

"It's beautiful." Jessa's brown eyes were wide with appreciation. "How long did this take?"

"A couple hours," Lark said, her anxiety easing beneath her coworkers' admiration.

"How did you do the flowers?" Jessa asked. "The roses look real."

"I use a frosting tip and something called a rose nail."

Marsha barely glanced at the three-layer white cake painstakingly decorated in a basket weave pattern with buttercream frosting and royal icing daisies, roses and forget-me-nots. "If it's not gluten free, I can't eat it."

"Sorry, I didn't know that."

"I don't know how. I talk about it all the time." But never to Lark.

"I guess I'm so focused on the patients." Lark realized even as she uttered the excuse that it was the wrong thing to say. "I haven't heard you mention it."

"And speaking of patients," Marsha said, shooting looks at both Jessa and Chelsea. "We'd better get in and check on them."

All three of her coworkers walked away, abandoning Lark at the desk with her cake and her disappointment. Her efforts to make friends with the other nurses these last few months had all been a bust. Marsha was top of the social order in the ICU and she didn't like Lark.

Not knowing what to do with the birthday cake that Marsha couldn't eat, Lark took it down to the surgical floor. She knew her former coworkers would appreciate the treat. Leaving the cake box on the desk of her friend Julie with a brief note explaining what had happened, Lark headed to the stairs.

One floor down from the surgery floor was the maternity ward. Lark had worked at the hospital for three years without ever setting foot on the floor where children were born until a fateful night three months ago when her niece was born. Estranged from her sister these last four years Lark hadn't been able to tell the medical staff when Skye was due, but they'd been able to surmise she was about twenty-eight or twenty-nine weeks along.

Reaching the third-floor landing, Lark headed to the door that would take her into the maternity ward. She put her hand on the door and pushed it open an inch, finding her way blocked by a broad shoulder clad in a navy blue cotton shirt. Dark brown hair in desperate need of a cut curled upward against the shirt's collar.

The tall, ruggedly built man on the other side of the door was Keaton Holt, brother of the man Lark's sister had run off. She seldom encountered him around Royal. He spent most of his time at the family ranch and only made occasional visits into town. She usually heard about those from her father, who complained every time Keaton showed up at the Texas Cattleman's Club.

All that had changed after the tornado ripped through town and a pregnant Skye had been discovered in her overturned rental car.

Keaton was talking on his cell, fully engaged in conversation, and hadn't noticed her presence. Lark would have to interrupt in order to get past. It would mean she'd catch Keaton's attention and have to brave the intensity of his sharp blue gaze that seemed to see straight through her.

As Lark debated retreating back down the stairs and

avoiding Keaton altogether, his words floated through the narrow crack between the door and frame.

"That's why I demanded we get the DNA test run. You're Grace's grandmother. You shouldn't be limited to staring at her through the NICU window."

"Of course Grace is his daughter. He and Skye were madly in love when they left Royal." Keaton's voice rang with arrogant confidence that chafed Lark's already frayed nerves. "He chose her over his family. And yeah, he's a stubborn jerk, but if things had ended between them, we'd know."

Lark leaned as far forward as she dared, her curiosity getting the better of her. Day after day she'd sat beside her sister's unconscious body, desperate to know what Skye had been doing in the years since she left town. Did Keaton have the answers?

"I don't know where Jake is." And Keaton sounded far from happy about that. For the last few months, Lark had rebelled against the possibility that Jake was Grace's father. He'd made no attempt to get in contact with Skye in the three months since she was hurt by the tornado that had devastated Royal. That was why Lark had resisted the DNA test as long as she had. What sort of man abandons his child and the woman he loves? A no-good Holt, that's who.

"I haven't been able to get a hold of him. I've called his company several times, but his assistant has given me the runaround. From some of his other staff I was able to find out that he's out of the country, but they refused to give me any more information, so I have no idea where he's gone."

Until this moment Lark hadn't realized that Jake didn't know about Skye. She'd just assumed that he hadn't rushed to Skye's side because their relationship was over. Skye wore neither an engagement nor a wedding ring, and her fingers hadn't borne any telltale band of paleness that indicated a ring had recently been removed. Given how passionate their love had been when they first left Royal, Lark couldn't believe Jake and Skye had been together four years without making some legal commitment to each other. Especially after Skye became pregnant.

"Of course I explained that Skye was hurt. His assistant…" Keaton's frustration was audible, but there was pain in his voice, as well. After a long moment, he continued. "The last time I called for Jake, she told me that she'd been informed he didn't have a brother."

Despite the animosity that existed between their families, Lark winced in sympathy. She and Skye hadn't had any contact these last four years either. She'd been shocked upon moving back to Royal to discover Skye and Jake were still involved and actively hiding their relationship from their parents. Several times in the few months between Lark's return to Royal and Skye's departure with Jake, Lark had warned her sister that she was making a huge mistake trusting a Holt. When Skye chose Jake over her family, Lark had said some harsh things.

She'd accused Skye of being selfish and inconsiderate. At the time Lark had believed her indignation was righteous, but as the years passed, she realized that what she'd perceived as concern for her parents was really resentment born of envy that her sister had chosen to be happy.

"It's okay, Mom. I get that Jake hasn't been able to forgive me for putting them in a position where they felt they had no choice but to leave town," Keaton said, his tone dark. "I can live with being disowned by him. But that doesn't mean I stopped caring about him or his family. He and Skye might not be married, but she is still family. That's why I wanted proof that Grace is his daughter."

"Excuse me." Someone had asked Keaton to step aside.

He nodded and moved out of the way before continuing. "The DNA test should be back today or tomorrow. In the meantime I hired an investigator to find out where Jake has gone."

Before Lark could move, the door she'd been leaning against was pulled away. Off balance, she stumbled into the hallway that led to the NICU. After she made a couple ungainly sidesteps, someone caught her by the arm, steadying her.

She glanced up at her savior. Softened by a thick fringe of black lashes, Keaton Holt's denim-blue eyes captured her full attention. At five feet ten inches, Lark rarely encountered a man she could look up at. Keaton towered over her, making her feel normal. Maybe even a little dainty.

The heat at her center had worked its way into her cheeks by the time she realized she wasn't standing on her own two feet, but still relying on his support. She should have regained her balance and gotten the heck out of there. Keaton and Gloria had to be wondering if she'd been listening in on their conversation. But the leashed strength of the man slammed into her like a runaway calf.

Gripped by what could only be described as a rush of lust, Lark floundered in confusion. Starting when she was a baby, her father's bedtime stories had revolved around the wrongs inflicted on her family by the Holts. She couldn't possibly want Keaton Holt.

"Thank you." She disengaged her arm and took an awkward step back. With effort she ripped her attention away from his sculpted lips. Twenty feet away the room that housed the smallest and sickest babies offered refuge. "Excuse me."

"Lark." Keaton's deep voice rumbled through her as she fled. "Lark, we need to talk."

His voice didn't recede the way it should if she was escaping him. Bracing herself, Lark stopped beside the door that led into the NICU unit.

"The DNA results are due shortly."

"I know," she mumbled, miserable at the idea that she'd have to share Grace with any of the Holts. Unfortunately and against her better judgment, she was also sympathetic to their plight. If she'd been denied access to her niece, she would be beyond miserable.

"We need to talk about what's going to happen next."

"Nothing is going to happen."

"That's not really the case, is it? Once the test determines that Grace is Jake's daughter then I have the same obligation to her as you do."

"Obligation?" Did he seriously think what she felt for Skye and Grace was born of responsibility? She loved her sister and would do everything in her power to take care of Grace. "You think it's your duty to step up because your brother is nowhere to be found." Lark's earlier compassion was trampled beneath an onslaught of annoyance. "You needn't bother. I have matters well in hand."

"I don't think of it as a duty, but I do feel responsible because Jake isn't here."

"And why isn't he?"

"I'm pretty sure he doesn't know what's going on." Keaton set his hand on his hip and gazed beyond her shoulder. "If he did, he'd be at her side."

Lark wasn't at all convinced. "What makes you think they're even still together?"

"My brother loves Skye. Grace is his daughter." Keaton's thick brows drew together. "That's all the proof I need."

Having had no way to reach her sister these last four years, Lark understood his frustration, but she wouldn't give him the satisfaction of admitting it. "Did you let him know Skye was hurt?"

Keaton's expression shifted into stoic lines. "I've spoken with his assistant, but she's refusing to forward any messages."

"That's quite an excuse." Lark blew out a breath. "If he and Skye were still together I believe he'd have moved heaven and earth to be here for her and Grace. I don't think he's her father."

But she wasn't as convinced as she pretended to be. Grace had Holt eyes and bone structure. That was why Lark had resisted the DNA test for so long. Her instincts told her Grace was Jake's daughter, but the feud that existed between the Taylors and Holts made it so hard for Lark to do the right thing. In the end Keaton's determination and threats of legal action had worn her down.

"Then who is Grace's father and where is he?" Keaton demanded.

Lark had no more idea what had been going on between Skye and Jake than Keaton did, and she wasn't going to pretend any different. "I don't have a clue. We haven't spoken since she left Royal." Seeing Keaton's surprise, Lark continued. "I didn't think running away with your brother was a good idea and told her so."

"Because you didn't think a Holt was good enough for her?" Keaton's neutral tone kept his comment from sounding bitter.

Lark didn't want to fight with Keaton. She was sick of their families being at war. "I knew my father would disown her if she left."

Skye had always been her parents' favorite. They understood her. Unlike Lark, she'd been pretty and popular in school. She didn't lock herself away in books. Their parents didn't care that Skye's grades were good enough to keep her in the top twenty-five percent of her class; they loved the fact that she was a cheerleader and voted prom queen her senior year.

"I guess we have more in common than either of us knew."

"Seems we do." Tightness eased in Lark's chest. Regret had been her constant companion for four years. It had been a lonely time. Her parents refused to talk about Skye, and Lark had been too ashamed at how she'd treated her sister to confide in any of her friends.

"Thank you for letting me do the test." Keaton's voice softened. "My mother desperately wants to visit her granddaughter."

Regret swamped her at his words. Lark wished her parents had similar desires. "My parents haven't seen Grace."

The words spilled out of her with more bitterness than she'd intended.

"But once she leaves the hospital, they can see her as much as they want." Keaton had misinterpreted Lark's meaning.

"The problem is they don't want to see her."

Despite the harm that had befallen their daughter, Tyrone and Vera Taylor hadn't set aside their resentment over Skye's choosing to run off with a hated Holt. Oh, they'd visited her in the beginning when she was first brought in and they acted genuinely concerned, but as the months passed and Skye didn't wake after the medical treatment that induced her coma ceased, they'd retreated into bitterness.

"I don't understand."

"They still can't forgive Skye for running off with your brother."

"Don't you think this thing between our families has gone on too long?"

"Maybe." Everything she'd ever been told by her parents made her want to keep Keaton and his family as far from Grace and Skye as possible, but deep in her heart she knew that if Keaton was right and Jake was Grace's father, the Holts deserved equal time with her. "But you can't expect decades of mistrust to evaporate overnight."

"Jake and Skye got the ball rolling. The rest of us have had four years to adjust."

His challenge settled a huge weight on her shoulders. She was supposed to mistrust him, dislike him even. Since the late 1800s their families had been fighting over the ownership of two thousand acres dotted with several lakes, owned by Lark's family, that bordered the Holts' ranch. She'd grown up listening to her grandfather and father rant about what liars and cheats the Holts were. Never to be trusted. How they were willing to do whatever it took to take what didn't belong to them.

Lark was sick of the feud. It had started with a bill of sale that had gone missing back in 1898. Edwin Holt claimed Titus McMann had sold him the two thousand acres in order to fund his trip to Alaska where gold had been drawing prospectors since the 1880s.

Unfortunately, Titus had died before he could leave town and when Holt's bill of sale couldn't be found in the town records, his brother subsequently sold the land to John Taylor. Although there was nothing overtly suspicious about Titus's death, the fact that both the money he'd received from Edwin Holt and the bill of sale had mysteriously disappeared caused Holt to insinuate John Taylor had been up to no good.

A hard headed, unforgiving man, John Taylor hadn't appreciated the trouble Holt's allegations caused his family and did everything in his power to ruin his neighbor's business and reputation.

Lark hated that her parents continued to be obsessed with the ancient land dispute. They couldn't just let it go. It would be one thing if they'd been the ones who'd lost the land, but they'd won and couldn't rise above their hostility. And she was ashamed that she'd let their spiteful rhetoric poison her against her own sister, something she'd give anything to fix. If only Skye would wake up.

"I heard they're going to release Grace in the next few days," he continued.

"I know." The news that her niece was healthy enough to leave the hospital brought with it both excitement and panic.

"Are you planning on taking her home?"

Something about the intensity in Keaton's manner warned Lark that this wasn't just an innocent question. "Yes."

"She's just as much my responsibility as yours."

"You don't know that. If you did, you wouldn't have asked for a DNA test to prove she's your brother's daughter."

"The test isn't for me," Keaton assured her. "I trust that Jake and Skye are together and want everyone else to know it too."

"What makes you so sure?" Lark asked, wanting him to reassure her.

"Your sister loves my brother. She'd never leave him."

Then why had Skye been returning to Royal and where was Jake?

"I have to start work in forty-five minutes," Lark said. "I really want to go spend some time with Grace before that happens."

"What are your plans for her care while you're working?" Keaton's blunt question caught her unprepared.

Lark usually worked four twelve-hour shifts in a row and then had six days off. She liked the schedule, but it was going to make being Grace's primary caretaker a little challenging. Lark had no intention of putting the tiny baby in day care and she didn't like the idea of a stranger watching her while Lark was at work. She'd hoped her mother might be willing to watch her grandchild, but thanks to Skye's estrangement from the Taylor family, Lark was pretty sure the answer would be no.

"I haven't finalized anything."

"Good."

"Why good?"

"Because I intend to be involved."

Keaton saw immediately that Lark didn't like what he had to say.

"Involved how?"

"I'm going to take care of her while you're working."

"You, personally?" She shook her head. "What do you know about babies?"

"What I don't know I can learn."

"Don't you have enough going on with rebuilding your ranch?"

When the tornado had torn through in October, the Holt ranch house had been demolished along with several of the outbuildings. Fortunately Keaton's parents had been out of town and most of the ranch hands had been miles away checking the fence line for breaks.

Keaton and a few of his employees hadn't been so lucky. Most of the men working nearby had made it to shelter before the tornado hit, but Keaton and his foreman had been in the barn. Jeb had suffered a minor concussion and Keaton's shoulder had been dislocated by flying debris.

Because of the number of people injured by the tornado, Lark had been working in the ER when Keaton drove himself and three other injured men to the hospital. He recalled the way his spirits had lifted at the briefest flash of awareness that had sparked between them as her eyes first met his. A second later she'd blinked and became all business as she sorted out the extent of their injuries.

The fleeting connection reminded him of simpler days when they'd been kids and he found her both appealing and a curiosity. The three-year difference in their ages and the feud between their families had given him plenty of reasons to give her a wide berth. But it hadn't stopped him from wondering about her.

"My foreman can supervise when I'm not there and call me if something needs my immediate attention." He was determined to protect his brother's paternal rights. "I'm not negotiating with you, Lark."

A mulish expression settled over her features. "Do you even have a place you can care for her? Where are you living while your ranch house is being rebuilt?"

"A hunting cabin."

"A cabin?" Lark crossed her arms over her chest. "I don't think so. A preemie's lungs are delicate. She needs to be in a clean, warm environment free from drafts and damp."

"My parents are staying with friends in Pine Valley. I could bring her there on the days you work." He made the suggestion knowing it would never fly.

"That would be a terrible imposition on your parents' friends."

"Then I'll watch her at your house."

Lark's eyes widened. Her mouth popped open, but she must have recognized the determination on his face, because whatever refusal she'd been about to utter didn't come. Her facial muscles shifted into unhappy lines.

"I don't really think…" she began before turning toward the door to the NICU. "Do you have any idea what it's like to take care of a baby?"

"Some."

Giving him a doubtful frown, Lark motioned for him to follow her. Her stiff posture demonstrated she wasn't happy with his determination to be involved with Grace. Too bad. As her uncle, he had as much right to be with the infant as Lark.

In silence they walked down the row of incubators to the crib that held Grace. The anxious burn in Keaton's chest whenever he visited his niece had faded. Born ten weeks premature at two pounds, two ounces, the baby girl had gained almost three pounds since then and was now free of all sensors, IVs, pressurized oxygen and the feeding tube.

Acting as if Keaton had ceased to exist for her, Lark carefully picked up Grace and settled her into the crook of her left arm. "Hello, beautiful. How are you doing today?"

"She's doing great," said Ginger. The nurse on duty was a plump woman in her midforties with keen brown eyes and an engaging smile. "Ready to go home in a few days."

"I'm really excited about that," Lark said, adjusting Grace's pink hat embroidered with the word *Miracle*.

"Are you ready?"

"I have tomorrow off. I'm going to go shopping for everything."

"We're going shopping," Keaton corrected her, drawing Ginger's gaze. "Grace is my niece, as well. I'm going to be involved with taking care of her."

Ginger's eyes brightened. "That's wonderful. Grace is going to need a lot more care than the average baby. I'm glad you're going to be helping Lark out." The NICU nurse gave his arm a pat as she moved off to check on another infant.

"It's premature to talk about your involvement," Lark muttered as soon as the other nurse was out of earshot. "Grace's paternity has not yet been determined."

"Today or tomorrow we'll have the results and you'll see she's my niece as much as yours." Seeing the way Lark's mouth tightened, Keaton continued. "I intend to share the responsibility."

"A lot of men wouldn't want the responsibility of a pree-mie."

"I know Jake would expect me to take care of his daughter."

He wasn't surprised when she didn't respond. Lark had always struck him as the ultimate wallflower. Quiet and reserved, she watched more than participated. Why had he noticed her at all? Probably because he had similar tendencies. He kept to himself, enjoying the solitude of his cabin beside the small five-acre lake after a hectic day spent managing the ranch.

Her preoccupation with the baby gave him a chance to study her at length. Dressed in pale green scrubs, her wavy blond hair cut in a short bob, she gave off an *ignore me* vibe. She might have gone unnoticed if she wasn't so tall. At five feet ten inches, she would have made a great basketball or volleyball player, but she'd been more of a bookworm than an athlete. She and Jake had been classmates, but despite the fact that he'd been secretly dating her sister all through high school, Lark had never been part of the same crowd.

Three years older than Lark, the single year they'd attended the same in high school, Keaton hadn't had any contact with her, but she'd been extremely intelligent and that intrigued him. With a perfect score on her ACTs and could have had her pick of colleges if she'd wanted to venture out of Texas.

"Can you hold Grace for a second?"

Keaton blinked himself out of his thoughts. "Excuse me?"

"Can you hold Grace?"

"Why?"

Lark's long lashes fluttered upward as she glanced at him in confusion. "Because she needs to be changed and I need to go get some wipes. This is out." She pointed to a box on a nearby shelf.

Keaton stared down at Grace with his hands at his sides. She was so tiny. And he was a big guy more accustomed to wrestling with querulous calves than handling fragile things like a five-pound baby.

Lark stood and held Grace out to him with an impatient "here."

Alarm flashed through him. Keaton took an involuntary step backward. Still staring at Grace's precious face with its soft, perfect skin, he clasped his hands behind his back, feeling the rough scrape of calluses. It wouldn't be right to touch her delicate skin with anything so abrasive.

"Keaton?" Lark's tone had softened. "What's wrong?"

"She's really small." He paused. "And…"

"You're afraid to hold her."

"No."

"How do you expect to help me take care of her when you aren't comfortable enough to hold her?"

He let a breath hiss out from between his clenched teeth before replying, "I'm going to be fine. I just need a little time to get used to her."

"No time like the present." Lark moved into his space, her manner determined. "Give me your left arm."

He resisted her imperious tone for only as long as it took her to lift her gaze to his. She had the greenest eyes, like spring grass after a week of rain. How had he never noticed how beautiful they were? She raised her eyebrows at him. Moving slowly, giving her plenty of time to change her mind, Keaton let his arm swing forward.

She took ahold of his wrist and placed his arm against

his abdomen. Her fingers were warm and light against his skin. His heart shifted off its rhythm.

"You need to support her head."

Her shoulder bumped against his chest as she placed the delicate bundle in his arms. The top of her head swept beneath his nose, offering him a whiff of whatever shampoo she used. It reminded him of summertime and his mom's strawberry shortcake. His mouth watered.

"I'm not sure this is a good idea." But his protest came too late. Grace lay along his forearm, her tiny body swaddled from chin to toes. The baby couldn't move, much less roll off his arm, but Keaton rested his right palm lightly on top of her.

"You doing okay?" Lark's soft lips wore a slight smile as she watched him cradle Grace.

"Fine." As long as she didn't fuss or move, he'd be great.

"I'll understand if you tell me you can't do this," Lark said. "Taking care of a baby is hard work."

"I'm not afraid of hard work." Keaton suspected she wanted him to back out. That was the last thing he was going to do. "I can do this. I just have to get used to how small she is."

"You do have rather large hands." Lark touched Grace's cheek with a fingertip. Her hand grazed his, making his skin tingle. "They make her look smaller than she is. But she's stronger than you might think."

He had a hard time believing that. Grace picked that second to yawn hugely and open her eyes. Her gaze latched on to his face, the expression wide and startled. Keaton stared back, mesmerized, until her eyes shut again. It wasn't until that happened that he realized his heart was thudding erratically.

Expecting Lark to laugh at his inexperience, he was surprised to find that she'd moved off several feet. Panic flared for a second. He noticed that Lark was watching him, gauging how he handled the situation. He was far out of his comfort zone. *Relax,* he told himself. He had to appear comfortable being alone with his niece if he was going to convince Lark that he could take care of the delicate infant.

He shifted Grace a little, learning the feel of her. Once again the baby opened her eyes. This time she let out a strange little grunt. Keaton didn't know if that was normal or not. He needed to do some research on preemies. A little knowledge would go a long way toward making him feel more confident.

"You really don't need to do this," Lark said, coming up alongside him once more.

"Yes, I do." He shoved aside any lingering doubts about his ability to take care of such a tiny baby. "She grunts."

"I noticed that. Might have something to do with her acid reflux issues. A lot of preemies suffer from it. Luckily Grace isn't too bad."

Another thing for him to worry about. Damn Jake. Where the hell was his brother? Skye and Grace were his responsibility. Keaton stared down at the sleeping baby. Jake's unavailability disturbed him. It wasn't like his brother to go off the grid. Something bad must have happened, but Keaton didn't have a clue where to start looking.

"Here, let me take her." Lark had stepped into his space once more.

Keaton liked how his body reacted to her nearness. Since Skye's accident and Grace's birth, he'd been at the hospital at least a couple times a week to check on them. He'd had plenty of time to notice Lark and indulge his curiosity about her.

"I've got her."

"But she needs to be changed." She gave him an assessing look. "Have you ever changed a baby before?"

"No. And before you say anything, let me point out that I intend to learn everything there is about taking care of a baby before you have to go back to work."

"Everything?" She looked doubtful.

"Everything."

"Why do I believe you?"

"Because like you, I graduated at the top of my class?"

Her lack of surprise at his declaration told Keaton that she'd known this about him. Logic told him her confidence in him would grow if she understood he brought intelligence as well as determination to the table.

"I suppose just about everything can be found on the internet these days," she agreed.

"So, are you going to walk me through changing her?" Keaton ignored the voice inside his head warning him how tiny and fragile Grace was. If he let any nervousness show, he'd never convince Lark to let him help.

"If that's what you want."

"It's what I want."

Two

The ranch house where Lark and Skye had grown up was a sprawling single-story structure with a cathedral ceiling over the enormous, open great room. Lark's father was an avid hunter, and the walls between the windows and ceiling were covered with trophies of white-tailed deer and bobwhite quail.

Above the dining table hung a chandelier made of antlers. A second one hung above the living room seating area composed of a brown leather couch and love seat. A fire crackled in the fireplace. Set into a sixteen-by-fourteen foot wall and surrounded by large river rock, it took up a corner of the room. As usual the television was on. Lark could tell her father wasn't home because it wasn't tuned to a sports program. Instead her mother had on the shopping channel.

Lark's rubber-soled shoes made no sound on the tile as she went across the room, shrugged out of her wool coat and draped it over one of the dining chairs. Her mother was in the open kitchen. Lark tried to gauge her mother's mood as she drew near.

"Oh, Lark. Must you wear those scrubs? They do nothing for your figure. And you really should do something about those dark circles under your eyes. They're not attractive."

Having just come from a double shift at the hospital because Marsha had called in sick again, Lark couldn't summon the energy to explain why she looked so tired. "Is that a new lipstick?" she asked. It made her mother happy to talk about herself, and Lark needed her in a good mood.

Vera Taylor smiled, obviously pleased that her daughter had noticed. "Passion's Promise." She dug into her purse and pulled out a tube. "It might be a good shade for you. Come closer and let me see."

Fighting down impatience, Lark let her mother apply the vivid red, knowing it would look ridiculous on her. She rarely wore make-up at all, much less something as eye-catching as ruby lipstick.

"And a little concealer." Her daughter's docility had prompted Vera to pull a bag of make-up out of her purse. It was a rare mother-daughter bonding moment. Skye had been the pretty one, the one Vera could relate to. "Some color in your cheeks."

Vera stepped back and regarded her daughter with something akin to satisfaction. Lark's chest constricted. No matter how much she loved her mother, Lark had never been completely sure her mother felt the same way about her. Vera's childhood in San Antonio had been composed of a string of beauty pageants starting when she was one. She'd grown up praised for her beauty and style. Lark was sure it had broken her heart to give birth to a child of average prettiness and no interest in fashion.

Her mother must have thanked heaven when Skye came along. Beautiful and personable, with an abundance of talent. A mini Vera. A doll for her to dress and mold into the perfect pageant princess.

"See, that took me no more than a minute and a half and you look so much better. Imagine what would happen if we did a little mascara and eye shadow. You really should take more care with your appearance. What will people think?"

Considering that her patients in the ICU were unconscious and their family members too distressed to notice anything but their loved ones, Lark doubted that it mattered what she looked like. "I'll make more of an effort."

Knowing it would make her mother happy, Lark went into the small bathroom off the entry and checked her appearance. To her amazement, her mother was right. The little bit of makeup had transformed her. She was pretty. Not beautiful like Skye or their mother, but maybe attractive enough to make Keaton give her a second look?

The instant the thought entered her head, Lark banished it. Depending on how her mother responded to Lark's request to babysit Grace, she might just be stuck dealing with Keaton on a much more regular basis. If that happened, the last thing she needed was to start wondering if she appealed to him.

First of all, there was the hundred and some years of fighting between their families.

Then there was the little problem of whether or not she could trust him. Skye had put her faith in Jake and look what had happened. He'd vanished when she needed him most.

Last, but certainly not least, Keaton's brusque manner and ruggedness were a little overwhelming. Granted, he'd handled Grace with an acceptable amount of gentleness, but he'd obviously been on his best behavior. Would he be as careful with her?

And would she want him to be?

Swept away by the thought of his large hands skimming over her body, pulling her tight against him as his mouth claimed hers in a vigorous kiss, Lark shuddered in delight. Her skin warmed as the fantasy heated her blood. She could almost feel the scrape of his rough chin against her neck. Desire lanced through her like an electric shock, leaving her knees oddly unsteady.

"Mom," she called, emerging from the bathroom. "I have a favor to ask you."

Vera frowned. "I'm not sure this is a good time. Your father is very distressed about the loss of the tree farm and the damage done to the irrigation pipes."

Lark recognized this tactic. Her mother was always using Tyrone as an excuse to avoid doing things she deemed too great a burden. Ignoring her mother's broad hint, Lark muscled on.

"Grace gets to leave the hospital in a couple days."

"So soon?"

"It's been three months."

And as far as Lark knew, Vera had only stopped by once. Lark thought about Keaton's mom, visiting both a child she didn't fully believe was her granddaughter and the woman who'd been instrumental in taking her son away. Gloria had just as much reason to take her anger out on Skye and the baby, but she'd chosen a path of forgiveness instead.

"Things have been so bad around here, I haven't noticed how much time has passed."

"I was wondering if you could help me out with her."

"I don't know how I can find the time. There's so much to do here."

Lark braced herself to beg. Her parents had always made it hard for her to ask for anything. "Please, Mom. Can't you help me out until Skye gets better?"

"Are you sure you're the best one to be taking care of your sister's baby, Lark?"

"If not me, who else?"

"There's the father." Vera arched one perfectly shaped eyebrow. "Has he shown up yet?"

"If you mean Jake…" She didn't dare defend a Holt to her mother. "I don't know where he is. His brother hasn't had any luck locating him."

"Does that surprise you? None of those people can be trusted."

"Grace is a Taylor, Mom." Lark wasn't comfortable misleading her mother, but she hoped that maybe Vera would be more inclined to help if the conflict with the Holts wasn't part of the equation. "None of us had heard from Skye in four years. We don't even know if she and Jake were still together."

Vera considered this and for a brief second, Lark thought her mother might have forgiven how badly Skye hurt them when she'd run off with a Holt. But then Vera shook her head.

"I heard that brother of his is doing a DNA test. We'll know soon enough, won't we?"

"Grace is so beautiful, Mom," Lark said, hoping if she appealed to what her mother valued most that Vera might be persuaded to put aside her hurt and embrace her granddaughter. "She looks exactly like Skye." Which wasn't completely true, but hopefully Vera would be so thrilled to have a mini Skye to smother with love that she wouldn't notice the Holt eyes and bone structure.

"I'm sure she's quite lovely." Vera could have been speaking of a stranger's child for all the warmth she showed. "I can see that you are quiet passionate about taking on the responsibility of your sister's baby. I just don't think you realize how challenging it will be with you working full-time. A normal baby is exhausting and she's bound to have special needs. I'll speak with your father about helping you out with the child care costs."

And Lark knew her last hope was gone. Her mother wasn't ready to forgive Skye for turning her back on her family and would resist warming up to Grace.

"I don't want a stranger taking care of her," she told her mother, letting her disappointment show. It was looking pretty certain that her options had dwindled to Keaton.

"She's had strangers taking care of her for the last three months," Vera retorted a touch impatiently. "I don't see the difference."

The difference was Grace had needed medical attention and the nurses in the NICU were experts in the care of preemies. "I appreciate your offer of financial help, but I really think we owe it to Skye to do the best we can for Grace, and that means having her *family* take care of her."

A layer of frost coated Vera's features at Lark's mild reproof. Almost immediately she wished she could take back her criticism. No purpose would be served by alienating her mother, but along with regret, Lark noticed a tiny buzz of triumph for having stood up to her mother.

Unfortunately, Lark's confidence quickly faded as the reality of her situation engulfed her, and she drove home in such a state of disappointment that she didn't remember Keaton had invited himself on her shopping trip for the baby until she noticed the four-door pickup parked in front of her house.

The clock on her dashboard said quarter after two. She was fifteen minutes late. Lark settled her car in the garage and headed down the driveway to meet up with Keaton.

"I forgot we were getting together today."

"You look different." His eyes narrowed as he surveyed her.

When his gaze settled on her lips, Lark remembered the makeup her mother had applied. "I went to ask my mother for help with Grace. She thought I looked tired so she put makeup on me."

"You look very nice."

"Thank you."

Nice wasn't beautiful, but it was better than tired and drawn. And there was something new about the way he stared at her. Something intense and interested that made her pay attention to the flutters in her stomach and the slow heat building in her core.

"Are you heading back to work?" He indicated her scrubs.

Lark shook her head. The slight breeze cooled her skin. "One of my coworkers called in sick and we're shorthanded as it is. I pulled a double shift." A sharp wind cut off any further explanation she might have made. "Do you want to come inside?"

"I picked up a few things this morning. I'll go get them."

"You did?" Lark wasn't sure whether to be pleased or dismayed. He was really determined to take care of Grace.

From the backseat of the pickup he unloaded two enormous bags printed with the logo of the local baby store. Lark hastened to open her front door so he could carry his bundles inside.

"What is all this?"

"Bedding, clothes." Keaton followed Lark into her living room and deposited everything on her couch. He glanced around. "I know you said you hadn't bought a crib yet. I thought that was something we could do together."

Curiosity drove her to investigate what he'd chosen. Rather than an ultra-feminine pastel-pink ensemble, he'd chosen pale yellow sheets, bumper, dust ruffle and comforter with fun jungle animals. Lark spied pajamas, bodysuits and pants, tiny socks, bibs and a towel.

"You look surprised," Keaton said.

"I am. You did a great job. How did you know what to buy?"

"I went online and found a list for what to have on hand when bringing home a baby."

"She'll need some diapers. I can get those later today."

"I already contacted a diaper service."

"I figured we would just use disposables."

"Cloth is better for the environment."

She couldn't argue with that. "I wasn't sure I wanted to deal with keeping dirty diapers around until they could be picked up." And the unpleasantness that went along with doing that.

"The person I spoke with said they have a hamper that keeps the smell contained."

"Sounds like you've done your research."

"I always do."

Lark was surprised at the resentment brewing in her gut. Why was she annoyed with Keaton for being helpful? After she'd worked back-to-back shifts, she should be relieved that some of the preparations for Grace's homecoming were done. So what if she wasn't the smartest person in the room?

Thinking of her double shift reminded Lark just how tired she was. Before she could contain it, an enormous yawn broke free.

"Sorry."

"You're tired."

"Back-to-back shifts are brutal."

"I can take care of the shopping and get the crib. I'm sure you have a list of everything you still need to do before Grace leaves the hospital."

While she realized he was only trying to lend a hand, Lark rebelled at the thought of him taking over the preparations. Grace was her responsibility. If she was too tired to shop for her, how was she going to cope once her niece came home?

"No." Lark gave her head a vehement shake. "I want to pick out the crib and finish up the shopping. It won't take long. And you're right. I have a list of what I need."

She should be annoyed that he'd presumed things about her habits when he knew nothing about her, but she found herself flattered by his accurate read. Few people noticed her much less paid attention to her practices.

A glow bloomed in her chest, banishing her tiredness. She recognized Keaton as the source of her abrupt sense of well-being. His proximity had a disturbing effect on her world. Long ago she'd learned that asking for help was likely to end up in a rebuff. So she'd grown used to muddling along without anyone noticing she needed help much less offering to pitch in. Now she had Keaton insisting on lightening her load and was more than a little afraid to trust what he was offering.

Dropping her gaze to the floor, she said, "I'll be okay on my own."

Stubborn, Keaton noted, just like her father. She was determined to make things more difficult for herself rather than let him help. Pushing down his irritation, he said, "Why don't I put this stuff away while you change?"

"I'll take care of it." She drew near and reached out for the bags. "I'm going to put the crib in my room. The master suite is on the opposite side of the house from the other two bedrooms, and I don't want her so far away."

Keaton surrendered the purchases and watched her retreat. As soon as she was out of sight he surveyed his surroundings. The house was a split-floor plan, just as she'd described, with bedrooms on opposite sides of an expansive great room/dining room/kitchen combination. The design was modern; the open flow of the place made it nice for entertaining.

The rooms reflected exactly what he'd expected her style to be. Like him, she preferred furniture that was comfortable rather than stylish. She'd always struck him as practical, but she'd chosen dreamy Texas landscapes for her walls.

Books overflowed the shelves that flanked the fireplace, leaving no room for knickknacks. Or family photos. More books were stacked on the coffee table and each of the side tables. Which wasn't surprising: his every memory of her had a book in it.

One of the most telling aspects of her décor, and where their taste was drastically different, was the lack of electronics of any kind. That included a television, stereo and video equipment. As rustic as his cabin was, one of the first purchases he'd made before moving in was a forty-inch TV. How could she stand not having such an important connection to the outside world?

"Is something wrong?"

Keaton turned his head and spied her coming his way. She'd traded baggy scrubs for snug jeans that hugged her curves and a dark green sweater with a scoop neck that showed a hint of cleavage.

Knowing he was staring at her in mouthwatering fascination, but unable to help himself, Keaton answered her question. "You don't have a television."

"No." She knotted a scarf around her neck, slipped into her coat and gathered up her purse and keys.

"Any particular reason?" With the most seductive aspects of her form hidden from view, Keaton was able to wrestle his thoughts back into line.

"What's the point?"

"It's television."

She focused a sharp gaze on him. "Mindless entertainment. I prefer to read or bake. I like feeling productive."

"Not everything on TV is mindless. There are educational programs." After gesturing her to go first through the doorway, Keaton stepped aside so she could lock the front door. "Some interesting stuff."

"I'll take your word for it," she murmured, looking completely unconvinced as he opened the passenger door for her.

His pulse kicked up as she whisked past him. Was his attraction for her going to cause problems? She was already as skittish as a feral cat. If she got any inkling that he craved a taste of her lips, it might ruin the fragile cease-fire they'd established.

Keaton slid behind the wheel. Although he wasn't much for small talk, he thought engaging Lark in casual conversation would be a good way to build rapport. "You have quite a collection of books. What do you like to read?"

"I alternate between classics and contemporary fiction."

Hearing her answer, he sighed in frustration. Their taste in books wasn't going to keep the dialogue flowing easily. "I like biographies and nonfiction."

She nodded and subsided into silence. Keaton shot her a sideways glance and noticed that she was gripping her purse as if it was a lifeline. He wanted her to relax in his company. If she decided he wasn't the villain her father made him out to be, he would have an easier time staking his own claim on Grace.

Tapping his fingers on the steering wheel, Keaton tried again. "I downloaded a couple books on preemies to my e-reader in an attempt to figure out what to expect with Grace."

"At this point her gestational age is that of a newborn. She's still tiny compared to most, but her need for specialized care is done."

"I realize that I missed being around for her early days, but the books talked about kangaroo care where the baby is held against her mother's skin to help with her development."

Lark nodded. "Because she couldn't leave the NICU, I would go in before and after my shift and hold her like that." Her voice took on a husky note. "I wish we could have put her and Skye together, but I did the best I could."

"You did a great job," he assured her. "She's thriving and ready to leave the NICU." Once again it struck Keaton just how much Lark had been dealing with on her own, and ir- ritation with his brother flared anew. Whatever Lark and Grace needed, he would make sure they were taken care of. "But I think you've single-handedly shouldered the burden for too long. From everything I've read, preemies are more work than an average newborn, which means you're going to be even more exhausted. Let me help."

"I would be lying if I told you I was completely convinced of my ability to take care of Grace on my own. Frankly, I'm terrified of failing. I owe it to Skye to do what is best for Grace."

The level of conviction in Lark's voice resonated with Keaton.

"That's exactly what I'm trying to do for Jake." And in his brother's absence, he intended to protect Jake's rights. The Taylors needed to understand that Grace was also a Holt— Keaton was convinced of that, with or without the DNA test—and that they had an equal say in her care.

"We share a common goal, then." She stared hard at the road before them. "I'm sorry if I've been suspicious of your motives, but I have to tell you that all my life I've had to lis- ten to how untrustworthy your family is."

"It's not true."

"I'm sure where the rest of the world is concerned it's not, but when it comes to my family, there's been so much strife over the years I can't shake my uneasiness. And then there's the fact that I haven't spoken with Skye since she left

Royal. I don't know what happened between her and Jake.
I don't know if I'm doing the right thing letting you be involved with Grace."

He wasn't sure what had happened between Skye and
Lark, but he had a feeling the Taylor-Holt feud had caused
the sisters' relationship to suffer the same the way his and
Jake's had. Whatever had happened, there was no question
that Lark bore her sister no lasting ill will. Her dedication
to Skye and Grace was unflinching.

"I assure you—" His phone began to ring before he
could finish the thought. Not recognizing the number, he
keyed the truck's hands-free option and answered the call.
"Keaton Holt."

"Mr. Holt, this is Sabrina from Dr. Boyle's office." The
doctor who had administered the DNA test.

Keaton glanced Lark's way and spied her somber green
eyes on him. "What are the results?"

"The kinship index was well over 1.0. You and Grace
show a strong chance of being related. That's a very good
indication that your brother is her father."

Because they hadn't been able to collect Jake's DNA,
they'd had to test Skye and Keaton for an uncle comparison.
It wasn't as definitive as a paternity test, but the results were
strong and should satisfy all but the most skeptical.

"Thank you, Sabrina. Please send the results to me by
email."

"Of course, Mr. Holt. And congratulations."

Keaton ended the call and waited for Lark's reaction.
They were nearing the furniture store where she intended
to get Grace's crib. In a minute there would be no time for
private discussion.

"That's it, then," she said, her voice low and without in-
flection.

"You don't sound surprised."

"Grace looks like Jake."

Her admission annoyed him. "But you fought me on the DNA test."

"I didn't want to believe my sister and her baby had been abandoned by your brother." Her eyes hardened. "How could he be so unreachable? They need him."

"They have us," Keaton reminded her. "I'm going to do everything in my power to take care of my niece. And your sister."

"I spoke with my mother today. She and my dad are busy because of the damaged tree farm and other things." She ducked her head, her posture defeated. "I think I'm going to need help taking care of Grace."

He was saddened, but not surprised, that the Taylors had chosen not to pitch in to care for their granddaughter. Skye had been disowned by her parents when she left with Jake. The Taylors were obstinate and inflexible. It was their intolerance that had forced their daughter to run away from Royal and further aggravate an already bitter war between their families.

He wanted to touch Lark's hand, to reassure her that he was on her side. "You and I are going to make a great team."

"That remains to be seen," she remarked, some of her prickliness returning. "I'm dreading the scene when my parents find out you and I are working together to care for Grace."

If that bothered her, she was really going to hate where his thoughts had taken him over the last twenty-four hours. "You're doing the right thing for Grace, and that's what counts."

"I hate having to choose between being a good daughter and a good sister and aunt." Lark worried her fingers along her jacket's zipper. "I suppose you think it's stupid that a twenty-seven-year-old woman is afraid of upsetting her parents."

From what he'd experienced of Tyrone Taylor's temper, Keaton understood Lark's desire to avoid her father's wrath.

He guided the truck into the furniture store parking lot and took a spot not far from the front door. Keaton shut off the engine and sat in silence for a long moment. He was overwhelmed by a strong desire to protect her from anyone who made her unhappy, but she wouldn't appreciate his opinion about her parents even if all he was doing was defending her.

At last he spoke. "We can't let this rift between our families keep us from doing what is best for Grace."

"You're absolutely right." She nodded fiercely. "Let's go buy some baby furniture."

If Keaton had expected to spend the next two hours bored to tears while Lark shopped, he was pleasantly surprised when she went straight to a crib in the middle row and gave it a quick nod.

"I want this one," she told the sales clerk who approached less than a minute later. "As well as that changing table."

"I'll get it all written up. When do you want it delivered?"

"The sooner the better."

"Let me check the schedule. We have tomorrow afternoon available."

Lark frowned. "I have to work."

"That will be fine," Keaton said.

"But I won't be home."

"I'll meet them." He could see immediately that she was uncomfortable with the idea. "You might as well get used to having me in your house. I'm going to be taking care of Grace there, after all."

"You're right." Lark shook her head. "I haven't had to share my space with anyone since buying my house two years ago."

"You're never lonely being on your own?"

"Sometimes." She offered him a tiny smile. "Mostly I love it. I walk in my front door and don't have to worry about anyone but me."

"Bringing Grace home is going to change that."

"I don't mean it the way it sounds. It's just that with Skye coming home, my parents are stressed out and things around the hospital have been really challenging since the tornado. I moved from the surgery team to ICU so I could be closer to Skye and am having a hard time with the nurses I'm working with. Everything I say gets twisted around. I feel as if I'm constantly walking on eggshells. It's exhausting."

"Sounds like you need a break."

"I'm taking a week off when Grace comes home." She gave a happy sigh. "I'll need it to get her settled in."

With the crib paid for and the delivery arrangements finalized, Keaton and Lark headed back to his truck. He scanned Lark's face as she buckled herself in. She looked worn to the bone.

"Can I buy you dinner before I take you home?"

She gave him a weary smile. "I'm too tired to be much company."

"How about takeout?"

"Are you always this persistent?"

Yes, when something was important to him, and Lark's well-being was rapidly climbing his priority list. "I don't feel right taking you home without feeding you."

Besides, he wanted to spend more time in her company. She intrigued him. They'd been neighbors most of their lives, their families had been at odds with each other for generations. He knew little about her beyond what was common knowledge, but had long harbored a sense that they could be kindred spirits if circumstances were different.

"Obviously you are not going to take no for an answer and I'm too tired to argue." She leaned her head against the back of the seat and closed her eyes. "But just because I gave in this once, don't think you can get your way every time."

He felt a smile tug at his lips as he started the car, but refrained from pointing out that ninety-nine percent of the time people did as he indicated because he was right. She'd figure that out soon enough.

Three

"I'm taking Grace home today," Lark told her comatose sister as she finished up her last shift for a week. "I hope you're okay with that. She's ready to leave and I'm her closest relative."

The closest one that wanted her, anyway.

"I wish we could get in contact with Jake and let him know about you and Grace. It would be nice if you could wake up and tell us where he is." She paused as her throat closed up.

The hope that Lark had clung to while her sister's coma had been medically induced had wavered in the days since the doctor had taken Skye off the Pentobarbital and she hadn't awakened. As a medical professional, Lark was well aware her sister's chances of ever waking diminished with each day that passed.

A couple deep breaths allowed her to go on. "Since Jake hasn't shown up yet, Keaton has offered to help me take care of her. We're going to trade off watching her at my house. Since the tornado demolished the Holt family ranch house, he's been living in a hunting cabin on the property and I'm sure it's no place for Grace."

Lark fussed with the sheet that covered Skye, hating her sister's stillness. Skye had always been so vivacious. So beautiful. So outgoing and personable. So not like Lark. Sometimes she wondered if they were really sisters or if one of them was the victim of a switched-at-birth scenario.

Skye's golden hair looked lank and listless against her

pale skin. There were shadows beneath her closed eyes. After three months in the hospital the bruises and scrapes that had marred her face and arms were long healed, as was her left earlobe, probably torn during the same impact that had caused her head wound. She'd lost the diamond out of her earring, but the screw back had kept the stud in place. The hospital had given Skye's jewelry to Lark for safekeeping, and because Skye's phone and luggage had never been recovered, the earrings were her only possession. The lack of any sort of ring continued to dismay Lark. What had happened between Skye and Jake these last four years?

"I bought her a crib and a changing table," Lark continued. "Keaton picked up her bedding. All by himself. It's really cute. Yellow with jungle animals. I set up the furniture in my sitting area, but it's pretty cramped. For the time being, I'm going to keep her in a bassinet. I think she'll feel more secure in a smaller space. Eventually I'll transition her to the crib. Or you can just wake up and take care of that yourself."

Holding her breath was fruitless and silly, but Lark issued the challenge at least once a day and hoped that her sister would respond.

"I don't want to fail you," she whispered. "I did four years ago and I've regretted it every day since." Lark wiped at a trace of moisture at the corner of her eye. "Did I mention what an annoying know-it-all Keaton is?" She needed to change the subject or risk further tears. "He seems to think if he researches something thoroughly enough that he becomes an expert."

A smile tugged at Lark's lips as she recalled how he'd looked the first time he held Grace. "And he's bossy. He decided that we were going to use a diaper service instead of disposable. Didn't even consult me. Of course, I like the idea that we won't be loading up the landfill, but I should have at least been given an opportunity to agree."

The wife of Skye's nearest neighbor came to visit. Her husband was suffering from sepsis, and his condition had been touch-and-go for the last week. Lark was happy to see he'd turned a corner toward recovery.

"I'd better get going," she murmured to Skye. "I'm supposed to meet Keaton in a few minutes. I'll bring Grace by to see you before we leave and then visit in a few days once I'm sure she's settling in okay and that Keaton is comfortable taking care of her. Before this he hadn't had any experience with babies, and I think he's intimidated by how tiny Grace is. But he's been handling her quite a bit these last few days and I'm surprised how deftly he manages her diaper and dressing her."

With a last squeeze of Skye's hand, Lark left the ICU. She waved to her coworkers as she walked by the nurses' station, but only Jessa gave her a smile and it was quickly gone. As Lark rode the elevator to the pediatric floor, she wasn't surprised how relieved she felt to have a weeklong break from the ICU nurses.

From the beginning they'd mistaken her shyness for superiority and now did everything in their power to shun her. Lark had a hard enough time opening up to people without having to overcome hostility.

As she stepped out of the elevator, it occurred to her that she'd never felt the least bit shy or uneasy with Keaton. The feud between their families should have made her anxious around him, yet from the moment she'd run into him in the hospital, she felt as if they'd known each other for years. Weird when he was the son of her parents' enemy. Or maybe she felt the connection more closely because of the bad blood between their families. Heaven knew she'd thought about him often enough. Him and Jake. Especially after Skye ran off with Jake and Lark spent a lot of time wondering what was so special about a Holt that would cause her sister to choose him over her family.

Her pulse kicked up a notch as she approached the NICU, but she didn't see Keaton. A glance at the clock showed it was fifteen minutes before their agreed-on meeting time. She'd caught a ride to the hospital with Julie. Since she was taking Grace home after her shift, Keaton was giving her and the baby a ride home. When Lark assured him she would be fine on her own, he'd insisted on being there. His steely determination had left her torn between relief and annoyance.

Lark approached Grace's basinet. She was wearing a pink dress one of the NICU nurses had crocheted. A matching pink headband encircled her head. This wasn't a normal practice, but nothing about Grace's situation had been normal thus far and Lark was one of their own.

"Thank you all so much," Lark said to her colleagues as she blinked back a rush of tears that flooded her eyes. "You've taken such great care of Grace."

"If you need anything or have any questions," Amy, the senior NICU nurse said, "just call."

"Thanks." She'd grown accustomed to leaning on each of these women for support and guidance. It was terrifying to be heading out on her own.

Except she wasn't alone. Keaton would be there to help her. Her skin prickled. She hadn't quite gotten used to the idea that he would be spending time in her private space. Buying a house and living alone for the first time in her life had been blissful. No more worrying about saying the wrong thing to her roommate's friends or hearing their whispers and knowing they were talking about the weird girl who rarely came out of the second bedroom.

"You're going to do great," said Nancy. The nurse with the most experience in the NICU, she'd been the one Lark had turned to about her anxiety.

"I don't know why I'm so emotional." Lark laughed self-consciously. At the hospital she worked hard to appear confident. Letting anyone glimpse her shy awkwardness might make them question her ability to do her job. "I guess I'm feeling a little overwhelmed."

"Oh, honey." Nancy wrapped her arm around Lark's shoulder and gave her a squeeze. "With your sister in a coma and this precious baby still so delicate, you've got a lot on your plate. Frankly, we'd be surprised if you weren't feeling that way."

Through the NICU's large window, Lark spotted Keaton. Her pulse gave a little leap as their eyes met. He nodded in acknowledgement, his grave expression and compelling gaze easing her turmoil a little. His presence reminded her that she wasn't alone.

Amy spoke up. "And it looks like Keaton Holt is going to be a big help." Her tone was sly, matching her wicked grin. "It's nice to see you two could put aside your families' differences."

Had they? Lark wasn't sure. A lifetime of hostility and accusations stood between them. Just because she and Keaton weren't at war with each other didn't mean they were going to get along. He was determined to the point of obstinacy and laser-focused when he decided he wanted something. While it might make him a successful rancher, it made fighting with him an exhausting enterprise. Lark tore her attention away from the tall, imposing ranch owner and redirected her thoughts to the five-pound bundle she held. For Grace's sake she and Keaton were just going to have to play nice.

Telling her pulse to settle down, Lark cradled Grace in her arms and gazed around the NICU for the last time. Burdened with a well-stocked diaper bag and the responsibility of her delicate charge, she threw back her shoulders and walked the gantlet of smiling nurses who'd gathered to wish her and Grace well.

"How is Grace this morning?" Keaton asked as she approached.

"Doing better than I am." Lark shifted her grip on the baby as Keaton slid the well-stocked diaper bag off her shoulder, lightening her load. "Thanks."

"Don't tell me you're nervous." His genuine surprise bolstered her confidence.

"I owe it to Skye to make everything perfect for Grace."

"It will be."

The hand he set on her back caused a shiver of awareness to travel up her spine. His touch was at once reassuring and stimulating. She wanted to lean into his strength. The urge gave her much to contemplate. For as long as Lark could remember she'd been a solo act. Growing up, she'd enjoyed solitude. Smart and independent, she'd been neither a leader nor a follower, but one of those quirky types who loved books and was perfectly content doing her own thing. Looking back, Lark wasn't sure if her isolation had been the cause or the result of her social awkwardness.

"If you don't mind, I'd like to stop by the ICU before we leave the hospital," Lark said as they walked down the hall to the elevators. "This is Grace's first time outside the NICU, and I want her to see her mother before we leave."

Lark didn't add that she was hoping that Grace's presence would somehow miraculously awaken Skye from her coma.

"Of course."

As always, she was discouraged by the sight of her beautiful, vibrant sister lying so still, the only sign of life the beep and electronic readouts coming from the machines that measured her vitals. But Lark's reaction today was worse than normal. Her throat closed up as misery swamped her. What if Skye never woke up? What if Grace never got to know how amazing her mother was?

"Damn," she muttered, wiping away the moisture that escaped the corners of her eyes. "I'm sorry," she said to Keaton.

"For what? Being sad that your sister is like this? It's terrible."

She wanted to smile in appreciation of his understanding, but her facial muscles were controlled by the ache in her heart, so she settled for a nod.

"Skye, this is Grace. You haven't had a chance to meet her because she's been too tiny to leave the NCIU. She's so beautiful. I wish you would open your eyes and see for yourself." Staying away from the wires that connected Skye to the monitors, Lark fitted Grace into the hollow between her sister's arm and her side. "She needs her mommy."

As soon as Lark finished speaking, Grace punched outward with both fists and opened her eyes. Lark half expected her face to screw up in distress, but the baby blinked and relaxed in a way that Lark had never seen before. Was it being snuggled against her mother for the first time in three months?

Keaton leaned forward to peer at Grace. His shoulder pressed against Lark's back. "She looks happy."

"The mother-daughter bond is alive and well."

How comfortable it would be to rest her head against his broad chest and pull his muscular arms around her body. The longing for his touch was so compelling, Lark had to dig her fingernails into her palms to keep from acting on the impulse. What was happening to her? She'd never been so physically drawn to a man before. Usually the men she dated were intellectually stimulating, but not exactly fantasy material. Not that they were unattractive, but their allure had been mostly cerebral.

Grace yawned and her eyes drifted shut. She knuckled one cheek. Her other hand rested on her mother's arm.

The anxious knot in Lark's chest tightened. "What if Skye never wakes up?" It was the first time she'd spoken the fear out loud.

"She will." Keaton's big hands settled on her shoulders. "As Grace gets stronger, so will her mother."

Keaton's words couldn't have been any more perfect. Lark's optimism surged.

"You're right." As much as she was loathed to disrupt the rapport that had bloomed between her and Keaton, she needed to get Grace home and settled. "Say goodbye to your mommy," she said to the baby, lifting her away from Skye. It hurt Lark's heart to separate mother and daughter, but she told herself it was only temporary. Before she left Skye's bedside, Lark turned to Keaton. "I want you to know how much

I appreciate everything you've done. I realized this morning that I'd underestimated how much I needed to get ready for Grace's homecoming. I couldn't have done it without you."

Her father would be furious to hear her say those words. But if he and her mother refused to step up and be grandparents to Grace, they had no right to criticize Lark for accepting Keaton's assistance. Unfortunately that wouldn't stop them from bombarding her with their opinions. Lark cringed away from thinking about her father's ire. Always volatile where the Holts were concerned, he'd become a powder keg since the tornado leveled his tree farm.

"You don't need to thank me," Keaton said. "We're doing this for Grace, remember?"

"For Grace," she agreed.

With Keaton a step behind her, Lark headed out of the ICU. As she neared the door to the hall, two people came into view. Her parents. They stood at the nurses' station, speaking with Lark's coworker Jessa and hadn't spotted Lark or Keaton yet.

She slowed her pace, all too aware of Keaton's towering presence behind her. In the rush of getting prepared for Grace's homecoming, Lark had neglected to mention to her parents that Keaton would be helping her with Grace. Or maybe she'd dodged the issue to put off dealing with her father's ire as long as possible. Lark gathered a breath to bolster her courage. This encounter promised to get ugly.

Her mother spotted her first. "Lark?" Her gaze bounced from her daughter to the man shadowing her. "What's going on?"

At Vera's sharp tone, Tyrone Taylor glanced around. His expression twisted with disgust when he saw Keaton.

"Grace is coming home with me today," Lark explained, stopping a good fifteen feet away from her parents, hoping distance and a soothing tone would keep her father's temper from flaring. "I brought her to see Skye before we left."

"And him?" Lark's father demanded. "What's he doing here?"

"I'm driving Lark and Grace home." Keaton's level reply was neither defensive nor aggressive. His body radiated calm confidence at Lark's side, but her tension didn't ease.

Lark had let Keaton take on the role of Grace's caretaker because her parents hadn't stepped up. Was that dawning on Tyrone and Vera or were they too consumed by their needs and desires to realize they would never be nominated for grandparents of the year?

"Since when are you two so chummy?" Tyrone demanded, his attention fixed on his daughter.

Lark felt her chin lift to a defiant angle in response to her father's hostility. "Keaton is Grace's uncle. We are both concerned about her welfare." She glanced down at the tiny bundle of pink sweetness they all should be concerned about, but failed to refocus her father's attention.

"I don't know why you've accepted Jake as Grace's father. He sure as hell isn't acting like it. What sort of man abandons his baby and the woman he claims to love?" Tyrone shot Keaton a hard look. "What does your brother have to say for himself?"

"I haven't spoken with Jake."

Lark's father made a dismissive noise, but his next words were for Lark. "I told your sister four years ago that Jake was going to ruin her life."

"He hasn't."

"He forced her to turn her back on her family and now he's abandoned her."

"You don't know that he did," Keaton said. "I know my brother. He loves Skye. If he's not here, there's a good reason why."

"And none of that matters at this moment," Lark chimed in, modulating her voice so as not to disturb the sleeping infant. "Grace and Skye need all our love and support. That's where our energy should be focused." Frustration ate at her.

She needed her father to put aside his dislike of all things Holt and concentrate on what was best for his daughter and granddaughter. "We should get going. I need to get Grace home." In the spirit of putting differences aside, Lark added, "It would be great if you could come by later this week and have dinner. You could spend some time getting to know Grace."

"Maybe you should bring her out to the ranch instead," Tyrone countered, his hard gaze still resting on Keaton.

"Preemie's lungs are always delicate," Lark explained. "It will be better for Grace if she doesn't venture out for the first few weeks. That's why I wanted you to come over."

"Will he be there?"

"We'll check our schedule and let you know what works for us," Vera said in a rush, her response geared toward ending the conversation. She fussed with the numerous bracelets on her wrist and glanced at the clock on the wall. "Tyrone, I have a meeting with my nutritionist in forty-five minutes, so we'd better go see Skye before we run out of time."

Lark said goodbye to her parents and headed for the elevator. She didn't realize how much she'd been dreading running into them until she let out a huge breath.

Keaton shot her a somber glance. "You okay?"

"That could have gone so much worse."

Keaton agreed. But it should have gone a lot better.

For the first time in his life, Keaton was having difficulty keeping his opinion to himself. The reserve Tyrone and Vera demonstrated toward their daughters irritated him. It was one thing to dislike Jake, Keaton and their parents based on grievances that had plagued generations of Taylors and Holts over numerous decades. It was another to let that animosity drive a wedge between them and their lovely, successful daughters.

"It's cool outside," he remarked as they stepped off the

elevator. "Why don't you wait in the lobby while I bring the car around?"

Lark settled into a seat by the door and he set the diaper bag beside the chair. Before he could leave, she stopped him with a light touch on his arm. "Keaton, I'm sorry about what my father said about Jake. My sister adored your brother."

He didn't like her use of the past tense. "I believe she still loves him. I don't know what's happened between them these last four years or why he's not here now, but until I know for certain that my message about Skye and Grace has gotten to him, I'm going to trust that they're still together and very much in love."

"I wish I had your faith."

Her melancholy expression weighed on him as he strode to the parking ramp where he'd left his car. Until he'd approached her about assisting with Grace's care, she'd never struck him as someone who needed help. Her competent exterior deflected anyone from noticing her vulnerability to harsh words and malicious intent.

Today, watching her in the NICU with the other nurses, seeing her anxiety, had cemented his perception of her as someone he should be taking care of.

The feeling had been building since the day he went with her to buy Grace's crib, working its way through his subconscious. Now it burst upon him like a solar flare.

Thanks to the land dispute between the Taylors and Holts she might not ever be his friend, but with Baby Grace's arrival, she'd become his family.

With this fresh insight firmly entrenched in his awareness, Keaton helped Lark settle Grace into her car seat for the ride home.

"I'm going to sit in the back with her," Lark said, fussing over the straps that secured the tiny infant.

"I'm sure she'll feel safe with you beside her." Keaton got behind the wheel and started the truck. As the vehicle eased away from the curb, he worried over every bump in the road. "How is she doing?"

"Great. She's still asleep."

"Good." Silence reigned as Keaton concentrated on navigating the traffic around the hospital. Lark's house was a ten-minute drive, but it seemed to take twice that long. At last they arrived and began the process of releasing Grace from her safety seat. "I've been doing a lot of thinking about our situation in the last couple days," he began as Lark unlocked her front door and stepped inside. Keaton followed her with Grace nestled in his arms.

"What situation is that?"

The baby was starting to wake and Lark offered to take her, but Keaton shook his head. Now that he'd grown accustomed to how tiny and fragile she was, he liked snuggling her against his chest and watching her yawn and blink.

"The one where we trade off taking care of Grace."

"You've decided you're too busy to help out?" She set her hands on her hips and regarded him with resignation. "I think she's hungry."

"Then this is a great time for you to show me what goes into one of her bottles." He waited patiently until she spun on her heel and headed into the kitchen, and then he followed with Grace. He watched how Lark went about measuring the powdered formula and mixing it with water. "Most new mothers get to take off six to twelve weeks off work. You're only taking a week. I think you're going to need me around to do more than watch Grace while you're at the hospital."

Lark turned with the bottle in her hand and eyed him. "You don't think I can manage?"

"I think you will wear yourself to the bone trying to take care of Grace and Skye while working full time."

"My mother already offered to pay for a nanny and I refused."

Keaton saw the hurt in Lark's eyes and voiced the idea

that had been cooking in his subconscious for several days. "I think I should move in here."

"Move in?"

It made perfect sense. Ever since the DNA results came back he'd been contemplating how best to stake a claim on Grace for the sake of his brother and the Holt family. Moving in with Lark would prove he was as dedicated to his niece's welfare as she was.

"You demonstrated last week that your schedule is subject to change," he pointed out, seeing his logic was encroaching on her doubts.

"That's true, but it's not exactly as if you have a lot of time on your hands."

She was right about that. Between his regular duties at the ranch, the rebuilding efforts there and in town, he was stretched thin.

"Grace is my family. I'm going to do everything in my power to take care of her."

Lark exhaled tiredly. "I appreciate that you feel responsible, but you don't actually have to move in."

His muscles relaxed as he heard the beginnings of capitulation in her voice. "It would be better for you if I was here full-time."

"How do you figure?"

"Have you considered what will happen if Grace is up all night? If I'm here we can take turns getting up with her." He could see she was weakening. "It makes sense."

"Let me sleep on it tonight?" She held out her hands for the baby.

This time, Keaton gave up Grace. "Sure."

Only she never got the chance to sleep. Neither did Keaton. Shortly after Grace finished eating, she began to fuss.

"It's probably just a little gas," Lark explained, setting the infant on her shoulder and patting her back encouragingly. "Once she burps, she'll be fine."

But Grace wasn't fine and neither Lark nor Keaton could get her to quiet. During the second hour of the baby's crying, Keaton got onto his tablet.

"She's dry, fed and obviously tired. Why won't she sleep?"

"Because it's her first day out of the NICU and she's overstimulated."

"It says here we can try white noise. Do you have a vacuum cleaner?"

Lark shot him a look. "It's in the laundry room." She pointed toward a door at the back of the kitchen.

Keaton plugged in the vacuum and turned it on. The hum acted like a swarm of bees against his eardrums, agitating him. If it had this effect on him, what must it be doing to a fussy baby? Closing the door behind him to muffle the sound, Keaton returned to the living room, where Lark paced and rocked Grace.

"Is it helping?" he asked, peering over her shoulder at his niece.

"I don't think so, but maybe we should give it a little time. She's pretty wound up at the moment."

But after an hour, it was obvious that the white noise was having no effect. Keaton returned to searching the internet for answers.

"How about wrapping her up?" he suggested. "Says here that babies feel more secure when they're swaddled." He cued up a video and watched it. The demonstration looked straightforward, but the woman used a doll, not a real baby. "Give me Grace and watch this."

After several minutes, Lark set the tablet aside. "We can try it. I'll go see if I have a blanket that will work." She returned with two blankets of different sizes. "Hopefully one of these will do the trick."

As Keaton had feared, swaddling a live, unhappy baby was a lot harder than an unmoving doll.

Lark braced her hands on the dining room table and stared down at the swaddled baby. "This doesn't look right."

Keaton returned to the video. "I think we missed this part here."

Grace was growing more upset by the second and she'd managed to free her left arm.

"Is it terrible that I have no idea what I'm doing?" Lark sounded close to tears. It had been a long, stressful evening.

"Not at all. I think every first-time parent feels just as overwhelmed as we do right now."

"Thank you for sticking around and helping me."

"We're helping Grace."

The corners of Lark's lips quivered as she smiled. "Not very well, as it happens."

And then, because she looked determined and hopeless all at once, Keaton succumbed to the impulse that had been threatening to break free all week. He cupped her cheek, lowered his head and kissed her.

Four

The press of Keaton's lips against hers lasted all of ten seconds, but they were ten of the best seconds Lark had ever experienced. With his granite features and steely nature, she expected his lips would be stiff, his kisses firm and unyielding. Therefore she was caught off guard by the softness of his mouth, the luxurious press and pull as he captured her sighs.

For ten seconds her brain stopped and her body came alive.

Then Grace's insistent protests came between them like a wedge, bringing reality back.

"Let's try the swaddling again," Keaton suggested, his long black lashes obscuring his eyes from her as his hand fell away from her face. "I think I know where we went wrong."

The next try went much better, but it wasn't snug enough for Grace's taste. Lark stood beside Keaton, her body alive with raucous cravings, her mind numb with disbelief, and watched his big hands wrap the cloth around the flailing infant. His confidence had grown in the last couple hours as he'd taken his turn trying to calm Grace. Lark's belief in his abilities had increased, as well. She appreciated how he'd not just stood by helplessly and let her figure out what was wrong with Grace, but he'd taken to the internet to find a solution to soothe the infant.

"She's still not happy," he commented as soon as the last corner was tucked away, creating a cocoon.

"Maybe she just wants it to be tighter."

"Do you want to give it a try?"

Lark shook her head. Their kiss was too fresh. Her body had yet to come down off the thrill. She couldn't let him see how her hands trembled. "You're doing great."

He shot her a doubtful frown as he unwrapped Grace. Lark stood as close as she could to him without touching to observe his next attempt. Despite the lack of contact, energy arched across the distance between them, setting her skin to tingling.

"I think you could go a little tighter," she offered, reaching out to demonstrate. Their hands brushed in passing, and the zap of contact caused her stomach muscles to tighten in reaction. She swallowed a gasp.

Fifteen minutes ago she'd decided to agree to his moving in. Now she wasn't so sure. Living in such close quarters was bound to lead to more inconsequential physical contact. And then there was that kiss to consider. She could easily write off Keaton's impulse as a reaction to the frustration of Grace's disquiet, but it hadn't been that sort of kiss. It had been tender and curious. He'd kissed Lark with focused deliberation as if that was the only thing on his mind. As if it had been on his mind for a while.

She trembled.

"I think we've finally got it right."

At Keaton's relieved words, Lark blinked and reoriented herself in the moment. The tight swaddle had done the trick. Grace had stopped crying and her mouth opened on a giant yawn.

"You did it."

"We did it," he corrected. "We're a team, remember?"

For the first time she didn't freeze up at his words. "A good team," she agreed, scooping the sleepy infant into her arms.

"I'm feeling more confident that we can do this." Keaton followed her to the couch where the bassinet waited.

"You weren't before?"

"Not once she started crying and wouldn't stop."

Lark had begun having doubts way before they left the hospital. Taking care of her sister's baby was a responsibility Lark didn't take lightly. Add in Grace's premature birth and the risks that accompanied such things, and the need for success grew proportionally more crucial.

"It's been a long night," Lark said, placing Grace in the bassinet before sitting beside her. After she'd confirmed that Grace slept on, Lark let her head fall back and closed her eyes.

"You do realize it's only midnight."

The cushion beside her dipped as Keaton joined her on the couch. The substantial differences in their weight caused him to sink deeper into the cushions and Lark slipped toward the resulting dip, reducing the distance between them. She kept her eyes closed and let her other senses come alive.

"That's all?" she murmured, revived by the rhythm of her vigorous heartbeat.

His shoulder bumped against hers. He smelled like soap and baby powder from Grace's last change. "She's finally quiet."

The sleeve of his crisp cotton shirt grazed across the top of her arms as he reached out to Grace. Sitting beside Keaton reminded Lark how long it had been since she'd let a man get close to her.

Although she'd had relationships in college and dated frequently the year she'd worked at Houston Methodist Hospital, since returning to Royal, Lark's love life had been limited to a few first dates with men she'd met online.

"But is she sleeping?"

"Not yet." His breath puffed against her temple.

She turned her head toward him and waited, wondering if he wanted to repeat their earlier kiss. When nothing happened, she opened her eyes. He was staring past her, gaze glued to a distant spot. Her lips parted as the longing for his kiss overwhelmed her. What would he do if she told him how she felt? Would he sweep her into his arms and drink deeply of her hunger or excuse the earlier kiss as a mistake?

Keaton withdrew his arm, and Lark's practical nature reasserted itself. What was she thinking? She couldn't get involved with Keaton. Look what had happened to Skye's relationship with their parents when the truth had come out about her and Jake. If anything happened between Lark and Keaton, there would be no running away. Keaton's life was the Holts' ranch, and Lark hadn't been happy living away from Royal. This was where she belonged. No, better that she and Keaton work together to take care of Grace and ignore whatever chemistry had sparked between them.

"You should move in." The blunt declaration came out of nowhere and surprised Lark as much as it did Keaton.

"Are you sure?"

"Absolutely. After tonight I can't imagine doing this alone."

"What about your parents? You know your father will object."

"Too bad." Annoyance smoldered in her gut. "If I can't count on their help, they lose the right to criticize what I do to ensure Grace's welfare."

"I'll bring my stuff by tomorrow. In the meantime, since this little lady is momentarily content, why don't you run off to bed and grab what sleep you can?"

"What about you?"

"Your couch is pretty comfortable. I'll just stretch out here."

"You're sure?" Lark was perfectly willing to keep him company. Perhaps too willing.

"Positive. Besides, you worked last night and no doubt are half-asleep already."

"Okay, just for a little while. When she wakes for her next feeding, get me up."

The road in front of Keaton's truck blurred for a moment, forcing him to give his head a fervent shake. A giant yawn followed. Three days of hard labor at the ranch. Three evenings of caring for Grace. Three nights plagued by the temptation of Lark sleeping a dozen strides away.

Damn. He was worn, frazzled and restless.

Grace's most difficult time of the day began as the sun went down. This was when she grew fussy and nothing they did seemed to satisfy her completely. That meant she didn't want to eat despite being hungry. Which meant she wasn't falling asleep after only half an hour of wakefulness. Tired and hungry, she grew more irritable by the second. And his inability to soothe her distress roused feelings of helplessness he'd never known before.

Lark wasn't faring much better. During the day Grace had decided she liked being held while she slept, so Lark wasn't free to take care of anything around the house. At first she resisted his suggestion that she needed a housekeeper to help, but on the third day after the laundry piled up and they'd eaten takeout three nights running, she'd caved to his insistence that she needed domestic assistance. Once Jen had started working, things had gone more smoothly with the household chores, but keeping Grace content remained a challenge.

Keaton's respect for parents had grown during the last several days. He'd never imagined how much work went into taking care of a baby. It made a twelve-hour day in the saddle rounding up cattle seem like a ride on a merry-go-round.

If either of them had considered revisiting the kiss they'd shared that first night, it was lost in feedings, diapering, swaddling and soothing Grace. Maybe that was a good thing. The brief taste of her lips had been a mind-blowing surprise. Who would have guessed a simple kiss could ignite his senses? He'd been deaf and blind to everything but the incredible pliancy of her lips, the way her breath had caught, how she'd quivered at his touch.

Had he ever kissed a woman who'd responded to him with such genuine longing? It had stunned him. Left him wanting so much more. Keaton shifted his weight to ease the sudden heaviness in his loins. If just thinking about Lark aroused him, what would it be like to make love to her? Was it madness to consider it? Hadn't enough trouble been caused by Jake falling in love with Skye? And what made him think that Lark was willing to risk a similar rift with her parents? She was far more practical and cautious than her sister. Less willing to make waves.

Look at how she'd struggled with her decision to allow him to help her with Grace and permit him to move in. If she hadn't been desperate, he doubted she'd have accepted his assistance. She was far too worried about her father's reaction.

Arriving at Lark's house, Keaton fetched his latest purchase from the back of the pickup. It was a windup swing for Grace. His foreman had suggested it and Keaton had headed straight to the store. He hoped Grace would find it a suitable substitute for being held so Lark could get a break.

He noticed an eerie stillness to Lark's house the moment he entered. For a second, his heart stopped. Because her premature birth meant Grace's lungs hadn't fully developed, Lark intended to keep her home unless absolutely necessary. Had something happened while he was at the ranch? Setting the box inside the foyer, he advanced into the living room. The succulent scent of roast beef struck him the same instant he spied Lark sacked out on the couch, a sleeping Grace splayed across her chest.

The adorable picture held him transfixed. Keaton had never imagined himself living with, much less marrying a woman. Every one he'd dated had satisfied his physical desires or matched him intellectually, but he'd never found the right balance. In three short days Lark had demonstrated the perfect combination of physical allure and mental acumen.

Keaton retreated to the kitchen and snagged a beer from the refrigerator. Twisting off the top, he drained half the bottle. He was tired. Not thinking straight. Why else would he have settled on the daughter of his family's archenemy as his ideal match?

His gaze wandered back to Lark. Her right hand rested against Grace's side, blocking the infant from accidentally sliding off. Not that it could happen. Grace was as limp and unmoving as a rag doll.

Behind him, a timer went off. The noise caused Lark to stir. Her eyes opened. She blinked a few times, then caught sight of Keaton.

"How long have you been home?" Not *here*, but *home*, as if she'd come to accept that her house was his, as well. At least for the time being.

"A couple minutes. You were sleeping so peacefully I didn't want to wake you."

She rubbed her eyes with the back of her hand. "What time is it?"

"About five."

Lark was struggling to sit up without disturbing Grace. Keaton set his beer on the counter and went to take charge of the baby. She didn't wake as he transferred her to the crook of his arm.

"I know you feel more comfortable having Grace in your bedroom," he began, broaching a subject that was loaded with land mines. He offered his hand in aid. "But I think you need to consider moving her into the nursery."

"I like her sleeping in my room." She let him pull her to her feet, but freed herself as soon as she was upright. "Having her clear across the house is just too far."

"But I'll be right next door." He gazed down at the sleeping infant in his arms. Grace's rosebud mouth puckered as if she were nursing. It was adorable. "I'll have a monitor and I'm a light sleeper." Keaton watched Lark grapple with his request and decided not to allow her too much room to think. "I know it drives you crazy that I have to go into your bedroom every time Grace needs a change."

Her discomfort had been palpable the first night he'd officially moved in. She'd been twitchy throughout dinner and wouldn't let Keaton near Grace even though she'd seen how capable he was the night before.

"No, it's fine."

"Besides, there isn't enough space between the crib and the changing table. And there's no room for her clothes." Keaton had a hard time with the disorder. Things being out of place were his hot button. Jeb, his foreman, was used to it, but Keaton knew it drove a lot of the ranch hands crazy. "I'm going to bring someone in to paint the spare room a soft yellow. Grace isn't sleeping in the crib at the moment. Let's just move it and the changing table out of your room. Meanwhile she can continue to sleep in the bassinet."

Lark looked as if she wanted to argue, but Keaton knew what he'd suggested made perfect sense. First he would get the nursery set up. Later he could work on convincing her that Grace should spend some of her nights there so Lark could get a full night's sleep.

"Can we talk about this later," Lark murmured. "I have to finish getting dinner ready."

"It smells wonderful," he said, willing to drop the matter for the moment.

Keaton was happy enough that he'd spoken his piece. Even if Lark didn't agree to his plan, he'd already stated his intention and he would get the ball rolling.

"My friend Julie from the hospital went grocery shopping for me today and stuck around long enough for me to get the roast in. I couldn't stomach another takeout meal."

"Sounds great. Home-cooked meals have been rare for me since the tornado destroyed the ranch house."

She opened the oven door and checked on the status of the roast. "That's a lot of pressure to put on my cooking abilities."

"If it tastes half as good as it smells, I'll be happy."

She shot him a suspicious look but discovered he was completely serious and visibly relaxed. "Do you mind holding Grace for a little while? I also baked a cake this afternoon, but I haven't had a chance to frost it yet."

Grace began to stir. "Not at all. I think she might be in need of a change. I'll go take care of that."

Grace's furniture had been set up in what was supposed to be a small sitting area. The space was designed to hold a single chair and ottoman or a small writing desk. Keaton barely fit into the space between the changing table and the crib. The latter was being used to store diapers, clothes and toys that Grace would one day play with.

Below the crib were some of the items that Keaton had bought on his first shopping excursion. Lark had been so focused on Grace's immediate needs she hadn't gotten around to unpacking everything yet. As soon as he changed Grace, Keaton leaned down to poke through the bag. He recalled the saleslady had suggested a number of items in rapid-fire succession. Having no idea what they did or didn't need for a baby, he'd bought everything she suggested. Now he pulled out an infant gym and some sort of wrap.

With Grace tucked against his chest, he carried both items back to the living room. From the kitchen came the sound of humming. He glanced toward Lark. She was completely focused on smoothing white icing onto a triple-layer yellow cake. Her pleasure in the task made it hard for him to look away. Only when Grace began to squirm did he switch his attention.

Since opening and assembling the infant gym was going to be impossible one-handed, Keaton sat down on the floor, stretched out his legs and settled Grace on his lap. The new perspective engaged her interest, and when she started to fuss, he bent his knees and bounced her a little until she calmed.

Once he had the gym mat placed on the floor and the various toys attached to the padded tubes that crisscrossed over the baby, he slipped Grace inside the structure and held his breath. A newborn's ability to focus was limited to a range of twelve inches, but he wasn't sure how that applied to pree-mies. Grace had been born some thirteen weeks earlier, but her adjusted age was closer to three weeks.

The bright-colored animals dangling above Grace were a huge hit. She gurgled in delight as she reached up and batted at a monkey. It swung wildly and Grace kicked in response. Keaton didn't expect much of a reprieve, so he turned to the second item, the wrap. It was a long, infin-ity scarf that had been designed to snuggle the baby tight against the wearer, thus freeing the hands. For a baby like Grace, who didn't want to be put down, it should enable Lark a little more freedom.

But first he had to figure out how to make it work. Like the swaddling, the trick was to manage all the folds of the fabric. After watching a video on his tablet, he used one of Grace's stuffed animals for practice. The soft bunny was smaller than Grace, so he wasn't sure how secure the wrap would keep her, but it would be worth a try.

"What are you wearing?"

Keaton looked up from tucking the toy bunny into the wrap and met Lark's amused gaze. His heart jumped at her relaxed expression. The lines of tension had faded from around her mouth, and the frown lines had smoothed out on her forehead.

"It's a wrap for carrying a baby. I thought if you put Grace in it, you could free up your hands."

"That certainly would be nice. Can you show me how it works?"

"I'm still trying to figure that out. Maybe together we can get it to function properly."

Although Keaton hadn't started out with ulterior motives when he began fitting the wrap around Lark's slim body, he quickly discovered the activity gave him the perfect excuse to skim his fingers all over her slender form.

"And then you wrap it around this way." He settled the

fabric into place, noticing the slight jump in her body as he accidently grazed his knuckles against her breast. "You should have two pockets. Here and here."

"Looks like I do." She sounded a trifle breathless. "Now what?"

"Now we take Buster Bunny and put him on your shoulder." After watching the video four times, Keaton felt pretty confident in the steps. "Next we settle his legs into this pouch and pull up the fabric around him."

"That doesn't feel very secure."

"We're not done. This side comes up like this."

He rocked the edge of the fabric up her torso, across her breasts and the stuffed rabbit tucked against her chest. Although he was working hard to keep his touch neutral, the intimacy of their proximity and the slight tremble in her muscles were eating away at his better judgment.

"That feels better," she said. "What's this piece for?"

"I'm getting there."

"I'm sorry, I didn't mean to rush you."

"Are you always so impatient?" He hadn't meant to sound flirtatious, but there was a teasing edge that had slipped into his tone.

"I'm not usually impatient at all." She bit her lip in confusion. "Something about this is making me anxious." With her hands she indicated the fabric wrapped around her torso.

"Is it making you feel claustrophobic?"

"I'm not sure that's it."

"Are you sure you want to keep going? I could take it off you."

The sensual tension in the room escalated. Lark vibrated with it. Keaton's body hummed in matching harmony.

"Keaton." She whispered his name as his hands encircled her waist, palms gliding up her rib cage. "What are we doing?"

He dipped his head and grazed her lips with his. "Save your questions for later."

"Okay."

With a groan he claimed her lips. She came alive in his arms, pushing up on her toes, tunneling her fingers into his hair. The bunny became trapped between them as he dragged his mouth over hers, tasting a hint of buttercream icing.

Her mouth was hot and sweet and welcoming and Keaton feasted on her lips like a man offered a gift from the gods. She matched his passion, held nothing in reserve. It was this openness that allowed Keaton to reel his wayward desires back in.

"That was crazy," she gasped as soon as he freed her mouth.

"Not crazy," he corrected, "wonderful." Keaton framed her face with his fingers and held her still so he could scrutinize her face. "If you cook like you kiss, I'm going to be in trouble."

"In trouble how?" Shadows were creeping into her eyes.

"I won't be able to stop myself from wanting more."

Color flooded her cheeks. She hooked her fingers around his hands and pulled them away from her skin. "I don't think you'll have to worry on either account."

"What makes you say that?"

"Because you've never struck me as a man who does anything that isn't good for him."

If that was her attempt at a warning, she was going to have to be a whole lot clearer. "What about kissing you isn't good for me?"

She set her hands on her hips and regarded him incredulously. "Have you forgotten the bad blood between our families? It already forced Skye and Jake out of town. Can you imagine how bad it would be if we were caught?"

"So what are we supposed to do with these feelings between us?"

"What feelings? It's just a simple case of proximity lust. Nothing more."

Keaton studied her, wondering if that was what she truly

believed, or if it was a way to let him off the hook. "Is proximity lust a scientific term or something you just made up?"

"It is what it is."

Five

Lark fled to the kitchen without removing the wrap, leaving Keaton to deal with Grace. She needed a second to regain her composure, and that wasn't going to happen if he offered to help her out of the yards of fabric.

She set about readying a bottle for Grace and plating the roast and potatoes for her and Keaton. Earlier she'd opened a bottle of red wine, but now she wasn't sure if drinking alcohol was a good idea after what had just happened between her and Keaton. The last thing she needed was for her guard to falter. Or had that ship already sailed?

"Why don't you eat while I feed Grace?" she offered, carrying both plates to the dining room. She'd set the table earlier and now wondered what she'd been thinking to bring out her crystal candleholders and best china.

"The table looks very nice, but you shouldn't have gone to so much trouble."

"No trouble." She relieved him of Grace and gestured toward a chair. "I opened a really nice Cabernet, or there's beer or whiskey." She was rambling because he was staring at her, his gaze inscrutable.

"The Cabernet sounds perfect. Let me get it. You sit and I'll get Grace's bottle too."

Lark dropped into her seat and discovered she still had the rabbit tucked into the wrap. With a wry grin, she plucked the stuffed animal free and shifted Grace's tiny form into the pouch. The baby's eyes widened as she settled into the sling, but Keaton had appeared with the bottle before Grace started to cry.

"I'm going to have to figure out the proper way to use this," Lark said, stabbing a piece of carrot with her left hand and lifting it to her mouth. "Being able to free up even one of my hands is really nice."

They traded off when Grace needed to be burped. Keaton had a knack for getting the infant to release the bit of air that she consumed with the formula. While he gently patted Grace's back, Lark quickly wolfed down her dinner. She hadn't realized how hungry she was until she popped the first bit of roast into her mouth.

"I don't think I ate lunch today," she remarked, shaking her head over her absentmindedness. "Grace was awake more than usual in the morning and then Julie came by and freed me up so I could get dinner ready. I don't know where the time goes."

"Babies take up more time than I imagined possible," Keaton agreed. "And I think establishing a routine with Grace will eventually help, but right now we're both learning about her needs and how best to meet them."

"Thanks."

"For what?"

"For saying exactly the right thing to stop me from feeling so overwhelmed. I just need to take it one day at a time."

"We," he corrected. "I'm here for Grace, as well. You don't have to do everything yourself."

Without warning, her chest tightened to the point of pain. Even though she'd let Keaton move in and surrendered part of Grace's care, she hadn't really let herself rely on him. In her mind he was an extra pair of hands that freed her up for short periods of time. Since bringing Grace home four days ago, she hadn't left the house, because to do so would be to fully relinquish responsibility for Grace to him, and Lark wasn't comfortable doing that.

"I haven't visited Skye since Grace left the hospital.

Would you be okay if I went first thing tomorrow? I'll only be an hour or so."

"That's not a problem. I have the electrical inspection for the ranch house tomorrow, but it's not until the afternoon." Keaton reached across the table for Grace's bottle and settled her into his arm so he could finish feeding her. "Don't worry about us, we'll be just fine."

"Keaton moved in to help me with Grace," Lark told her sister after glancing around to make sure she couldn't be overheard. Her nerves were already a tangled mess. She didn't need the added stress of becoming the focus of hospital gossip. "The day we brought Grace home he suggested the idea and I should have turned him down flat. I mean, what was he thinking that I couldn't handle things?"

Hands moving compulsively across Skye's bed linens, smoothing, straightening, Lark let her thoughts revel in the previous night's kiss. It was what she really wanted to talk to Skye about, but she'd never been one to share something so private and needed to warm up to the telling.

"But then Grace had a bad first night. Oh, don't worry. She didn't get sick or anything," Lark rushed to assure her sister. "But I think the transition from the NICU to my house was a little jarring. She couldn't calm down and then we had trouble swaddling her."

Of course, recalling that night revived the memory of that first, brief kiss and how soft Keaton's lips had been. Lark closed her eyes and swayed a little as she relived the delicious sensations she'd experienced.

"Apparently she likes being swaddled really tight." Lark noticed that she'd grabbed fistfuls of Skye's blanket, and released her grip with a soft exhalation of self-disgust. Was Julie's theory of proximity lust the best explanation for the way her body awakened to his slightest touch? "It took us quite a few tries to figure that out. And somewhere in the middle of all that, he kissed me."

Lark half expected her sister's eyes to fly open at such shocking news, but Skye remained unconscious. "It was a nice kiss. Impulsive. Didn't last long."

Spilling this first secret had taken its toll. Lark bustled around, checking the equipment in a feeble attempt to calm her pulse and restore normal breathing. When it became apparent that her emotions were messing with her body's electrical signals, Lark decided the best thing to do would be to spill everything all at once.

"He kissed me again a few days later. This one was longer and more premeditated. He made me feel as if I was the sexiest woman alive. Is that how Jake makes you feel?" She felt a little stupid asking. "Of course, that's why you left with him, isn't it? I've never had anyone treat me like that before. I wanted to…"

Confession might be good for the soul, but Lark had only just admitted to herself what she'd wanted that night. Her hormones, on alert since the night before, quickened. A mild ache invaded her body.

"Funny about Keaton," she continued. "I expected him to be the kind of guy who got in and got things done." Not exactly a flattering description, but he was always so stern and efficient. "How was I supposed to know he'd be so passionate? Such a great kisser. I…I didn't want him to stop."

There. She'd said it. The truth was out in the open. She wanted to have sex with Keaton Holt. Lark clapped her hands over her mouth and stared at Skye. Why wouldn't her sister wake up and give her advice about how to handle things with Keaton? She was completely out of her depth. No man had ever made her long to tear his clothes off and take big bites out of him. Well, not literally.

It was just the thought of both of them naked. His big body pinning her to the mattress. Or a wall. While he drove inside her…

Lark gave her head a vehement shake to clear it of such thoughts. She couldn't want those things with Keaton. He was a Holt. She was a Taylor. Her sister and Jake had left Royal in order to be together. The town was too small to hide a romantic relationship. Word would get out. Her parents would never forgive her.

Keaton was standing in the middle of Lark's empty third bedroom, slowly rocking Grace, when he heard the door to the garage open. In a couple days Lark would be going back to work and he was going to take over the baby's care. He wanted Grace in the bedroom next to his so he could handle her late night feedings.

"What in heaven's name is that?" Lark's normally soft voice, coming loud and clear from the living room, rang with shock and dismay.

Obviously she'd discovered his newest purchase. Keaton strode into the living room and found Lark staring at the sixty-inch flat-screen television that had been delivered this morning.

"A television," he responded. "Surely you've seen one before."

"That's a television?" She set her hands on her lush hips and faced him. "It takes up the whole wall."

"The better to watch the play-offs and not miss anything."

"Play-offs?"

"Football..."

Although he'd never considered himself much of a TV watcher, he hadn't realized how much he enjoyed unwinding after a long day with a beer and a sports channel until he couldn't. Granted, both Lark and Grace were plenty entertaining. He found a great deal of satisfaction in watching Grace sleep and Lark read. But after they went off to bed, he had far too many hours to keep his mind occupied and paperwork wasn't cutting it.

All too often, his thoughts strayed in the direction of Lark's bedroom. He contemplated if she slept in pajamas or nightgowns. Cotton or silk. She owned a queen-size bed and he liked picturing her in the middle of it, asleep on her side, her body curved, hands beneath her cheek. He doubted she snored, but it amused him to wonder if she did. Did she puff out her breath in little spurts? Maybe she drooled.

This last should have turned him off, but he found the image intriguing. In the short time he'd been living with her, he'd discovered she wasn't much of a morning person. Until she got a cup of coffee into her, she was downright grumpy. But at the same time her defenses were down and she was far more likely to smile. Naturally she reserved her happiest expressions for Grace, but what Lark didn't realize was that even though her grins weren't directed at him, he got to enjoy them, as well.

"It will only be here as long as I am," Keaton assured her. "Or until the ranch house is finished enough to receive it."

Lark gave the television the evil eye and then turned her back on it as if what she couldn't see didn't exist.

"It's getting late," she said. "Let me take Grace so you can get going."

Despite his need to be at a meeting at the Texas Cattleman's Club in thirty minutes, Keaton was reluctant to give up his niece. He'd enjoyed their time together. Since bringing her home, Lark had been Grace's primary caregiver, making Keaton feel like an unnecessary third wheel. Today, being alone and in charge, he'd been able to relax fully. Granted, Grace had slept through most of Lark's absence, but if she'd needed anything, he would have been ready and able to take care of it.

"The remote is on the coffee table," he said as he handed Grace over. "If you want to check out the TV."

Lark wrinkled her nose. "Not really my thing."

"When I get home later, we can watch the Discovery Channel together. You might find that you like what you see."

"You are persistent, aren't you?"

"If by persistent you mean bullheaded, then yes." He'd hoped for a smile but had to settle for a sparkle in her moss-green eyes. "I won't be home until around eight tonight. I have a dinner meeting. Will you be okay?"

"We'll be fine."

Reluctant as always, Keaton headed out to his truck. As he backed down her driveway and pointed the vehicle in the direction of the Texas Cattleman's Club, he wondered why leaving her and Grace took so much effort. Although he'd shared the ranch house with his parents until the tornado wiped it out, the place was big enough that he didn't spend all that much time with them.

Basically he was accustomed to being alone.

But since moving into Lark's cozy house, sharing space with her and Grace, he'd adapted to their company. When Lark visited her sister in the hospital, her house had an empty feeling about it that nagged at him. He liked being with her. More than that, he craved her companionship.

It was an unexpected development for a lone wolf like him. Then he remembered that wolves were pack animals. Maybe he'd just been waiting for the right woman to come along. Was the change temporary? When he and Lark stopped playing temporary family, would all his longing for her dissipate? That he hoped it wouldn't trouble him.

She'd made it pretty clear that she didn't trust him. For years her parents had filled her head with inflammatory rhetoric against the Holt family. He might have overcome her reservations regarding his right to help with Grace, but despite the soul-stirring kisses they'd shared and her acknowledging a case of proximity lust, Keaton doubted she'd want to have anything to do with him once Skye and/or Jake claimed Grace.

Too bad she was such a tempting package. If he hadn't been driving, he might have shut his eyes to better savor the memory of her curves beneath his hands. Full breasts, narrow waist, flaring hips. Add to all that her long legs and the way she'd fit into his arms. Most men didn't notice her latent sensuality. She'd spent her entire life building a defense of invisibility.

It had never worked on Keaton. She'd always stood out to him. A tranquil pool amidst the white-water rapids of the people around her. Her still waters ran deep and he found this endlessly fascinating.

Keaton put his mulling aside as he parked his truck beside the rambling single-story building that housed the Texas Cattleman's Club and strolled toward the clubhouse's front door. The interior decor was classic men's club. Dark paneling, lots of leather chairs and the walls were lined with hunting trophies.

A few years earlier the club had opened its doors to a few women. This had caused a great deal of consternation in many of its members. They'd grumbled and fussed, but the women had remained and then proceeded to ruffle even more feathers by transforming the billiards room into an on-site day care.

Keaton had sat back and watched the entire drama unfold, saying little, but throwing his support toward the women. It was long past time the Texas Cattleman's Club stepped into the twenty-first century. Watching Tyrone Taylor sputter in ineffectual annoyance had merely been a satisfying bonus.

The status update meeting had already begun when Keaton entered one of the private meeting rooms and took a seat in the back. President Gil Addison stood at the front of the room, running through the list of all the ongoing projects the members were in charge of.

"How are our tarp teams doing?" he asked Whit Daltry, owner of Daltry Property Management. His task had been to coordinate small groups of people to make sure damaged roofs were covered until repairs could be made.

"They were keeping up pretty well until the wind kicked up last week. At least we haven't had much rain."

A murmur of agreement went up around the room. Keaton nodded. He'd volunteered to coordinate the club's efforts to clean up the demolished town hall and preserve whatever records hadn't been damaged by the tornado. Much of the building's rubble had been cleared and they were close to being able to get at the filing cabinets. Depending on the ability of the old cabinets to withstand a building coming down on them, it was going to be dicey getting the records out intact. For the last few weeks he was wishing he'd volunteered to head up the chainsaw team.

When they finished the official business and Gil concluded the meeting, Keaton waved at a few of the other members, but didn't linger to chat with anyone. The meeting had run longer than he'd expected and he was late for an appointment with the acting mayor to discuss his concerns about moving the town's records.

As he drove, his phone chimed and the truck's electronic voice announced that he'd received a text from Lark. He listened as the message was read to him and then smiled. She'd sent him another of those artistic pictures of blissfully sleeping Grace dressed like a fairy amongst flowers or sailing in a boat. Lark used fabric to create the scene on the floor and then set Grace into the tableau.

At a stop sign, he checked the photo she'd sent him and chuckled at the sight of Grace as Rapunzel in her tower. Lark's creativity surprised him over and over. If she wasn't baking and decorating cakes, she was seeking other outlets for her rich imagination.

Suddenly he was glad she'd spent her entire life building a defense of invisibility. If she'd let more people see who she really was, she might have gotten married before Keaton wised up.

But despite the soul-stirring kisses they'd shared and her acknowledging a case of proximity lust, Keaton wasn't sure she wanted him to stick around once Skye and/or Jake claimed Grace.

And not for the first time that uncertainty was accompanied by a heaviness in his chest and a weighty sense of dread.

* * *

Lark felt sluggish and dull as she left her car parked in the hospital's employee lot and leaned into the chilly January wind on her way to the entrance. Grace had developed a case of the hiccups after her four o'clock feeding, and Lark hadn't been able to get her back to sleep until almost six. By then it was only an hour until she had to get ready for work, so she'd decided to bake a batch of cinnamon rolls to share with her fellow nurses since Marsha wasn't on duty and couldn't complain about the treat.

It was her first day back since bringing Grace home, and already Lark could feel anxiety getting the better of her. Keaton would be annoyed if he suspected how she was feeling. They'd had several tense conversations regarding her reluctance to let him be fully in control. Well, today she didn't have much choice.

Lark swung by the surgical floor to drop off half the cinnamon rolls for her former coworkers. Even if her stint in the ICU hadn't been difficult and lonely, she would have missed the camaraderie she shared with Julie, Yvonne, Hazel and Penny. They were smart, hardworking women who functioned like a team and had little interest in hospital gossip.

Julie was in her office when Lark stopped by. Although she hadn't known the pretty brunette more than a couple months, Lark felt a real connection with her. Born in South Africa, Julie had traveled extensively around the world before coming to Royal to work with Dr. Lucas Wakefield, the brilliant surgeon who'd saved Skye and Grace.

"I brought treats," Lark announced, setting the pan of rolls on Julie's desk.

"Isn't that just like you to think about everyone but yourself? You look half-dead on your feet." Julie's brown eyes narrowed in concern. "How are things going with Grace?"

"Better, but it's something new every day. Last night she had the hiccups."

"Oh dear." Julie popped the lid on the rolls and inhaled deeply. "They're still warm. How did you find time to bake?"

Lark covered a yawn with one hand while waving away Julie's concern with the other. "I had a free hour this morning."

"You are amazing. How is living with Keaton going?"

"Fine. We had the talk."

"The one where you told him nothing was going to happen between you two?"

Lark thought back a few days. Had she spelled it out that succinctly? "I'm not sure. I told him your theory of proximity lust." She paused. Had she actually said there would be no more kissing? "I know I mentioned how bad it would be if we were caught..." She trailed off.

"But you didn't actually tell him to keep his lips to himself."

"I don't think I did."

"Because you don't want him to?"

"I guess." Was it lack of sleep that was making her ambivalent or something else? "I mean, no."

"You're not sounding very clear." Julie grinned at her. "I think you like him and are afraid of the repercussions because of what happened with your sister."

"I do like him. He's intelligent and a huge help with Grace. He's been a strong advocate for his brother even though none of us understand why Jake hasn't been in contact."

"Not to mention he's incredibly sexy in an intense, silent way."

Goose bumps rose on Lark's skin as she recalled the heat of his kiss and the way he'd watched her afterward. "He's tall. I actually have to look up at him."

"And he's built like he could wrestle calves all day and never break a sweat."

Lark laughed. "What do you know about wrestling calves?"

"Only what I've seen on TV, but it's enough to know you need to be tough."

"Okay, he's definitely on the rugged side and that's very appealing, but I would be crazy to think of him as anything but the one man in Royal that my father would never forgive me for getting involved with."

"Except that you're already involved with him. He's living in your house."

"To help me take care of Grace." Lark cringed when she thought of her father's inevitable reaction when he found out. "It would be so much worse if he thought we were sleeping together."

"So you're just going to ignore the chemistry between you?"

"That's the plan."

"Good luck."

Waving goodbye to Julie, Lark headed toward the ICU. Her nerves were a tangled mess. She'd been gone from the house, leaving Keaton in charge for a whopping half hour, and already she wanted badly to call and see how things were going. What bothered her was that only part of her wanted an update on Grace; she mainly desired contact with Keaton. He'd gotten under her skin in a very short period of time.

As a compromise between instinct and logic, she sent him a text instead of calling. This way she satisfied her need to connect with him but maintained her distance. It was going to be a balancing act until she got her emotions under control. It would be hard—living in close proximity, desiring his hands against her skin, quelling the urge to press her body against his while maintaining a casual, unaffected demeanor. Lark shuddered in dismay.

The ICU nurses' station was slammed when Lark arrived. Apparently Marsha had gone home with a headache halfway through her shift and one of the surgical patients who had undergone a routine knee replacement had developed a blood clot that had moved into his lungs.

This meant Lark wouldn't have the opportunity to ease

back into her job and wouldn't have more than five minutes to stop by Skye's bedside. With time running short before her shift started, Lark pulled out her phone for one last thing. She set it on Skye's chest, right over her sister's heart, and hit the play button.

"I brought you a video of Grace doing this weird grunting thing that is typical of preemies. She's lying in the infant gym that Keaton bought her and playing with the monkey. It's her favorite animal. I know you can't watch her yet, but I hope her voice reaches you." Lark started the video and watched Skye's face for some reaction. She had no idea if her sister was aware but if anything could reach a new mother, it was adorable baby noises, and Grace made more of those each day.

"Keaton bought a sixty-inch flat-screen and put it in my great room," Lark complained, cuing up the video to play again. "Apparently he can't live without football. The thing is monstrous. He insisted we watch a show on the Discovery Channel. It was interesting, but the programing on the History Channel was more to my taste. And then there's this show about women in search of the perfect wedding dress." Lark had found that one on her own. The gorgeous wedding dresses had left her contemplating what sort of bridal gown Skye would choose.

Lark surveyed her sister's bare hand. Surely when she'd gotten pregnant, Jake would have proposed. He'd want to make sure Grace had his name. Lark shied away from considering that Keaton's brother wasn't the honorable sort. Had Skye been the one who'd balked? Why, when she'd adored Jake for so long?

After she'd connected with her sister, the rest of Lark's day bordered on frantic. At least being busy kept her from worrying how Grace and Keaton were doing. Halfway through her shift, she was able to take a twenty-minute break to grab lunch and check her messages. Her inbox was filled with pictures of Grace sleeping peacefully in her bassinet or the mechanical swing Keaton had bought. Her relief was instantaneous. Why had she worried? Grace was in good hands.

Six

Keaton kept his ear tuned to the swing in the living room where Grace slept while he checked out the job the painters had done on what would become the nursery. He'd bought odorless paint, but until it was completely dry and the fumes had cleared, he didn't want Grace in here.

He hoped Lark would be pleasantly surprised. After seeing her weariness this morning, he'd determined the best thing for her would be moving Grace into her own room so Lark could sleep through the nights she had to work the following day.

"Looks great," he told the artist he'd hired to decorate the newly painted walls with images plucked from the crib bedding.

"Thanks." Tracey had placed a monkey above where the changing table would go and a smattering of jungle creatures on the wall opposite the crib. "I hope your wife likes it."

Keaton didn't correct her. To explain the complicated relationship between him and Lark would take too much of his energy. Better that he say nothing. "Monkeys are Grace's favorite, so I'm sure Lark will approve."

Although Lark hadn't been overjoyed that Keaton had hired painters, her scowl carried less punch than when he'd first brought up the idea of hiring Jen to clean house and prepare meals a couple times a week. He'd wanted her full-time, but Lark refused. She hadn't quite given up her determination to do more than was physically possible, but Keaton had his own streak of stubbornness. Grace needed her aunt to be in tiptop shape, and Lark needed to be at full strength to support Skye. He intended to do whatever necessary to see that she was.

From the living room, his satellite phone beeped, announcing a call. Cell coverage had been disrupted at the ranch since the tornado damaged the equipment on the nearby tower. Keaton had picked up a couple satellite phones that he and the foreman used to keep in touch with the various contractors they had working on repairs.

Grace slept peacefully despite the phone ringing nearby, but Keaton decided to take the call in the kitchen. It was close to her feeding time, so he might as well get a bottle ready.

"Keaton, how are you?" His mother sounded relaxed and happy. "How are things at the ranch?"

"Fine, Mom. Everything's fine. How are you and Dad?" His parents were shopping for retirement property on the Alabama gulf coast.

"We're enjoying the beach, but your father is frustrated with the real estate market here." His mother sounded amused. With Keaton in charge of the family ranch, David Holt had been free to throw his abundant energy into finding his wife the perfect home.

"Sorry to hear that."

"And I think he's anxious about the ranch. So we're coming home in a few days."

"I hope he's not disappointed with the progress."

"Do you think Lark would mind if we came over there and spent time with Grace when we get back to town?"

Keaton was pleased his mother no longer sounded suspicious when she spoke of Lark. Initially his parents had had a very negative reaction to his announcement that he was moving into Lark's house, but they trusted his judgment and he'd plied them with stories of Lark's earnestness and devotion to her sister and Baby Grace until they'd come around.

"I think she'd be glad to have you. Let me check with her when she comes home tonight."

In truth, he wasn't sure how Lark would react to his mother's request. She'd yet to receive an answer to the invitation she'd extended to her parents despite having called twice since Grace had come home from the hospital. The lack of contact agitated her. Keaton hated seeing her distress. As angry as his parents had been when they found out that Jake had been secretly seeing Skye through high school and college, as the years had gone by without contact with their son, their attitude toward Skye and, by extension, the rest of the Taylors had mellowed.

If only the Taylors felt the same way.

"I'll give you a call later tonight and let you know what Lark says," he told his mother before ending the call.

No more than five minutes later Grace began to fuss. Pleased that he was developing a sixth sense where she was concerned, Keaton headed for the swing before she had a chance to let out her first wail.

Lark let herself into the kitchen and pushed the button that would close the garage door. All the way home she'd been dreading what sort of chaotic mess she'd find her house in. To her delight, there were a neat row of drying bottles lined up on the countertop and a delicious smell wafting from the oven. Soothing music poured from her stereo speakers. Keaton had found her collection of interpretive piano CDs.

Before she shrugged out of her coat, Keaton appeared at her side with a glass of white wine. "Dinner will be ready in twenty minutes if you want to grab a quick shower."

"You did all this?"

"I had a very smooth day with Grace. That left me with enough free time to stay caught up." He took her coat and handed her the wine. "How was your first day back?"

"Awful." She sipped the wine and sighed. "Is there really time for me to take a shower?" The thought of letting hot water wash away her stressful day sounded blissfully perfect.

"There's time." He gave her a little shove in the direction of her bedroom. "Just don't fall asleep in there."

Drifting in a fog of pleasure, Lark sipped her wine and peeled off her scrubs. Leaving them in a pile on her bathroom floor, she started the water running in her shower and blinked to restore moisture to her dry eyes. The last twelve hours were beginning to feel like a bad dream. She took another sip of wine and felt the knots in her shoulders begin to unravel. She'd never imagined how wonderful it would be to have a family to come home to after a long day.

Ten minutes later, wrapped in a thick terry robe, her hair still damp, Lark reentered her bedroom and stopped when she realized Grace's crib and changing table were no longer in the little sitting area. She and Keaton had talked about moving Grace into the third bedroom, but Lark wasn't ready to have the baby so far away. Instead of respecting her decision, he'd gone ahead and done what he believed was best.

Lark stalked out of her bedroom and headed for the kitchen, where Keaton was sliding a cookie sheet covered with dinner rolls into the oven. "I thought you understood that I wasn't ready to have Grace move."

Keaton closed the oven door and turned to face her. His eyebrows drew together as he took in her damp hair, robe and bare feet.

"Grace will be fine in her own room. You need to be able to sleep the nights you work, and this way I have freer access."

His calm explanation had the opposite effect on Lark. "This is my house," she reminded him, her temper flaring. "I should be the one who decides what happens here. You've already insisted on hiring a housekeeper and brought in a huge TV. Now you've moved Grace."

"Look, it's going to be okay." He took her upper arms in a strong grip and gave her a little shake. "You just need to let me help."

All the fight went out of Lark as her body became immediately aroused by Keaton's touch. Despite the thickness of the terry cloth, Lark could feel his heat. It flowed into her in a rush, igniting the desire she'd worked so hard these past few days to ignore.

"Keaton." Her voice cracked on his name. She had no idea how to verbalize what she needed. Her skin longed for the imprint of his hands. The ache between her thighs flared, demanding relief from the endless hours of anticipation. Her instincts took over. "Kiss me."

His body stiffened at her plea…demand…whatever it had been. Concerned that she'd been too bold and embarrassed by his inaction, she was on the verge of explaining that she'd been kidding when he growled.

"Damn it, Lark." His lips dipped toward hers but hovered before he made contact.

"What are you waiting for?"

His grip on her arms tightened. The corner of his mouth jerked. "You Taylor girls are nothing but trouble."

Stung, she pulled back. Keaton's long fingers held her prisoner. "What's that supposed to mean?"

"Just what I said. You're trouble."

"I'm not the one who demanded we share responsibility for Grace or suggested you move in. That's all on you."

His fingers refused to relax their grip and she couldn't risk struggling to free herself or he would get an eyeful of her bare form. As if he read her thoughts, Keaton's gaze raked down her body.

"You have gorgeous breasts," he murmured. "Why do you insist on hiding them?"

The awe in his voice was such a contrast to his annoyance a moment earlier that Lark was at a loss. "How do you know what my breasts look like?"

"There's a great lake for swimming on the edge of Taylor land. When it was hot, you used to ride there and go swimming on the days you weren't working at the mall."

As soon as Lark had been old enough to get a part-time

job, she started working a minimum of twenty hours a week. The income allowed her to buy her first car and limited the amount of time she was at home, enduring her mother's nonstop criticism.

"How did you know that?" Then she realized what he hadn't said. "You watched me?"

"Are you kidding? I was a horny college student and you wore a tiny yellow bikini."

Her skin burned as she thought back to those days. Believing herself alone, she'd shed her inhibitions and reveled in being sensual and free.

"But that was my family's land."

"And it pissed me off that you had the best swimming hole for miles around. So I trespassed." His lips twisted into a humorless smile. "A lot."

"Why didn't you ever tell me you were there?"

"Because as long as you thought you were alone, you were like some wild water nymph. If you'd had any idea I was there, you'd have chased me off with that shotgun you always carried with you."

"I needed it to keep the predators at bay," she replied. "Looks like it worked."

"Now that you understand that I've been crazy about your beautiful body for a long time, will you please go get dressed." Keaton gently shoved her an arm's length away and set her free. "And hurry. Dinner will be ready in five minutes."

Knowing it would be supremely reckless to bait him further, Lark retreated. To her dismay, her knees had developed a perilous wobble and she had to sit on her bed for two minutes before she felt steady enough to dress. Slipping into jeans and a bulky sweater, she returned to the kitchen in time to help Keaton dish up the meal.

"This looks amazing," she said, hoping some mundane conversation would disperse the last bit of tension between them. "What is it?"

"Chicken covered in mayo and shredded Parmesan cheese. I saw the recipe on a commercial and it seemed easy enough."

"You are a man of many surprises," she murmured, carrying their plates to the dining room. Glancing over to where Grace slept in her swing, Lark realized the chance of distractions during the meal was low. She sat down and smiled up at Keaton as he topped off her wineglass. "You know, I think I've used this dining table more since you moved in than in the two years I've owned the house."

"Where do you usually eat?"

"At the breakfast bar." She smoothed her napkin across her lap, avoiding looking at Keaton.

Tonight he'd substituted a long-sleeve Henley in dark gray for his usual cotton button-downs. The knit material clung to his wide shoulders and highlighted his sculpted chest muscles. Heat flooded her cheeks as she recalled the solid wall of his torso pressed against her the last time they'd kissed. A five-foot-ten-inch girl with substantial curves would be crazy not to swoon over a man who was strong enough to manhandle her and smart enough to know when she wanted him to and when she didn't.

So far Keaton was that guy. He'd demonstrated both passion and restraint. If only his last name wasn't Holt.

"My mother called tonight. She and my dad are coming back to town in a few days," Keaton began, appearing oblivious of her musing.

What a relief. Usually he demonstrated an unsettling ability to read her thoughts and anticipate her needs.

"That's nice."

"Mom wondered if they could come over and spend some time with Grace. I thought maybe a family dinner?"

The word *family* gave her a jolt. Did he want her there? Or would he choose a night when she was working?

"Sure."

"You're off Wednesday, right?"

"I am." The strength of her relief speared through Lark, shocking her. "That should work great."

"And I don't want you to worry about dinner. I thought we'd fix steaks and keep things simple."

"I don't own a barbecue," Lark reminded him.

"That's okay. I've got it taken care of."

Taken care of how?

"Having your parents over for dinner is a great idea," she said. "They deserve to get to know their granddaughter." If only her parents were so inclined. "And thank you for asking me."

He didn't look at all chastened by her subtle reproof.

"Of course. It's your house."

He had to be kidding. Irritation flared. "That hasn't slowed you down thus far."

"I know I should have told you my plans for fixing up Grace's nursery," he said, returning to the disagreement they'd been having earlier. "But see it from my perspective. When Grace sleeps in your bedroom, I'm not able to do my fair share." He lowered his lids to half-mast and peered at her from beneath his lush lashes. "Unless, of course, you want me in your bedroom late at night."

She couldn't restrain the grin that tugged at her lips. "Stop trying to distract me from being annoyed with you."

"I'm not trying to distract you, I'm simply pointing out the reality of our current situation." Keaton rested his forearms on the table and leaned forward, his expression earnest. "I'm not going to pretend I understand what you're going through. With Skye in a coma and Grace's health a constant concern, you've got to be consumed with anxiety. All I'm trying to do is take some of the burden off your shoulders. Let me help."

Lark drew a shaky breath. With her stomach in knots she'd lost her appetite. "It's just so hard to let go. I keep worrying that she'll need me and I won't be there."

"Remember that she was on her own in the NICU for the first twelve weeks of her life."

"I know, but that makes me all the more determined to keep her close."

"And I'll be right next door with the baby monitor on my nightstand."

She knit her fingers together in her lap and struggled to overcome her compulsion to control every aspect of Grace's well-being. "Let's start tomorrow. Give me the night to get used to the idea."

Keaton nodded. "That sounds good."

"And if she hates being all by herself, we go back to what we've been doing."

"With one difference." Keaton picked up his fork and speared a broccoli floret. "I will be visiting your bedroom every two or three hours throughout the night."

Keaton lay on the bed in Lark's guest room, his hands behind his head, his feet crossed at the ankle, and stared at the dark ceiling. Even though it was Lark's night to get up with Grace, he couldn't sleep. Over the last few days he'd grown accustomed to his niece's schedule and woken every few hours just as she was beginning to stir. He glanced at the clock and decided to get up and get a bottle started. Maybe if he could catch Grace before she made a sound, he could give Lark a few more hours to rest.

For a man who spent his days directing the operations of an extensive ranch and getting dirty on occasion working alongside his hands, he was rather surprised how well he'd managed with Grace. Everything about her was so tiny it had taken him forever to master slipping on her doll-sized socks and days before he was completely confident in his ability to change her diaper and dress her without worrying that he might accidentally be too rough with her.

Each time she focused her gaze on his face, his heart took a severe hit for his absent brother. Jake was missing so much. And then there was Skye, still locked in a coma. There were so many firsts they both were missing.

Right on cue, Grace was beginning to wake up when he entered the nursery. He immediately turned down the baby monitor so if she did make a sound, Lark wouldn't hear. Pleased with his timing, Keaton lifted the infant into his arms and settled into the rocking chair he'd bought. As soon as he brought the bottle to her lips, Grace latched on and began sucking with enthusiasm.

"Hungry little thing, aren't you?"

It pleased him how the baby was thriving. Tomorrow was her first wellness check since leaving the hospital. He and Lark had agreed to go together, and if all went well, they were going to attempt an early dinner out. That should start the tongue-wagging, he thought, remembering how getting caught having dinner together had led to Jake and Skye running away from Royal. But then, they'd been in love. He and Lark were simply co-babysitting.

Yet if that was all it was, why did his thoughts circle back to her all day and much of the night? Getting up to feed or change Grace hadn't been much of a hardship since his sleep was all messed up by the temptation of her sleeping twenty feet away. Nor could he get out of his head the night she'd picked a fight over the nursery while wearing nothing more than a robe. Did she have any idea how close she'd come to driving him over the edge?

By the time Keaton resettled Grace in her crib and watched her fall asleep, his own exhaustion had caught up with him. But he knew it was nothing compared to how Lark must be feeling.

"Is something wrong with Grace?" Lark's soft voice, tense and filled with concern, came from the doorway behind him.

"She's fine," he reassured her, pitching his volume equally low. Turning his head in her direction, he caught her staring at him in dismay. What would it take for her to stop worrying so much?

"Why are you up, then?"

"I was awake and figured you could use the sleep." Since

she seemed to be unable to shake her doubts, he held out his hand and beckoned her close. "She's all right, really."

Once she'd seen for herself that Grace was sleeping peacefully, Lark heaved a huge sigh. Then her attention shifted to him and her gaze sharpened.

"You aren't wearing a shirt."

He glanced down at his bare chest, unsure what to make of the accusation in her voice. "I don't usually wear one to bed."

"But you're not in bed."

"Obviously."

Since she seemed determined to pursue the odd conversation, he decided they'd be better off having it where they wouldn't disturb Grace. Taking Lark by the arm, he escorted her out of the nursery and deposited her stiff form in the middle of the living room.

"I've got everything under control. Go back to bed."

"It's my night to take care of her." Her lower lip jutted out, making her look like an adorable toddler in a temper.

Keaton set his hands on his hips above the waistband of his pajama bottoms, and struggled not to grin at how cute she looked. "I promise to sleep as soundly as a hibernating bear tomorrow. Now go to bed."

"Damn it, Keaton, you can't tell me what to do." She was in a transfixed stupor, staring at his half-naked form.

Again he glanced down at himself, wondering what she found so utterly fascinating. Then he looked at her.

Lark wore pale blue, long-sleeve pajamas that covered her from neck to ankle. Modest in fit, they still managed to accent the provocative swell of her substantial breasts and failed to hide the tightening of her nipples against the soft fabric.

His body came to life with such ferocity he almost groaned. "You should listen to me when I'm giving you good advice," he growled, unsure how much longer he could keep his hands off her.

She tipped her head back and met his gaze. Her eyes were clear, the look in them bold. "What makes your advice so great?"

"It will keep me from doing something that won't make you very happy."

Her eyebrows rose. "Like what?"

Sexual tension flared between them at her defiant tone.

"Like this." Plagued by too many long nights of temptation and incensed that she'd dared him to act, Keaton seized the edges of her pajama top and tore it open. Buttons flew in all directions. Shocked by the ferocity of the desire she aroused in him, Keaton froze.

They were both breathing hard, but the ragged rise and fall of their chests was the only movement. Keaton searched Lark's stunned expression and waited for her to speak, to yell at him for stepping across the line.

Her hand came up, but not to slap him. She slid her palm up his chest, the caress brimming with sensual intent, and tunneled her fingers into his hair. Rising on tiptoe, she pressed her bare breasts against his chest and slid her cheek against his.

"Kiss me."

His lips were halfway to hers when she spoke the words.

This was no tentative, exploratory kiss. Lark's mouth was open and eager as he claimed it. He wasted no energy on preliminaries, just plunged his tongue deep, and was rewarded by the ardent thrust of her pelvis against his growing erection. Her moan made his head spin.

Leaving one hand to cup her head, he let the other skim down her back. He savored every curve and dip as her skin slipped like silk beneath his questing fingers. When he reached the waistband of her pajama bottoms, he hesitated only briefly before diving beneath. The fullness of her butt was a temptation he could no longer resist. They groaned in unison as he filled his palm with her flesh, fitting her more firmly against his raging hardness.

If he didn't get her naked soon, he was going to descend into madness. Or perhaps he'd already plunged down the rabbit hole. He was fast losing track of which way was up, and when Lark stroked him through the cotton fabric covering his erection, he shuddered. She touched him with more curiosity than eroticism, but the contact was earth-shattering. With only a matter of moments before he could no longer stand, he eased down on one knee. Bracketing her lush hips between his hands to hold her still, he placed his lips against her flat stomach between her rib cage and belly button.

She quivered as he kissed a path across her abdomen and smoothed her hand across his shoulders. He needed a moment to gather himself for what came next. At long last, confident that he was ready, Keaton set his forehead against her body and spoke.

"If you go back to bed right now, we can both pretend that this was nothing more than an incredibly realistic dream."

Fabric whispered through the air as it fell to the floor. Seconds later Lark guided his hands up her body. Understanding what she wanted, he cupped her breasts, marveling at their perfection. The hardness of her nipples fascinated him. Her breath caught as he gave them a light pinch. She was so incredibly sensitive. He couldn't wait to make her body sing.

Eager to begin, Keaton lowered her to the carpet unable to make the long trek to her bedroom. As soon as her back met the floor, he moved over her, capturing her lips in a slow, drugging kiss. Her hands moved down his back, nails digging in, as he released her mouth to suck gently at the spot where her neck and shoulder met.

Beneath him her hips shifted restlessly, inciting his passion with each thrust against his overly stimulated flesh. Breathless, he licked his way down her chest and sucked her nipple into his mouth, distracting her momentarily. He brought his hand up to knead her other breast, and a soft mewling sound broke from her lips. Smiling, he used tongue and teeth to keep her attention fixed where he wanted it, but he underestimated her—she wasn't willing to be a passive participant.

Before he knew what she was up to, she'd spread her legs and tugged the waistband of his pajamas down past his hips. In an instant he was pressed against the heat between her thighs, the only barrier between them her pajama bottoms.

She slid her hand between their bodies and found him. The sensation of her bare skin on his hot shaft was too much for his willpower to bear. Keaton slid down her body, breaking contact. He trembled in the aftermath of what could have been a very quick end to their foreplay and trailed his mouth across her stomach. She lifted her hips to aid him in stripping her bare and he smiled as his lips dipped into the hollow near her hip. With her pants no longer in his way, he shifted his shoulders between her knees and gathered her butt in his hands.

"Keaton?"

It was all she managed before he put his mouth against her hot, sweet center.

Seven

With his tongue trailing fire around and over the most sensitive part of her body, Lark arched her back and quaked with pleasure unlike any she'd ever known. Keaton's mastery stole her voice and rendered her muscles useless. Her entire world became his mouth and the rapid building of pressure centered between her thighs.

He seemed to understand exactly what drove her wild. His touch was both clever and commanding. She rose higher and higher. An unbridled moan grew in her throat, the rumble vibrating through her as her orgasm built. It was crazy how fast and hard she was coming. She tried to slow it down, to linger in the moment, but Keaton slid two fingers inside her and touched a spot that sent her off like a rocket.

Blind and deaf, she shook with the intensity of her climax. For several heartbeats time stopped and she floated. Then she crashed back into her body and gasped.

"That was amazing."

Keaton kissed her stomach. "Glad you enjoyed it."

He lay between her thighs, with most of his weight supported on his arms, and watched her through heavy-lidded eyes, a half smile on his gorgeous lips.

"You look awfully pleased with yourself."

"Any time a man can get a woman to come like that, he has a right to feel smug."

"Is that so?" Before he guessed her intention, Lark wrapped her thighs around his waist and used the element of surprise to knock him off balance.

With Keaton flat on his back, she took a second to appreciate the width of his chest and all the fine muscles that made up the ridges of his abdomen. She drew her fingers over his collarbone and across his pecs to the flat disks of his nipples. He shuddered as she scraped her nails over them and with that her confidence ballooned.

Behind her, Keaton's erection bumped against her lower back. She reached for it and watched his eyes widen as she cupped him lightly. Immediately a familiar hum began below her belly button. She rocked her hips in a gentle arc. The motion stirred her body back to wakefulness, making her smile.

"What are you thinking about?" Keaton asked, cupping her breasts in firm fingers.

Lark pushed into his touch and gripped him more firmly. "I'm thinking that I've never been with anyone that makes me feel the way you do."

"And what way is that?"

"Like I'm hungry all the time. When I'm in the same room with you, all I can think about is this." She moved her fingers in provocative swirls, and Keaton's face screwed up as if in pain. "How it would feel to have you inside me."

She leaned forward and kissed him sweetly on the mouth. Her tongue licked along the seam of his lips, tasting the lingering flavor of her arousal, and when he parted for her, it dipped in to tease and tantalize.

When Keaton cupped her face and deepened the kiss, she let him. Her hunger spiked, driven to new heights by the passionate bite of Keaton's fingers and the ferocity of his kiss. Soon she knew she needed him to fill her. She broke free of Keaton's mouth and gasped in a great lungful of air. At the same time she shifted so the tip of his erection nudged at her, eager for what she offered.

With a sharp curse Keaton caught her hips in a firm grip. "Wait. We need protection."

She shook her head. "It's okay."

"Are you on something?"

"No, but I'm at a safe point in my cycle." She pried his hands off her and with a whooshing exhale, took him in.

An exclamation of surprise burst from her. She'd known he was big, but she wasn't prepared for the reality of how completely he filled her. "Wow."

"Are you okay?"

"I'm good."

He didn't look convinced. "You have a funny look on your face."

"I'm just getting used to all of you."

"Take your time." He caressed her thighs with a casualness that belied the tightness around his mouth, but when she started gyrating her hips, he sprang into action.

Before her mind recognized movement, Keaton rolled her beneath him and captured her lips in a sizzling kiss. At the same time he shifted his hips back and thrust slowly into her. The friction was amazing and Lark wrapped her legs around Keaton's hips as his rhythm built.

As they moved together she noticed that his earlier intensity had been tempered. He made love to her with deliberate concern for her needs. As much as she appreciated his thoughtfulness, she didn't like that he was holding back. She liked the wildness he aroused in her. It unleashed a sense of freedom missing in her life.

She bit down on his shoulder and dug her fingernails into his back. "Stop being so gentle," she growled when he stared down at her in confusion. "I'm not going to break. Give me all you've got."

"Fine." After uttering that single word, he kissed her hard and drove into her powerfully.

Lark grabbed handfuls of his hair and let her tongue duel with his. His need surrounded her, filled all the lonely places she'd gotten so good at ignoring. This was what it felt like to be truly wanted. No one had ever made love to her with such determination.

"Yes, yes, yes," she chanted when he let her breathe. "More, just like that."

An orgasm was rushing forward to claim her. Words poured from her. She heard them in her ears but could make no sense of the flow. They seemed to have an effect on Keaton, however, because he began to pound harder into her. Lark pried her eyes open and watched his face, sensing that he was close and wanting to see him come.

As a cry broke from his lips, the first shudders of her own climax claimed her. His body jerked, his lips pulled back in a savage grin. He looked down, caught her gaze with his and held her captive as they exploded together.

"That was not appropriate," Keaton muttered, shifting his weight off Lark. His chest rose and fell in exaggerated breaths as he sat up and stared down at her.

She punched him in the shoulder. "The postcoital words every woman wants to hear."

The hit barely hurt, but it was enough to make her point. She might not expect flowery, romantic phrases, but she wasn't interested in stark realism either.

"I meant not using protection."

"I figured, but we'd already covered that issue before it happened. I told you it was not going to be a problem."

He raked his fingers through his hair, disturbed by what he'd done. "I don't have unprotected sex." He was furious with himself for the lapse.

"That's good to know." Heedless of her nakedness, she pushed to her feet and snatched her pajamas from the floor. "I don't either. I'm sorry if I made you do something so out of character."

She was halfway to her bedroom before he realized she'd misread the target of his irritation. By the time he leaped to his feet to pursue Lark and apologize, she was in the process of shutting her door firmly in his face. Ignoring the blatant "get lost" signal, he knocked.

And knocked again.

"Look," he called. "We need to talk about what happened."

The door muffled her voice, but her words were clear. "No, we don't."

"What just happened between us caught me off guard and I put my foot in it."

"You put your entire leg into it." She sounded closer, but no less annoyed.

"Open the door and I'll do better."

"I don't believe you can."

"No one has ever made me lose control the way you just did."

A long pause followed his words. "I'm listening."

"The reason I didn't insist on protection was that I couldn't stop. Never have I done something like that before. I couldn't bear to have anything come between us. But it was stupid and put you at risk."

The door cracked open. Lark peered at him through the narrow space. "Never?"

"Not once."

"You didn't put me at risk." She gave him a small smile. "But thanks for your concern."

And to his astonishment, she shut the door again, leaving him alone in the hallway. He retraced his steps back to the living room and scooped up his discarded pajamas. Well, what had he expected after he'd ruined the moment? A night of cuddling and maybe more lovemaking?

Unsure what their next encounter would bring, Keaton had a hard time falling asleep. Or maybe it was the way he kept reliving the taste of Lark and the feel of her curvaceous body beneath his. He remembered glancing at the clock around five-thirty. The next thing he knew it was seven-fifteen and he was running late.

Lark was in the kitchen, humming an off-key ditty when he emerged from his bedroom. She looked well rested and happy. Her cheeks wore a lovely shade of rose and her eyes danced in merriment as she alternately flipped French toast and tickled Grace.

The smell of bacon and fresh-brewed coffee hit his nose at the same time. His stomach growled in appreciation. The noise was loud enough to alert Lark that he was there. She poured him a cup of coffee and added the perfect amount of creamer. With a sweet-as-peaches smile she extended it to him.

"You look rested," he remarked over the rim of the mug.

"I conked out the second my head hit the pillow and slept until Grace woke me at quarter to six. That was almost five hours. I feel amazing."

Keaton considered his own restless night and grimaced. Obviously he'd been the one most impacted by their late night interlude. "I'm glad to hear that."

"I appreciate you getting up with her last night, but I'm off for the next few days, so you need to get a good night's sleep tonight."

So she was going to act as if nothing had happened? It was not how Keaton had imagined the morning going, but far less awkward than if they'd rehashed what had been a colossal mistake. And he wasn't just talking about their lack of protection. He should never have kissed her or let things get so out of hand that their first time together had been on the living room floor.

"I'm sure that's what will happen." Keaton's gaze wandered to the spot in the living room where they'd made love the night before. "Lark," he began, only to have her shake her head vigorously. "We should talk."

"Do you still want to come with me to Grace's checkup?" she asked. "It's at four."

"Yes." He watched her closely as she dished up two slices of French toast and piled bacon on the side. The urge to kiss her rose in him so fast he was reaching for her before his conscious mind registered the impulse.

She blocked him with the plate. "Eat up. You have a busy day today. What time is the contractor expecting you at the ranch?"

"Nine."

"And then you've promised to help move the storage files at the town hall." She shooed him toward a bar stool and went to fill a travel mug with coffee. "How are things going with the cleanup?"

Obviously she was eager to get rid of him. Keaton wasn't sure whether or not that was a good sign. What had happened between them the night before bothered her more than she let on or she wouldn't be making such an obvious effort to act as if nothing had happened.

"Most of the big debris has been cleared. I'll know more when we get under the tarps they stretched over what used to be the records room and start moving the cabinets."

"I imagine some of those files go back to the 1800s."

Back to a time before the Holts and Taylors fought over two thousand acres of prime land. Land rich with the water so essential to sustain large herds of cattle through the dry season. Keaton's gut tightened at the reminder of how much animosity existed between their families. He hadn't been thinking about repercussions when he made love to Lark last night. Or the consequences of letting his feelings for her develop.

She wasn't her sister. Growing up, Skye had been confident and popular. The apple of her father's eye, she'd been unafraid of disappointing her parents. She'd loved Jake passionately and turned her back on everyone she cared about to be with him.

Lark wasn't like that. Brilliant, sensitive and mostly ignored by her parents, she'd been shy and reserved. If their families hadn't hated each other and his brother hadn't secretly been seeing her sister, he probably never would've noticed her. What a shame that would have been.

Much as Lark wasn't like Skye, Keaton wasn't like his

brother. Jake could leave Royal and their ranch, knowing that Keaton would stick around to take charge. He doubted that Jake had ever considered whether Keaton wanted to do something else with his life. Or that their parents might desperately miss the younger Holt.

Damn. His brother could be a hardheaded, selfish idiot. When Jake finally showed up in Royal, Keaton might have to take his brother down hard before letting him anywhere near Skye and Grace.

"Keaton?" Lark's worried voice broke through the haze of irritation that gripped him. "Are you okay?"

"Yeah. Fine." He rubbed his temple to ease the ache there. "I was just thinking about Jake."

"About beating him bloody?"

"What?" Her accurate read of his thoughts caught him off guard.

"You looked pretty angry." And from the look on her face, she'd been worried he was mad at her.

"Sorry. It's just every time I ask myself why he hasn't called or shown up, I can't imagine what could be keeping him away."

"Hopefully we'll find out sooner rather than later."

Once she'd gotten Keaton out the door, Lark released a gigantic sigh of relief. He'd so obviously wanted to rehash what had happened between them the night before and she wasn't sure she knew what to say.

Yes, it had been a mistake. A glorious, wonderful, spectacular mistake. One she'd repeat anytime and as often as she could.

Except she probably wouldn't get the chance.

She closed her eyes and let the memory of his hot kisses and fierce possession wash through her. Nothing in her life came close to those moments he'd made love to her, and she wasn't sure how she was supposed to go forward.

With Grace's needs taken care of for the moment and a

housekeeper coming in twice a week to cook, clean and do laundry, Lark found herself with a few precious hours of free time. Normally she would pick up a book and get lost among its pages, but her mind was far too restless to concentrate. Instead she carried Grace in her bouncy seat into her bedroom and went to investigate her closet.

One of the nice things about the years she hadn't lived in Royal was the freedom she'd enjoyed from her mother's criticism. Vera Taylor had an opinion about everything when it came to a person's appearance, and her daughters faced the lash of their mother's judgment the most. The constant badgering to *do something* about her appearance had turned Lark into an antifashionista.

All through high school, she'd owned several pairs of jeans and a variety of nondescript shirts that she rotated through her closet and the laundry. When it grew cold, she'd add a bulky hooded sweatshirt. In the summer she wore cut-offs and T-shirts. Her resolve to blend in drove her mother absolutely crazy. Vera lived to be complimented and envied for her carefully chosen outfits, flawless skin and perfect hair.

It wasn't until Lark arrived at college that things changed. Her freshman year roommate was a fashion major and had gently guided Lark to break out of her rut. Without being compared to her beautiful sister all the time, Lark had discovered a sense of confidence. Karen had shown her how wearing jeans with the right top and a cute pair of flats could make her feel pretty, even sexy. By the end of the first semester, she'd added several skirts and even a couple dresses to her wardrobe.

From the very back of her closet, Lark pulled out a garment bag. In it were four dresses that she hadn't worn since returning to Royal and one she'd never taken the tags off. She considered each one as she arranged them on her bed. Two were casual daytime dresses, something she'd wear to go shopping with friends or grab drinks at happy hour. The third one was a fancy cocktail dress she'd bought her senior year of college to attend a Christmas party at her boyfriend's law firm. Her gaze came at last to the fourth dress.

She'd bought it on Karen's recommendation because her roommate insisted that every woman needed an LBD in her closet. This particular little black dress showed off Lark's curves to great advantage. The wrap design drew attention to her hourglass shape and left her arms bare. Lark had never worn the dress because she felt so blatantly sexy in it, and that was significantly outside her comfort zone.

Lark stripped off her jeans and sweater and slipped the dress over her head. Before she looked at her reflection in the mirror, she fetched her one pair of heels. Basic black pumps that pushed her height over the six-foot mark. A pair of gold earrings completed the outfit. Gathering a deep breath, Lark regarded herself in her full-length mirror and gasped.

She looked amazing.

And not unlike herself, something she'd discovered the last time she'd tried on the dress. That had been four years ago, before she'd moved back to Royal. Returning to her hometown had caused Lark to regress into what had been comfortable and familiar. Once again she was that wall-flower who worked hard and received little notice. She spent quiet nights at home reading or decorating cakes. Once in a while she went out with her coworkers, but she was never the girl men wanted to flirt with.

Now, for the first time in what seemed like forever, she craved someone's attention. Longed to see a man's eyes to light up when he spotted her. For him to be a little tongue-tied when she smiled his way.

And she wanted that man to be Keaton Holt.

Keaton arrived home much later than he intended. He glanced at Lark's closed bedroom door before checking on Grace. The infant was sleeping peacefully in her crib. It was about half an hour before her four o'clock wellness visit.

Work at the town hall wasn't going well. The delicate process of unearthing over a century of the town's records had suffered yet another setback.

After a quick, hot shower Keaton put on a pair of khaki slacks, a striped shirt and a navy sweater. With the restaurants on the west side of town destroyed by the tornado, they had only the Royal Diner or Claire's to choose from. As much as he enjoyed the diner's fifties décor and terrific food, the place was a hotbed of local gossip. If he and Lark showed up there with Grace, they would be mobbed with questions and the focus of far too much speculation. Better that they dined at Claire's, which boasted a more refined ambience and an upscale menu.

Lark must have decided the same thing, because she was wearing a black trench coat and heels. His eyes were immediately drawn to her bare calves. She had great legs. Long. Toned. He loved riding his hands up their smooth length, relishing the power of her muscles as she wrapped her thighs around his hips.

Desire pulsed through him, a languid, sensual tug on his hormones. Until they'd made love, he'd been mostly preoccupied by her perfect, luscious breasts. Now he was having trouble deciding which turned him on the most.

"Ready?" Lark questioned, picking up Grace's carrier and giving him a strange look. She'd dusted her eyelids with gray shadow and darkened her lashes with mascara, making her green eyes stand out. A soft pink gloss covered her lips, drawing his attention there next. "Grace's appointment is in ten minutes," she prompted, her voice edged with smoke.

There was something different about her today and it wasn't just the stylish trench or the makeup she'd applied. She wore confidence like a favorite accessory. He had a hard time keeping his thoughts from straying to what dinner might lead to.

"Here, let me take that." He relieved her of the carrier and gestured her ahead of him out the door.

Since Grace hadn't left the house since they brought her home from the hospital, her car seat was still in Keaton's truck. He settled her carrier into it and made sure everything was secure while Lark clambered into the passenger seat.

"Where to?" he asked, backing slowly down the driveway.

"The medical building just south of the hospital."

They rode in silence the ten minutes it took to navigate the short distance. Keaton kept his eyes on the road in front of them, but his attention was half on Lark. He was accustomed to her unadorned beauty, appreciated her naturalness, but the bombshell seated beside him was whipping up his appetite.

Once they were inside the lobby, they looked up the doctor's office on the wall directory and made their way there. "So, I was thinking Claire's for dinner," he said as they stepped off the elevator on the third floor. "We run a better chance of an uninterrupted meal."

"That sounds nice."

Her quiet reply nagged at him. She didn't seem withdrawn or angry with him, but the camaraderie they'd enjoyed these last ten days was missing. And he didn't like it one bit. He'd come to relish their particular blend of arguing and amity. Most days she kept him guessing and when she wasn't stimulating him intellectually, she was inspiring his baser urges.

"I thought since it's where Jake and Skye had their last official date in Royal," he said, holding the clinic's door open for her, "that it should be the place where we have our first."

She halted halfway to the receptionist's desk and gave him a blank stare. "Our first...?"

"Date."

"Can I help you?" the receptionist asked brightly.

"We have an appointment with Dr.—"

"Reedy," Lark supplied, her gaze not leaving Keaton's face.

"For our niece, Grace Holt-Taylor."

"If you can fill out this paperwork." The receptionist

pushed a clipboard and a pen across the desk toward them. "I'll let the doctor know you're here."

Keaton sat beside Grace's carrier and watched Lark fill out the baby's pertinent details. As he waited for her to finish, he was bemused at the anxiety that tightened his chest. She'd been caught off guard when he described their dinner as a date, but she didn't protest the notion. Did that mean she was willing to give things between them a shot?

Before he found out, they were being escorted into a tiny exam room. The nurse who led them there brought in a scale and a tape measure to take Grace's measurements. Between them the nurse and Lark peeled Grace out of her fleece onesie. Not liking the cool air on her skin, Grace began to protest. In record time the stats were recorded on her chart and then the nurse left them alone to calm the baby.

Rather than dress her again, Lark wrapped Grace in a blanket and held her against her shoulder. It only took a bit of rocking for the infant to calm. Once the room was silent, Keaton spoke.

"I've spent the entire day thinking about you," he said. "I think we have a connection that goes beyond taking care of Grace or simple physical attraction." The words that had been racing through his mind all day spilled easily from his lips.

"I like you too," she said, her voice and expression solemn. "It's just that dating means we're going down a path that ended badly for Jake and Skye."

"They decided to run away from trouble rather than face it. We're both stronger than that."

"You might be, but then your parents are way more sensible and forgiving than mine."

The door opened before he could respond and Keaton was left to mull her words.

"Good afternoon, Lark," Dr. Reedy said, flashing his teeth in a boisterous grin. In his midfifties, the pediatric physician had pronounced crow's-feet at the corners of his eyes and strong laugh lines bracketing his mouth. He stuck his hand toward Keaton. "I'm Dr. Reedy."

"Keaton Holt."

The doctor nodded. "Grace's uncle. So, how is our little angel doing?"

Lark and Keaton spoke at once.

"Terrific."

"Wonderful."

"Fantastic," Dr. Reedy said. "Well, her weight has increased nicely. She's a little ahead of where we'd expect she'd be at this time."

Keaton appreciated that bit of good news. At least when his brother showed up, Keaton could feel confident that he'd done everything possible for Grace. "And her reflux?"

"We're still giving her the drops and that's working great."

"She's sleeping okay?"

Keaton and Lark exchanged glances.

"Pretty well," Keaton said. "At first she wanted to be held all the time, but she's adjusted to her bouncy chair and swing really well in the last few days."

"Sounds like everything is going nicely."

After that Dr. Reedy began his exam. Grace hated every second of being checked and let the entire building know. He had a list of questions for Lark and Keaton as he worked and they traded off answering.

"I'd say she's doing great," Dr. Reedy pronounced, giving the two adults a pleased smile. "We'll need to see her in another month. You can schedule that before you leave."

From the way Lark's mouth drooped, Keaton suspected she was hoping her sister would be able to bring Grace to that checkup. Keaton agreed and hoped his brother was in town to drive her. The next time Keaton attended a baby wellness visit, he wanted it to be for his own son or daughter.

Eight

After leaving the doctor's office, Lark sat in the backseat of Keaton's truck and pulled out Grace's bottle.

"Do you want to skip the restaurant and do dinner at home?" Keaton offered, watching them from the front seat.

The baby was still agitated from being checked out by Dr. Reedy, but she quickly settled down. "I think she'll be okay after she has something to eat. She's really hungry these days. I've started preparing four-ounce bottles and she can almost get through the whole thing."

"It's amazing how much has changed in the ten days since she's left the hospital."

With the bottle half-consumed, Lark took it away and handed the baby and a burp cloth to Keaton.

"And who would've guessed you'd be so good with babies?"

"Certainly not me."

"I think your mother was a little shocked." As soon as Grace expelled the gas trapped in her stomach, Lark handed Keaton the bottle and let him finish the feeding.

Watching the two of them together, she noticed how her fondness for him increased a little more each day. If things kept going this way, she was going to start thinking in terms of the *L* word that wasn't *like*. To her surprise, this didn't give her the qualms it might have a week ago. For one thing, it wasn't as if she could stop the inevitable from happening. Keaton was a wonderful man with everything going for him.

If she wasn't a Taylor falling for a Holt, she would feel free to revel in her happiness.

Lark executed a quick diaper change before Grace drifted off to sleep. "I think that will buy us a couple hours at least," she said, switching back into the passenger seat.

The late afternoon sun hit Keaton's blue eyes, making them glow. "Then we won't have to rush." He slipped on a pair of sunglasses and started the engine.

Finding herself oddly breathless, Lark clasped her hands together and set them in her lap. It was a good thing they were avoiding the Royal Diner's bright interior. At least in the soft lighting at Claire's her flushed skin and feverish gaze would be less obvious.

The hostess led them to a four-top toward the back and replaced one of the chairs with a stand that Grace's carrier fit into. While Keaton got Grace settled, Lark slipped out of her coat and draped it over the empty chair beside her. When Keaton looked in her direction, his eyes widened.

"You look amazing," he murmured, a hoarse note in his voice. "That dress suits you."

"I was worried it was too much." Lark ran her hands down the dress, smoothing the fabric over her hips. "I bought it in Houston but never had a reason to wear it."

"It's perfect."

She loved the way his gaze clung to her as she sat down and dropped the napkin in her lap. His intensity heightened her confidence and made it easy to shoot him a flirtatious glance.

"I haven't ever been here," she said, scanning the menu. "What do you suggest?"

"That we skip dinner and go straight home."

Her stomach executed a back flip. "But I'm hungry," she protested.

"So am I." And his steady regard left her no doubts about where his mind had gone.

Excited by the hot lust in his gaze, Lark surrendered to

the smile tugging at her lips. Already she was on fire for him. Her nipples hardened against the silk of her bra. An ache throbbed between her thighs.

All her life she'd existed in her head. She read books and imagined faraway places she'd probably never visit. Baking cakes gave her a way to express her creative side, but it was a hobby that involved precise measuring and exact bake times. Her buttercream flowers were a work of art, but they took hours and meticulous attention to detail to get just right.

The way she felt around Keaton was so completely foreign. Her blood simmered. She grew rash and wild. They'd made love on her living room floor last night. Just ripped off their clothes and dove straight in. There'd been no preset number of dates before the event. Hell, they weren't even dating. She wanted him naked, his strong body heavy on her while he plunged into her over and over.

"Are you okay?"

Keaton's question broke through her sensual fog. Unclenching her hands, she discovered half-moon indents in her palms where her fingernails had dug in. Lark picked up her water and sipped it. She wanted to put the cool glass against her heated cheeks, but that would be a dead giveaway. "I'm fine. Why?"

"You were staring into space with such a fierce expression on your face. What were you thinking about?"

Well, she certainly couldn't tell him the truth. "There's a woman I work with. She hates me." Lark was surprised by her own vehemence. She hadn't told anyone about her frustration with Marsha. It wasn't her style to complain.

"I can't imagine anyone hating you." Another man might have used that line to flirt. Keaton was completely serious. "You're kind, thoughtful and intelligent."

She wasn't upset that he didn't describe her as beautiful. She wasn't. Her mother was right to complain that she did nothing to make herself look more attractive. Besides, the way he focused all his attention on her was so much better than a bunch of flattery she wouldn't believe.

"I'm also efficient, hardworking and intolerant of people who don't pull their weight." Lark stared in fascination as Keaton's mouth curved into a wry line. "From the minute I walked into the ICU, she's acted like I'm the most annoying person she's ever met."

"So she's intimidated."

"Why should she be? She has seniority in the department and everyone except the head nurse defers to her."

"Everyone except the head nurse and you," Keaton guessed. His eyes glowed. He seemed to understand something Lark wasn't grasping.

"She's lazy and sloppy. I've tried to be nice, but I draw the line at pandering to her ego."

"And she's working in the ICU where your sister is. You told me you transferred from surgery to the ICU to watch over Skye. Why did you feel that was necessary?"

Lark caught her breath. Was that it? She didn't trust Marsha to take good care of Skye, and the other nurse had picked up on that? In the days following the tornado, Lark had been frantic about her sister's condition. She'd spent long hours at Skye's side, overseeing her care like a fierce mama bear. Looking back, Lark realized she probably hadn't made any of the nurses' lives easy, but Marsha's least of all because her level of care had been subpar in Lark's opinion.

A week later, Lark had requested a temporary transfer to the ICU. Marsha couldn't have been happy. No wonder she'd been so unfriendly.

"I really need to work on my people skills," Lark muttered. "I did not connect the dots."

"How do you feel now?"

"Better. At least I have an idea why Marsha hates me. It will make dealing with her a lot easier."

Her father often complained about how aloof Keaton was. Said the Holt boy thought he was too good for any of them.

After spending time with Keaton, Lark decided her father was wrong. Keaton didn't believe himself superior. Rather, he was focused on his ranch and spent more time thinking than talking. Thus, when he had something to say it was worth listening to.

During dinner their conversation turned to the town's recovery efforts and the projects Keaton had been involved in. Lark had no idea how much he'd pitched in.

"I haven't really kept up with what's been going on," Lark said, pushing vegetables around her plate. "I should've pitched in."

Keaton shook his head. "You've had your hands full taking care of Skye and watching over Grace and we haven't been short any volunteers."

"I feel like I should be doing something."

"Most of what's going on now involves demolition or construction, but I can check and see what other things might be available."

"That would be great."

Despite the easy flow of conversation during dinner, Lark's tension grew. They were minutes away from heading home and she hadn't yet figured out how to take advantage of the camaraderie they'd achieved. Her mind and body were eager for another round of lovemaking, but she didn't know how to go about communicating that to Keaton.

It didn't help that his relaxed manner gave no clue if his thoughts ran in the same direction. She declined dessert. Even if her mouth hadn't been dry and her stomach in knots, she wouldn't have enjoyed anything sweet. She was far too eager to get Keaton alone. Maybe in the privacy of her home she could tempt him to kiss her and maybe that would lead to more.

While they awaited the check, a dark-haired man clapped Keaton on the back, but the newcomer's curious gaze was fixed on Lark.

"Keaton, good to see you out enjoying yourself for a change."

"Hello, Gil." Keaton stood and greeted the tall man with a hearty handshake before turning in Lark's direction. "I'm not sure if you two have met. This is Lark Taylor." He gestured toward the carrier beside him. "And Grace, our niece. Lark, this is Gil Addison, president of the Texas Cattleman's Club."

"Both Keaton and my father have spoken of you." Lark smiled. "It's nice to put a face with a name."

"You're Tyrone's daughter?"

She nodded, seeing the way his eyes narrowed as if surprised she and Keaton were so relaxed with each other.

"Okay, date night is on." A tall woman with shoulder-length wavy brown hair appeared at Gil's side. "There's no emergency at home."

"This is my wife, Bailey," Gil said, putting his arm around her waist before finishing the introductions.

"Nice to meet you," Lark murmured, realizing how much she'd isolated herself these last few years.

The couples chatted for a few more minutes before Gil and Bailey returned to their own table where the waiter had just delivered their appetizer.

On the ride back to her house, Lark realized her earlier anxiety about the rest of the evening had dissipated. Gil Addison's surprise at finding her and Keaton together reminded Lark how many obstacles stood between them. Letting herself get further wrapped up with Keaton would be asking for trouble. She was better off chalking up their single encounter as a lightning strike. Life-altering and never to be repeated.

Keaton took charge of Grace as they entered the house and pushed Lark in the direction of her bedroom. "Go get into your pajamas," he commanded, no hint of playfulness anyway in his manner.

Her stomach clenched in reaction. "But it's not even seven o'clock."

"You owe me at least an hour of…what did you call it? Postcoital? You owe me an hour of postcoital snuggling."

"What are you talking about?" Heat rushed up her neck and set fire to her cheeks.

"You ran off before I had the chance to hold you in my arms and savor how great you smell and how soft your skin is."

Embarrassed laughter bubbled in her chest. "I ran off because you acted like an insensitive jerk."

"Stop trying to pick a fight with me or I'll change my mind about the pajamas and make you cuddle dressed exactly as you were when we ended."

Unsure why he thought threatening her with snuggling naked was at all intimating, Lark decided not to argue further. What was the point when all she wanted was for him to hold her in his manly arms and kiss her breathless?

Since the pajama top she'd been wearing the night before was ruined, Lark had to find something else to put on. Most of what she wore in the winter she'd purchased to combat the cool nights, and she didn't like the notion of her skin being so completely inaccessible.

"That's not what you were wearing last night," he said as he showed up in her bedroom, wearing pretty much the same pajama bottoms he'd had on the night before.

"You tore off the buttons, remember?" She glanced down at the sleeveless cotton nightgown. "It might not be pajamas, but it's sleepwear."

His frown told her he wasn't fully convinced, but he held out his hand. "Do you want to do this here or on the couch?"

Although the couch's limited space would force their snuggling to be extra close, she preferred the bed's potential. "Here."

"A good choice." Lifting her off her feet as if she weighed no more than a dry leaf, Keaton placed her in the middle of the mattress and settled down beside her. He put his arm around her and pulled her against his side.

She laid her cheek against his shoulder but had a hard time relaxing. Hunger raged through her, firing her blood and awakening an insistent thrumming in her loins. While cuddling with him had sounded wonderful, what she really wanted was his hands on her skin, driving her mad with pleasure.

"What's wrong?" he asked, his voice deep and content.

Lark shook her head slightly and gazed up at him. His eyes were closed. She envied his tranquility.

"It just doesn't seem like this is how we would have ended up last night."

"Why not?"

"Something about it doesn't feel organic."

"Organic?" The corners of his mouth twitched. "What do you suggest?"

"I think we should get into the position we were in just after we finished last night and take it from there."

He cracked one eye open and regarded her for a long moment. Then with a huge sigh, he sat up. "I just have one question." He paused and let his fingers drift down her cheek. "With clothes or without."

"Definitely without."

And just like that they were kissing and rolling across her mattress, shedding her nightgown and his pajamas. The foreplay was feverish and focused, leaving little breath for words. And just when Lark thought she was going to explode with anticipation, Keaton sheathed himself in one of the condoms she'd squirreled away in her nightstand and slid inside her. Their breath mingled as they rode the escalating waves of pleasure. If it had been great last night, it was even better now because they were just a little bit more familiar with each other.

Lark climaxed first, her body reaching completion mere seconds before Keaton pounded to his own finish. With their energy deliciously depleted, Keaton rolled onto his back and draped Lark's boneless body across his chest.

"You were right," he agreed, lifting her hair aside so he could deposit a kiss on her damp cheek. "This is much more organic."

"I knew it would be," she murmured, convinced that she could stay like this forever. "I was feeling really awkward before because I didn't know where to put my legs or the best place for my hands. Now I can't feel either, so it really doesn't matter."

Beneath her cheek his chest lifted and fell with his chuckle. "I have a great antidote for that when you're ready."

"I'm sure you do." She nuzzled his throat and smiled.

Already fresh desire was stirring at the edge of her consciousness. Her hunger for Keaton astonished her. In the past she'd never been driven by a need to tear someone's clothes off and have sex at the spur of the moment. She'd enjoyed intimacy with the men she dated, but the lovemaking was more like canoeing on a calm lake compared to the ocean storm she enjoyed with Keaton.

"Next weekend Paige Richardson is throw a party at the Double R to celebrate her barn raising," Keaton said, his fingers trailing a soothing path up and down Lark's back.

"Hmmm." Mesmerized by Keaton's caress, she had little more to offer.

For the last three months there'd been a lot of opportunities for the townsfolk to pitch in and help each other out. She knew the co-owners of R&N Builders, Aaron Nichols and his business partner, Colby Richardson, brother of Paige's deceased husband, had assisted Keaton with some aspects of rebuilding the Holt ranch house and outlying buildings. But with the high amount of devastation suffered throughout the town, the professional builders were spread thin.

So anyone with a free day or afternoon and a willingness to wield a hammer or a saw could easily find a project to work on. Lark knew Keaton had hosted a party at his place the weekend the town gathered to help with the roofing of the ranch house and his main barn.

"I think we should go together," Keaton continued. "And bring Grace."

Lark's contentment vanished as anxiety flared. "Sure."

"You don't sound convinced it's a good idea."

"I thought we were going to keep our situation as quiet as possible."

"We're co-caretaking Grace," he reminded her. "We were seen having dinner together at Claire's. I'm living with you. You don't think that speculation about us has circled town three times already?"

"You're right." But as long as she didn't have to confront a bunch of knowing smiles, she could at least pretend that no one would run to her parents with the news that she'd invited the family enemy to live with her.

Keaton kissed her shoulder. "You know I'm here for you, right?"

Lark knew his promise wasn't given lightly. Even though his parents hadn't treated her with the same disdain shown by Tyrone and Vera, Lark had gotten the distinct impression that they were hoping nothing was going on between her and Keaton. They didn't want to lose another son to a Taylor girl. With the feud between the families, it would be just a matter of time before conflict arose again, and that would mean trouble for everyone involved.

"What's bothering you?" Keaton asked.

"Nothing."

"You've sighed four times in the last two minutes."

"I'm really relaxed."

"They weren't sighs of contentment. You're worrying about something."

"I was just thinking your parents wouldn't be overly pleased to learn we've taken playing house—literally."

"You're wrong. They like you."

"Sure, as the woman who's taking care of their granddaughter. Not as the woman in their son's bed."

"Technically their son is in your bed."

She made a sour face at him. "It's not like you to take things so lightly." And then it occurred to her that she had no idea if that was true. How much did she really know about the man sprawled naked beneath her?

"Uh-oh. What now?"

"I'm just realizing how little I know about you."

"You know more than most."

"I do?" She considered what she'd learned in the last ten days.

"Why do I keep to myself?"

"Your ranch keeps you busy. You like your own company. I've heard you make polite conversation if you have to, but I think you prefer more straightforward discussions."

"I dislike pretending to feel something I don't, and often that rubs people the wrong way."

People like her father, Lark realized. Tyrone Taylor never appreciated when the reality of a situation conflicted with his version of the truth.

"We've got that in common," Lark admitted, thinking back to those awful days after Skye ran off with Jake. "Sometimes I miss social cues, and that gets me into trouble. Luckily most people take me at face value, but once in a while, I encounter someone who takes offense at my cluelessness." Like Marsha at work, who needed the entire world to revolve around her. "Sometimes it's just easier being alone."

"You've felt like that for a long time. I remember as a kid you were always in your own world, either reading or standing around with a grumpy look on your face. What were you thinking about?"

"Usually stuff I'd been reading about earlier or how long before I could escape whatever I'd been dragged to."

He laughed. "Did that happen a lot?"

"Less as I got older. Most of the time when I was a kid, my parents forgot I existed. The older I grew, the more invisible I became."

"That can't possibly be true."

"It is. Skye could have been an only child for all the impact I made on their lives." Lark shook her head, remembering how she'd alternated between resenting her younger sister and rejoicing that Skye was their mother's focus. "The times I remember being most happy were when I was lost in a story. While Mom coached Skye on her pageant walk or spent hours trying out new hairstyles or planning the next routine, I was up in my room or down by the creek, reading."

"I remember Jake complaining about you all through school."

"Complaining about me?" She thought back to those days and couldn't remember ever so much as making eye contact with him even though they'd been in the same grade and he'd been so friendly with her sister. "Why?"

"The teachers were always using your work as an example. You weren't just bright, you worked really hard."

"I don't know that I worked all that hard. I just made sure I got everything done. It's an easy thing to do when you're inept socially and have only a handful of equally awkward friends to hang out with."

"What else do you know about me?"

"You do crossword puzzles in pen. Most people would find that impressive."

"But not you?"

"I've known for a long time that you're extremely smart. In fact, there were a lot of people who figured you'd end up in a think tank somewhere after you graduated from UC Berkeley."

"I had offers, but in the end what I really wanted was to come back to Royal and ranch."

"I understand that. For a year I considered staying in Houston, but my heart was here." And no one was more surprised by that fact than Lark. All through high school she'd been eager to get away. Only it was a case of the grass not necessarily being greener on the other side. "But do you ever feel as if you wasted four years getting a degree in mathematics?"

"It's actually worse than that," he said, looking slightly abashed. "I completed my master's and began working on my doctorate."

"Wow." She regarded him in amazement. "But you prefer ranching?"

"I'm not built to spend my days indoors. Ranching suits me. And before you think I've completely wasted my education, I do consulting work for a company outside Boston."

"When do you find time?"

"Evenings. Anytime I need a break from the ranch. Meeting deadlines has been challenging in the days since the storm, but the only thing that's suffered has been my social life." His expression grew momentarily wry. "Which isn't saying much."

"We are a lot more alike than I realized." Lark regarded him with a sinking heart. The compatibility between them was going to lead to deeper feelings. How could she help but fall for him? He was handsome. Brilliant. And he understood her.

"I wonder what would have happened if we'd been closer in age the way Jake and Skye were," he mused, echoing something she'd caught herself pondering several times in the last few weeks.

"You mean would we have become friends against our parents' wishes?" She shook her head. "I was too sure your family was evil." And too afraid of disappointing her father.

"And now?"

"The feud might have started for a good reason, but it's idiotic that we haven't found a way to settle things. Your parents have done a better job supporting Skye and Grace than my own, and that makes them friend, not foe, in my book."

"And me?"

Her gaze met his. The concern darkening his eyes to a somber shade of blue made her heart lose its rhythm.

"You know how I feel about you."

"I really don't." This wasn't a flirtatious game. He was regarding her as if he really wanted to hear her opinion.

How much did she dare tell him?

"I like you."

"Just like?"

Although there was a trace of amusement in his tone, Lark couldn't tear her gaze from his. "Very much like. I wouldn't have…you know…"

"Made love?"

"Exactly. It's not something I do lightly." Or often. "When I'm with you I believe I can handle everything."

"We've made a good team."

But it was a temporary alliance. Soon Skye would wake and take Baby Grace back to wherever she'd been living. Or Jake would come to town in search of his daughter and the woman he loved and reawaken old hurts. Her parents would demand that Lark stand at their side once more. Against her sister and the Holts.

"What are you worrying about?" Keaton asked.

"I'm not Skye," she explained. "I've never had the strength to go against my parents." She snuggled her cheek against his shoulder, ashamed at her weakness. "If they find out about us, I'm not sure my choices will make you happy."

Beneath her, Keaton's chest rose as he gathered a great breath in his lungs. "You don't know what's going to happen or when. Until then let's make sure we make the most of the present."

Nine

Lark's home sparkled with cleanliness and order by Wednesday night. Despite the already pristine nature of the housekeeping, Lark had attended to every corner and out of the way surface to make sure it was free of dust and dirt.

It hadn't been Keaton's intention that she work like a maniac in advance of his parents' visit, but every attempt to make her stop was met with stony determination.

"Enough," he commanded, plucking the surface cleaner and rag from her hands and dragging her from the kitchen. Scooping Grace from her swing, he handed her to Lark. It was the only way to pause her obsessive housework. "My mother is not going to notice your house. She'll have eyes only for Grace."

"Does she look okay?"

The dress Lark had bought for Grace was pale pink with a scalloped hem and white flowers embroidered on the bodice. Her hair had grown noticeably in the last couple weeks, but the fine texture and white-blond color didn't make it seem as if she had much going on. Lark fussed with the tiny rosebud clip she'd attached to the silky strands.

"She's perfect," Keaton assured her, refraining from adding that his mother wouldn't judge what her granddaughter was wearing.

The doorbell rang, announcing his parents' arrival.

Lark started at the sound and gazed frantically toward her front door. "Maybe you should hold her?"

"Relax." He tilted Lark's chin up and kissed her softly,

letting his lips linger far longer than he'd intended. "Everything is going to be fine."

He left Lark standing in the middle of the living room, a dazed expression on her flushed face, and went to welcome his parents. He wasn't surprised when his mother brushed right past him with barely a hello and went in search of Grace. The intensity on her face as she approached the pair made Lark's body stiffen.

"There she is." Gloria stopped short of plucking Grace from Lark's arms, but touched the infant's cheek with gentle fingertips. "Oh, she's absolutely precious. And I think she looks a little like Jake through the chin."

"Would you like to hold her?"

"You're sure it's okay?" Keaton's mother looked delighted.

Lark's gaze went past Gloria and fastened on her son. "Absolutely."

Grace barely stirred as she went from her aunt to her grandmother. Hearing the volley of questions begin, Keaton turned to his father and gestured with his head toward the kitchen.

"I think they'll be occupied for some time. Can I get you a beer?"

His dad grinned. "Always."

Keaton showed his father the steaks he'd bought for later and David Holt nodded approvingly over the thick cuts. Although Keaton had insisted that Lark didn't need to worry about fixing dinner, she'd made half a dozen side dishes to accompany the main course from two types of potatoes to three cold salads.

"How are things going?" Keaton's father nodded toward Lark.

"Fine." His gaze lingered on the pair of women in fond amusement. "Taking care of a newborn, and a preemie at that, has been easier than I expected."

"And the Taylor girl?"

Something in his father's tone set Keaton's radar buzzing. "You mean Lark? What about her?"

"You're living here, right?"

"Yes."

What was his father getting at?

"She's a lot prettier than I remember."

"Your point?" Keaton quizzed, although he had a pretty good idea what was on his father's mind.

"Just want to make sure you know what you're doing."

Having his father doubt his judgment took Keaton by surprise. "Why would you think I don't?"

"Don't take that tone with me," his father said. "Your brother got involved with a Taylor girl and look what happened."

So his father had learned nothing in the last four years. "Seems to me he's been living quite happily with the woman he loves," Keaton retorted, making no effort to moderate his irritation.

"You don't know that. We haven't had any contact with him in four years. Anything could have happened."

"They have a beautiful baby girl. That speaks for Jake and Skye still being together."

"Then why isn't he here?" Grief showed in David Holt's gaze. "If they're so happy, why hasn't he made any attempt to be here for Skye and Grace?"

"The investigator I hired was able to find out Jake is in the Middle East, he just doesn't know where yet."

"I don't understand why his assistant won't just give you his number."

"She...." Keaton hesitated, unsure if his mother had shared the next part with his father. "Told me when I identified myself that Jake didn't have a brother."

David sucked in a sharp breath. "Did you tell that to your mother?"

"She knows."

"One of you should have told me." The news had obviously landed a huge blow to Keaton's father.

"I honestly thought he'd be here by now and that there wouldn't be anything to tell."

"I'll call her," Keaton's father said. "She'll give me his number or I'll—"

"David," Gloria called. "Come over here and hold your granddaughter."

"Mom already tried calling," Keaton told his father. "The assistant won't budge. There's something a little off with her."

His father snorted. "A little?"

"The investigator will find him," Keaton said, sounding more confident than he felt.

"See that he does." With those parting words David crossed to where his wife snuggled their granddaughter. Lark offered a shy smile as she passed Keaton's father. He responded with a brief nod. While she bustled about the kitchen, pulling out side dishes and heating the oven, Keaton assessed her state of mind. She was looking agitated again. He had to block her between his body and the counter in order to gain her attention.

"Relax," he said.

"You keep saying that, but it's not going to happen." She scowled at him. "Do you think I didn't notice the way your father was looking at me? He isn't happy about our arrangement."

"He said you were pretty."

The stern look Lark leveled at him would have started a lesser man sputtering apologies. "And then proceeded to warn you that Taylor girls bring Holt boys nothing but heartache?"

"Not in so many words."

Lark set her hand on his stomach, intending to push him away. Keaton grabbed her wrists and pulled her arms around his waist. She stiffened, but he held firm.

"They'll see," she hissed.

He couldn't care less. When Jake and Skye had fallen in love, the connection between their feuding families began to transform. With Grace's arrival, there was yet another string binding them together. A sound relationship between Keaton and Lark would put an end to multiple generations of fighting.

"That's the idea." And then he kissed her.

Her lips quickly grew pliant and responsive. He kept the contact romantic, ignoring the passion that flared between them. There would be time enough to satisfy that later. When he was sure he'd made his point, he released her and stepped back.

"Keaton?" His mother's voice had a slight warble as she spoke his name.

"Yes, Mom?" He kept his gaze on Lark, letting her glimpse what was in his heart.

"Are you and Lark...together?"

He shifted one eyebrow up and waited for Lark to tell him what to answer. Her nod was barely perceptible, but it released all the tension in his muscles. "Yes. We are."

Lark's whole body felt as if it was on fire, although whether desire or embarrassment was the dominant cause, she wasn't sure.

"Okay, you've made your point," Lark muttered to Keaton, stepping around him to go back to dinner preparations. She didn't glance into the great room to see how Gloria and David Holt reacted to their son's announcement. She imagined their faces reflected horror.

"Is this a new development?" Gloria sounded closer than she'd been moments earlier.

Unsure what she should contribute to the conversation, Lark kept her back to her guests and focused on getting her side dishes into the oven. She still had a green salad to pull together. After agonizing over which recipe would be best received, she decided to go with a simple collection of lettuce, carrots, grape tomatoes and cucumber. Along with that, she'd offer four different types of salad dressing.

When she'd told Julie about her limited entertaining experience and tools, the research assistant reached out to the surgical nurses for help. They'd plied her with serving dishes and favorite recipes. Lark had come home with more than enough to satisfy Keaton's parents.

"Relatively," Keaton said. "We were three years apart in school and never had a chance to get to know each other. If not for Grace's arrival, our paths might never have crossed."

With everything as ready as it could be for the moment, Lark had no more excuses to avoid her guests. "Can I get you something to drink?" she asked Gloria. "Water? Soda? Tea? Coffee? Wine?" She ran out of offerings and snapped her mouth shut.

"I have a bottle of your favorite Shiraz," Keaton suggested.

"Maybe with dinner. For now I'll take a glass of water."

"Flat or sparkling?"

"Sparkling."

"Plain? Lemon? Raspberry?"

Gloria shot her son an amused look. "No wonder you like her. She's prepared for everything."

Lark's cheeks burned, but the remark hadn't been unkind. "I wanted to make sure I had a variety of things on hand."

"Lemon." Gloria stepped into the kitchen and shooed her tall son out. "What can I do to help?"

Lark hovered near the refrigerator, a glass in one hand, a bottle of water in the other. "With ice or without?"

"Without is fine." Keaton's mother relieved her of the items with a gracious smile. "What can I do to help?" she repeated.

Knowing she would be all thumbs with Gloria in the kitchen, Lark gave her head a vigorous shake. "You came here to see your granddaughter, not to help me. Dinner's in great shape. Most everything is ready to go."

"Good. Then you can come sit with me and tell us everything about you."

Although Lark wanted to protest, Keaton's mother had her neatly trapped.

"There's not much to tell." She glanced at Keaton's father, noting his stern expression, and wished she was anywhere but here.

"I'm sure that's not the case," Gloria replied, drawing Lark onto the couch and motioning for her husband to hand over Grace. "David, why don't you go help Keaton with the steaks? You know how I like mine cooked."

Lark was able to relax a little when the Holt men headed out back to the enormous grill Keaton had recently purchased. David Holt so obviously disapproved of her and Keaton being together. She wasn't yet sure where Gloria's opinion lay, but she suspected she was about to find out.

"My son is obviously taken with you."

"I care for Keaton a great deal. I'm not going to hurt him. I hope you know that." The three rapid-fire sentences left Lark breathless. She stared at Grace, longing for an ounce of the baby's current tranquility.

"We've upset you. I'm sorry about that. It's just that learning about your relationship with our son like this has come as a little bit of a shock."

As much as Lark wanted to let her guard down with Gloria, she'd been fooled by someone's appearance of niceness before. Not that she thought Keaton's mother was manipulative. With her thoughts spinning in confused circles, Lark kept her lips pressed together.

The silence didn't seem to bother Gloria. "I don't want you to think that we're prejudiced against your relationship with Keaton because you're a Taylor." She paused. "Well, perhaps my husband is a little distressed... But some of what's caught us off guard is that Keaton has always been a private person. We know he dates, but he hasn't brought a single girl around since high school. He must be pretty serious about you to share with us what's going on between you." She paused again to let her words sink in. "And so soon. How long have you been…seeing each other?"

Lark had a strong desire to shift uncomfortably, and held still with effort. "A couple weeks. Since he moved in here. I know things seem like they're happening fast, but I'm not sure Keaton is as serious as you think. We've been thrown together by circumstances."

But in truth, she wasn't sure how Keaton felt. He made love to her with tenderness and passion, but that was in his nature. Lark doubted Keaton had left a string of casual one-night stands in his wake. At the same time, he was a man and not exactly ruled by his emotions. For one thing, she was pretty certain that of the two of them, she was the one falling harder.

"Is that how you feel about him?" Gloria asked. "That this is just a convenient fling?"

This wasn't a conversation Lark wanted to be having with Keaton's mother. Surely Gloria would understand that what happened between Lark and Keaton should remain between them.

"Neither one of us has spoken about the future. Right now we're focused on Grace." That said, Lark stood. "I'd better get everything ready. Those steaks are going to be done in no time, and I would hate for them to get cold while we wait for the rest of the food."

Lark didn't care that her retreat was graceless and desperate. She was prepared to satisfy the Holts' culinary preferences and assure them her housekeeping skills were adequate. What she hadn't equipped herself to do was explain what was happening between her and Keaton.

"You look a little pale," he remarked as he came in to get the steaks.

"Your mother had questions about what's going on with us."

"What did you tell her?"

His frank curiosity irritated her. "That I had to get dinner ready. Can we talk about this later?"

"Did you mention that I have a hard time keeping my hands off you?" He took her backside in one large hand and gave a provocative squeeze.

The urge to laugh struck her. "Stop it this instant." She kept her voice neutral and low so his mother wouldn't know anything untoward was going on. "What has gotten into you?" Where was the solitary man who spoke little and kept everyone guessing?

The wicked glint in his eyes faded. "I'm sorry my mom gave you a hard time. I've already explained to my father that I won't tolerate any attempts to make you uncomfortable. I'll drop off the steaks with him and have the same chat with my mom."

His earnest declaration made her head spin. No one had ever jumped to her defense before.

"Oh, please don't." The last thing Lark wanted was for Keaton's relationship with his parents to suffer because she couldn't handle a little admonishment. "She's just worried about you. Besides, don't forget I've been dealing with my mother, the tiger lady, all my life. By comparison your mom's a pussy cat."

He scrutinized her face for a long moment. "Are you sure?"

"Positive."

But it was nice that he wanted to defend her. It was something she could get used to. Not that she should. She was telling the truth when she'd told his mother that they hadn't discussed the future.

Proximity lust. She could never have used the term with Gloria, but it was an obvious explanation for what was going on with Keaton. Two people of the opposite sex thrown into everyday contact with each other. It was only a matter of time before desire exploded between them.

But while proximity lust described how the sparks had ignited between them, Lark wasn't sure it justified why her desire for Keaton grew stronger each day or how badly it made her heart hurt when she imagined living alone in her house once more. That was more likely caused by how hard she was falling for him.

Keaton steered his truck into an empty space along the Richardsons' driveway and cut the engine. Since the dinner with his parents, Lark had grown even more difficult to read, but not impossible. Looking at her now, he could tell she was a nervous wreck. A classic introvert, she'd admitted she wasn't at her best in crowds. And their very public appearance together was going to cause rampant speculation.

He lifted Lark's hand and dusted a kiss across her knuckles. Her arm muscles jerked at the contact. She scanned the area around the truck as if searching for someone. A second later she slipped her hand free.

"Sorry," she said, her voice husky with embarrassment. "I guess I'm a little more wound up than I thought."

"You know it's going to be okay, right?"

"Not if my parents are here."

"Chances are they won't be since neither of them has been any help in the recovery efforts and this party is to thank everyone who helped raise the Richardsons' barn." Keaton kept reproach from his tone as he pointed out her parents' shortcomings, but Lark looked as if she'd been kicked in the gut. "I'm not saying anything you don't already know."

"You're right." She shot him a half smile. "I think this is the first time I'm glad my parents are so self-absorbed."

Keaton detached Grace's carrier from the car seat and met Lark by the hood. As much as he wanted to hold her hand the way he had during the drive from her house, he sensed she needed him to maintain a casual distance. Not easy, considering the way her perfume made his head spin and her soft skin begged to be caressed.

As they strolled through the guests, Keaton noticed almost the entire Texas Cattleman's Club membership was in attendance. Often since the tornado had struck Royal, Keaton was glad he'd joined the club. His original purpose for joining hadn't been social. Making small talk to pass the time wasn't his idea of fun. Sure, he'd sometimes found the other members a good source of information on the market.

But in the beginning, he'd joined because he knew it would drive Tyrone Taylor crazy.

"People are staring at us," Lark murmured, her eyes darting from one group to another.

Keaton saw curiosity and speculation in the expressions of the folks they passed. "Maybe if we stopped and spoke with someone, we could answer the questions on everyone's mind."

"Like who?"

He scanned the crowd and spotted a likely pair of candidates. "How about Drew and Beth?" Keaton switched direction without waiting for Lark's response. Her discomfort worried him. He didn't want her to feel like a fish in an aquarium.

"Keaton, we haven't seen much of you lately," Drew said, reaching his hand out. "How are things going at the ranch?"

"Coming along. The outbuildings will be finished the end of next week, and the interior work is beginning on the house."

"That's great."

"Drew and Beth, you remember Lark Taylor. And this is our niece, Grace."

"I heard what happened to your sister," Beth said, peering into the carrier Keaton held. "Oh, she's darling. But so tiny."

"She was ten weeks premature," Lark explained, her voice soft and hesitant. "But she's doing really well."

Beth paused in her cooing at the baby. "How's Skye?"

Lark sighed. "She's still in a coma. Dr. Wakefield, the trauma surgeon who saved her life, said with the type of brain injury Skye has, she could wake anytime."

Or not at all.

Keaton knew what Lark feared. She'd broken down and spoken of her anxiety two nights ago after spending an hour sitting at her sister's bedside. All the pressure of Skye's coma and Grace's early birth, not to mention her parents' inflexible attitude toward their daughter and grandchild, was taking its toll.

"I hope it's soon. This beautiful baby needs her mama." Beth caught the attention of a redhead with long straight hair and bright green eyes. Megan McGuire, manager of Royal Safe Haven, the local animal shelter. "Megan, come meet Lark and her niece, Grace."

"Why don't I take Grace for a while?" Lark suggested to Keaton, her eyes brighter than they'd been a few minutes ago. She looked more confident since running into Beth. "Would you mind putting my cake on the dessert table?"

"Not at all." Although he'd promised not to leave her side, she was obviously comfortable enough to send him away. They exchanged burdens and Keaton headed toward the heavily laden food tables with Drew strolling beside him.

"Forgive my curiosity," Drew said, "but did you introduce Grace as your niece, as well?"

"Lark's sister and my brother, Jake, left town together four years ago. Grace is their daughter."

"Interesting. And now you and Lark?"

This was where things got sticky. Lark wanted to keep the truth hidden. Keaton wanted to shout his happiness from the rooftops. An unusual urge for him.

"We're just co-caretaking Grace until Skye wakes up or my brother gets to town."

"Oh." Drew frowned. "Sorry. I assumed you two were together."

Was the horse breeder unusually perceptive or were Keaton and Lark giving off a couple vibe? Knowing that wouldn't make her happy, he frowned.

"Are we that obvious?" Keaton asked with a low laugh. "I was trying hard to behave."

"Maybe not obvious to everyone." Drew glanced around. "But ever since Beth and I got together, I see budding romances everywhere I turn."

"Really?"

Keaton looked around. "I guess a few couples have fallen in love since the tornado." Besides Drew and Beth, their acting mayor, Stella Daniels, and Aaron Nichols were such a couple. "It makes sense. Tragedy can bring out strong emotions."

"And with so many people thrown together who wouldn't normally be." Drew paused. "Like you and Lark. Don't the Holts and Taylors have some dispute between you?"

"A long-standing feud over land. It's kept our families fighting for years."

"That must have been hard on your brother and Lark's sister."

"They left town because of it."

Keaton understood Lark's worry. Unlike his sibling, Keaton let his responsibilities keep him tied to the Holt Ranch and by extension the town. Nor did he think Lark had any desire to live elsewhere. They were committed here. Sacrifices would be necessary if they intended to be together. At this point he was pretty sure whom she'd choose between her family and him.

"That's tough," Drew said.

"I could use a beer." Keaton checked to see how Lark was doing and found her surrounded by women. "How about you?"

"Sounds great."

It took Keaton another forty-five minutes to make his way back to Lark's side. By the time he reached her, he expected she'd be furious that he'd left her, but she simply took his arm and smiled up at him.

"You two doing okay?" he asked, peering at a sleeping Grace.

"Just fine."

"Sorry I was gone so long."

"It's okay. You'd have been bored standing around while all the women oohed and aahed over Grace and asked dozens of questions about preemies."

"I'm sure you had answers for each and every one of their questions."

"Of course." A smile flitted across her lips, catching his attention. "We're experts now, aren't we?"

"We're getting there." He'd known that inviting her to accompany him today had been a risk, but so far it seemed to be paying off.

"And Grace wasn't the only thing they wanted to know about," she said, a hint of slyness in her tone. "A few asked if you and I were together."

"What did you tell them?"

"What we agreed on." Basically the same thing he'd told Drew.

"And that satisfied them?"

"Of course not. Each and every one believes you and I are together."

Her matter-of-factness confused him. Wasn't this what she'd been most afraid of?

"Are you worried it will get back to your parents?"

"I knew it would when I agreed to come."

"So why did you?"

"I've been really happy these last couple weeks, and that's because of you."

He didn't push her for more. "You and I are good for each other."

"And we're not the only ones who think so."

He doubted that would be enough to sustain her when her parents began pummeling her with their negative opinions. "Drew asked me if we were together too. He said since he and Beth have fallen in love he's paying more attention to the relationships around him."

"It's funny that he would say that," Lark said. "I've noticed myself being more interested in other people's love lives. There's a few people here who've started dating recently. And I can't help wondering if something is going on between Paige Richardson and her brother-in-law."

Keaton glanced over at their hosts. "Like what?"

"Not like they're together," Lark assured him, but frowned thoughtfully. "They're really in sync. I suppose it could be shared grief over losing someone they both love. Except I think Paige is less sad than she used to be. Is that weird?"

Now that Lark had pointed it out, Keaton noticed the way Colby stayed close beside his brother's widow but never touched her. Not even a casual brush of arms or hands. It was as if he took care to maintain space between them.

"Not weird. But maybe we've fallen prey to the same affliction that Drew has?"

"But Drew and Beth are in love," Lark began, her voice trailing off as she caught Keaton's gaze.

"Why don't we say our goodbyes and get out of here?" Keaton suggested, letting her glimpse the flash of sexual intent in his eyes. Suddenly he was very impatient to get her home. "I think Grace has had enough excitement for one day, don't you?"

"Sure." But she sounded a little nervous as she agreed. She sucked her lower lip between her teeth as her color began to rise.

"I think everyone will understand that preemies are more delicate than the average newborn."

"They are." Her gaze clung to his. "It was good to bring her out, but I don't want to push it."

"Absolutely." To anyone listening nearby, their conversation would seem mundane enough, but heat flared between them at their unspoken accord. "I'm glad we're in agreement."

Ten

Lark entered Royal Safe Haven in a distracted state. Even after a fifteen-minute drive, her body still hummed from Keaton's goodbye kiss. At Paige Richardson's party, Lark had met Megan McGuire, the shelter's manager, and agreed to volunteer with the dogs for a couple hours. Basically, they needed some human contact, a little fussing over.

Keaton had encouraged her to go. For the last three and a half months, Lark's entire world had been the hospital, her comatose sister and Baby Grace. He'd insisted that doing something outside her narrow world would clear her head. Lark felt guilty for leaving him alone with Grace again on the heels of four days of twelve-hour shifts at the hospital, but secretly she'd been excited to try something new.

Almost immediately she was struck by a sense of sadness that so many pets had lost their owners because of the tornado or other hardships. In the days following the storm, her focus had been Skye and Grace. She'd spent all her time at the hospital, either working or alternating between the two intensive care units. Except for the damage done to the hospital's west wing and the branches down all around in her neighborhood, Lark hadn't seen the town's widespread devastation.

Stories had filtered through the hospital of the fine job Stella Daniels had done working with FEMA, the National Guard and local agencies to bring in the help they needed. The Texas Cattleman's Club had stepped up and organized many of the cleanup projects around town. Colby Richard-

son and his partner had brought their construction exper-
tise from Dallas to assist in the repair and rebuild efforts.

All this made Lark wish she'd pitched in more.

"Hi, Lark. Thanks for coming." Megan came out from
the back, her smile welcoming and addictive. "Let me show
you around."

The tour was brief and informative. By the end, Lark
was really glad she'd come. "What do you want me to do?"

"We've got a couple dogs that aren't adapting very well to
being locked up. They'd love a twenty-minute walk."

"That sounds easy enough."

The first dog she walked was a beagle mix named Bugsy
that started out by dragging her down the street. Before she'd
left, Megan had handed her a pouch with dog treats and offered a brief lesson on loose leash training. By the end of the
twenty minutes, Lark was surprised that the dog had stopped
sniffing every tree and bush and was paying attention to her.

"Nice job." Megan approached while Lark was returning
the dog to its pen. "Feel like trying another?"

"Sure."

The next dog Megan picked for her was an Australian
shepherd. The shelter manager described the dog's color as
red merle. She had a mottled blond and chestnut coat with
touches of white.

"Aussies are incredibly smart and used for herding,"
Megan explained. "Nicki was Agnes Baker's dog. Agnes's
place was hit by the tornado and she was badly hurt. I know
it just about killed her to leave Nicki behind when she went
to live with her daughter in Dallas, but there was no way
she could take her along. For a couple months I'd hoped that
Agnes would make a full recovery and come back to Royal,
but her healing is progressing slower than anyone hoped."

Suddenly Lark was fighting back tears. "Oh, that's terrible."

Megan nodded. "Nicki is a great dog. Where we run into
problems with her is that she's too smart for most people.

And she's used to a lot of exercise, so she gets destructive if left on her own for eight or more hours a day."

Lark dropped to her knee beside the dog and smoothed Nicki's thick coat. As if sensing her sadness, Nicki nudged her nose beneath Lark's arm and their gazes met. The Aussie had the most beautiful golden eyes dotted with blue. And intelligence sparkled in them.

"She likes you," Megan said.

"You sound surprised." Lark fondled Nicki's ears and the dog half shut her eyes.

"One of the reasons I've had trouble placing her is that she doesn't warm up to people. The two who took her home on a trial basis did so because of her coloring and her intelligence. They had no idea what they were getting themselves into."

What was supposed to be a twenty-minute walk turned into half an hour. Unlike Bugsy, Nicki understood the concept of walking on a loose leash. She showed little interest in the tantalizing scents along the way, but kept her attention mostly on Lark. And this wasn't due to treats either, because she'd forgotten to grab the pouch on her way out of the shelter.

Absolutely smitten, Lark was reluctant to put Nicki back in her pen. She took out three more dogs, all with various levels of leash training, but couldn't stop thinking about the Aussie. After promising to return the following week, Lark drove home, wishing she'd followed her instincts and adopted the Australian shepherd.

But Megan's comments stuck in her head. A dog like Nicki needed to stay busy. She couldn't be left alone for eight hours, much less the twelve Lark worked. Granted, right now there was someone home all the time with Grace, but Lark couldn't ask Keaton to help out. And it wasn't as if he was going to be around forever. When Skye woke, she would take over responsibility for Grace and Keaton would return to his cabin. Or perhaps even the Holt ranch house.

The thought of that caused a lump to form in Lark's stomach. She'd known all along that this was a temporary situation. But knowing was different than facing the reality. Especially when she and Keaton had been dancing around the consequences of committing to a serious relationship.

Lark drove home in a somber mood. She couldn't get Nicki's keen gaze out of her mind and couldn't shake the certainty that she and the dog had made some sort of instant connection. Surely she was simply bummed that soon Grace would leave and Keaton would have no reason to keep living with her. A dog wouldn't fill the void created by their departure, but it would keep her house from feeling empty.

Keaton was in Grace's room as Lark entered the kitchen. She could hear him talking to Grace as he fed her. Usually this would make Lark smile, but today her heart was too heavy.

Baking had always been a solution for whatever ailed her, so Lark pulled out the ingredients for a rich chocolate cake and began to measure. This particular recipe was a family favorite, something she'd always made for her father's birthday. Maybe she would take it over later. It had been over a week since she had any contact with her parents. The last conversation had been stilted and cool. Her parents were still unhappy that Keaton was helping her with Grace.

"You're home." Keaton sounded surprised as he emerged into the great room, the bright-eyed infant cradled in his arms. "How did it go?"

"Fine." She tried to inject a light note in her voice, but wasn't completely successful.

"What happened?"

"It was just so sad. All those dogs without homes."

"You didn't have any fun?"

"Oh no. It was great. There was one dog in particular that I absolutely fell in love with."

"Have you thought about adopting a dog?"

She shook her head. "It wouldn't be fair to leave one home all day while I work. Besides, the one I liked is a trained herding dog who is used to being busy and gets destructive if left alone."

"What sort of herding?"

"Sheep and cows. Although Megan told me Nikki had worked with ducks to earn some of her titles."

Keaton looked thoughtful. "I've never worked with dogs before, but I know other ranchers who have."

This seemed like an opening. "You should meet her. She's the most amazing dog. Smart. Focused. If she's titled, I'll bet she's really well trained too."

"I'll do a little research tonight. Is she any particular breed?"

"Australian shepherd. I gather she was bred as a herding dog."

"Maybe I can go by the shelter tomorrow on my way to the ranch and meet her."

Lark was so excited she was close to bursting. "I'll let Megan know you'll be coming."

Keaton was surprised that Lark rose with him the next morning. Usually she took whatever opportunity she could to sleep after her four twelve-hour shifts. While he showered, she made coffee and a hearty breakfast of eggs, bacon and toast. He watched her while tucking away the meal. Her eyes were clear and bright. Her body hummed with energy.

She'd been even more passionate than usual the previous night. Although her innate shyness had never manifested in the bedroom, she'd taken a while to trust him completely. Last night, she'd seemed determined to smash any lingering barrier between them.

Was all this because of a dog she felt sorry for? It amused him that she was so easy to please. He'd dated women who expected expensive dinners and elaborate birthday presents. Not one of them would be delighted with a dog. It was part of Lark's charm that she was so grounded. And focused on what was truly important.

"Call later and let me know what you think after you meet her," Lark said, following him to the door. "I don't want you to feel pressure or anything." But her eyes glowed with fervent eagerness. "I'm just really curious about your opinion."

"Sure." He slid his palm into the small of her back and pulled her close for a leisurely goodbye kiss. His heart was thumping enthusiastically by the time he lifted his lips from hers. "I'll call you when I'm headed to the ranch."

On the way to the animal shelter, Keaton caught himself humming along with the radio and shook his head in bemusement. He couldn't remember ever feeling this content. Living with Lark wasn't without its challenges, but he looked forward to coming home to her and Grace every evening, to their quiet family dinners, the passionate lovemaking after they put Grace to bed.

He liked doing whatever it took to make Lark smile. Even though he hadn't known much about her when they were kids, he suspected that she hadn't enjoyed the happiest, most carefree upbringing. It made him look for ways to bring her joy. Like going to meet the dog she'd fallen in love with. He wanted to be Lark's knight in shining armor. If that could be accomplished by rescuing Nicki, that was what he'd do.

The instant Keaton was introduced to the Australian shepherd, he understood why Lark had been so taken with her. There was a lot of intelligence in her unique parti-colored eyes and he decided, unless there were obvious temperament problems, he would bring the dog with him to the ranch to see how she got along.

"Lark really fell hard for her, didn't she?" Megan commented as Keaton stroked the dog's coat.

"She did." He was equally smitten. So much so that he was contemplating the complications that went along with co-owning the dog with her. "Lark said she's a herder. I was hoping I might be able to take her to the ranch and see how she gets along."

Megan grinned. "I've got a little paperwork for you to fill out first."

In half an hour, Keaton was on his way to the ranch. The dog curled up on the backseat of his truck for the ride as if this were just a normal day in the life. It wasn't what Keaton had expected. He figured Nicki would take a while to get used to him. As promised, he dialed Lark's cell.

"What did you think?" she asked without bothering to say hello.

"Nice dog. I've got her with me right now. We're heading to the ranch."

A long pause followed his words. "Oh."

"Megan let me take her on a trial basis," he explained. "I want to see how she is with the cows."

"If she does okay, will you adopt her?" Hope vibrated in Lark's voice.

"I thought we could discuss that over dinner tonight."

"Sure. Shoot, Grace is crying. What time will you be home?"

"Around six."

"See you then."

Keaton hung up, musing about the last time he'd included anyone in his decision making. Now it seemed that he was consulting Lark about everything from what he ate to how he spent his time. It should bother him that he had to consider someone else's opinion. In fact, he liked being half of a team. Team Grace.

Not for the first time he became aware that when her parents returned to the picture, he and Lark would have nothing more tying them together. Was this why he was considering sharing a dog with her? So they could remain in contact no matter how much pressure Tyrone and Vera put on her to cut him out of her life?

When he arrived at the ranch, Keaton's foreman gave him an odd look as he released Nicki from the truck, but one of the newer hands approached with a wide smile.

"That's a nice-looking Aussie," Treat commented, bending down to fondle the dog's head. "Where'd you get her?"

"Royal Safe Haven," Keaton explained. "Apparently she's a good herding dog. Thought I'd see how she handled herself."

He glanced down at Nicki and was surprised to see she watched him as if waiting for instructions. Keaton had half expected the dog to take off the second he let her out. Instead she glanced around, taking in the situation, and then sat at his side.

"You ever handled a herding dog before?" Treat asked.

"No, but I watched a few videos online last night and got an idea how it works."

"My uncle used to breed and train Australian shepherds. I know a little. Want me to help you out?"

Keaton glanced at his foreman. "If Jeb can spare you for an hour or so."

Jeb shrugged. "Shouldn't be a problem."

For the next thirty minutes Keaton learned the signals to guide the dog around the corral. At the end of the hour, Nicki had driven three cows into a narrow chute and Keaton was feeling pretty pleased with their teamwork. He called the dog to him and could swear she was smiling as she trotted in his direction.

"Sweet," Treat said. "She's really well trained."

"And fast," another hand said.

Keaton looked around and realized their herding exercise had drawn an audience. Jeb stood nearby. A traditionalist when it came to ranching, the old foreman wore an expression of grudging admiration.

"I can see where a few dogs like this could come in handy, especially when we're trying to move the cattle for the vet or shipping," Jeb said. "She managed them really well."

For the rest of the day wherever Keaton went, Nicki stayed within ten feet. Her eyes roamed the yard and the barns, alert and interested. By the time they headed home, Keaton knew the answer to whether Nicki was going back to Royal Safe Haven. He just wasn't sure what sort of arrangement he and Lark would come to about the dog.

When he arrived back at Lark's house, Nicki at his side, her eyes bright and alert after working cattle all day, Lark met him at the door with a cold beer and a hopeful smile.

"How'd it go?" She stood with her weight balanced on the balls of her feet, searching his expression.

"Terrific." Physically he'd been ready for Lark's enthusiastic embrace, but the strength of her jubilation sent his emotions reeling. "She's a great dog."

Lark broke off the hug and bent to love up the Aussie. "I knew you'd like her."

Keaton watched the pair with bemusement. When had making her happy begun to rule his world? "She fit in at the ranch like she'd always lived there."

"I'll bet she was happy to be working again."

"So, are you thinking about keeping her?"

He'd stopped by the pet store and bought the necessities. Food, bowls, a comfy bed for Nicki to sleep in.

"Let's see how she does with Grace."

Lark's eyes widened. "I never thought about that. She's probably never been around children, much less babies." The dog had finished wolfing down dinner and now bumped against Lark's legs. She squatted down and took Nicki's face in her hands. "What are you going to think of her? I wonder."

Grace woke shortly before dinner and Lark put her in her swing while she prepared a bottle. Keaton was in the living room, working on reports, when he heard Lark laugh. He glanced up and caught sight of the dog staring at the baby in the swing. Nicki's head was cocked in a quizzical manner, but she was completely calm. Grace was wide-awake and staring back.

"Grace is too far away to see the dog, isn't she?" Keaton asked.

"I think she can see Nicki, but maybe not perfectly."

While they watched, the Aussie nudged the swing with her nose and it moved. Grace grunted in her preemie baby way and waved her arms.

"I think they're bonding," Keaton said, setting aside his paperwork.

"Whatever they're doing, it's awfully cute."

With his heart thumping harder than normal, Keaton stared at the scene and felt a stab of envy for his absent brother. Even though Jake wasn't here to share these first few months with Grace, Keaton had no doubt that his brother would eventually show. Then it would be Skye, Jake and Grace together and both Lark and Keaton would be alone once more.

Unless Keaton took steps to keep their story from heading down that path. Lark was worth fighting for. Being with her made him happier than he'd ever been. What he needed to do was find a way to convince her they should take a shot at a relationship. And he'd better get on that fast before Skye woke up or Jake came to town, because if he waited too long, she might slip right through his fingers. And what a loss that would be.

"Keaton and I adopted a dog." Lark was sitting beside Skye's bed two days after Keaton brought Nicki home. "At least I think we both have. I'm not really sure whom Nicki actually belongs to. She's an Australian shepherd. If you've heard about the breed, you know they're really smart and good at herding." She paused. "I guess since they have shepherd as part of their name, it makes sense that they'd been good at herding."

These one-sided conversations with her sister had gotten easier in the three and a half months that Skye lay asleep. And if Lark kept up a rambling monologue, it was easier to ignore that her sister never responded.

"I know I've said it before, but I totally understand now why Holt men are so attractive. But Keaton isn't anything like Jake. He's quiet and serious. Jake was outgoing and great with people. They're as dissimilar in personalities as we are. And yet they each manage to be our perfect match."

Lark glanced around. She was keeping her voice low, but she worried that Marsha or one of her minions might over-hear. The last thing she needed was for that bit of gossip to make its way around the hospital. She'd be the laughingstock of the ICU staff if they thought she had feelings for Keaton. Several times she'd made it completely clear that her rela-tionship with Keaton was strictly about taking care of Grace.

"I think I'm falling in love with him, Skye." Lark set her forehead on her sister's hand and struggled to draw air into her tight lungs. "That makes me some kinda hypocrite, doesn't it?" With her voice muffled, she continued. "I was so awful to you when I found out you were running away with Jake. I couldn't understand how you could pick him over our family."

Four years later, Lark flushed with shame at the way she'd spoken to Skye. Lark had been convinced her sister was doing the wrong thing. She'd been smugly confident that as the older sister, she knew what was best. What would have happened to Skye if she'd listened to Lark? Grace never would've been born. Vera would have continued to hammer at Skye's spirit, criticizing every choice Skye made because it wasn't what Vera would have done.

Lark hadn't realized how much Vera had focused on Skye until she'd left town. It was once her critical eye had turned to Lark that she'd begun to understand why it hadn't been a hardship for Skye to leave her family behind.

But after such a long period with no communication, why had Skye suddenly decided to come back?

"I wish I knew something about your life these last four years. Are you still a graphic artist? Do you like your job? What was it like to discover you're pregnant and how did Jake react? I'll bet he was excited about becoming a father."

Lark paused as doubts crept in. If that was true, where was he?

"Do you have a house or an apartment? I suppose if it's the latter you're going to want to move. Grace will need a yard to run around in. Maybe even a dog. She really likes Nicki. It's funny watching them together. Nicki nudges her with her nose and Grace wriggles like crazy." The memory made her smile. "I can't wait until you wake up and can see for yourself."

Please wake up.

A familiar wave of grief swamped her, bringing a sting of tears to her eyes. In the months since Skye reappeared in Royal, Lark had been in an almost constant state of anxiety and sadness. Only in Keaton's arms did she get any relief. He had a knack for distracting her from her problems and making her exist solely in the moment.

Feeling safe was something she'd never really known before. Nor had she realized it until she'd surrendered to Keaton being in charge. The peace this brought her was temporary and addictive. Letting someone share her burden hadn't come easily, but now that she had done so, Lark was dreading being alone again.

"It's time for me to start my shift," she told Skye, clearing her throat a couple times to purge the huskiness from her voice. "I'll be back to check on you later."

"Lark?"

She jumped at the sound of her name. Turning, she spied Gloria Holt.

"Hello," she greeted. "I was just visiting my sister." Way to state the obvious. Lark's whole face felt on fire. "What brings you here?"

"Same as you."

"You're visiting Skye?"

"I try to come by at least once a week when I'm in town."

Lark shook her head. "I've never seen you before."

"I've tried not to come when I know you're working." Gloria put out her hands in a calming gesture. "Oh, that didn't come out right. What I mean is I didn't want you to be upset that I was visiting your sister."

"Why would I be?"

"There has been tension between our families for a long time."

And that tension had ruined a lot of lives.

"It's nice of you to visit Skye," Lark said. "I'm sure she appreciates the company."

Vera Taylor would have scoffed and said that Skye was unconscious and incapable of knowing that someone was nearby. Gloria Holt pulled out a book.

"I've been reading to her," she said.

"What a great idea. I've been telling her about Grace. I've heard stories where patients wake up from comas and remember conversations going on around them."

"I have a hypnosis tape I listen to as I'm falling asleep at night. It's for stress. I got it not long after the tornado came through town." Gloria grimaced. "When the ranch house was hit we lost so much that can't be replaced."

"I'm sorry to hear that, but at least no one was hurt." Lark froze as she realized she'd made another of those blunt remarks that some people took the wrong way. She hadn't meant to irritate Keaton's mother.

Fortunately Gloria took no offense. "You're absolutely right. We were more fortunate than some." Her expression clouded for a moment. "Anyway, I found that I wasn't hearing the entire recording because I was falling asleep. My hypnotherapist insisted my brain still processed the message."

"Has it helped?"

"I think so." Gloria gave her a wry smile. "I know it's having an effect on David. Despite all our losses, he's never been so calm. And he's done a great job of letting Keaton handle things."

"Your son is very determined to get things done."

Keaton's organization had impressed Lark. He worked everything on his tablet, from mind-mapping each project to formulating a process to reach his goal to tying the individual tasks to his calendar. She'd always been more comfortable doing things on paper, but after he'd shown her some of the software he used, she was beginning to see the advantages of going electronic.

"He was that way as a child. Always focused on a goal."

Lark found her curiosity aroused. She'd been in school with Jake and remembered him as a noisy, confident kid. But Keaton had been three years older and the only time he registered in her conscious thoughts was when her father complained about the *Holt* boys. "What was Keaton like as a child?"

The question surprised Gloria. "He was quiet. When he wasn't working around the ranch, he spent a lot of time reading and studying. Everything fascinated him, but math was his true passion."

"I remember that he graduated top of his class."

"When Keaton went off to college, David and I wondered if he'd want to come back to Texas and ranch. Or if he even should."

"But he came back to Royal." As she had. Lark knew she belonged here. She wondered if Keaton felt the same way or if he felt obligated to take over the family business.

"Ranching is what he wants to do." Gloria gave a "who would have guessed?" shrug.

Lark glanced at her watch. "I'd better get going. My shift starts in a little bit."

"It was nice talking to you," Gloria said.

"It was nice talking to you too." Lark gave Keaton's mom a genuine smile as she started past. "And thanks again for visiting my sister."

"She's family." Gloria's next words caught Lark by surprise. "You are too. I hope that's okay."

"Sure." What else could Lark say? Despite the animosity

between their families, Lark had nothing bad to say against Gloria. Besides, with the birth of Grace, the Taylors and Holts were forever connected to each other whether any of them liked it or not. "Of course."

"Good. I know it's a lot of change for all of us, but I hope we can set aside the past and start fresh. It's what's good for Grace, and she needs to be our top priority."

"I couldn't agree more."

Before she checked in at the nurses' station, she went to the visitors' lounge and dialed Keaton. "How are things going?"

It wasn't odd for her to check in with him, but it didn't usually happen until partway through her shift.

"Fine." His deep voice was steady and reassuring. A life preserver for her to cling to. "Are you okay?" His perceptiveness never ceased to amaze her.

"Everything's fine. Nothing has changed with Skye. I told her about Nicki and how cute she and Grace are together." What she should tell him was how hearing his voice calmed her. But he probably already suspected that. "I'm getting ready to start my shift and wasn't sure I'd have the chance to call before you went to bed."

"You didn't answer my question. How are you?"

"Sad. Skye's been in her coma so long. I'm worried that she might not ever wake." There. She'd said it. This was where she needed him to reassure her that everything would be okay.

"I know it's hard, but you need to stay strong. Skye will come out of this just fine."

Lark's shoulders sagged. "Thank you."

"No need for that. I'm not just here for Grace. I care about you and I know how stressed you've been." The deep note of concern in his tone was exactly what she needed to rally. "Why don't you call me as you're leaving the hospital? I'll have a hot bath and a cup of tea waiting."

She'd never lived with a man before, but she knew

Keaton's thoughtfulness wasn't the norm. "You know I like coming home to you, right?"

"I'm glad because I like coming home to you, as well."

Silence followed their mutual confessions.

"And you know there's room enough for two in my tub."

"Won't you be too tired?"

"To take a hot bath with you?" She chuckled, feeling much better than she had ten minutes ago. "Never."

Eleven

Keaton cradled Lark's left foot in his hand and pressed his thumb into her arch. The low moan she made was almost sexual and caused his temperature to climb.

"That's amazing," she murmured, her head thrown back, eyes closed.

The water lapped against her chest, pushing a crest of bubbles almost to her throat. It was a little after nine in the evening. As promised, Keaton had drawn her a bath for her arrival home, but before she could slide into the heated water, she'd fallen upon him with determined vigor. They'd made love in slow, silent appreciation of each other and the passion between them.

Her bath had cooled by the time sweat coated their bodies, but lovemaking had done more to relax her than a dozen hours of soaking in hot water. Later, she'd watched him from the doorway that separated bedroom and bathroom, her eyes lazy with contentment as he emptied and refilled the tub. Naked and completely at home in her skin, she bore little resemblance to the shy, self-contained woman she became outside her home. A tigress lurked beneath her skin. He loved being the only one who got to feel her claws.

"My parents came by today to see Grace and have dinner," he remarked, switching his attention to her other foot. "Mom made her famous lasagna. There's leftovers if you're interested."

"As much as I've been dying to try your mom's lasagna," Lark said. "I'm way too comfortable to move at the moment."

The sound of her cell phone came from her bedroom. Keaton recognized the caller because Lark had set Carly Simon's "*You're So Vain*" as her mother's ring tone. There was little love lost between mother and daughter, yet Lark remained unwilling to make waves with her parents.

"She's been calling me for the last three days." Lark's huge sigh spoke volumes. "I'm guessing she or my dad heard that you and I showed up at the Richardson party together and she wants to tell me how stupid I am for associating with you."

"You haven't spoken with her yet?"

"Why bother when I know what she's going to say?"

The support Keaton wanted to offer would only cause Lark more grief with her parents. This was a battle she had to face on her own, and that frustrated him.

"My parents found a condo they like on the beach in Gulf Shores, Alabama, and put in an offer. It's on the tenth floor and has great views." Keaton couldn't imagine his active father settling into beach life, but his mother had been thrilled by the four bedrooms. "I guess each floor is a single unit, and there are three-hundred-and-sixty-degree views."

The conversation was mundane enough to allow Lark to relax. "Sounds fantastic, but it's a long way from here."

"My mother has always been fond of the beach."

"What about your dad?"

"He likes making my mom happy. Says he's going to work harder on his golf game." In the years since Keaton took over supervision of the ranch business, David Holt had begun playing a round or two a week. "And they have friends that bought in the same building several years ago."

"Is this a full-time move?"

"At this point I don't think so." Keaton recalled his mother's glowing descriptions of the town and the unit. "But I think they were leaning that way before the tornado hit."

Of course, that was before Skye had shown up and Grace had been born. Lark picked up his train of thought.

"We don't know that anything has changed really. Jake hasn't shown up yet and there's no reason to believe Skye has any intention of staying in Royal."

"My mother is afraid that she's never going to see Grace again after Jake and Skye take over as parents."

Lark looked worried. "Surely the fact that Skye was coming back to Royal is a good indication that she was ending four years of silence."

"Is that what you think?"

"Why else?"

"It still bothers me that she was alone." Keaton turned his attention toward the baby monitor set up on the sink. A faint cry rose from the speaker. "That she didn't contact anyone and let them know she was coming."

They both stopped speaking when they heard another cry. Sometimes Grace made noises in her sleep and then subsided. In silence they waited to determine what would happen next. It was quiet for several seconds, so Keaton spoke again.

"You'd think she'd want Jake with her when she came to tell everyone she was pregnant."

"Or maybe that would have made things so much worse?" Lark sighed. They'd speculated on every sort of scenario and hadn't settled on a single one.

Another cry pierced the silence. This time both adults jumped into action. Keaton waved Lark back into the water as he stood and grabbed a towel.

"I'll get her. Stay and relax."

She shook her head. "I'm already feeling like a prune. Besides, I should probably call my mother back."

Water ran down her body as she stood. Soap bubbles clung to her nipples and dotted her midsection and thighs. Keaton stared at her in absolute fascination, only half-aware that Grace's unhappiness was escalating.

"Keaton?" Lark caught him staring at her as she turned from releasing the tub drain.

"Have I mentioned how gorgeous you are?"

Her face, already flushed from the hot water, grew even rosier. "Several times today." She let her gaze rake down his body in slow deliberation. "And right back at you. I'm not sure I'd ever get tired of looking at you."

"We should institute naked Sundays."

Seeing he was completely serious, she laughed. "It's January."

"True."

Instead of handing her the towel she pointed to, he wrapped it around her. The kiss he gave her was hard and quick. Mostly he'd wanted a second to enjoy the softness of her breasts crushed against his chest. He kept his hands away from any naked skin. Touching her silky wet skin would only delay getting to Grace.

"I guess I can wait until it warms up in April." And with a provocative pat on her towel-clad backside, he exited the bathroom.

Lark stared at Keaton's retreating form while his words played over and over in her mind. April? He was thinking they would still be living together three months from now? Surely he didn't believe that Skye would still be in a coma or Jake would continue to be missing. That meant he expected to still be together even after they no longer had Grace's welfare to look after.

A shiver raised goose bumps on her arms. She grabbed a quick shower and washed her hair, then dressed in a pair of her new silky pajamas. Keaton enjoyed running his hands over the slippery material, and she adored having every inch of her curves caressed by him. The thought made her smile. Even though her desire had been sated by their earlier love-making, it took very little to rouse the ache between her thighs.

Telling her body to behave, Lark headed into the kitchen to find Gloria's lasagna and open a bottle of red wine. Another perk of having Keaton living with her was that she'd learned to appreciate the finer vintages. Luckily the Holts' wine cellar hadn't been damaged during the storm and he enjoyed sharing his favorites with her.

While she heated up the lasagna, she kept one ear tuned to the nursery. Grace had calmed. Keaton certainly had the magic touch with her. The baby had probably woken wet or messy. She was very particular where her diaper was concerned. Someday she'd probably be equally determined about her fashion. Something that might make her acceptable to her grandmother.

From the time Skye was a toddler, she'd been thrust onto the pageant circuit by their mother, whose obsession with appearance and winning had been extreme. Lark remembered visiting Skye's room when she and their mother were gone for the weekend and trying on her sister's massive crowns or whatever sequined, tulle-enriched dress had been left behind. There'd been dozens in Skye's closet, some of them for the pageants that required specialty routines.

One time her father had caught her and paddled her backside hard. She wasn't sure which had hurt more, the spanking or his disappointment. Fortunately he'd kept the tale from his wife or Lark might have been punished worse than she had. In later years, when she'd begun to understand the value of things, she'd discovered those silly, overembellished dresses cost between five hundred and a thousand dollars apiece.

Keaton carried a very wide-awake Grace to the infant gym and laid her beneath the arches. He then joined Lark in the kitchen, where she offered him a lingering kiss. The microwave dinged before they got too carried away and Lark fetched her dinner. She decided to break her rule against eating on the sofa so she could join Keaton while he watched another one of those educational shows he'd introduced her to.

As they sat in companionable silence, attention alternating between the enormous television and their niece happily batting at the animals suspended above her, Lark decided not to broach the question tickling her since Keaton had teased her about naked Sundays. Instead she let herself enjoy the weight of his hand on her thigh and the familiar jump in her pulse as he kissed her neck and shoulder during the commercial breaks.

At long last, nerves mellowed by Keaton's solid presence, a delicious meal and two glasses of wine, Lark called her mother. Keaton offered to leave the room, but she needed his strength beside her. With her arm linked with his, she waited for her mother to pick up. By the fifth ring Lark was convinced there would be no answer and had moved her thumb to end the call when she heard her mother's voice.

"Yes?"

"Hello, Mother. It's Lark. I was just returning your call."

"It's about time. I've left you five messages."

Lark hadn't realized that. She avoided looking at her phone log since her mother had begun calling. "Sorry." She had no excuse. "What's so urgent?"

"Haven't you listened to any of my messages?"

"No."

"That's very inconsiderate. What if something had happened to your father?"

"Has it?"

"No."

"Then what's the problem?" The question came out a little more bluntly than she'd intended.

She'd had no contact with her parents since the little incident outside the ICU, and the silence had been nice. Immediately guilt lashed at her. This was her mother. As little as they got along, Lark owed her respect. Or if that wasn't possible, civility.

"The problem is I was ambushed at the beauty shop about you and that Holt."

Lark wasn't sure what to say so she kept silent.

"Are you *involved* with him?" Vera made the word *involved* sound like a mortal sin.

"He's helping me take care of Grace. You knew that."

"You didn't tell us that he'd also moved in."

While it was on the tip of her tongue to snap that she was twenty-seven years old and perfectly within her rights to do whatever she wanted with the house she'd bought, Lark knew that her mother would never hear the logic of that.

"It's made things much easier."

"Are you sleeping with him?"

Keaton's fingers moved between hers in a soothing caress. This was the moment she'd been dreading since her feelings for Keaton had begun to surface. She would be forced to choose between her parents and the man she was falling in love with.

"The feud between the Taylors and the Holts isn't my fight," she said, admitting nothing. "I'm sick of being caught in the middle of it."

"You are." Her mother gasped, assuming the worst from Lark's lack of swift and immediate denial. "Your father will be devastated."

"Keaton is an honorable man. He cares about Grace and about me."

"He's using you," her mother spat. "You're nothing but a convenience."

Even knowing how vehemently her parents hated the Holts, it still shocked Lark that they would turn so completely against her. Was this what Skye had experienced? And then Lark had gone and heaped more disapproval on her sister's slender shoulders. Shame rose to choke her.

"I'm sorry you feel that way, Mother," Lark said, forcing her voice to remain steady. "I have to go." And without giving her mother another opportunity to spew more negativity, she hung up.

Keaton's arms came around her and pulled her tight to his chest. His lips drifted over her cheek toward her ear. "I'm sorry you had to go through that."

His solidness absorbed the tremors that racked her body. "She can't understand."

"She doesn't care about your happiness," he said as he ran his hands up and down her spine. "Or Skye's. Neither of them does."

To her relief, he didn't ask her why she hadn't admitted to being involved with him, but had let her mother draw her own conclusions. Lark felt as if she'd betrayed him, been disloyal to the relationship developing between them. If she truly was falling in love with him, why hadn't she proudly claimed him?

"It's been a really long day." Lark looked at the baby. Grace was showing no signs of fading. "If it's okay with you, I think I'm going to turn in."

"Sure. Grace and I will watch a little basketball. You get some sleep."

With a nod, Lark left the couch and washed her plate and wineglass. Nicki chose to follow her into the bedroom. As the Aussie curled up on her bed, Lark slid between the cool covers and lay shivering. Although she'd been truthful about being tired, sleep was a long way away. Now that her parents knew she and Keaton were together, how long would it be before they started issuing ultimatums and forced her to choose between them and Keaton?

Worse, Lark wasn't sure whom she'd pick. Even though she wasn't their favorite, she was still their daughter. Outside of Skye they were the only family she had, and Lark had no idea what sort of relationship she'd have with her sister when Skye woke up. They hadn't spoken in four years. Wasn't that a pretty good indication that Lark hadn't been forgiven?

Keaton had given her no direct indication just how deep his feelings for her ran. What if she chose him only to find out he wanted little beyond great sex and companionship? His parents weren't as rigid as hers, but she suspected they weren't wild that Keaton was with her. From what Skye had told her before she left, they'd been furious to learn about her romance with their son. Their anger had driven Jake from Royal. He'd been the one who persuaded Skye to leave.

That wouldn't happen with her and Keaton. He was tied to the ranch. They would be forced to stick around and bear the brunt of their parents' vehement disapproval. Lark almost choked on a ragged exhalation. Keaton might be strong enough to cope, but was she? And what damage would it do to their relationship? In the end the Taylor/Holt feud would tear them apart.

When Keaton came to bed an hour or so later, Lark rolled toward him and pressed against him from breast to thigh. He claimed her mouth without hesitation and made love to her with fierce passion. She left her mark on him, her fingernails scoring his back as she climaxed. Keaton followed her seconds later with a powerful orgasm of his own.

No words passed between them as they lay gasping for breath. As soon as they'd sufficiently recovered, Keaton shifted her into the perfect niche at his side and smoothed her sweat-damp hair off her face. Lark snuggled her nose into his neck and breathed his unique musk. Exhausted from her long day and their vigorous lovemaking, she resisted sleep. How many more nights would she have him like this?

"Go to sleep," he murmured as if sensing her mind's restlessness. "There's nothing you can do about anything at the moment."

She lifted her head for his kiss and smiled beneath his lips. Only a very foolish woman would push this man out of her life because she was too afraid to upset her family. And Lark was many things, but she'd never been called foolish.

Keaton neared the ruins of the town hall, his thoughts far from the task ahead. After a great deal of deliberation and consultation with the construction contractor, a plan had been created for recovering the city's records. In the weeks leading up to today, much of the rubble had been cleared from the site. Today, the tarp that had been thrown over the records storage area was gone and heavy machinery stood at the ready to begin the delicate task of lifting the large chunks of concrete off the sturdy filing cabinets that held the town's records.

"I guess we were lucky that someone had the foresight to move everything into fireproof cabinets," Stella Daniels commented as Keaton approached. The acting mayor was no longer the nondescript town hall administrative assistant she once was. In the months since the tornado had landed Richard Vance, Royal's major, in the hospital, she'd blossomed into a stunning woman who'd taken charge during the crisis and performed brilliantly. "Fireproofing means more than just heat resistant, you know."

"When I first got started on this project, I did a little research," Keaton admitted. "They're waterproof and designed to survive short falls. As long as nothing too heavy landed on them, we should find the cabinets intact."

Stella eyed him. "I just knew you were the right man to take on this job."

"This town has given a lot to the Holt family," he said, tugging on the brim of his cowboy hat. "I'm happy I can pitch in and help."

Which was true. Although he participated in very few social activities around town, Keaton's problem-solving abilities had been unanimously welcomed. He'd been surprised how quickly he was caught up in the community spirit. Helping where he could, he'd been involved with over a dozen repair or cleanup projects. But except for a few simple construction jobs like the Richardsons' barn, he left the major rebuilding to the experts.

"I see the crews are assembled," Stella said. "Shall we get started?"

The delicate process of removing concrete from the area where the records room had once been was tedious and slow. In addition to the large chunks of building material, there were several yards of pulverized debris that had once been walls and ceiling to sift through. It was late afternoon when there was enough cleared away to begin the removal of the files.

Moving carefully through the rubble, Keaton inspected each of the cabinets before they were hauled away and was pleased that despite the dents to the metal caused by the building's collapse, the contents were intact and mostly undisturbed.

In addition to the modern files, there were several antique cabinets that no one had ever bothered to remove. These had not fared as well. Keaton thought there might have been four or five of them on the far side of the room. It was hard to tell an exact number, as they had mostly been reduced to kindling.

One cabinet had fared better than the others. Although one side had been crushed, the other had six drawers still intact. He pulled out one of the drawers, surprised that it rolled smoothly, and noted that it was empty. Keaton felt foolish as he investigated the other five drawers in the same way. Did he really expect to find some lost piece of paperwork that proved his family were the true owners of the two thousand acres of lakes and superb pasture now part of the Taylors' ranch?

Stella, accompanied by her fiancé, Aaron Nichols, had stopped by to see how the work was going. They were picking their way toward Keaton.

"You've made amazing progress," Stella said, stepping around a small pile of twisted metal that had once been a light and stopping beside Keaton. "How amazing that part of this cabinet looks unscathed while the rest of it is destroyed."

"As are three or four others." Keaton gestured at the other cabinets.

"Was there anything in it?" She pulled out a drawer the same way he had.

"No. I'm guessing they were original to the building, but no one bothered to get rid of them when the fireproof ones were brought in."

"They look old enough to have been worth something before the tornado struck."

The cleanup crew had been steadily working in their direction, and now they began to toss bits of the shattered cabinets into the bucket of the loader idling nearby. While Keaton gave Stella an update on the progress made that day, the loader moved off to empty its bucket into the nearby construction dumpster. When it returned, Keaton and Aaron stepped to opposite sides of the mostly intact cabinet and picked it up.

They'd shifted it several feet when Stella called out, "Wait! There's something caught underneath it."

Keaton glanced in her direction as she ducked down and came up with a yellowed piece of paper. "Is that it?"

"I think so."

He and Aaron finished moving the cabinet to the loader, checking for more loose paper before returning to Stella. They found her studying the document with interest.

"What is it?" Aaron asked, peering over Stella's shoulder at the paper she held.

"Looks like a bill of sale for some land back in 1880." Her gaze shifted to Keaton. "Is Edwin Holt any relation?"

Something about the way she asked the question made Keaton's heart thunder in his chest. "My great grandfather many times over."

"Good thing we found it. I think it's the bill of sale for your land."

"My family settled here in the 1860s."

"Are you sure?"

Keaton nodded. "Edwin Holt came here not long after the Civil War ended."

"Maybe they didn't buy your family's ranch until much later. Take a look."

But even as Stella held out the document, Keaton knew what he'd see. And yet it seemed impossible. All the times he'd hope the bill of sale would be rediscovered had been little more than wishful thinking.

He stripped off his gloves in order to handle the aged paper with utmost care. With his thoughts a chaotic swirl he had a hard time discerning the words. After blinking a few times, the thin, spidery script began to make sense. He grew lightheaded at what he read.

"What is it?" Aaron pressed, as the silence dragged on.

Keaton lifted his gaze from the document, scarcely believing what he'd seen, mind reeling at the implications. "I think it might be the missing document that started the feud between my family and the Taylors."

And the basis for a new cycle of conflict between the families.

Twelve

Lark rubbed her eyes and yawned. At three in the morning, the ICU was relatively peaceful. Machines beeped and whirred, keeping their patients alive. Once again Marsha had called in to say she couldn't make it, so Lark had agreed to stay on a few extra hours. How much longer was the senior nurse going to tolerate this? By Lark's estimate, Marsha was out for one reason or another three or four times a month. Marsha had probably gotten away with it this long because of the way she made her boss feel sorry for her.

"How are things going?"

Turning, she spotted Becky Jones, the head nurse in charge of ICU. "Fine. It was a quiet day, which is turning into a peaceful night."

"You look half-dead on your feet."

"Grace had a hard time settling down after her feeding last night and I missed a few hours of sleep."

Even though it had been Keaton's night to get up with Grace, she'd been so miserable that she and Keaton had taken turns trying to calm her. In the end it was Nicki who'd convinced the baby to settle down by gently nudging her until Grace stopped crying. After two hours of frantic crying, the abrupt quiet had been nothing short of amazing.

Becky smiled in sympathy. "I remember my two at that age. I swore there was some magic switch that flipped on in them as soon as the sun went down." She shook her head. "The good news is it won't last long. Pretty soon she'll be sleeping through the night."

"I hope so."

"Judy should be back from her break in a couple minutes," Becky said. "Why don't you go sit with Skye for a while? I can handle things here."

"Thanks."

"No, I should be thanking you. It's been great having you here in the ICU. I'm going to miss you when you go back to surgery."

Lark smiled at the compliment. Becky wasn't usually one to hand out praise. "It was nice of you to let me transfer into your department so I could stay close to my sister."

"She needed you. And it turns out we needed you, as well. Our efficiency has gone up dramatically thanks to you."

"I didn't do much, just saw a few places where our processes varied and pointed them out. You were the one who implemented the changes."

"I know that hasn't made you popular among some of your fellow nurses."

Lark shrugged and tried to keep her expression as neutral as possible. "I can be a little forthright. It's gotten me into trouble in the past."

"I see it as speaking your mind for the good of the department. And you didn't say anything that wasn't true." Becky's lips tightened. "Not everyone can face that there's always room for improvement."

Was she speaking of Marsha? From what Lark gathered, Marsha's absences had escalated since the tornado hit Royal. She'd been on duty that day and not far from the west wing when it collapsed. She hadn't been hurt, but it was possible that she was suffering from PTSD.

"Change can be hard," Lark said. "Especially when it originates from a know-it-all newcomer."

Becky gave a light laugh. "Go sit with Skye. Talk to her about Grace. Maybe if she knows her baby needs her she'll wake up."

"Good idea."

Lark didn't tell her boss that she'd already been doing that. She drew up a chair beside her sister's bed and took Skye's hand. For a while she didn't know how to begin. Then she began as she always did and let her words flow from there.

"Grace is thriving. I swear if you stare at her long enough, you can see her grow. I don't know if you recall that we have a dog now. Nicki has turned out to be a terrific addition to the family." Lark paused and swallowed the lump in her throat. "Keaton bought this wrap thing that I wear when Grace wants to be held and I need to keep my hands free. On the warmer days I put Grace in it and take Nicki for a walk. I swear since I've started doing that she's doubled her formula consumption. I think the fresh air is good for her."

While she talked, Lark stared at the monitors that surrounded her sister's bed. They registered all Skye's vitals, their beeps and flashing numbers soothing.

"Mom's been calling. She found out that Keaton and I had gone to the party at the Richardsons' together. She guessed that Keaton and I are sleeping together. I don't need to tell you how angry she is. I haven't spoken to Dad. I don't imagine he'll want to have anything to do with me now that I've gone over to the dark side." Bitter amusement darkened her tone. "I know I've said it plenty already, but I'm sorry. I really screwed up when I found out you were leaving Royal with Jake. I didn't appreciate then how hard our parents were on you or how painful it must have been to have to choose between him and us."

Lost in her misery, Lark barely noticed the minute pressure against her hand. But she saw Skye's finger twitch. Too scared to blink lest she missed it again, Lark stared at her sister's pale hand and willed it to move again. Nothing happened.

"The difference between Keaton and Jake, though," she continued, hoping that maybe something she'd been saying had reached her sister, "is that while Jake loved you with all his heart, I'm not sure if Keaton's thinking of forever and me in the same sentence." Still no movement from Skye, so Lark kept going. "Mom told me he's using me. She's convinced that as soon as we're no longer taking care of Grace, he'll head back to the Holt Ranch and never give me another thought."

The pain her mother's words had caused was reflected in Lark's voice, but it all vanished in an instant when Skye's fingers moved again, more obviously this time. Maybe all this time Lark had been using the wrong stimuli to reach her sister.

"It hasn't happened yet, but they're going to make me choose. The same way they made you choose. I'm not as strong as you. I'm worried that I'll end things with Keaton, but that Mom and Dad still won't want me as their daughter."

Another pulse came from Skye's hand. This one stronger than ever.

"You're waking up," Lark exclaimed, dropping her head over her sister's hand. "You're finally waking up." And as pain tore through her chest, she began to cry.

At six in the morning, Keaton was awake and troubled over the empty bed beside him. Lark should have been home a little after midnight. Something was wrong. He bolted up and reached for his phone. Nicki leaped to her feet and came over to nudge his hip with her nose. He absently stroked the Aussie's head as he checked for messages.

A three-word text explained where she was.
Skye's waking up.

He was in the middle of responding when he heard the garage door and slid out of bed. He met Lark just inside the door between the kitchen and the garage. Without a word, he threw his arms around her and spun her off her feet. Nicki frolicked around them, animated by their excitement.

"I just got your text," he explained, setting her on her feet so he could frame her face with his hands and survey her expression. "How is she?"

"She only came to for a couple seconds, but it was fantastic. Her doctor told me she'll go back and forth between conscious and unconscious for a while with the periods of consciousness growing with time."

"This is fantastic news." News he longed to be able to share with Jake. Not wanting to dampen Lark's euphoria, Keaton pushed his annoyance aside. This was a time to celebrate. "Do they have any idea how long her recovery will take?"

Lark shook her head. "It's too early to tell." She leaned her head against his chest, wrapped her arms around his waist and squeezed tight. "It's going to be all right."

"I never doubted it."

Keaton set his cheek against her soft hair and pushed his own news to the back of his mind. This was not the time to tell her about the documents he'd found in the wreckage of the town hall. And until his lawyer was able to verify their validity, there was no reason to stir up trouble. That was why he hadn't told his mother. She'd feel obligated to tell her husband, and Keaton's father would waste no time confronting Tyrone Taylor. Keaton wanted to handle the delicate situation with Lark before the news got to her father.

"Is it okay if I grab a couple hours of sleep? I wasn't sure what your plans were this morning."

"I'm supposed to be back at the town hall around nine. Do you want me to call my mom again and see if she can come by?"

"No. I'll be fine with a quick nap. I'm used to sleeping when I can, so I'll grab naps while Grace sleeps."

With the way her eyes were sparkling, Keaton wondered if she'd sleep at all. "Are you sure you don't want to go back to the hospital and sit with Skye after you get some sleep?"

"She's in good hands and it will take a while before she'll be coherent enough for conversation. I'll go check on her tonight. If anything happens between now and then, the hospital will call me."

"And you'll call my mother?"

"Definitely."

They grabbed a leisurely shower together and Keaton felt Lark's muscles loosen beneath his hands. As tempted as he was by her soft murmurs of pleasure and the skimming of her palms over his own soapy flesh, Keaton tucked her into bed without exhausting her further. She was fast asleep before he dressed and left the room.

Grace lay awake in her crib, her eyes fixed on the mobile above her. Unlike her father, she tended to wake happy in the morning. Keaton recalled Jake dragging himself blurry-eyed to school every morning.

"Good morning, sunshine," he crooned, lifting her into his arms. She blinked at him, her blue eyes not quite able to focus. "Your auntie Lark has come home with great news. Your mother has come out of her coma and she will be so excited to meet you."

Keaton wondered how long before mother and child were reunited. He hoped for Grace's sake it was soon. Although he and Lark had done a good job, Grace needed her mother. And her father.

As promised, Lark woke in two hours and took charge of Grace so Keaton could get back to the town hall. Between feeding, burping, changing and a stint in the infant gym, Grace was ready to go back to sleep.

Lark put the baby down, kissed Keaton on the chin and shuffled off to the bedroom once more. She was half-asleep; her extra-long shift and the excitement over her sister's recovery had drained her. Keaton wanted to stay home and watch over both her and Grace. With Skye awakening from the coma, his time with the pair was growing short and he hated the empty hollow in his chest at the thought.

There was nothing he could do about losing Grace. She belonged with her mother. But preventing Lark from slipping from his life was something he could control. The previous day's discovery gnawed at him. As close as he and Lark had grown these last several weeks, there was no question in his mind that the revelation of the misplaced bill of sale would put a strain on his relationship with Lark if she sided with her father on the issue.

He might just lose her forever.

Yet he owed it to his family to fight for the land the Taylor family currently claimed. They needed the lakes on the disputed property to keep their cattle fed. Because of the water, this area was abundant with grass. They could shift the herds until they could complete repairs on the damage the tornado had done to the system they used to irrigate their current pastures and buy more lightweight calves to increase their herd.

Keaton realized the implications of the choice he had to make. Jake had prioritized love over family. Keaton had no idea if his brother was happy with his decision, but if he had to guess, he'd say the answer was yes.

But Keaton had never been one to lead with his heart. He acted based on facts and logic. Choosing a technical approach to the cattle business, he'd altered the type of grass in the pastures and set up irrigation. The plentiful, high-quality forage allowed them to double the number of cattle per acre. This had enabled the ranch to become wildly profitable.

Logic told him to do what was good for his family and the ranch. He and Lark had known each other for less than a month. They'd been involved for two weeks. No matter how intense the chemistry between them and how much his heart ached when she snuggled against him, was he really ready to choose something as intangible as love over something that would benefit his family for decades to come?

The answer was very clear.

Lark sat in the chair beside her sister's bed and reached for her hand. From what Jessa and Ivy had told her, Skye had awakened twice since Lark left the hospital earlier. Both times, she'd only been conscious for a few minutes, but she knew her name and although she seemed surprised to be at Royal Memorial Hospital, she recognized the town she grew up in.

"Your baby is eager to be held by her mommy," Lark said, willing Skye to open her eyes. "The sooner you start getting better, the faster you two will be reunited."

A tall man in white approached the bed. "How's our patient today? I heard she's woken up quite a few times."

The smile Dr. Lucas Wakefield sent Lark's way was supposed to fill her with encouragement. The handsome, accomplished surgeon oozed confidence in the operating room where he excelled, and at a patient's bedside. It was hard to feel anxious when he was around.

"Yes," Lark said. "I can finally breathe again."

"I know this has been very hard on you," Dr. Wakefield said. "And I hope you realize that she has a long recovery ahead of her. There will be physical therapy and it sounds like she may have gaps in her memory."

"There's more than you're saying." Lark braced herself. "What else are you worried about?"

"She might have trouble doing everyday functions. The memory loss may be extensive and permanent."

"You're trying to say she may not be back to a hundred percent."

"We'll know more as she stabilizes and begins to respond to stimuli."

Ever a pragmatist, Lark struggled against being swallowed by anxiety. Dr. Wakefield was simply trying to prepare her. She briefly closed her eyes and longed for the support of Keaton's strong arms.

"Thank you for everything you've done," Lark said. "I know my sister wouldn't have survived without your skill."

Dr. Wakefield smiled. "Thank you. I'll check back in later."

Left on her own once more, Lark fought back tears and tried to remember a time when her emotions had run away with her like this. Falling in love with Keaton had brought her feelings into sharp focus.

"Lark?" Skye's voice sounded blurry and far away.

"Skye." She stood up and leaned over her sister. Brushing her fingers against Skye's pale face, she met her sister's green eyes and smiled. "I'm so glad you're awake."

"I'm in the hospital."

At least her short-term memory was okay. "Do you know how we can get a hold of Jake?"

"Where is he?" Skye's gaze searched past Lark. Panic tightened her face. "I need him."

"I know." Lark fought to keep her voice calm and soothing. "Do you have his cell number?"

"Phone." Her lids drooped, voice fading.

"Your phone is gone." But it was too late. Skye was out once more.

Lark suspected that her sister would have no idea what Jake's number was. She'd probably programmed it into her missing phone and never given it another thought. But if she remembered her own number, then perhaps they could get a hold of a bill and Jake's number should be on it.

But that wasn't going to happen soon, and Lark settled back to wait for her sister to return to consciousness.

Keaton paced his lawyer's office. The document had been authenticated, but the battle was far from over.

"It could take months before the courts agree that the land belongs to your family," Sean Abbot said, "and that's if the Taylors don't decide to tie things up with a counterclaim."

If that happened, the battle was going to be ugly, and the one who would suffer would be Lark. Skye was waking up. She would contact Jake and the two of them would spirit Grace off, perhaps never to return again. Keaton's heart lurched at the thought.

"Any idea how to keep that from happening?"

Sean had been the Holts' lawyer for the last twenty years.

He'd been involved in every lawsuit and countersuit that the two families had thrown at each other.

"I've heard you've been staying with Lark and helping her out with your niece. Does she have any pull with Tyrone? Maybe if she spoke to him."

Keaton shook his head. "Even if I thought it would help, I'd never ask her to do that. This is my battle with Taylor."

"Well," Sean said, his expression somber, "that's what it's going to be. A battle. Do you want me to get the court documents started?"

Keaton hesitated before answering. He picked up the envelope with a copy of the bill of sale. "I'll call you in a couple hours." Before he moved forward, he had to tell Lark and then her father.

He wasn't looking forward to either conversation. Lark deserved to know before anything happened, but she was preoccupied with her sister's recovery and didn't need to be worried about how the discovery of the lost document was going to impact her family. She'd probably insist on going with him to confront her father.

Tyrone was going to rant and threaten and end up taking his frustration out on Lark because he would view her as a traitor for suggesting they try for an amicable solution.

She was at home when he called looking for her. This relieved him. He wouldn't have told her at the hospital where her reaction might have been noticed by her coworkers. The twenty-minute drive gave him plenty of time to prepare the best strategy for approaching the subject of the long-lost bill of sale. He hoped that she'd be sensible when she found out he intended to take the land back.

The woman who greeted him at the door wasn't the bubbly, optimistic woman who'd headed for the hospital earlier that day. She threw herself into his arms and clung as if he was the only thing keeping her safe.

"What's wrong?" he murmured against her hair, wondering if something had happened to Skye. "Is your sister okay?"

Lark pushed out of his arms and ran her fingers under her eyes to scoop up the moisture. "I'm such a mess."

"You're beautiful." He cupped her cheek in his palm and leaned down to kiss her. His heart thumped against his ribs as she yielded beneath his lips. Before the chemistry between them flared, he broke off the kiss and drew her toward the couch in the great room. "Tell me what's going on."

"Dr. Wakefield came to see Skye today while I was there. He's concerned about her memory and warned me she may never be back one hundred percent."

Keaton had done some reading on head trauma and knew the recovery was slow and sometimes not complete. He hadn't said anything to Lark about it, figuring as a medical professional she already knew the odds and didn't need him heaping worry on her.

"But she's young and strong. And she has a beautiful baby girl to motivate her."

They sat down on the couch and Lark made a move to kiss him. Keaton drew back and she regarded him in confusion. Now it was her turn to ask what was wrong.

"While moving the records at the town hall, I made a discovery." He began his tale in gentle tones, knowing what was to come would be jarring.

"What sort of discovery?"

"An old bill of sale that's been lost for years."

She stared at his face, and her expression froze. "The one our families have been battling over for years?"

"That's the one. It was behind one of the antique filing cabinets in the records room."

"Rather convenient that *you* found it," she said, her tone flat.

"It's not a forgery if that's what you're implying. It's been authenticated." In his rush to avert her suspicions, he didn't consider the conclusions she'd draw from that.

She shifted away from him. "How long ago did you find it?"

"A few days."

"Days?" She looked stricken. "How many?"

"I found it the day Skye woke up for the first time."

"We've been together a bunch of times since then." She scurried off the couch. "We…we made love. You should have told me. I deserved to know."

"You were worried about Skye. I didn't want to distract you."

She clenched her hands into fists. "Distract me? Seems more like you wanted to deceive me. I trusted you."

"You still can." Keaton stood. Had he subconsciously known her deep-seated distrust of his family would overwhelm any faith she'd placed in him? Was that why he'd waited so long to tell her? "I didn't want to upset you unnecessarily if the document wasn't valid."

"What are you planning to do?"

"The land belongs to Holt Ranch."

"So you're going to just take it?"

"It's not like that. The land isn't yours."

"You can't just take it back. My family needs those lakes to irrigate our tree farm and water our cattle."

He tried to assume a placating tone. "If your father would see reason for a change and work with me, we could offer him a water lease." It was more generous than Tyrone Taylor had ever been with the Holts.

"You intend to charge us for what's been ours for decades?"

So it was *us* now. After how her parents had treated Lark. The way they'd refused to help with Grace. Their abandonment of Skye as she lay in her hospital bed fighting for her life.

His anger with her parents, specifically her father, boiled over. "It's Holt land."

Immediately he knew he'd chosen the wrong tack. She looked as if he'd slapped her.

"We'll fight you." Her voice quivered with dismay. "With everything we have."

"Lark, be reasonable. Let's talk about this."

"Reasonable?" The word carried the weight of all her distress. "Why do I have to be reasonable? My father was right about you. You Holts will do anything to get what you want." Her breath caught. "Even sleep with me."

Her accusation struck him like a whip. "You can't really think that."

"My mother said you were using me. She was right."

"That's not true. I only wanted to help you with Grace."

"You did a little bit more than that." She spoke the words as if they tasted bitter.

"You're right," he said, all passion leaving his voice. "I also fell in love with you."

Thirteen

He was lying. Lark stared at Keaton in horror. The room around her grew fuzzy, but his face remained crystal clear. How had she been so stupid? She'd actually believed that he cared about her when all along he was manipulating her emotions so that she'd turn against her family.

One part of her brain reminded her that the discovery of the missing document had only recently happened and they'd been intimate for weeks. He knew she had no ability to sway her father. Skye was the sister who wrapped their father around her little finger.

"You don't love me," she said, the denial struggling to escape her tight throat. "We barely know each other. No one falls in love that fast." But hadn't she? Could she honestly deny that she loved him with her whole heart? "You just want me on your side against my father."

"I want you *by* my side, but only because in the last few weeks you've become my world."

He looked so earnest. Believable. "Then can't you forget you found the bill of sale?" In her heart she knew it was unfair to ask him.

"I don't want to lose you." He closed his eyes and his face turned to granite. When he met her gaze once more, his expression was bleak. "But I can't sacrifice my family's future either."

From the beginning Lark had dreaded this moment and now she knew she'd been right to worry. She wasn't romantic and passionate like Skye, who'd willingly turned her back on her family and entrusted her whole world to the man she loved. "Then you must do what you believe is right." Her whole body went cold. "And so must I."

She backed away and fled to the nursery, confident he wouldn't follow. Sensing her distress, Nicki had stuck to her like glue. The closed door and white noise player that helped Grace sleep drowned any sound of the front door opening and closing. Lark sat in the room's rocking chair and absently stroked Nicki's head until she'd recovered enough to process the last ten minutes.

Did she really believe that Keaton had used her? She rubbed her temples. Surely if he wanted a partner for sex, he could snap his fingers and have a dozen gorgeous women flock to him. He might have been oblivious of the stir he'd created among several of the women at the Richardsons' party, but she hadn't. But with her mother's vile suspicions bolstering a lifetime of social awkwardness, Lark had fallen into a familiar mind-set.

But love? That seemed too far-fetched. Nor had he looked particularly happy to admit it. He'd chosen his family over her. The same way she'd chosen hers over him. They weren't at all like Jake and Skye. Those two had given up everything they'd ever known to be together. Neither Keaton nor Lark was willing to make that sort of sacrifice. That proved, however much they cared about each other, it wasn't truly love.

Calmer by the moment, Lark at last felt strong enough to stop reacting and move forward. She called her friend Julie and asked if she could watch Grace for a couple hours. Her parents needed to know what Keaton had found. It was important that they knew what was coming.

An hour later, she turned her car onto the long driveway that led to the Taylor ranch house. Leaving Nicki in the car, she approached the house. It wasn't until she set her hand on the doorknob that she realized she'd been so consumed about talking to her parents that it hadn't occurred to her to call and make sure they were home. To her relief, her father was in his favorite chair in the great room.

"Lark, what brings you here?" Her father set aside the file he'd been reading and gestured her into a nearby chair. "You're upset. Nothing is wrong with Skye, is it?"

She'd called her parents yesterday with the news that Skye had awakened from her coma, and to her relief they'd rushed to the hospital. For a little while they'd been a family once again, maybe not a particularly happy one, but at least for the duration of the visit, their focus had been on Skye.

"No, nothing like that," she assured him, sitting down on the edge of the chair. "It's about the land that borders the Holt property."

Tyrone's eyes narrowed to slits. "Let me guess, that Holt boy has convinced you the land belongs to his family."

Lark ignored the acid in his voice. "He found the bill of sale at the town hall that predates the one that entitles us to that land."

"Oh, he just found it." Her father eyed her in disgust. "You were always book smart and not very good with people."

She couldn't deny her lack of social skills, but she'd seen no evidence that any of the Holts lied or cheated. They'd been nothing but kind to her and considerate of Skye and Grace. Lark's head spun. Or was that what she wanted to believe because she'd fallen in love with Keaton?

"Can't you at least sit down and talk with Keaton? It would save both sides a huge legal battle."

"A legal battle we are going to win."

Although she'd known this would be her father's answer, disappointment swept over Lark. In the back of her mind, she'd held on to the tiniest bit of hope that her father would be reasonable for once in his life.

"You don't know that. What if the land isn't ours? You're going to waste money and time fighting a losing battle."

"It's Taylor land."

His vehemence threw Lark back into her childhood. For

a moment she wasn't a twenty-seven-year-old woman, but a girl of eight watching from the front seat of a pickup as her father drove his fist into David Holt's jaw. The blow had been followed up by another to his opponent's stomach. It wasn't the fight that had frightened her, but her father's savage delight. It had taken three men to restrain him.

Suddenly Lark had heard enough. "I'm sick of this stupid feud," she cried, pushing to her feet. "It's a couple thousand acres of land. Fighting over it has done nothing but hurt people. It drove Skye away. She left because she fell in love with Jake and no one could accept it."

"She didn't run away," Tyrone said. "When I found out she'd been sleeping with that Holt boy, I threw her out."

"What?" All this time Lark believed her parents had given Skye an ultimatum and that she'd chosen Jake. "She was your favorite. You loved her."

"She betrayed us." Her father rose.

Lark couldn't believe what she was hearing. "She didn't betray you." Again her thoughts turned to Skye and what she must have gone through in those days after her relationship with Jake had been discovered. Lark would give anything to take back her unsupportive behavior and longed to ask her sister how she'd coped. "She fell in love."

"Is that what you did? Your mother tells me you're sleeping with the elder Holt boy."

The change of topic caught Lark off guard. She should have come prepared to defend herself, but her emotions were too raw for clear thinking. "He's not using me, if that's what you think."

"What I think is you didn't have much experience with boys in high school. I'm guessing that continued in college. The Holts are liars and cheats. You should have known better than to let him trick you."

"I haven't." But wasn't that what she'd accused him of doing? Before she'd had dealings with them, Lark had always assumed there was something shifty about the Holts. She'd trusted her father's judgment, but now that she'd gotten to know Keaton and his parents, she had a different perspective.

Her father turned fierce blue eyes on her. "He created a fake document that he's going to use to cheat us out of our land."

"Keaton wouldn't do that."

"Sure he would. He's a Holt, isn't he?"

"That's ridiculous. Keaton is honest and honorable. He would never do something so underhanded."

Where had this reasonableness been an hour ago when she was throwing accusations at Keaton? Maybe if she'd taken a moment to think it all through she wouldn't have treated him so unfairly. Would he ever be able to forgive her?

"You are no different than your sister, siding with them against your own family."

"I'm not siding with anyone against you, but if he's had the document authenticated, surely that means something went wrong a hundred years ago."

"That's impossible. It was lost years ago."

"Lost?" At first Lark was too shocked to understand; then as her father's meaning penetrated, she gasped. "The Holts have always claimed there was a bill of sale. You've always claimed there was no such document. Now you say it was lost. Which is it?"

Her father glared at her, but uncertainty flickered for a moment in his gaze. "The land is ours."

"But did the Holts buy the land first?"

"There might have been a sale, but there was no official record."

"Because proof of the sale wasn't recorded." Appalled, Lark saw that her father wasn't as certain of his position as he'd been moments before. Her heart softened. Had he taken his aggressive stance against the Holts all these years because of fear? "The land does belong to the Holts."

Any doubt she'd glimpsed in her father vanished at her words. He stalked to the door and opened it. "Get out of my house and don't bother coming back until you change your tune."

While father and daughter stared at each other, a large figure filled the open doorway.

"Lark?" It was Keaton. He gazed from her to her father, assessing the situation. "Is everything okay here?" He hadn't entered the Taylor home, but looked prepared to do so on Lark's word.

Her heart floundered in her chest. What was he doing here? The concern in his gaze sent regret and shame rushing through her. She'd been so wrong to accuse him of using her. She'd let fear and old prejudices guide her to make terrible assumptions.

"I came to tell my father about the bill of sale you found." She began to edge toward the door, toward Keaton, giving her father a wide berth. "I asked him to sit down and discuss the situation rather than getting the courts involved."

Keaton looked surprised. She tried to convey her apology without words, but he'd switched his attention to her father. "Tyrone." Keaton pitched his voice in polite and moderate tones. "I want to work out something with the land that will benefit both our families."

"It's not your land."

"I have a bill of sale that says it is."

"It's a fake."

Lark could see her father's conviction had flagged. Yet he was a stubborn, single-minded man who'd been fighting a battle against the Holts all his life. He'd never admit that what he knew as truth might be wrong.

"Father, please listen to what Keaton has to say." As she spoke, she moved to stand beside Keaton. His solid strength comforted her, enabled her to feel safe for the first time since she'd entered her father's home. "He's fair and honest. You can trust him."

Tyrone's upper lip curled in derision. "So you've chosen.

Very well. From here on out, you are no more my daughter than that sister of yours."

"Father!" Lark took an involuntary step backward. The movement put her outside the house on the wide front porch. She bumped into Keaton and felt him grip her upper arms, steadying her. "You don't mean that."

"I do indeed. You've placed your loyalty with the Holts. I am finished with you."

Her father closed the door with an emphatic finality, underscored by the sound of a dead bolt being thrown.

Conscious of Keaton's worried expression, Lark descended the porch steps. Her emotions whirled and dipped like a carnival ride. She'd just been tossed out of the family. Had her father lost his mind? Was two thousand acres of land worth more than her and Skye?

"Lark, I'm so sorry," Keaton said, catching her arm and turning her to face him. "I never meant for any of that to happen."

Of course he hadn't. That was the sort of man he was. He'd suggested working with her father to give him a lease on water rights from the disputed property. Lark knew her father would never have made a similar offer to Keaton.

"It's okay." She raised her hand and put it on his chest.

He immediately covered her hand with his. "No, it's not. Your father just disowned you."

"Really...?"

To Lark's amazement she felt lighter, less encumbered, than she'd ever known. Was this what Skye had felt when she left town with Jake? Had she felt free to do and be whatever she wanted without the weight of their parents' expectations and disapproval dragging her down?

Lark sucked in a huge breath, and the fresh air infused her with glee. At last she was free to love the man standing before her without agonizing over what would happen when her parents found out and how angry they'd be. She was her own person. The only person she had to worry about disappointing was herself. And she would be terribly unhappy with herself if she pushed Keaton away again.

"It's okay." She beamed at him. "I'm okay."

Unsure if Lark was suffering from hysteria or shock, Keaton scrutinized her closely. "I don't understand. Aren't you upset?"

"I might be later, but for now all I feel is relief."

When he'd left her house he went straight to his parents and told them about the bill of sale and Lark's reaction to the news of its reappearance. He'd been certain that he'd lost her and determined to do whatever he could to win her back. He'd offer to split the land. Even compensate the Taylors for their loss. But he couldn't do any of that without his parents' approval.

He'd never expected to turn up at the Taylor Ranch in time to hear her side with him against her father. She'd chosen him over her family.

"Relief?" he asked. "Why?"

To his delight, she lifted up on tiptoe and wrapped her arms around his neck. "Because I love you and I don't care who knows it." She planted a hard kiss on his lips and pulled back to grin at him, her smile one of wild, unfettered joy.

His arms went around her and pulled her tight. She loved him. Hearing her say those words made him happier than he'd ever been. "You chose me over your parents."

"I was stupid not to do so a long time ago. You are the most caring, intelligent, sexiest man on the planet, and until today I hadn't fully appreciated how lost I would be without you."

"I'm glad to hear you say that, because this afternoon I was terrified I'd lost you. In fact, after our fight, I realized what needed to happen and went back to the house looking for you. Julie told me you were here and I came to lend you my support."

"Of course you did." Her eyes were bright and trusting. "Thank you."

"Let's get out of here," Keaton suggested, all too aware that her father could be loading a shotgun at this very moment with the idea of running him off Taylor land. "I have something I want to talk to you about. Follow me in your car."

She looked puzzled by his request but nodded. Halfway down the Taylors' driveway, around a curve and out of sight of the house, Keaton turned onto a little-used track that wound past the tree farm and entered the land that had been in dispute for so many generations. He was sure Lark had an idea where he was heading, and when he at last stopped the truck and got out to meet her, he could see she was smiling.

"The swimming hole I used to come to in the summer," she said, her eyebrows raised. "Where you used to spy on me."

Keaton took her hand and led her down the path to the water's edge, the Aussie frolicking around them. "I was old enough to know better," he admitted, watching Nicki chase a rabbit that was darting for cover. "But I couldn't bring myself to stop. It was the only time I'd ever seen you truly happy." He cast a sideways glance in her direction. "And then there was how you looked in that bikini."

"It was one of Skye's old ones. We weren't exactly the same size, so it didn't fit all that well."

In fact, it had been incredibly indecent on her lush curves. And she hadn't cared in the least. Keaton had loved every second she'd spent near or in the water. Her laughter had been infectious. Her sexy strut along the beach, laughably awkward and all the more delicious for its unconventional style, had sent his hormones into a tailspin.

"You were gorgeous in it." His voice had lowered into a husky murmur. "Any chance it's languishing in a drawer somewhere?"

Lark laughed. "Not likely."

"Pity." He pulled her along the edge of the water. The ten-acre lake wasn't the largest on the property, and the Taylors didn't use it to irrigate the tree farm. But it sat exactly in the middle of the two thousand acres that had been in dispute.

"But I didn't bring you here to reminisce," he explained, looping his arm around her. "I've decided this land needs to be claimed by both our families, so I intend to build a house here."

She surveyed the lake. "It'll be a fantastic spot. But won't that mean the ranch house will be empty a lot of the time now that your parents have bought property in Alabama?"

"I think a married man ought to have his own house, don't you?"

"Sure." She drew the word out. "Your wife would want the freedom to decorate and run her own household." She peered at him from beneath her lashes, her expression leaning toward somber. "And it's about time you thought about settling down. You're not getting any younger."

"You sound like my mother," he groused, but a smile lurked in his tone.

"But you said the land should be claimed by both our families, so what else did you have in mind? Some sort of compound where I live on the opposite side of the lake? And maybe Jake and Skye would consider a vacation home here."

"I'm not really sure that would work for me," Keaton said, pulling her close. "You'd be a little too far away for my taste."

Her eyes widened with pleasure. "You want to live together?"

"That's been working out pretty well this last month."

Her brow furrowed as she considered his proposition. "I've really enjoyed spending time with you, so I say let's do it."

"You've enjoyed spending time with me?" he echoed. "Ten minutes ago you claimed you loved me."

"Well, yes. I do."

"And you may recall that I told you at your house that I had fallen in love with you, as well."

"You meant that?"

"Of course I did. Do you think I run around telling women that I'm in love with them when I'm not?"

"Have you been in love with a lot of women?"

Keaton snorted. "Only you. Which is why…" He reached into his pocket and pulled out a small burgundy box. "Lark Marie Taylor." He popped the top on the box and watched her eyes widen at its contents. "Will you marry me? I want to build our dream house on this spot and live happily ever after with you."

Her eyes glowed like twin emeralds as she answered, "Absolutely."

He slipped the ring from the box and onto her trembling finger. As they sealed their pledge with a long, deep kiss, the rest of the world faded. Much, much later he felt the cool breeze against his hot skin and realized they'd been lost in each other for a quite a while.

"We should probably continue this at home," he said, setting his forehead against hers. "I'm sure Julie wasn't expecting you to be gone this long and may be worried."

"I sent her a quick text before getting out of the car and let her know we'd been delayed."

And that was one of the things he loved about Lark. Always considering others and acting with efficiency. Opposites might attract, but what had drawn Keaton to Lark was all the ways she understood and accepted him.

"You know what this means," Lark said, laughing with joy. "We've officially ended the Holt/Taylor feud. After us there will be no more generations of your family and my family. It will all be our family."

"I think that sounds pretty great," he said. "And speaking of our family, how eager are you to start one?"

"Very," she admitted. "Having Grace around this last month has made me anxious for children of my own. How do you feel?"

"The same."

Her smile grew wicked. "Then what are we doing standing around here?"

Chuckling, he drew Lark back to where they'd left their

vehicles. The afternoon sun was fading toward the horizon, painting the lake and surrounding trees with a golden light. He gave the scene a final look as he opened Lark's car door, picturing a big house by this lake with children running in the yard. It was going to be a perfect place to build a life with her. He imagined their sons and daughters growing up on the land that had kept their families at odds for decades, their happiness banishing old resentment.

"What do you see?" she asked, noticing his distraction.

"Our future." He brushed his lips against hers. "And it looks absolutely wonderful."

* * * * *

"I wish to kiss you."

Hearing the words melted Sunny's resolve to stay strong and not succumb to his charms. "I wouldn't exactly be uncomfortable, and I certainly wouldn't take offense. But I might regret it."

Rayad smiled halfway. "Do you not trust my skill?"

She worried he had too much skill. "How do I know you're not the kind of man who kisses and tells?"

His expression went suddenly somber. "Whatever transpires between us will remain between us."

Oh, heavens, she was going to do it—invite him to put her in a lip-lock. She had to know how it would feel. How she would feel. "In that case, show me your skill."

Keeping his arms at his sides, he leaned forward to press his lips against hers, making a brief pass, then another, as if testing the waters. Then, as if she'd become someone else, Sunny wrapped one hand around his neck, signaling she needed more. He answered that need by delving into her mouth with the soft glide of his tongue.

Skilled was an enormous understatement.

ONE HOT
DESERT NIGHT

BY
KRISTI GOLD

MILLS &
BOON

Published in Great Britain 2015
by Mills & Boon, an imprint of Harlequin (UK) Limited,
Eton House, 18-24 Paradise Road, Richmond, Surrey, TW9 1SR

© 2015 Kristi Goldberg

ISBN: 978-0-263-25244-6

51-0115

Harlequin (UK) Limited's policy is to use papers that are natural, renewable and recyclable products and made from wood grown in sustainable forests. The logging and manufacturing processes conform to the legal environmental regulations of the country of origin.

Printed and bound in Spain
by CPI, Barcelona

Kristi Gold has a fondness for beaches, baseball and bridal reality shows. She firmly believes that love has remarkable healing powers and feels very fortunate to be able to weave stories of love and commitment. As a bestselling author, a National Readers' Choice Award winner and a Romance Writers of America three-time RITA® Award finalist, Kristi has learned that although accolades are wonderful, the most cherished rewards come from networking with readers. She can be reached through her website at www.kristigold.com, or through Facebook.

To my future son-in-law, Christopher.
We are so blessed to have you in our family.

One

Sheikh Rayad Rostam had blood on his hands, a bounty on his head and a burden he had carried for years.

Though at times he longed for peace, he had lived on the edge for so long, he knew no other way. And today, as he stared out the palace window to the mountains towering over Bajul, the pain in his side reminding him of his recent face-off with possible death, his never-ending mission still urged him to continue.

"You cannot return to your duties until you are medically cleared, Rayad."

An order issued by the king, who happened to be his cousin. He despised any attempts to dictate his choices and a life where family loyalty and royal decrees prevailed. Battling anger, he chose to keep his attention focused on the familiar landscape to avoid Rafiq's scrutiny. "I do not see why I cannot return immediately. I have suffered much worse than broken ribs and will probably do so again."

"And the next time you could very well sustain wounds that will not heal, particularly if your cover was breached."

That sent him around to face Rafiq as he struggled to suppress his fury over the reminders of his downfall. A tragic event that had set his life-long course. "I learned from my mistake many years ago, and since that time no one has learned my identity. As far as my safety is concerned, that is a risk I take to fulfill my duty to this country."

Rafiq leaned back in the chair situated behind the massive desk and streaked a palm over his goatee, seemingly unaffected by the ire in Rayad's tone. "You go beyond the limits of risk-taking, cousin, as you continue your futile quest for elusive killers that you will most likely never find."

Bordered on losing control, he braced his palms on the edge of the desk and leaned forward. "I will never stop searching until I locate and punish those responsible."

Rafiq raised a brow. "And if you do not find them?"

He straightened, hands fisted at his sides. "I will die trying."

"And that, Rayad, is exactly what I fear will happen if you do not reassess your goals. I have accepted that I will never know the true circumstance behind my

mother's death. I have also accepted Rima's death was
no fault of my own."

"My situation is very different, Rafiq. You speak
of a possible accident or suicide. I speak of murder."

"Some answers are not meant to be known, but life
is meant to be lived. You should rebuild yours as I have.
You should honor your royal heritage by continuing the
legacy with an heir."

A concept that was not feasible in light of the tragedy that remained foremost on his mind. "Unlike you
and your brothers, Rafiq, my duties prevent me from
considering taking a wife and bearing children."

"I am ruler of our country," Rafiq said. "Zain has established a water-conservation system that will secure
Bajul's future. Adan is the commander of our armed
forces. We have all been successful in our endeavors to
bear children and keep our wives satisfied."

Since Rayad's recent arrival at the royal palace, all
signs pointed to that success every night during the
evening meal when he had been subjected to several
miniature Mehdis, and Maysa, the king's very pregnant wife. "I commend you on that achievement, Rafiq.
However, I am personally not interested in attaining
domestic tranquility."

Rafiq narrowed his eyes and studied him a lengthy
moment. "Are you so lost in your thirst for revenge that
you no longer crave the company of a woman?"

"I am not celibate, yet there are very few women I
trust enough to bed."

"How long has it been since you have been with a
woman, Rayad?"

Too long to admit to any other man. "I have been infiltrating several insurgent encampments for the past eight months, or do you not recall giving that directive?"

Rafiq released a rough sigh. "Perhaps you should take this opportunity and use it to locate a suitable mate."

He had heard the same suggestions from his parents, as if they expected him to discard the pain and remorse. Clearly, no one understood that he only wanted to sate his natural desire, not settle into an ordinary life. "Even if I consented to wed as you and my father suggest, suitable brides in Bajul are rare, Rafiq. Most are married or too young."

Rafiq scowled. "Must you make this so difficult? You are free to travel to another region if necessary. I am certain your father can locate prospects in Dubai."

In an effort to quell the subject, Rayad returned to the window where he glimpsed the official armored limousine arriving at the entrance. When the driver rounded the car and opened the door, a lithe woman exited the vehicle, the afternoon sun glinting off her long blond hair. Her clothing was somewhat conservative and nondescript, yet she moved with the grace of a gazelle. As she removed the sunshades covering her eyes and glanced up at the window where he now stood, Rayad was struck by her beauty, and immediately reminded of his unwelcome abstinence.

Forcing his gaze away, he regarded Rafiq over one shoulder. "Are you expecting a guest? Specifically a female guest?"

"That is accurate," Rafiq said. "She will be staying here for an indeterminate amount of time."

He thrust his hands in his pockets and slowly began to pace the area. "Is she wed?"

The king presented his best scowl. "No, she is not, but I caution you to stay away from her, Rayad."

He paused midstride and turned toward his suddenly irritable cousin. "Why? Are you interested in bedding her?"

"Of course not," Rafiq said. "If you recall, I have a bride."

He could not resist the urge to bait the king. "This is true, but perhaps you have decided to reinstate ancient customs and populate a harem."

Rafiq's venomous look revealed he did not appreciate the conjecture. "The woman is Adan's sister-in-law. Should you trifle with her, you will have to answer to him, your commander in chief, as well as Piper, his wife."

That did not deter Rayad from exploring all possibilities. "Does this woman have a name?"

"Sunny McAdams. She is an international correspondent, and I highly doubt she would be interested in engaging in a temporary affair with you, if that is what you are considering. It is my understanding she has recently dissolved a relationship with a colleague."

What better way to temporarily move past loss than with mutual passion? Of course, she would have to be willing. He had never taken from a woman what she refused to give. He never would. "I appreciate your counsel, cousin," he said as he backed toward the door.

"I assure you I will take your concerns into consideration." *And promptly ignore them.*

"That would be wise, Rayad, and I suggest…"

Rayad closed the door on the king before he had a chance to finish his lecture. At the moment, he intended to give the palace guest an appropriate greeting.

He thrived on the chase, lived for the challenge in all aspects of his life and at times yearned for a respite from his mission of revenge. Erotic fantasy was his specialty, sex his second calling. When he set his sights on a conquest, he ignored all obstacles that stood in the way of achieving his goal. Yet one goal he had never achieved…

Refusing to relive the regrets, Rayad decided the woman with the golden hair would be worth his best efforts to know her, if only for a brief time. If they decided they did not suit each other, so be it. Yet if they did, then the world was rife with possibilities, including a journey into pure pleasure…and a brief escape from the sins of his past.

Although the mountainous terrain qualified as breathtaking, and the majestic palace looming before her storybook-worthy, Sunny McAdams didn't have the presence of mind to appreciate the enchanting scenery. She sought only solace, a refuge in which to reclaim her courage and return to the woman she once had been.

A few months ago, she'd come to this obscure Middle Eastern country called Bajul to visit her beloved fraternal twin sister, Piper, who'd married a bona-fide Arabian prince. That day, she had been happy with life, secure in her job as a journalist and comfortably settled into a casual relationship with a really good guy. Two weeks later, everything had fallen apart. Now she felt terribly sad and a whole lot alone. Beaten down, but not broken. No one could ever break her, even those who had tried.

Yet for some reason, she felt as if someone might be watching her. Then again, her paranoia had grown by leaps and bounds since the kidnapping. Lately everyone appeared to be the enemy, from cab drivers to convenience-store workers.

As much as she hated to admit it, she needed family now, Piper in particular. Their personality differences had never interfered when it came to sensing each other's emotional needs. And that connection had led to her sister's invitation to visit for however long it took for Sunny to regroup.

As she stood by the car and waited for further instruction, she didn't possess enough energy to insist that she was quite capable of opening her own door and carrying her own luggage. *Luggage* was definitely an overstatement when describing the lone duffel bag and small carry-on case now in the hands of an attendant all decked out in white muslin. She'd learned to travel light and pack very little in the course of her work. Covering breaking news in some of the most obscure places on earth required only minimal supplies. At least today she'd exchanged the khakis and T-shirts for black slacks and a white, tailored, buttoned-up blouse, as dressed up as she'd been in quite a while.

When the driver gestured toward the entry, two

beefy guards opened the heavy, wooden double doors, allowing her access to the ornate Mehdi palace. And after she stepped inside, her footsteps echoed in the three-story foyer as she followed the man with her bag, passing several golden statuettes and exquisite artwork.

The attendant paused before the towering staircase, turned and set the duffel onto the polished stone floor near Sunny's feet. "If you will kindly wait here, I will summon your sister," he said, his tone thick with a Middle Eastern accent.

"Of course," she replied politely, although she wasn't sure why she had to wait. She couldn't imagine Piper had forgotten she was due to arrive at this hour. Then again, considering her sibling had stepped into the role of mother to the sheikh's infant son, she could have been detained by a wet diaper.

As the minutes ticked off, Sunny passed the time studying several portraits of regal-looking royals lining the stone walls, including the current king, the stoic and darkly handsome Rafiq Mehdi and his debonair brother, Zain. She then paused at the painting depicting the lighter-haired Adan, the youngest Mehdi son, and her new brother-in-law. She had to admit Piper had landed herself one good-looking pilot-prince, and the person who'd painted this picture had nailed every detail, right down to the guy's dimples.

After Sunny leaned over to better see the artist's signature, she immediately straightened from shock when she noted her twin's familiar handwriting. She then backtracked and checked every painting to find that Piper had created each and every one, and she'd done a darn good job. Finally, her sister had realized her overdue dream of becoming an artist. And she'd become a princess in the process. Amazing.

"Not too shabby at all," she muttered aloud. "It's about time you were wrested from our grandfather's clutches."

"Parental influences can be a challenge."

Sunny's hand automatically went to her throat as she spun around in search of the owner of the darkly masculine voice…and contacted the most intense near-black eyes she'd ever seen. He shouted military man from the top of his close-cropped black hair, to the bottom of his brown combat boots, yet his jaw was spattered with whiskers, as if he hadn't shaved in a while. The tan fatigues and black T-shirt pulled tight over his extremely toned chest, the short sleeves revealing standard-issue muscles that said he meant business, proved to be quite the distraction. So did his self-assured stance and the somewhat arrogant lift of his chin.

As he boldly assessed her from forehead to feet, Sunny's journalist's instinct kicked into overdrive, bringing with it a series of descriptors. Stealth. Mysterious. Sexy as hell.

The impact of the last thought caused heat to fan over her face and snake down her throat as the overwhelming need to escape took hold. She refused to give in to that urge.

When he didn't speak she offered her hand for a shake. "I'm Sunny McAdams. And you are?"

He stepped forward and enveloped her extended

hand in one very large palm. "Greatly pleased to meet you."

Two more words came to mind—practiced player. After he released his grasp, Sunny hugged her arms to her middle as if that somehow guarded her from the impact of his inescapable aura of power. "Do you have a name or should I try to guess?"

"Rayad," he replied without even hinting at a smile, but his gaze never faltered. Oh, no. He just kept staring at her as if trying to read her mind. Hopefully he couldn't, because she harbored too many secrets she would never reveal to a stranger.

Sunny inclined her head and studied him straight on, showing him she wasn't about to cower under his assessment. "Ah, a man of few words who apparently doesn't have a last name."

"You made it!"

She tore her attention from the stranger and brought it to her dark-haired, blue-eyed bubbly sister practically bounding down the stairs to the right. Before Piper reached the bottom landing, Sunny risked a glance to find that the mystifying Rayad was nowhere to be found.

As soon as Piper's feet hit the floor below the final step, she drew Sunny into a voracious hug. "I'm so glad you're here."

"So am I," she said after they ended the embrace. "And I can't tell you how much I appreciate you letting me hang out here for a while."

"You're welcome to stay as long as you like," Piper said as she surveyed Sunny's face. "You look terrible."

That could explain why Mystery Man had been staring at her nonstop. "Gee, thanks, sis. I didn't know the invitation came with insults."

Piper rolled her eyes to the gold-bedecked ceiling. "I meant you look exhausted. You couldn't look terrible if you tried."

Oh, but she did. She was well aware how badly her blond hair needed a trim and how pale she'd become since she'd left the field. "I'm in dire need of some sun and sleep, that's for sure. Spa treatments couldn't hurt."

Piper grinned. "Well, you've come to the right place. Or maybe I should say the right palace."

Sunny felt as if she'd been transported back to a better place and time, when she and her twin hadn't had a care in the world, in spite of the fact they hadn't had a caring mother. "Very funny, Pookie Bear."

Her sister scowled. "Please don't let my husband hear you call me that, Sunshine. He'll grab on to the nickname like a fish on a worm and won't let go."

"Tell you what," she said. "You can the *Sunshine* and I'll forget the *Pookie*."

"But your name is Sunshine."

"And you know how much I hate that."

"All right, it's a deal." Piper hooked her arm through Sunny's. "Now I shall escort you to your accommodations. For this visit, I've selected the first-floor guest quarters reserved for very special guests. Lots of privacy."

Unlike the last stay at the palace, this time Sunny needed privacy and a place to hide away, at least when

she wasn't expected to socialize with the in-laws. "I
only require a bed and a bath."

"Oh, you'll have both," Piper said as she led her
down a lengthy corridor off the foyer. "And your own
private garden."

"As long as I don't have to tend it, that sounds great."

After they navigated a narrow hallway flanked by
more polished rock walls, Piper paused in front of a
pair of gleaming wooden doors and opened them wide.
"Enter this chamber fit for a princess. Or the princess's
sister."

Sunny stepped over the threshold and visually
searched the massive room, awed by the absolute gran-
deur, including an intricately carved headboard, red
satin spread and a scattering of matching red and gold
chairs. She turned to Piper and smiled. "Where's my
tiara?"

"I'll have one sent up," she said. "Bathroom's to the
right, complete with massive soaking tub and a car-
wash-size shower, in case you want to have a party with
a companion or ten."

She didn't even have one companion, let alone ten.
When the image of the patently sexy, albeit elusive
Rayad jumped into her brain, she mentally shoved it
away. But she couldn't dispel the suffocating imagines
of confinement at the hands of a criminal. She couldn't
rid herself of the concern that she might never function
as the normal sensual woman she'd once been. "Do you
have a few minutes for a brief visit, or do you have to
tend to royal duties or baby stuff?"

Piper plopped down onto a gold brocade divan.

"Sure. Sam won't be up from his nap for another half hour or so."

Sunny joined her on the less-than-comfortable sofa. "So how is my nephew these days?"

Her sister revealed a mother's smile. "He's fat and sassy and a very active eight-month-old. He started crawling fairly early, and now he's pulling up on furniture poised to take off on his chubby little legs at any time. But I really expect him to climb before he walks."

She expected Piper to burst at the seams with pride at any moment. "I assume the supermodel hasn't given you and Adan any trouble since the adoption."

"Not one bit. As far as everyone in the kingdom knows, Sam is my son."

Sunny took her sister's hand. "He is your son in every way that counts."

"You're right," Piper said. "And not only am I a mother, I have been commissioned as the official palace portrait artist. It's been a juggling act over the past few months, but I've had a lot of help with Sam from the staff and my gorgeous husband. I just finished Adan's painting two days ago and I hope it's up to speed."

Sunny smiled. "I saw the paintings, and Piper, they're beautiful. I'm so glad you tore yourself away from our grandfather's business so you could finally do what you've wanted to do for years."

Piper shrugged. "Believe me, if I hadn't met Adan, I'd probably still be acting as the company's goodwill ambassador. However, that position directly led to my husband."

Sunny grinned around an unexpected nip of envy.

"You must have shown him some mighty fine goodwill, among other things."

After they shared in a laugh, Piper's expression turned suddenly serious. "Enough about me. How are you doing?"

She'd been dreading this part of the visit—recounting the details of what led to her breakup with Cameron. Horrific details that she'd relived every day and night since the traumatic experience. "I'm doing much better than the last time we spoke. I've moved past the anger and on to acceptance." Though she would never quite accept her former lover's abandonment when she'd needed him most.

"It's not your fault," Piper said, as if she could read her thoughts. "He wasn't good enough for you if he couldn't face what happened."

"He tried, Piper. I was a mess."

"He didn't try hard enough, and that makes him a jerk."

"He was dealing with his own guilt for not following me that day so he could ride in and save me."

"Stop making excuses for him, Sunny. You were brutally attacked and abducted and that's not something anyone can get over in a matter of days. If I'd been through the same thing, I know Adan would have stuck by me."

Something suddenly occurred to her. "You haven't mentioned the attack to Adan, have you?"

Piper shook her head. "No. He thinks you're here because of the breakup. I don't like keeping things from him, but I did promise you I wouldn't say anything."

She'd known she could count on her sister for dis-
cretion. "Thank you. The network decided to keep it
under wraps."

Piper frowned. "Why? Are they afraid you're going
to sue them?"

"No. They're respecting my privacy. They know if
word gets out, I'll be headline news instead of covering
it." She sighed. "I keep trying to tell myself we knew
what we were walking into. What we'd been walking
into for the past three years. Greed breeds criminals,
but you never really know who they are until you meet
up with one on a dark street. And in one moment of
carelessness, your whole perspective on life changes
when facing possible death."

Piper leaned over and hugged her. "I hope you're
going to consider staying in the States when you resume your career."

She had considered it, then nixed that idea altogether,
a fact she chose to withhold from her twin for the time
being. "That's going to be up to the network, provided
they even want me after I've been on leave for two
months."

"The network adores you, Sunny. I'm sure they'll
welcome you back with open arms. Do you still have
your apartment in Atlanta?"

Sunny shook her head. "Nana convinced me to give
it up when my lease ran out while I was staying with
her and Poppa. My things are in storage in Charleston."

"Well, you can always live in the guesthouse permanently since I've vacated the premises."

She'd rather eat collard greens. "A little bit of the

grandparents goes a long way. If I decided to work solely in the U.S., I'd move back to Atlanta."

Piper gave her another quick hug. "I hope you do. I wouldn't have to worry about you fending off poisonous snakes in some rain forest."

At least she hadn't brought up unseen attackers. "You could have gone all year without mentioning those foul creatures," she said, followed by a yawn.

Piper came to her feet and smiled. "You apparently have a lot of catch-up to do on your sleep. So feel free to take a long nap."

If only it were that simple. Sleep hadn't come easily, at least nightmare-free sleep. "That sounds good, but it's not that long until bedtime."

"True, but don't hesitate to try the giant bathtub before dinner," Piper added.

Sunny stood and stretched her arms above her head. "Speaking of dinner, who'll be joining us for the evening meal?"

"Everyone," Piper said. "My husband, of course. Zain and Madison and their toddlers since they've recently returned from Los Angeles. King Rafiq and an extremely pregnant Queen Maysa. Oh, and a cousin, Rayad Rostam, who showed up two days ago."

Finally, Mystery Man was no longer quite the mystery. "Since his last name isn't Mehdi, how is he related?"

"His father and the former queen were siblings, I think, but I don't know much more. I haven't had the opportunity to speak with my husband for three whole days, thanks to some top-secret training mission where he flies planes at warp speed. But I'll be sure to introduce you to Rayad tonight, and you can interview him."

"I met him," Sunny blurted without thought. "While I was waiting for you in the foyer. But he didn't say much more than a few words."

Piper's smile arrived full-force. "He's gorgeous, isn't he?"

Unfortunately. "I didn't notice, and you're not supposed to notice since you're now a married woman."

"But I'm not blind, and neither are you."

Her twin knew her all too well. "Fine, he's gorgeous. Satisfied?"

Piper's expression said she wasn't. "Maybe you should get to know him while you're here. It's my understanding he is presently unattached."

Sunny held up both hands, palms forward. "Stop right there. I'm not in the market for a man, if that's what you're thinking."

"I'm thinking you could use a diversion after the idiot left you high and dry."

"It's too soon, Piper. Cameron and I haven't been apart that long." And her internal wounds resulting from the attack had yet to heal. Wounds she had yet to reveal to her twin.

"And by your own admission, Sunny, you loved Cameron, but you weren't *in love* with him."

She'd argued those points with herself, but that hadn't eased the hurt. "Color me gun-shy."

Piper's features softened into a sympathetic look. "Maybe it's time you make a sincere effort to rejoin the land of the living, Sunny. I'm not suggesting you sleep with Rayad. I'm suggesting you use your skills to find out what he's all about and leave all options open. A challenge of sorts to get your mind off your troubles. And lucky for you, he's staying in the room right next door."

She found that somewhat odd, and a little disconcerting. "Doesn't he have a house of his own?"

"Since he's undoubtedly rich as sin like the rest of the family, I assume he does. But Maysa told me that Rafiq insisted he stay here while he's recovering from an injury he sustained during some kind of incident."

He'd looked perfectly healthy to Sunny. Very healthy. "What did he injure?"

Her sister grinned. "I'm not sure. Why don't you ask him? Better still, why don't you request he show you?"

"Not interested," she said, worried that she might never be able to experience true intimacy again. "Besides, I've never really been drawn to the strong, macho, silent type."

Piper barked out a laugh on her way to the door. "Yeah, right, Sunshine. Aside from Cameron, that's the only type that's ever held your interest."

Bristling from the truth, Sunny trailed behind her sister and prepared for a debate. "Don't you dare do anything stupid like try to fix me up, Pookie."

Piper spun around and scowled. "You promised you wouldn't call me that."

"You promised, too."

"Okay, you're right. No more Pookie or Sunshine."

"It's a deal."

"And I also promise not to play cupid," Piper continued, "although Madison tells me Rayad's a really nice guy if you can get past all that machismo. Just something to consider between now and the evening meal."

After Piper closed the door behind her, Sunny perched on the edge of the mattress and toed out of her flats. She'd already surmised Rayad Rostam was a testosterone-ridden military man, and that should be all she needed to know. Yet her innate inquisitiveness urged her to learn more about him. She craved peeling back those personality layers to reveal the man behind the steely persona. She truly needed to investigate him further, from a solely journalistic standpoint, of course. Even if she proved to be drawn to him on a physical level, a virile man like Rayad wouldn't want the closed-off, fearful woman she'd become. Not even a nice guy could handle that—case in point, her former lover, Cameron.

Rayad Rostam a nice guy? She frankly had her doubts about that.

Two

Macho Man had a squirming toddler in his lap, and he didn't seem to mind.

Seated across from Rayad Rostam at the lengthy dining table, for the past ten minutes Sunny had witnessed his remarkable patience with brown-haired, chatty, two-year-old Cala, daughter of the former playboy prince, Zain Mehdi, and his wife, Madison, the resident palace fixer of all things scandalous. The patient sheikh didn't seem concerned that the little girl had dotted his T-shirt with cheese cracker remnants. He didn't appear to care when she poked at his mouth, as if it held some sort of magic. Sunny suspected it probably did. The tolerant sheikh simply kept his lips sealed against the intrusion and gently extracted her hand from his face, followed by a kiss on her palm.

She certainly couldn't fault a guy who apparently had an affinity for children. She also hadn't been able to ignore the furtive glances he'd tossed her way during dinner, even though the to-die-for skewered chicken, tasty cheese and hummus side dish should have earned all her attention. Fortunately, no one else seemed to notice, thanks to the ongoing adult conversation and occasional screech from an overstimulated infant, namely her nephew, Sam.

When Cala wriggled from Rayad's lap, Sunny noticed discomfort pass over his face as his hand went to his upper right side. The wound Piper mentioned apparently involved his rib cage. Another mystery solved, several more to go, including the hint of sadness in his eyes as Cala turned and waved to him before claiming a spot in her father's lap.

But at the moment, the effects of jet lag had Sunny considering putting off her sheikh fact-finding mission until a later date. And when the queen and king rose from their chairs and excused themselves, followed by Zain and Madison and their twins, she saw that as an excuse to make her escape.

Sunny tossed her napkin aside, came to her feet and regarded Piper, who was seated next to the silent Rayad. "Dinner was great," she began, "but I really need to retire before I nod off in the dessert plate."

Piper stood and removed Sam from his highchair then turned him around to face Sunny. "Tell your auntie good-night, sweetie." The baby responded by flailing his arms around and making motoring noises.

"A chip off the old pilot block," Adan said, displaying

a dimpled grin as he stood with Rayad following suit. "I do hope you find your quarters satisfactory, Sunny."

"They're more than satisfactory," she replied as she rounded the table to kiss her nephew good-night, very aware that Rayad visually followed her movements. "I'm sure I'll sleep well as soon as I take my nightly walk. Any suggestions where I should do that?"

Adan nodded to the open dining room doors. "After you exit, take a right, and you'll find the entry to the courtyard."

"But be careful," Piper cautioned. "The grounds are like a maze. You might want to grab some bread crumbs and leave a trail, just in case."

"I have a fairly good sense of direction, so no worries."

After giving her twin a hug, and bidding everyone good-night, Sunny left the room and immediately located the doors leading to the expansive garden. She followed the labyrinth of stone walkways using the three-quarter moon as her guide, occasionally glancing behind her to keep the palace within her sights. When the path ended at a low retaining wall, she paused to study the twinkling lights dotting the valley below. A warm November breeze ruffled her hair, bringing with it the scent of exotic flowers. Back home the weather would be much cooler, and much of the fragrant foliage gone until spring. But not in this region. Most days brought pleasant weather, according to her hosts, yet rain had been forecasted in the next couple of days.

Feeling surprisingly serene, she looked up at the night sky to study the host of diamond-like stars. She welcomed the sense of peace she experienced for the first time in quite some time…

"Have you lost your way?"

For the second time that day, Sunny's heart vaulted into her throat. She spun around to face the familiar man standing in the shadows behind her. "I'm not lost, and do you have some bizarre need to scare me to death?"

"No. I was simply concerned for your well-being."

"Look, Mr.…Sheikh… What exactly is your official title?"

He took a step toward her, his handsome face only partially revealed in the limited light. "You may call me Rayad."

She'd like to call him a few unflattering names at the moment, and she would if he wasn't so darn intimidating—in an overtly male sort of way. "Look, Rayad, I have traveled to some of the most remote places in the world and navigated some of the most treacherous terrain. I can handle a palace garden."

"A garden that has been known to house deadly insects and asps."

Just when her heart had returned to its rightful place, he'd mentioned her biggest fear. Correction. Second biggest fear, if the truth were known. "Really? Snakes?"

"Yes."

She refused to let him see her uneasiness. "Would that be the reptile or human variety?"

"I have not personally encountered either in this garden," he said without even a touch of lightness in his tone. "However, I have been conditioned to protect women. Therefore, I feel it is necessary to ensure your safe return."

Her perfect opportunity to get to know him, but then he went and ruined it with the whole he-man posturing. Now she was determined to make a hasty escape and prove she could make it back to safety on her own. She had survived much, much worse. "Not all women need protection, Sheikh Rostam. Have a nice night."

After Sunny brushed past him, she paused to survey four directional options, crossed her fingers and chose the path to her right.

"You are going the wrong way."

Somewhat annoyed by his interference, and her irritating female reaction to the sexy timbre of his voice, she reluctantly faced him again. "I'm sure every way eventually leads back to the palace."

He moved closer. "Not necessarily. If you continue on your current course, you will reach the road leading to the village. And if not careful, you could tumble down the cliff if you lose your footing."

Wasn't he just the bearer of good news? If she refused his offer, she could be allowing pride to overrule safety, a mistake she'd already made that had brought about severe consequences. If she accepted his aid, she could find out what made him tick, and avoid falling to her death. Option two sounded the most favorable, although not completely without risk. "Fine. Lead the way."

After Rayad chose the trail heading in the opposite direction, Sunny came to his side and kept her focus straight ahead. And as they walked a few yards in silence, she mentally dashed through a list of subtle questions, choosing the most logical query to begin her impromptu interview. "Piper mentioned you'd recently suffered an injury during military training."

"Broken ribs."

"Did you run into something?"

"A fist."

Definitely a man of few words, or two words, as the case might be. "Must've been some tough hand-to-hand combat. Is training troops primarily your duty?"

"No. Intelligence."

Figured. "So you're a spy guy, huh?"

"In a manner of speaking."

"I bet you have a code name like Scorpion, or perhaps Snake."

"That information is classified."

She wondered if he ever let down his guard, or smiled, for that matter. "How long have you been serving?"

"Twelve years. I entered the military at the age of twenty-one."

Progress. She now knew his age and that he was only six years her senior. Not too bad. Not that their age difference should matter one iota. "Are you married?" Now why had she asked that when she already knew the answer?

"No, I am not."

"Have you ever been married?"

His long hesitation was a bit telling, or maybe she was reading too much into it. Then it suddenly dawned on her that he might think she was interested in him.

Time to set the record straight. "I ask because I've known quite a few military men who find it difficult to maintain a marriage. Understandably so when they're away much of the time. And I can relate with my line of work. Covering global news isn't conducive to having a serious relationship."

He paused, reached down to his right, snapped a plumeria from one grouping and offered it to her. "Have you been wed?" he asked as they continued on.

Both the question and the gesture caught her off guard. "Thanks, and I've never been married."

"Are you currently involved with anyone?"

Somehow the interviewer had become the interviewee. "I was involved briefly with a colleague, but that's been over for a while now."

"The man who apparently drove you to seek out your sister."

He presented the comment as a statement, not a question, leading Sunny to believe he knew much more about her than she knew about him. "You're right in a manner of speaking. How did you learn that?"

"Rafiq mentioned this to me when I inquired about you."

She'd expected her sister had been the messenger, not the king. "What else did he say?"

"He warned me to stay away from you."

One more shock in a series of several. "Seriously? Does he think I have the plague or homicidal intent aimed at men?"

He almost cracked a smile. "Do you?"

"No, I do not, and I have a hard time believing Rafiq believes that, either."

A slight span of silence passed before he spoke again. "The king believes you are too great a temptation for a man such as myself."

"Oh, I see." And she did, very clearly, even if his expression remained unreadable. "He thinks that if you attempt to seduce me, I'd be too vulnerable to resist. Clearly, he doesn't know me at all." Or at least the woman she used to be.

"Perhaps that is what he believes, but I do not view you as a vulnerable woman."

The compliment and the flower earned him a few points, even though she did inexplicably feel somewhat defenseless around him. His mystery and aura of power threw her mentally off-kilter. "I'm happy we've established I'm not some simpering Southern belle who needs saving."

"I do not understand the term *Southern belle*, but I do believe you are a highly sensual woman."

She loosened the chokehold she had on the poor plumeria. "What brought you to that conclusion?"

He slipped his hands in the pockets of his slacks and failed to look directly at her. "You are passionate about your work. You have put yourself in danger many times for the sake of your career."

She forced away the sudden terrifying images, with great effort. "Rafiq told you details about my occupation, too?"

"No. I perused your network's website."

She should probably be a bit wary that he'd conducted an internet search, but she was actually curious. "What prompted you to look me up?"

He sent her a fast glance, giving her a drive-by view of his damnable dark eyes. "When we spoke in the foyer today, I was intrigued by you."

She couldn't fault him since she'd felt the same about him. "Maybe I should search the net so I can learn more about you."

"You will find nothing."

Apparently he worked deep undercover, or he could be attempting to divert her from discovering information he preferred she not know. "In that case, tell me about yourself. The man, not the soldier."

He streaked a palm over the back of his neck. "I am the only child of a sultan who resides in Dubai with my mother."

"Considering how well you handled Cala tonight, are you sure you don't have a secret baby hidden away like your cousin, Adan?"

As he glanced her way, some unnamed emotion reflected from his eyes then disappeared as quickly as it had come. "I have no children."

"Then you have a gift."

He continued to focus on the path and not her. "Children are a gift. Too often they are used as pawns during war."

He'd probably witnessed unspeakable acts in his tenure as a soldier. That could explain why he'd seemed so sullen after Cala returned to Zain. She did find it odd that with his royal lineage, he would choose the military as his occupation and serve a country that obviously wasn't his homeland. "How did you end up in Bajul?"

"Adan and I attended the same military academy in the United Kingdom, though I was three years ahead of him. After I graduated, he encouraged me to consider joining him in the armed forces. My father gave his blessing, as well."

"You evidently didn't pick up the British-speak like Adan. In fact, you don't really have an accent at all, and your English is perfect."

"I am required to know many languages."

"How many?"

"Ten."

Incredible. "Do you fly jets, too?"

He shook his head. "No. I am strictly involved in ground forces."

She lifted the flower to her nose and drew in the wonderful scent. "If I were in the military and had my choice, I'd definitely learn to fly. Piper, on the other hand, hates planes. Ironic that she would marry a pilot."

"Reason is not always present when human emotion is involved."

How well she knew that. "Since I'm positive you can't be all work and no play, do you have any hobbies? Any interests beyond your job?"

"I have a weakness for beautiful women such as yourself."

Had she'd known she'd walk right into the typical playboy trap, she wouldn't have asked. "You don't get out much, do you?"

"Do not question my ability to recognize beauty," he said. "However, I do find humility very attractive."

False flattery would get him nowhere, especially since she hadn't felt attractive in quite some time. "I personally find arrogance off-putting."

Finally, he smiled—a small one—but a smile all the same. "Do you believe me to be arrogant?"

"I believe you're the kind of man who uses compliments to your advantage."

As they neared the palace entrance, Rayad paused beneath one of the lights lining the walkway, giving Sunny a good look at his handsome features, particularly his expressive eyes. "I am simply a man who speaks the truth," he said.

She hugged her arms to her middle, the flower wilting in her grasp. "Would that be all the time or only when it's convenient?"

"I am forced to withhold some information for security reasons. Yet when it comes to my attraction to a woman, I have nothing to hide, and I find I am extremely attracted to you."

She suspected many a woman had willingly given him anything he'd requested with only the crook of his finger and a come-hither look. She had no intention of doing that for many reasons. "Please explain to me how you could even remotely find me attractive after knowing me such a short time."

"Attraction is at times immediate, and oftentimes without explanation."

She couldn't exactly argue since she had to admit she found him illogically attractive, as well. And that in itself could be dangerous. "You're referring to *physical* attraction."

"That is the bait that encourages two people to explore the possibilities."

As Rayad studied her face, his gaze coming to rest on her mouth before trekking back to her eyes, she could imagine several possibilities. Tempting possibilities. Inadvisable and unattainable possibilities in light of her recent past.

Forcing herself back into reality, Sunny pointed the posy at the double doors. "Since it's getting fairly late, we should probably call it a night. Sleep well."

He inclined his head and narrowed his eyes. "Do you sleep well, or do nightmares plague you?"

Her entire body tensed with the fear he knew more about her than she'd first assumed. "Why would you believe I have nightmares?"

He leaned back against the stone ledge behind him and folded his arms across his broad chest. "I know you have seen carnage in your line of work. And with that carnage comes images that haunt you in dark and daylight."

Somewhat relieved he evidently didn't know everything, she wanted desperately to deny his accurate assumption. But she sensed he possessed an expert ranking when it came to character study, and therefore chose a partial lie. "I've had a few bad dreams, but it's not an every-night occurrence."

"Then you are fortunate," he said.

She took a step toward him in an effort to better read his reaction. "I take it you speak from experience."

He lifted his shoulders slightly in a shrug. "I am not immune to dreams that disturb my sleep."

"Then you've seen your share of horrors."

"Many in the past, and I expect more in the future."

Sheer curiosity to dissect this enigmatic man drew her to his side. "At the risk of sounding idealistic and illogical, I don't understand why the world has to be that way."

"Evil," he said, a strong cast of anger in his tone. "I have seen unspeakable acts forced on innocents by those with no conscience."

"So have I." She had been the victim of that very thing, though she refused to see herself as a victim. "It has made me rethink my career choice. I'm considering returning to the States when I go back to work."

"You will never be happy."

She faced him, leaned a hip against the wall and rested her elbow atop the ledge. "You're very bold to make that presumption."

Finally, he turned toward her and made eye contact. "I know your kind. You live for adventure and the thrill of chasing the story. You said in your biography you choose to ignore danger to seek the truth."

Damn the internet. "Yes, I did, but I'm not sure I feel that way anymore."

He gave her a look of surprise laced with suspicion. "Has something happened to change your attitude?"

The question had hit too close to home. If not careful, she might start confessing. "Burnout, I guess you could say. And it's definitely time for me to retire. If I'm lucky, this little jaunt through the snake-ridden garden has tired me out enough to drift off fairly quickly. Thanks so much for the companionship. I truly enjoyed it."

When Sunny turned and started away, he quickly clasped her hand. The sudden action caused her to wrest away and turn toward him, a knee-jerk reaction she'd developed since the attack.

"I do not wish to harm you," he said in a tempered tone.

She shivered slightly. "I know, and I apologize for my jumpiness. Just a little fallout due to the job. I've learned to always be on guard."

He pushed off the wall and approached her, leaving a scant few inches between them when he stopped. Then without warning, he reached out and pushed a tendril of hair from her cheek. "I find you very captivating, Sunny McAdams, and I hope I have the pleasure of speaking with you at length again."

"That's definitely a possibility," she said then hooked a thumb over her shoulder. "But if I don't get some rest, the next time you see me I might be babbling like a mad woman."

He smiled again. A fully formed smile that lessened the intensity in his eyes, but not his appeal. Not in the least. "Should you require assistance during the night, I am residing in the room next to yours."

That fact certainly wouldn't do a darn thing for her insomnia. "Thank you, but I'll be fine. I'm sure I'll see you tomorrow."

"That would be my pleasure."

The way he'd said *pleasure*—in a deep, sensual

tone—prompted some fairly sexual images in Sunny's muddled mind. And long after she left Rayad to settle into bed, she allowed them to fully form—only to have horrendous memories interrupt the welcome bliss.

She wondered if she would ever move past her fears and resume a normal life. If she would ever forget the harrowing experience. If she would ever be able to trust a man again.

For some reason, she truly wanted to trust Rayad Rostam, but she wasn't certain she could.

Three

He had never met a woman who recoiled at an innocent touch…until tonight. Rayad had pondered Sunny's reaction as he stripped off all of his clothing and stretched out on his back on the bed, naked.

He had wanted to kiss her and would have attempted it if not for her response. She had not necessarily been repulsed, but she had been afraid. He suspected that fear stemmed from a recent experience. He had seen it in her eyes, heard the wariness in her voice when he had asked about her decision to return home. Unless he knew the cause of her fear, he could only speculate. Yet he truly believed Sunny would not be forthcoming with that information. In that regard, she was very much like him, withholding details due to a lack of trust. However, one person would mostly hold the answers he sought.

Though he should wait until morning to question Piper, Rayad's thirst for the truth drove him from the bed. He retrieved a guest robe from the closet and slipped it on before entering the hallway. He strode through the corridors and sprinted up the staircase to the living quarters. Once there, he paused and attempted to discern which room belonged to Adan and his new bride. Fortunately, a meek-looking, dark-haired woman walked out one door to his immediate right and met his gaze, obviously surprised to find a nearly-naked man standing in the hallway.

After recognition dawned in her expression, she bowed her head slightly and muttered, "Your Highness."

He tightened the sash on the gaping robe. "I need to locate Sheikh Adan's room."

"At the end of the hall," she said, keeping her eyes averted as she pointed to her right. "But they do not wish to be disturbed. That is why I am tending to the young prince tonight."

If he retained any decorum whatsoever, he would take his leave. This mission was too important. "I will make certain you are not held responsible for the disturbance."

With that, he headed to the designated quarters without glancing back. Once there, he rapped twice on the wooden surface and waited. He had almost given up when the door creaked open to reveal his disheveled cousin, also dressed in a robe. "Bloody hell, Rayad," Adan muttered. "I hope you tell me we've gone to war, the only excuse I will accept for you showing up here in the middle of the night."

"There is no war, but I must speak to your wife."

"*My* wife is not presentable at the moment, and why would you need to speak to her?"

"I need to inquire about her sister."

Adan narrowed his eyes. "If you are entertaining thoughts of garnering permission to seduce Sunny, discard them now. She does not need to have you hounding her under the circumstances."

Perhaps he could bypass Piper after all. "Which circumstances would those be?"

"She was thrown over by some bastard and has suffered a severe broken heart. Those were my wife's exact words."

Siblings had been known to withhold truths from one another before, as it had been often with his cousins Adan and Zain. Or perhaps in this matter a wife was withholding information from her spouse. "And you are certain Piper is not concealing other details pertaining to her sister?"

He presented a stern scowl. "I have no reason not to believe what she told me. Now what is this all about?"

"I sensed there is more to Sunny's sabbatical than the end of a relationship when I was with her this evening."

Adan took on a murderous expression. "Define *when I was with her.*"

"We took a walk together in the garden."

"And where, Rayad, did you end your walk?"

He realized exactly what his cousin was implying. "We ended the walk in the garden, and that is when I realized she has unexplained fears."

"Of what? You?"

"Indirectly, yes. When I attempted to touch her—"

"*Where* did you attempt to touch her?"

"Her hand."

"Are you bloody sure you didn't reach a bit higher than that?"

Adan's question echoed loudly through the hallway and apparently disturbed his bride, who suddenly appeared in the doorway. "If you two don't lower your voices, you're going to wake the entire palace, including our son and the twins. What in heaven's name has you both so worked up?"

Adan pointed at Rayad. "This cad made a pass at your sister."

His wife seemed surprisingly calm. "She's an attractive woman, honey."

Rayad felt the need to defend his honor. "I only attempted to take her hand, yet her reaction to that innocent gesture has led me to believe she has possibly suffered a recent trauma."

"I told him it was a traumatic breakup," Adan said. "With the soundman."

Piper frowned at her husband. "He's a cameraman, Adan, and what kind of reaction are you referring to?"

"She startles easily," Rayad answered. "It is as if she is fearful of many things."

Piper's gaze briefly faltered. "That's understandable considering she throws herself into some fairly precarious situations due to her job."

Her lack of eye contact, coupled with the slight tremor in her voice, served to support Rayad's suspicions. "I have seen this behavior before in those who have experienced violence in some manner. It can be indicative of post traumatic stress disorder."

Adan raised a brow. "It is probably indicative of your penchant for making unwanted advances on an unsuspecting woman."

He despised having his honor questioned. "I never force myself on unwitting women, Adan. And you have no cause to make accusations. At one time you were much worse in regard to making advances."

Adan took obvious offense over the affront. "I have always been noble when it comes to the fairer sex, cousin."

Patience waning, Rayad glared at him. "As have I, *cousin*."

"Rayad's right," Piper interjected, drawing both their attention.

Adan regarded his wife with a confused expression. "Forgive me, Piper, but you haven't known Rayad long enough to make that character judgment."

She shook her head. "He's right about Sunny. Something did happen to her a couple of months ago."

"Why did you not tell me this before now?" Adan asked.

"Because she made me promise not to say anything," she replied. "But frankly, I'm worried about her. Even more so now." She both looked and sounded extremely concerned.

Exactly as he'd predicted. Rayad now needed all the details Sunny's sibling could give him. "What precisely happened to her?"

"She was in a small village in Angola," Piper said.

"Late one night she went for a walk on the streets. She was ambushed and attacked by some unknown assailants. They held her captive for a few hours before she managed to get away."

"Was she sexually assaulted?" Adan asked before Rayad had the opportunity.

"No," Piper stated adamantly. "She was very clear about that. Thankfully, nothing was broken aside from her spirits, but it did take a while for her to recover, according to her. In my opinion, she still hasn't."

Two questions weighed heavily on his mind—why had her former lover not sought her out, and had anyone been held accountable? "Did they apprehend the assailants?"

"They never did," she said. "Sunny told me a lot of people travel there to mine for diamonds, so it could have been anyone from anywhere in the world. She doesn't expect to ever find out the identity of the responsible parties."

How well he knew that concept, yet he refused to accept that conclusion. He had lived with his own mystery for many years, and lived his life for revenge. "Thank you for providing this information, Piper. It does explain her behavior. And now I know how I should handle the situation."

"Leave her be, Rayad," Adan demanded. "She's come here to be alone and heal her wounds."

His cousin's cautions would not deter him from his goal. "And she cannot tend to that herself. I can provide the support she needs during her visit here in Bajul."

"It's your idea of support that concerns me," Adan said.

"Maybe Rayad's help is exactly what Sunny needs," Piper interjected. "She's not going to listen to me. If he can get through to her, he has my blessing."

Adan pointed at him. "Do not do anything inadvisable, Rayad."

He nodded his acknowledgment. "I will handle the situation with the greatest of care."

And he would, despite his desire for the beautiful, troubled Sunny McAdams. Perhaps this would be his chance to engage in an honorable endeavor. An opportunity to prove he had not completely lost his soul. Perhaps he could save this woman where before he had failed another. Perhaps he could prove to himself that he was a man worthy of salvation—not the soldier who had no hope for redemption.

"Wake up, sleepyhead."

Frightened and disoriented, Sunny jolted her head up from the pillow and attempted to focus on the figure before her. Thankfully, the familiar face and smile helped calm her raw nerves and bring her back into reality. Not that she was overly happy with her sister's sudden appearance, nor did she understand why she had her arms full of garment bags.

Sunny threw back the covers, climbed out of the too-tall bed and sighed. "You could've knocked, Piper."

"I did. Twice, in fact. And I'm really sorry if I scared you."

"I'm not scared." The slight tremor in her voice belied her confidence.

"It's okay, Sunny. I know it's been tough to overcome the effects of your ordeal."

Her twin couldn't even imagine what she'd been through. "What time is it, and did you raid the local dry cleaners?"

Piper looked down at the bags as if she didn't remember what she had clutched in her arms. "It's close to noon, and no, I did not raid the dry cleaners. I did, however, raid the local boutique earlier this morning to find you something suitable to wear."

Lovely. Just what she needed after a restless night— wardrobe criticism. "You told me to pack what I normally pack."

"Yes, but tonight we'll be attending an event that requires something a bit more formal than cotton and khakis."

Sunny swept her mussed hair back with one hand and adjusted the top of her sleep shirt to better cover her neck. "What event?"

Clearly bent on avoiding the question, Piper laid the bags across the end of the bed and unzipped the first of three garment bags. "This is my personal favorite," she said as she withdrew a black, slinky dress.

The plunging neckline would never work, not when she needed to hide the reminders of her recent torment. "Too much bling, and you still didn't answer my question."

Piper tightened the band securing her dark auburn hair into a low ponytail before smoothing a palm down her flowing peach-colored sundress. "It's no big deal, really. Just a simple state dinner Madison arranged several months ago. A few dignitaries hoping to hold court with the king. Some schmoozing. That kind of thing."

The kind of thing that made her head hurt. "Am I required to attend?"

"No, but you'll miss a lot of great food." Piper withdrew another dress and held it up. "What about this one?"

She eyed the satin evening gown that reminded her of a shiny hothouse tomato. "You know I look horrible in red, and I've had fancy food before. Just bring me a take-out box after you're finished schmoozing. Or I'll scrounge around in the kitchen after the festivities if I get hungry."

"You can come to the banquet and leave early if you'd like." Piper brought out the final evening wear selection. "I'm sure Rayad wouldn't mind seeing you in this one."

"That's perfect." Sunny was caught off guard by the verbal seal of approval that spilled out of her mouth without thought. One mention of the mysterious sheikh, and she was ready to party. What in the heck was wrong with her? "I meant it would work if I decide to go, and it really is immaterial to me whether Rayad is there or not."

Her sister sighed like she'd lost her best gal pal. "Stop being so stubborn, Sunny. You need to get out and socialize a while. Meet new people. Get to know those you've already met, better."

She needed to stay in and lick her wounds. "Believe me, I had enough socializing to last a lifetime in my youth. I swore at our debutante ball I'd never put on another ball gown again."

Piper chuckled. "I remember how much you hated being a deb."

"And I remember how much you loved the attention, although I don't know why. That has to be the most antiquated tradition in the history of womankind."

Her sister's blue eyes sparkled with amusement. "It was worth it seeing you in that hoop skirt. Now promise you'll attend tonight or I'll post pictures of that on the web."

Sunny snatched the gown from Piper's clutches. "Fine. I'll put on the darn dress and parade around for fifteen minutes, thirty tops."

Piper frowned. "Funny, I thought this royal blue one would be your least favorite. And I know how much you detest a high neck."

Not when she had an obvious scar to hide. She didn't dare let her sister see the wound for fear she would have to explain, and she wasn't prepared to reveal the details yet, if ever. "I like the overall cut of the dress. Sleeveless, satin and simple, yet elegant."

"And also loose fitting," Piper said. "You won't be able to show off your figure that I've envied since we were teenagers."

She didn't care one whit how it looked on her. Much. She admittedly yearned to catch a glimpse of Rayad, and maybe continue her interview. "It's fine, Piper, and I've envied your curves for years. And that you got the blue eyes and I got stuck with green. Besides, I'm sure no one will notice me at all."

Piper barked out a laugh. "Sure, Sunny. Just keep telling yourself that. I'm fairly certain I know at least one man who'll be staring at you all evening, just like he did at dinner last night."

Darn if her sister hadn't noticed. "I have no clue what you're talking about."

"Rayad. He eyed you like you were dessert."

"He did not."

"Did so."

Sunny was simply too sleep-deprived to get into this now. "Go take care of your son."

"Aren't you going to try it on?" Piper asked, followed by her patent scowl.

Only after she was assured she had complete privacy. "I need to shower first, but I'm positive it will fit."

"We have yet to discuss your shoes."

Obviously her twin was intent on playing dress-up. "I have shoes."

"Heels?"

"What does it matter? The gown is floor-length so no one will see my feet anyway. And I promise not to wear sneakers or hiking boots."

"Or you could wear these." Piper reached into the pocket of one garment bag to retrieve a pair of silver sandals with three-inch heels. "The perfect finishing touch, and they'll give you a little height, although at five-six you really don't need that."

Her sister's long-time height envy was now showing. Sunny snatched the platform torture shoes and set them at the foot of the bed. "Great. I'm all set. Now if you don't mind, I need to bathe."

Piper gathered the remaining dresses into her arms and sighed. "If you're hungry, the chef has some lunch for you in the kitchen. Wear a little extra makeup to-night, and if you need your hair done, Kira is a master."

She'd only briefly met the palace staffer and frankly didn't trust anyone with her hair. "I can handle my hair, so if you're done giving me orders, you can run along now."

Piper backed toward the door, grinning. "You are so going to totally blow Rayad away."

Her sister quickly left the room before Sunny could insist she didn't need to impress anyone, let alone a man who was virtually a stranger. She did need to get on with the day and ignore thoughts of that man that had played on her mind much of last night.

After making the bed, she made quick work of her routine and emerged from the shower feeling some-what more human. Then she caught sight of the raised horizontal welt right above her collarbone and cringed. They'd told her she could eventually have a plastic sur-geon repair it, but in time she hoped to be brave enough to wear it as a badge of honor. A reminder that life could end on a moment's notice with one flick of a switchblade.

Pushing the recollections aside, she dressed in a light blue T-shirt that concealed the evidence, put on a pair of white cotton shorts and slipped her feet into plain beige flip-flops. Next step—finding food.

After twisting her damp hair into a knot at her nape, Sunny walked out the door and strode down the lengthy corridor, all the while considering the sinfully sexy sheikh…until she realized she had no idea where she was going when she hit a dead end in the hallway. She could turn right or left, and decided on right, only to discover Rayad heading her way, as if she'd somehow conjured him up.

He continued to walk as he focused on a document in his hand, giving her a prime opportunity to covertly check him out. From the confident gait to the broad chest and all points up and down, he would be the kind of man worthy of a magical love spell. The kind of man who drew attention the moment he entered the room, or a confusing corridor in this instance. Then she remembered how she looked at the moment—wet-headed and bare-faced—and heat flowed over her cheeks, most likely leaving crimson in its wake.

Who cared if she wasn't dressed like a prom queen? So what if her appearance was barely fit for public viewing? It truly didn't matter what he thought. She didn't give a rat's patoot if he caught sight of her, turned and ran away.

Yet when he looked up and met her gaze, he continued to move toward her, a hint of a smile curling the corners of his sexy mouth. As the space disappeared between them, he stopped and tucked the papers under one arm. "Good afternoon, Sunny."

The sound of her name on his lips made her think about warm desert breezes, the whisper of his voice in her ear, making love at midnight beneath the stars…

Heaven help her, she had died and gone to Southern belle hell, where romantic ideals were as common as mint juleps.

She managed to clear her throat, but she couldn't quite clear her mind of the silly notion that he would ride in and save the day, complete with a sword and horse. "Good afternoon to you, too, Rayad. And before you ask, yes, I'm lost. Which way to the kitchen?"

He pointed behind him. "Maintain your current course and take a left immediately before the staircase, then follow the scent."

The only scent she discerned at the moment was him. An earthy, exotic scent that gave the flower the night before a run for its money. "I take it you've already had lunch."

"Yes, and breakfast several hours ago."

He probably thought she was an absolute slug. "I slept in."

"Apparently, yet this is a good thing. Did you rest well?"

As well as anyone plagued by visions of masked villains. "Fairly well. And you?"

"Not as much rest as I perhaps should, but I require little sleep."

"Oh." Now what? Ask him about his reading material? What he had planned for the day? Could she come along for the ride? Ride as in... "I guess I'll go grab something to eat."

No sooner than she'd said it when a silver-haired, golden-skinned gentleman dressed in white muslin came toward them at a fast clip, a tray balanced in one hand. Sunny stepped to one side to get out of his way, but he paused and afforded her a quick glance before addressing Rayad. She knew a few Arabic words, but the exchange was spoken so fast, none of it made much sense. Then Rayad seemingly barked out an order before pointing down the hall.

The man sent her an oddly apologetic look, lowered his head and continued on his way.

"What was that all about?" she asked after he disappeared.

"Your meal. I instructed him to place the tray in your room immediately after he asked if I had seen you. I told him you were standing before me."

Sunny shrugged. "That's understandable. He wouldn't have any reason to know me. I hope you weren't too hard on him."

"Only after he made the mistake of assuming you are my lover and not the sister of a princess."

She swallowed around her self-consciousness. "So he thought I was your mistress?"

"Precisely, yet he did apologize when I clarified your identity, although it was tempting to allow him to believe we are involved."

She leaned a shoulder against the wall as the need to be somewhat coy, even flirtatious, overcame her. "In your dreams."

He moved closer and nailed her with those damnable dark eyes. "I did have those dreams last night."

She playfully slapped at his arm like a fourteen-year-old with a first crush. "You did not."

He sent her a half smile. "Yes, I did. One cannot control the subconscious."

Clearly, she was having trouble controlling herself around him because at the moment, she really, really wanted to kiss him. "I agree with you on that. But I also know that you and I have no business dreaming about each other."

He inclined his head and studied her for a moment. "Did you have dreams of me?"

If only that were true. If only she were that well-adjusted. "Actually, no, but don't take offense. I was extremely tired and I fell asleep the moment my head hit the pillow." And that happened to be one colossal lie.

"My dreams of you were very interesting," he said, his voice low and compelling.

"In what way?"

He reached out and streamed a fingertip down her cheek, a gentle and almost comforting gesture, as if he sensed she needed that. "You were very spirited in my imaginings. I believe you are that way in all your endeavors."

Her recent past came crowding in on her. "At one time, I suppose I was, but lately that's not necessarily true."

"Is this due to lack of confidence due to your lover's disregard or has some other event changed you?"

His intuitiveness took her aback. Yet for the first time, she was very, very tempted to confess. "No, it's because…" She had no reason to tell him anything, though somehow she sensed he'd understand. "Let's just say things happen when you least expect it. Some not so great things, and we'll leave it at that."

After a brief bout of silence, Rayad took a step back. "Should you wish to speak to me of these *things*, it would be my honor to listen, and you may trust what you say will remain between us."

How badly she wanted to believe him, but she really couldn't. Not yet. "Thanks for the offer. I appreciate it."

He offered a warm smile. "I suppose you should return to your room before your meal turns cold."

"You're right," she said as she pushed away from the wall, clear disappointment in her tone. "Have a productive day."

"Will I see you tonight at the gathering?" he asked.

"Unfortunately, I'm required to make an appearance. But I only intend to stay long enough and mingle very little."

"If you are inclined, will you mingle with me?"

That would not be classified as a chore on any level. "I suppose I can add you to my dance card."

He frowned. "I do not believe there will be dancing at this event."

She laughed. "I know. That's just a saying...never mind."

He surprisingly clasped her hand and brought it to his lips for a soft kiss. "I will look forward to the moment when we meet again."

After he released her, Rayad turned and retreated in the opposite direction, leaving Sunny's mind in a serious state of confusion. She'd begun to discern a soft side to the tough guy, but perhaps his consideration only covered his true goal—seduction. She refused to fall in the frail-female trap. Or maybe she'd become too jaded to believe any man's motives. After all, she thought she'd known Cameron well, and she'd been terribly wrong. What true friend and former lover turned his back on someone in their hour of need? A man whose own guilt overrode his compassion. A man looking for a way out of a relationship that had grown static due to both parties' opposite goals and vast differences. She, in part, had played a role in their demise by pushing him away.

If she ever decided to have a serious relationship with someone else, Sunny vowed to choose a man who believed in open, honest communication. She honestly doubted Rayad Rostam would be that man because soul-deep, she suspected he had his own serious flaws and secrets.

Tonight she would converse with him, be cordial and try her best to ignore his charms. How hard could that be?

Four

The man's name should be Bond. Sheikh Bond.

Exactly Sunny's first thought when she glanced to her right to witness Rayad Rostam's grand entrance. She hadn't seen this much neck-craning since she'd been involved in a twenty-car pileup in Los Angeles.

He'd shaken and stirred almost every female in the packed ballroom—every size, shape, age and nationality—as they seemed to instantaneously notice the darkly gorgeous, debonair man dressed in black tie. She tried not to notice, honestly she did, but he was extremely hard to disregard.

When Sunny caught his glance, she refused to count herself among his admirers, even if she'd like nothing better than to go to him and request he take her away from the crowded ballroom. For that reason, she immediately turned her attention back to Maysa Mehdi, who looked beautiful in her flowing aqua gown, her waist-length brown hair woven into a loose braid. She also looked as if she could give birth at any minute. "Do you need to sit down?"

The queen pressed a palm into her lower back. "I *need* to go into labor."

"Hopefully not at this moment."

Maysa smiled. "That would definitely make the evening much more interesting."

Sunny couldn't argue that point. "When are you officially due?"

"Two weeks. As a physician, I know it's best if I complete the gestation period. As a woman with swollen ankles, tomorrow would not be too soon."

Standing not far behind Maysa, Sunny noticed the darkly handsome and somewhat fierce-looking man she'd last seen at Piper and Adan's wedding reception. "It seems Tarek Asmar is still on the guest list for all important royal events."

"Yes, he is. My husband is quite impressed with his business acumen."

"And that young woman seems quite impressed with him, too."

Maysa subtly glanced over her shoulder. "That is Kira. She basically runs the palace now that Elena has decided to retire."

The woman looked as if she'd like to run off with the billionaire. Or perhaps she was only being polite to an honored guest. Nope. Sunny recognized serious flirtation when she saw it.

Maysa presented a bona-fide frown, something she rarely did. "I believe you are being summoned, Sunny."

She followed the queen's gaze straight to Rayad, who was holding up the wall adjacent to the double doors, towering over several people in his vicinity. When he crooked a finger at her, she laid her hand above her breast and mouthed, "Me?" He answered with a nod.

She could fail to respond to the request, or she could see what he wanted. At the very least she should wait a bit so as not to appear too eager. But as if he'd morphed into some high-powered magnet, Rayad drew her toward him with only a sly, sexy smile.

As Sunny attempted to work her way through the crush of people, Piper clasped her arm, halting her forward progress. "Are you leaving so soon? We haven't even sat down for dinner yet."

Food wasn't quite as appealing as a striking guy in a tux. So much for ignoring Rayad. "I'm just going to grab some fresh air. It's a little warm in here."

"Will you be gone long?"

Not if she could help it. "I'll be back before the first course."

As soon as she reached Rayad, he clasped her hand and guided her to a corner away from the crowd. "May I say you look very beautiful tonight?"

She couldn't resist rolling her eyes. "Yes, you may, and I've heard that one before."

"It certainly bears repeating, and often."

Odd how he knew all the right things to say, and she felt the need to return the favor. "You look very handsome yourself, Your Highness."

He also looked as if he'd eaten a mouthful of pickled eel. "I prefer not to be burdened with an official title by someone with whom I have a personal connection."

They were definitely up close and personal at the moment, thanks to the middle-age woman wearing the purple silk caftan standing behind her, practically pushing Sunny into the sheikh. "All right, Rayad. Personally speaking, for such a thoroughly macho military guy, you wear refinement very well."

Amusement flashed in his dark eyes. "I truly appreciate your somewhat dubious compliment. Now if you would please come with me, I have something to show you."

All sorts of possibilities ran through Sunny's mind, none of which she could repeat in a social setting, unless it happened to be a biker bar. "Is it bigger than a breadbasket?"

Rayad's smile melted into a frown. "I am not quite clear on your meaning, yet I believe you will find it interesting."

Too bad she didn't know what *it* was, but her inherent sense of curiosity propelled her answer, and she couldn't discount the benefits of spending time with him. After all, she hadn't completely learned what made him tick. "I suppose I'm game since the noise in here is stifling. But you do realize if anyone sees us leaving together, rumors will spread like wildfire."

"They will only envy me due to my good fortune of having your company," he said, followed by the kind of grin that could drive a woman to write a poem in praise of his perfection.

But not her. Never her. She wasn't that taken with him. Much. "Since you put it that way, let's go."

As Sunny followed Rayad into the red-carpeted foyer, she cursed her apparent weakness where he was concerned. She ran through a mental laundry list outlining all the reasons why she couldn't become involved with him, if only temporarily. Reasons that hadn't existed until recently. Reasons she wished would just go away and allow her to be carefree again.

Together they navigated a labyrinth of hallways until they reached a steep, narrow staircase leading downward. "Is this the way to the dungeon?" she asked when Rayad stepped aside.

"No. It is a place of great historic interest."

That should make her feel better, but as she descended the stone steps on the stupid spiked heels, the claustrophobia began to hinder her breathing. Fortunately, the stairs weren't substantial in number, and she reached the bottom winded but without incident. Rayad joined her to open a heavy wood door, allowing her entry into a large room that resembled a museum, complete with glass cases.

"What is all this?" she asked him over one shoulder.

"Artifacts," he said as he walked to the display to her right. "The history of Bajul's past."

Sunny moved closer to him and studied the primitive pottery, glossy stones and weathered scrolls. "I'm no historian, but that all looks rather ancient."

"It is. Most of these relics were excavated in the desert region to the south of the mountains."

"That must have taken several years."

"It did take some time, yet it was worth my efforts."

She shot him a surprised look. "You found all this?"

"Yes. On the land I own approximately eighty kilometers from here."

While she mentally converted that into fifty miles, Sunny went back to surveying the artifacts. "Interesting. Is it a mountainous area?"

"No. The terrain is flat, and the climate much more arid."

One thing about Bajul—its topography was as varied as the state of Texas. "Do you prefer the desert?"

He inched a little closer to her side. "Yes. It holds a certain magic, particularly in the evening."

Cue the return of the midnight lovemaking fantasies. "Yes, it does. There's nothing quite like a warm breeze on your face while stargazing. I remember that from a trip to the Sahara."

"Would you wish to experience it again?"

"Experience what?" she asked, the rasp in her voice indicating her recent penchant for wicked yearnings.

"The desert and my land."

"Now?"

"Perhaps tomorrow would be better."

She called on her wit to cover the unsettling excitement. "Would we be traveling by camel?"

He released a low, sensual laugh that acted on Sunny like a potent aphrodisiac. "All-terrain vehicle. We could journey there during the day and return late into the evening."

She would be an absolute fool to agree. "Maybe that wouldn't be wise."

Taking her by the shoulders, he turned her to face him. "It would be very wise. The place I wish to take you is a healing sanctuary."

This time she laughed, a cynical one. "Honestly, my heart isn't that broken."

"Perhaps your soul is."

This conversation made little sense...unless... "Has Piper said something to you about my reasons for being here?"

"Yes, but you should not direct your anger at her."

Oh, but she would. "Piper had no right to tell you about the..." Even now she had trouble saying it. "What I went through."

He tenderly tucked a lock of her hair behind her ear. "If you feel it necessary to blame someone, then blame me. I sought her out to confirm what I suspected after our time in the garden."

She wasn't that transparent. Or was she? "I don't know how that's possible."

"I know the signs of trauma," he said. "You exhibited them several times, though you attempted to hide them from me."

She sighed. "Okay, I admit I've been jumpy since the incident. But I'll be fine. I just need a little more time."

He raised a brow. "Are you certain?"

Not exactly. "I've been told the memories will eventually pass."

"Allow me to assist you," he said as he cupped her jaw. "Allow me to take you to this safe haven. I expect nothing more than your company."

If only she could believe he had honorable intentions.

If only she wasn't waging her own war between accepting his friendship and wanting to feel whole again. To regain her inherent sensuality. Her trust. "I promise I'll think about it and give you an answer tomorrow."

He looked resolute. "You will go."

"You are entirely too confident."

"I know you better than you believe, Sunny. You once longed for adventure, yet your understandable fear prevents you from pursuing that which you desire. Let this journey be the catalyst to return you to who you once were."

Such a lofty goal. "You sincerely believe that will happen in one day?"

"With faith comes great reward, if you are open to all possibilities."

She was open to a lot of things, namely a kiss, yet she couldn't gauge how she might react. If the way he studied her mouth was any indication, she might find out. Instead, he took a slight step back and thrust his hands in his pockets.

"We should return to the reception," he said. "Otherwise, what I am considering could very well offend you."

"And that is?"

"I wish to kiss you, yet I do not wish to contribute to your discomfort due to my own cravings."

Hearing the words melted her resolve to stay strong and not succumb to his charms. Knowing he wanted her gave her unexpected courage. "I wouldn't exactly be uncomfortable, and I certainly wouldn't take offense. But I might regret it."

He smiled halfway. "Do you not trust my skill?"

She worried he had too much skill. "Oh, I trust you on that front. But how do I know you're not the kind of man who kisses and tells?"

His expression went suddenly somber. "Whatever transpires between us will remain between us."

Oh, heavens, she was going to do it—invite him to put her in a lip-lock. She had to know how it would feel. How she would feel. "In that case, show me your skill."

Keeping his arms to his sides, he leaned forward to press his lips against hers, making a brief pass, then another, as if testing the waters. Then, as if she'd become someone else, Sunny wrapped one hand around his neck, signaling she needed more. He answered that need by delving into her mouth with the soft glide of his tongue.

Skilled was an enormous understatement. The man was an expert. A kissing prodigy. She wanted to be closer to him, feel his arms around her. Yet when he drew her into an embrace, Rayad inadvertently triggered a series of frightening images from deep within her psyche—suffocating recollections that caused her to break the kiss and wrest away.

"I'm so sorry," she muttered around her labored breathing. When she noted the disappointment in his expression, she felt the need to explain. "This has nothing to do with you. It's me."

He narrowed his eyes and nailed her with a serious look. "What did your abductors do to you?"

"It's not what you're thinking." But it so easily could

have been, had she not had the good fortune to get away. "It's about the confinement."

He streaked a palm over the back of his neck. "My apologies for crossing a boundary I should not have crossed."

The sincerity in his tone touched her deeply, and led her to believe he truly was a "nice guy." "Rayad, I wanted you to kiss me, but I have serious issues due to the kidnapping. Maybe I'll tell you a few details to-morrow."

He couldn't mask his astonishment. "Then you will come with me?"

Rescinding her agreement seemed prudent. The urge to say "yes" won out over all her concerns. "All right. You win. I'll go."

He looked entirely too satisfied, and gorgeous. "We will leave before dawn so that we will have enough time to enjoy our day together."

Spending even a few hours in his presence seemed extremely appealing. "Then I suppose we should say good-night now so I can join my sister for dinner and get to bed a little earlier than planned."

"As much as I would like to stay with you a while longer, I will escort you back to the soiree for the eve-ning meal."

After they returned to the hallway in silence, Rayad gently clasped her hand, turned it over and kissed her wrist. "You will not regret your decision to spend the day with me."

She sincerely hoped not. "I guess I'll see you in the morning, bright and early."

"That will be my pleasure."

He turned and started away then paused and faced her again. "Bring a swimsuit with you."

That could pose a problem on several levels. "What if I didn't pack one?"

He brought out his best smile, and it was oh so good. "Then I suppose we will have to improvise."

With that, Rayad walked away, one hand in his pocket, the other dangling at his side, looking every bit the debonair devilish sheikh turned spy.

Sunny did own a swimsuit, and she'd brought it along. She also owned a scar she'd worked hard to hide. To most, it probably wouldn't appear that hideous, but it could lead to hard questions. And tomorrow she'd have to decide whether she would tell Rayad Rostam everything.

For the second time in two days, Sunny's dear sister had arrived at her suite to deliver a morning greeting, only this time she wasn't alone.

Piper stood in the corridor outside the guest suite with a sleepy baby, dressed in blue footed pajamas, resting on her shoulder. "I'm surprised you're up at this hour," she said as she breezed into the room. "I was walking this fussy little guy and thought I heard you stirring."

Sunny didn't care that Piper had stopped by or knocked loud enough to disrupt her sleep, had she been sleeping. She did have some measure of concern over what her twin would see. And after she saw it, the questions would start rolling in. Lots of questions. "Just thought I'd get an early start with my day."

When Piper laid little Sam on the unmade bed, the baby rolled to his belly with his knees bent beneath him, popped his thumb in his mouth and stuck his bottom in the air as if he wanted to show off the cartoon-airplane appliqué strategically positioned there.

So cute, Sunny's first thought. Such a big responsibility, her second. A responsibility she didn't welcome at this point in her life. Maybe someday she'd change her mind on her own without any pressure from those who believed it was past time for her to settle down.

As Piper turned from the bed, Sunny purposefully shook off the unwelcome recollections of her last argument with Cameron. But she couldn't shake the fact her sister was bound to see the evidence of her plans.

And no more had Sunny thought it, Piper did it— shot a look straight at the open bag set on the divan. She brought her attention back to Sunny, her blue eyes wide with surprise. "Are you going somewhere?"

She could lie, or she could play the avoidance game. "I'm not leaving permanently, if that's what you're asking."

"Are you going on an assignment?"

"In a manner of speaking, but it's not work-related."

"Are you being intentionally vague?"

Absolutely. "If you must know, I'm about to tour the countryside."

"Alone?"

Sunny brushed past Piper and shoved a couple of

T-shirts, a swimsuit and two pairs of shorts into the duffel. "No, mother hen. I have an escort."

"Do I know this escort?"

"Maybe."

"You're going with Rayad, aren't you?" Piper asked a little louder than necessary.

Sunny zipped up the bag, set it on the ground and turned to her meddlesome sister. "You might want to keep your voice down so you don't wake the baby."

"He can sleep through a sonic boom, and you haven't answered my question."

Time to reluctantly come clean. "Since I suppose you'll find out sooner or later, Rayad invited me to spend the day exploring his land."

Piper released a shrewd laugh. "I'm sure that's not all he wants to explore."

No matter how hard Sunny tried to fight it, a few wicked images invaded her brain. "Look, as bad as I hate to admit it, you were right. He's a nice guy. The perfect gentleman." And a stellar kisser. "Besides, you're the one who encouraged me to get to know him."

"True, but I thought if the two of you liked each other, maybe you'd start with dinner and a movie. I didn't expect you to go gallivanting all over Bajul with him for heaven knows how long."

"This is why I didn't want to tell you, Piper. You're blowing it way out of proportion. It's only a day trip."

"Then why are you packing extra clothes?"

Good question. "Because I like to be prepared, just in case."

"In case he wants to hold you captive?" Remorse

passed over Piper's expression the moment the sarcastic question left her mouth. "I'm so sorry. Poor choice of words."

Sunny hated pity of any kind, but she'd give her sister a free pass—at least on this count. "You don't have to evaluate everything you say to me, Piper. The abduction happened, and it's over. And while we're on that subject, why did you tell Rayad about it?"

"Because he came to me," she replied. "He sensed there was something going on with you beyond your breakup with Cameron. He also wants to help you with the aftereffects."

Now she wondered if Rayad's invitation had more to do with sympathy than with the desire for her company. A question she'd definitely ask him for the sake of clarity. "Like I said, he's a decent guy, and he expects me to meet him downstairs in less than twenty minutes. So if you don't mind, I need to dress."

Without saying another word, Piper gingerly picked up her sleeping son and returned him to her shoulder. "Just be careful, Sunny. I'd hate for you to have your heart shattered all over again."

Funny, her split with Cameron wounded her pride more than her heart. "Since I have no intention of getting involved with Rayad beyond a casual relationship, you have no need to be concerned."

Piper crossed the room, patting Sam's bottom as she went. "I didn't intend to fall for Adan, either." She paused at the door and smiled. "I want a full report when you get back this evening, and have fun. Just not too much fun."

With that, she disappeared, leaving Sunny alone to prepare for the trip with Rayad. She returned to the bag, opened it again and added a few travel-size toiletries, like they might somehow get stranded on a desert island, or perhaps in the desert. A ridiculous assumption, but he did mention swimming, so maybe it wasn't so far-fetched. She'd also learned the hard way that one never knew what the future might hold. And that unknown factor drew her in like a moth to a porch light. So did the prospect of spending the day getting to know Rayad even better.

The thought of an adventure exhilarated her. Thrilled her. If luck prevailed, she would have an experience she wouldn't soon forget, with a man she quite possibly would never forget.

Five

"Would you be so kind as to tell me where you are taking my sister-in-law?"

Leaning against the passenger door of the customized black Mercedes SUV, Rayad maintained his calm in light of Adan's heated tone. "Would you be so kind as to inform me why this is your concern?"

"She is my wife's sister, and she deserves to be treated with respect."

Rayad's own anger began to build, yet he refused to reveal it. "You may rest assured she will receive the utmost respect."

Adan pointed at him. "If you so much as make one inappropriate advance, you will have to deal with me."

As it had been when they were in their formidable years, he took great pleasure in tormenting his younger cousin. "Then I am to assume that I may make an *appropriate* advance?"

Adan's features turned fierce. "You bloody know what I mean, Rayad. No advances whatsoever. She is very fragile."

He would not describe Sunny as fragile. Wounded, yes. Fragile, never. "If it puts your mind at ease, Rafiq warned me to take care with her from the moment she arrived."

"My brother is a wise man," Adan said. "And if you find having both of us taking up verbal arms against you disconcerting, I promise you do not wish to deal with my wife."

That instilled more fear in Rayad than Bajul's entire armed forces setting their sights on him. "Again, you need not worry. We will only be gone for the day."

"I hope I didn't overpack."

Rayad turned his attention to Sunny standing behind Adan, a large olive-green bag clutched in her arms.

Adan shot him a suspicious glance and said, "I believe you stated you are going on a day trip."

"We are," Sunny said, a slight flush coloring her cheeks. "I'm one to prepare for any scenario, like a car breaking down. Earthquake. Monsoon. That sort of thing."

"You cannot be too prepared." Rayad opened the door and held out his hand to assist her. "Let us be on our way."

Adan glared at him. "I expect you to have her back here before dark."

After he helped Sunny into the Mercedes, he closed

the door and regarded his cousin again. "I have long since passed the time when I needed fatherly warnings, Adan. We will return when I see fit to return."

Without awaiting a response, Rayad rounded the vehicle, climbed into the driver's seat and turned the ignition. He sped away, glancing in the rearview mirror to find Adan still standing under the palace portico, appearing as if he would like to chase after them in his bathrobe.

"Nice ride," Sunny said as she ran a slender hand over the console dividing their seats.

The gesture, no matter how innocent, caused Rayad to shift slightly against the tightening in his groin. "It is adequate."

"I'd say the satellite radio, leather seats and moonroof qualify it as more than adequate. Company car?"

"Personal vehicle."

"I should be so lucky," she said. "My personal vehicle is a subcompact, but then I don't really drive that much."

He would gladly escort her anywhere she dared to go, particularly in a carnal sense. Yet he had to move slowly and accept that any intimacy between them might not come to pass.

Settling into silence, Rayad concentrated on navigating the steep descent away from the palace. Yet when Sunny's sigh drew his gaze, he saw her hide a yawn behind her hand. "You clearly are tired."

"Well, since the crack of dawn is still sealed," she began, "and I didn't get into bed until after midnight, I'm still a bit sleepy. But I'll wake up as soon as we get where we're going, wherever that is."

He felt the need to prepare her for the first step of their journey. "The place I am taking you will involve climbing, if you are willing."

"How much climbing?"

He sent her a glance to find her frowning. "Minimal, and I will assist you."

"As long as it's not Mount Everest, I can handle it."

He had no doubt she could.

When he noted the sky had begun to turn a lighter blue, he picked up speed, taking care to stay close to the side of the cliff as they ascended to their destination before they reached the village.

"Is it necessary to go this fast?" Sunny asked, a hint of concern in her tone.

"Only for a few more minutes."

And after those minutes passed, he pulled over at the road's bend and put the vehicle in Park. "We have arrived."

Rayad left the Mercedes and rounded the hood, only to find Sunny had exited without his aid. He knew better than to debate his duty as a gentleman. She was fiercely independent, one of the many aspects that had earned his admiration, though it warred with his protective nature.

As Sunny stretched her arms above her head, her shirt rode up above the waist of her beige cargo shorts, exposing bare skin that earned his immediate notice. "What now?"

He considered several answers to the query, yet what he desired to do, and what he should do, were in direct contrast with each other. "We will climb the precipice to your right."

She turned to survey the rock surface before presenting him with a less-than-pleased look. "It's definitely steep."

"Only from here. Once we begin our ascent, you will see it is not so difficult."

"If you say so," she said as she made a sweeping gesture toward the side of the mountain. "You go first, and I'll be right behind you."

Not at all what he had planned, yet he would refrain from arguing with her for the time being. "I will be happy to help you if the need arises."

"I appreciate your concern, but I have hiked quite a bit in my lifetime."

"Then perhaps it is time to test your skill."

She presented a smile that brightened her emerald eyes. "I'm always up for a challenge."

He happened to be up for several challenges, though one he did not particularly favor—resisting her feminine wiles. Yet he must resist so to prove he still retained some honor in light of his oftentimes dishonorable— though necessary—profession.

As the sky began to turn a pale blue, Rayad realized they would have to hurry to enjoy the advent of dawn. "Perhaps it would be best if you go first," he told her as he walked to the base of the rock wall. "I will remain close behind you."

She moved beside him and scowled. "To check out my butt, no doubt."

He had not considered anything but her safety, yet since she had mentioned it… "I wish to remain behind you in the event you stumble."

"And if I do, that means I'll fall back on you, and we could both plummet to our deaths."

"The peak is not as high as you might believe. If we fell, we might—"

"End up in a full body cast?"

"Suffer a few scrapes and bruises and possibly a broken bone."

"Or neck." She lifted her shoulders in a shrug. "But if you're willing to break my fall and be my cushion, who am I to argue?"

She smiled at him over one shoulder before she began to ascend the rock, carefully choosing her footholds, as if she had done this before. Perhaps she had, and that came as no true surprise to Rayad.

She fascinated him. She made him feel emotions he had long since learned to bury. She made him feel as if he were a whole man again. Many years had passed since he had experienced such strong, unwelcome emotions.

Surprisingly, she reached the top of the cliff with expediency, and once there, she turned and favored him with a smile. "You're as slow as a snail."

The insult sent him up to join her in a matter of seconds. "You clearly are a skilled climber," he said as he came face-to-face with her.

"I've done my share in some pretty rough regions, and apparently, so have you."

If she only knew where he had been, and what he had been forced to do at times, she would probably scurry back down the mountain and run to the palace. "I have, yet it is not often I have been graced with such a beautiful companion."

Her smile returned, soft and overtly sensuous. "And I've never known anyone who so easily threw out the compliments."

"Do not doubt my sincerity, Sunny, for as I have said before, I know true beauty."

With that in mind, he clasped her shoulders and turned her to face the east. The first fingers of light had begun to reveal themselves above the mountain range, giving the sky an orange cast. "This is why we are here. To pay homage to your namesake."

He remained close to her side to witness her reaction firsthand to that which he had so often taken for granted. Without speaking or moving, she stared at the sun as it rose in the distance. A warm breeze ruffled her blond hair, yet she seemed oblivious to her surroundings, and him. Though he should not be concerned by her inattention, for some reason he was.

"It's breathtaking," she finally said. "Seeing the dawn of a new day gives you hope that the world isn't such a terrible place after all."

Yet his world could be a terrible place on a constant basis. "I find this scene gives me a sense of peace, as well."

She sighed. "Sometimes peace is hard to come by so you look for it wherever you can find it."

He knew that to be all too true. "You will have peace again, Sunny. You are a survivor."

"Actually, you're right, and like I told you last night,

I'm going to be fine." The slight break in her voice belied her conviction.

"You are not yet *fine*, but you will be as soon as your soul is on the mend."

She turned her gaze to his, a hint of frustration calling out from her green eyes. "Really, it's okay. As far as I'm concerned, my breakup with the ex-boyfriend was long overdue."

"I am referring to your abduction."

Rayad could tell by the way her body stiffened that she relied on denial to dampen the memories. "I try not to think about it too much for the sake of my sanity."

Sensing she needed comfort, he laid his palm against her lower back, relieved when she did not recoil at his touch. "There are certain experiences in life that haunt us for many years. Circumstances that will lessen in impact, yet never be entirely forgotten. Fortunately, the passage of time does aid in gaining perspective."

"What events are haunting you, Rayad?"

Because his attempt at counsel had led to his transparency, he would only supply a half-truth. "I am serving in the military. Oftentimes that regretfully entails witnessing revolting acts imposed by men on other men. Unfortunately, I am not at liberty to provide details." Nor would he reveal his own personal tragedy.

"I understand." After a brief span of silence, she asked, "Is that the baby-making mountain over there?"

That brought about his smile. "*Mabruuk*. And yes, if you believe in the legend, it has the power to render women fertile within a hundred-mile radius."

"I'm not saying I believe in the legend, but would

you mind keeping your distance? Just in case." She followed the comment with a coy smile.

He did not care to keep his distance or acknowledge that he gave the folklore credence. "I do not believe that *Mabruuk's* powers would enable me to impregnate you with only a touch of my hand."

"I suppose that would be miraculous."

"And it would take away the pleasure of the process of procreating."

Her cheeks flushed slightly as she lowered her eyes. "True. But the process doesn't have to be only about procreating, does it?"

"No, it does not." Should they continue this conversation, he might attempt to begin the process. Yet when it came to Sunny, vigilance should be paramount.

When she failed to speak, he felt an apology was in order. "I am sorry if I have upset you with my talk of procreation."

"Not at all," she said. "In fact, for the first time in a long time, I'm starting to feel like myself again. That kiss last night didn't hurt."

He tipped her chin up, forcing her to look at him. "If you believe nothing else about me, believe this. I would never intentionally do anything to make you uncomfortable."

"I know that, otherwise I wouldn't be with you. But there is something you can do for me."

"Whatever you wish."

"Kiss me good morning."

He struggled with what he wanted and what she needed. What he must do to win her trust so that he might guide her through the crisis. Yet refusing a beautiful woman's request for a kiss was foreign to him. Still, he vowed to proceed carefully from this point forward, and chose to press a chaste kiss against her lips.

She did not look at all pleased. "Very sweet. Not what I had in mind, but nice."

He cupped her cheek in his palm. "Had I kissed you the way I wish to kiss you, we might spend all day on this mountaintop. And though that might be pleasurable, we need to continue our adventure before the storms arrive."

Sunny turned her face to the skies. "I don't see even one cloud."

"The deluge is coming," he said. "But you will see no rain where I am taking you." A destination where he had never taken another woman since... He pushed away the bitter realities to focus on his companion.

"Can you give me just a little hint about where you're taking me aside from your land?"

"You will soon see for yourself. I will tell you it is unlike any place you have ever been before."

"I've been quite a few places."

"Trust me on this point."

"That remains to be seen."

Though she had said it with a touch of amusement, Rayad realized he would have to earn her confidence. And should anyone discover where he was taking her, he could be stripped of his duties and his honor, or worse.

Sunny McAdams would be worth the risk.

* * *

Rayad hadn't been kidding about the lack of rain. For the past twenty minutes, Sunny had yet to see any water whatsoever. The landscape had flattened into desert, the ground covered mostly in sand as far as the eye could see. Aside from one scant patch of grass supporting a small herd of sheep, the route they were taking showed few signs of population. And the farther they drove, the more desolate the surroundings became.

She adjusted in the seat to get a better look at Rayad and marveled at the perfection of his profile. The fit of his dark green T-shirt. She even sneaked a peek at his extremely masculine legs exposed because today he wore a pair of khaki cargo shorts and hiking boots. She also couldn't help but ponder the possibility of a real kiss later today—provided he actually cooperated. If she accomplished nothing else, she vowed to convince him she wasn't some broken, needy female who had to be treated with kid gloves. Okay, maybe she was a bit broken, but she felt as if she might be on the mend, thanks to him.

"So exactly where does your land begin?" she asked to disrupt the silence that had gone on way too long.

"We passed the property's boundary twenty miles ago."

"Wow." All she could think to say in light of the revelation. "You obviously own half of Bajul."

"Not quite half."

"How did you manage to wrangle the property away from the royal family?"

"A portion of the land was willed to me upon my

aunt's death. The rest I purchased since the area is not conducive for development."

"I can understand that. Most people don't care to live in the middle of nowhere."

"I am not most people."

That personal assessment wasn't remotely up for debate. "Is that why you haven't built your own palace?"

"I have no need for a palace," he said, his tone surprisingly serious. "I travel much of the time."

"I assume you have no need for a wife and kids, either."

"Not presently."

She would have sworn she heard a touch of wistfulness in his voice. "How much longer until we get where we're going?"

A split second after Sunny posed the query, Rayad took a sharp right turn and stopped the Mercedes in front of a fortress-like entrance, complete with barbed, ten-foot fencing. He then lifted the console, took out a remote control and pointed it at the heavy steel gate that opened wide to allow them entry.

She felt as if she were entering a prison and that resurrected memories she was hard-pressed to ignore. "What is this place? Some kind of military compound or maybe a sheikh commune?"

"You will see soon enough," he said as he drove forward.

If she wasn't so darned inquisitive, she might have demanded a better explanation before she allowed him to proceed. But crazy as it seemed, she didn't consider him threatening. "I'm looking forward to it."

They traveled down an afterthought dirt road that narrowed between two large stone formations. After threading the rocky needle, they finally reached a wider spot next to one of the behemoth boulders.

Rayad put the Mercedes in Park, turned off the ignition and shifted to face her. "Before we enter, you must promise me you will never speak of this place to anyone."

Sunny did a quick visual search but found nothing that even remotely resembled a structure. "I don't even see a *place*."

"Promise me."

Rayad's stern tone said he meant business. "All right," she conceded. "I promise to keep my mouth shut, like I do when I'm protecting an anonymous source. But if you want me to climb that wall, you should know I didn't bring any spikes or rappelling equipment."

"No climbing will be involved at this juncture." He opened the SUV door and told her, "Come with me."

When Rayad walked to the back of the Mercedes and retrieved what looked like a cooler, Sunny reached back to grab her own bag. She slid out of the seat and retraced his path, her mind caught in a web of confusion when he stopped in front of the mini-mountain. That confusion turned to blatant curiosity when he set the cooler down and opened a hidden panel set in the red-orange rock face, revealing a hi-tech keypad. While she looked on, he punched in a series of numbers, and just like that, the seemingly smooth stone parted. Definitely the stuff spy movies were made of. She wouldn't be a bit surprised to find a houseman greeting them with a tray of martinis.

After Rayad stepped aside, Sunny moved forward to find no servants, but she did discover another set of narrow stairs descending into darkness. Fortunately, this time she'd had enough sense to wear sneakers, not stilettos. Unfortunately, her heart began to beat at an accelerated clip when she noticed the narrow walls. "You seriously want me to go in there?"

"I promise it is safe."

She shifted the bag's strap to her shoulder. "No bats?"

"No. Or asps."

She could use some oxygen after hearing the reference to reptiles. "Thank goodness for small favors."

Rayad put the cooler down again, picked up a torch leaning against the wall, retrieved a lighter from his pocket and transferred the flame to a pair of sconces on either side of the steps. Then he turned and pressed a button to his left, closing the door behind him. "Follow me, and take care with your footing."

He certainly didn't have to worry about that. She'd take care all day long if necessary. While she followed behind him, Rayad lit more sconces as they traveled downward into the abyss. The scent of earth and a slight chill assaulted her. Luckily, she didn't smell fire and brimstone, although right now she wouldn't be surprised if they came across Hades.

Much to Sunny's relief, they eventually reached the final stair where she exhaled slowly when her feet hit the dirt floor.

Rayad paused and flipped a switch that illuminated several overhead lights, revealing a lengthy corridor. "A generator provides electricity, but I use it sparingly."

Sunny joined him and did a quick survey of the room to her right that held no real furnishings but a lot of electronics. "What is all this?"

"My means to communicate with the outside world."

Awareness began to dawn. "Is this a covert military installation?"

"In a manner of speaking," he said. "It's a natural bunker available for the royal family should Bajul come under attack. I discovered it several years ago."

"And that's when you found the artifacts."

"Yes. I have spent many days here exploring the surroundings and modifying the caverns to house occupants. I come here often when I am not on duty."

Now it all made sense. "So this is also your own personal hideout."

"Perhaps some would view it as such."

Including her. She couldn't help but wonder exactly what he might be hiding from. Granted, he'd claimed to be involved in military intelligence, but she sensed there might be more to the story. "Is this all there is to it?"

"No. I will show you the rest."

And he did, beginning with one room that held several bunks and what appeared to be an adjoining latrine. "This is huge. Do you sleep here?"

"I have my own private quarters that you will soon see, and you may leave your bag here."

She really didn't see much of anything other than a

long, narrow hallway. "Can't wait," she said as she set her duffel on the dirt floor by the door.

They continued on to a stockroom with rows of shelves holding what appeared to be military K-rations. A self-contained, primitive hostel. "I take it you don't have a refrigerator."

He placed the cooler on a table in the corner then faced her again. "No, but since the cave holds steady at fifty-eight degrees, spoilage is not an issue when I have fresh fruit delivered."

"All the way out here? That must cost a pretty penny."

"Money is not a concern when comfort is involved."

Of course it wasn't. The man probably had a fortune holed up in a wall somewhere. "Did you bring some fruit with you today?"

"Yes, and some other supplies," he said as he rejoined her in the corridor. "Should we require more, several outlying villages are not far away."

"Since we're only going to be here today, I'm sure we have enough to get us by."

"Perhaps," he said. "Let us now continue the tour."

After they traveled a few more feet, the hallway hit a dead end at another stone wall. Sunny assumed the tour was over, until once again Rayad revealed a keypad much like the one at the entry.

"What you have seen has been designed solely for security," he said. "What you will soon see is designed solely for pleasure."

He then punched in another code, and the walls parted like that proverbial Red Sea. The view he revealed absolutely stole her breath, but not because the area seemed confining. On the contrary, the place was massive—and mystical. The palace-size cavern, with glistening stones dotting the natural walls, could best be described as a fantastical, natural wonderland. Across the way, stalactites hung from the towering ceiling while stalagmites jutted up from the ground. And in the middle of the Caribbean-blue pool of water, a beam of light shone down from a large circular opening in the cave's roof.

A few moments passed before she recovered enough from her amazement to speak. "This is unbelievable. It reminds me of Jeita Grotto in Lebanon."

"Yet not quite as large," Rayad said from behind her. "And it is virtually untouched by man."

She couldn't seem to tear her gaze away from the remarkable sight. "It's truly a desert oasis. Where does the water originate?"

"From an aquifer fed by runoff from the mountains. Another of Bajul's hidden treasures."

Amazing. "Water is definitely in short supply in the region."

"That is why Zain has begun the conservation efforts. Eventually, it will be exported and in turn, secure the country's future, as well as save lives."

"Zain has seen what the lack of water can do to people. So have I."

She heard footsteps and sensed Rayad's presence before he said, "Are you not curious about my personal quarters?"

Sunny turned to find he was only a foot or so away. "Actually, I am."

"Then look behind me to my left."

Only then did she see the makeshift bedroom carved out of the rock. And on the raised ledge, a huge bed covered in dark blue satin and draped with a sheer canopy. A cave boudoir definitely fit for a prince. "Incredible. Do you have an en-suite bathroom? Maybe a steam shower and a whirlpool tub?"

He smiled. "Who needs those accoutrements when you have your own pool?"

"You bathe in the pool?"

"At times I have."

That unearthed some fairly naughty images involving a very masculine, well-toned body wet and slick with soap... "I suppose that makes you a modern caveman."

His low, sexy laugh echoed off the walls of the cavern. "I suppose that would be accurate."

She crossed her arms beneath her breasts against the onslaught of shivers, resulting from the cool temperature and his overt sensuality. "Well, as long as you don't beat me with a club and drag me by my hair, I can deal with that."

His expression went suddenly somber. "I would never do such a thing."

"It's a joke, Rayad."

"My apologies, but I find no humor in abusive behavior toward women."

Evidently he didn't bring his wit along with him. She also suspected a story existed behind his attitude. "I truly appreciate that. And in case I haven't said it before, I feel very safe with you."

Rayad surprised her by drawing her into a light embrace then rubbed his palm gently up and down her back. Funny, she hadn't even flinched, demonstrating how her trust in him had grown.

A few moments later, he framed her face in his palms and kissed her forehead. "Your faith means a great deal to me."

She smiled. "You're welcome. And now that you have me here, what's next?"

"We still have much to explore," he said as he kept his arms around her.

"Oh, really? What will we be exploring?"

"The cavern, of course."

"Too bad." Her face heated over her spontaneous comment. "I'm sorry. I meant I'm getting kind of hungry."

He stroked his knuckles softly up and down her cheek. "We will take a brief tour, then we will have lunch."

"Not that food in the supply room, I hope."

"No. I have brought something special from the palace." He studied her eyes. "I am very glad you are here."

"So am I."

And she was. By day's end, Sunny hoped that still remained true.

Six

He'd traveled through the tunnels many times before, yet seeing the cavern through Sunny's eyes made the experience seem new to Rayad. But when they had ended up in tight quarters several times, she had inadvertently brushed against him, stirring his body and his fantasies.

Even now, as he walked behind her and watched the gentle sway of her hips, he wanted her greatly. His fantasies took flight as he imagined Sunny naked, her long legs wrapped around his waist. He wanted to know how her bare flesh would feel against his palms, how she would feel surrounding him as he buried himself deep inside her.

Shaking off the images, Rayad remembered his vow to move slowly. He must accept that quite possibly nothing would come of his desire for her.

"Which way should I go?" she asked when they met a crossroads.

"To your right."

Once they emerged from the passageway, she turned to him and smiled. "We're back where we started."

"Yes, we are."

She snapped off the flashlight. "Any chance we can have lunch now? I'm really, really hungry."

As he was, but not only for food. "I suppose I could accommodate you."

"Gee, thanks. I'd hate to start foraging for wild berries since I doubt I'll find any."

"Berries actually are a possibility."

She rolled her eyes. "Please don't tell me we're about to trek through the desert to pick berries."

She brought about his smile that arrived more often in her presence. "No need for that. Now if you will follow me, I will bring our meal to you."

"Gladly."

He guided her around the bank of the aquifer and across the small wooden bridge he had built with his own hands. Once they reached his private quarters, he told her, "Wait here, and I shall return shortly."

"Hurry," she called out to him as he entered the bunker. "Or I'm going for the granola bars I brought with me."

He strode into the supply room to retrieve the container housing their meals. After he returned to Sunny, he nodded toward the pair of large crimson pillows next to the bed. "We will sit here to dine."

Sunny lowered herself onto the cushion and crossed

her legs before her. "I've heard of breakfast in bed, but never lunch next to the bed. So what's on the menu?"

After he took his place on the opposing pillow, Rayad opened the cooler, lifted the platter, set it between them and uncovered it. "This is the palace chef's specialty. *Shawarma* on taboon bread, topped with hummus and olives."

She picked up the sandwich, studied it briefly and then took a bite. "This is delicious," she said. "And I can't wait to dive into the dates and cheese."

He might have to dive into the nearby pool if he kept watching her mouth as she ate—and imagining how that lovely mouth would feel on his body. Instead, he handed her a bottled water, small silver plate and white cloth napkin. "Please eat as much as you would like. We have another tray for our dinner if this is not enough."

She paused midbite and frowned. "I thought we'd be heading back before dinner."

He tamped down his disappointment, with effort. "I had planned to have the evening meal here, beneath the stars."

Sunny mulled that over for a moment before she addressed him again. "I have to admit that sounds tempting, as long as you have me home before midnight in case I turn into a pumpkin."

"Pumpkin?"

She laid the sandwich down and dabbed at her mouth. "You know the story. Fairy godmother. Handsome prince. Young girl with evil stepsisters... Never mind. I tend to forget we're not culturally on the same page."

"Actually, I do know the fairy tale. Yet if my recollections are accurate, the young woman's gown turns to rags at midnight. I do not recall the threat of becoming a pumpkin."

Her laughter gave Rayad surprising joy. "Apparently, you can be very literal in your interpretation of folklore."

"Do you believe in these fairy tales?"

"If you're referring to happily-ever-after, I'm on the fence. My grandparents have been married for over fifty years and seem to still be in love. But my mother, and I use that term loosely, went from one man to the next, so obviously, she's never found what she was looking for in a relationship."

"And your father?"

She turned suddenly sullen. "I have no idea who he is. I did some investigating a few years back and after seeing the possible prospects, I gave up the search. Some things are better left unknown."

He would have to agree with that in terms of his past. "My parents have been wed over thirty years, although their marriage was arranged. However, they seem genuinely fond of each other."

"Fond isn't the same as love. I sincerely hope for Piper's sake that forever love does exist. But I'm certainly not looking for a charming prince to ride in to rescue me."

"You do not strike me as a woman who needs to be rescued."

"Are you sure that's not what this is all about?" she asked. "The noble sheikh attempting to save me?"

He would be foolish to believe he could save her when he had already failed another. Yet in some small way he needed to try in an effort to atone for his transgressions. "I am an ordinary man spending time with an extraordinary woman who needs a respite."

"You're definitely not ordinary, and I'm anything but special. But I do appreciate the compliment and that you're concerned about my well-being."

He reached out and touched her face. "As I have said before, I appreciate a beautiful woman whose humility prevents her from realizing her true worth. However, beauty is not only about physical traits. It involves the soul, even one that is injured. Yours might be wounded, yet it makes you no less attractive."

"Before we head in that direction," she began, "I'd rather talk about something more pleasant."

At some point he hoped she would talk to him about her experience. Since that would not happen in the imminent future, he opted for a suggestion that did not involve conversation. Perhaps not his first option but one that best suited her situation. "Would you wish to swim?"

She averted her eyes. "I'm not sure I'm ready for that."

"Did you not pack your suit as I suggested?"

"I have it." She finally raised her gaze to his. "I also have a reminder of my recent experience. A not so pretty scar."

"Show me."

"Maybe later."

Needing to encourage her, Rayad pulled his shirt

over his head and tossed it aside, revealing his own scars. "I received this six years ago," he said as he pointed to the jagged line on his left side. "The bruise on my right is from the broken ribs. On my back you will find a random pattern of slashes, compliments of a murderous insurgent who held me hostage and attempted to beat information from me."

Her green eyes widened. "How did you escape?"

Barely with his life. "My captor made the mistake of freeing my hands to move me to another chamber. He suffered a broken jaw for his efforts, and I managed to steal away without detection."

"I know all about fighting for freedom." Her tone hinted at a very real fear.

"Each scar we earn in our lifetimes has a story, Sunny. Every wound marks a challenge that we have overcome. If you will not show me your scar, then I implore you to tell me your story."

She drew in a deep breath and exhaled slowly. "If I do this, will you promise not to tell Piper the details?"

He worried the details were much worse than he had first presumed. "As I told you previously, what is shared between us, remains between us."

"I'll try to be brief."

"Take as much time as you need."

When a long span of silence passed, he thought she had reconsidered. Then finally she began to speak. "We were staying in a small village in Angola, covering a story on a group of aid workers. We knew going in that the area drew a dangerous criminal element due to the diamond trade. I don't think I realized how dangerous until that night."

As she hesitated again, Rayad took her hands into his. "You believe your attackers were a part of this element?"

She shook her head. "I'm not sure. I never saw them. They spoke broken English, and their accents had a Spanish note to them, but that's not what they were speaking because I know Spanish."

"How did you come upon them?"

She shifted on the pillow, a certain sign of discomfort. "Cameron and I were staying in a small bungalow in the center of the village. We'd had an argument about our future. He wanted to settle down and return to the U.S. and get married and have kids. I wasn't ready for that, and he knew it, but he kept pushing me. When I told him it might be best if we parted ways since we didn't want the same things, he demanded I leave and find somewhere else to spend the night. He insisted he didn't want to spend even one more minute in my presence. I decided to go for a walk until he calmed down."

He muttered an oath aimed at the man's disregard for his partner's safety. "He should not have allowed you to leave. He should have been the one to leave."

She sighed. "He realizes that now. He feels very guilty about the whole incident."

"As he should." In an effort to return to the abduction, Rayad asked, "What happened when you went on the walk?"

As if she could not tolerate the contact, she wrested her hand from his and gripped the pillow on either side of her thighs. "I was upset, so I wasn't aware of my surroundings. I passed by an alley and was ambushed. Someone pushed me to the ground and taped my mouth shut before I could even scream. They blindfolded me before I could get a good look, but I know there were at least two of them. One held me down, and the other tied me up."

"Is that where they kept you captive?" he asked, though he knew that most likely was not the case.

"No," she answered, confirming his suspicions. "Someone carried me to a small house, although I didn't know that at the time. I only knew I was put in some sort of tight space, like maybe a closet. I heard a door close, but I couldn't see a thing, and I could barely breathe, thanks to the tape on my mouth. I felt like I'd been buried alive."

"And that is the cause of your fear of enclosed spaces."

"Yes, it is," she continued. "I did get a periodic break when every now and then, I'd get yanked out, put in a chair and slapped around for unknown reasons other than I was an American journalist, or so I assumed."

His stomach pitched at the thought of anyone raising a hand to her. He had to pose a question that, depending on the answer, could change everything. A question he had presented Piper, yet he could not trust the answer. "Forgive me for asking, but were you sexually assaulted?"

She released a laugh that held no humor. "One of them tried. He came into that closet, closed the door and pawed me. He whispered things in my ear that I didn't understand, but I could just imagine what he was saying, and it wasn't pleasant. I still remember the way he smelled, like booze and sweat, as he climbed on top of me and tore at my clothes. I try not to think about it."

When Sunny seemed to mentally wander away, Rayad asked, "Do you wish to stop now?"

"There's more," she said, as if unburdening had become a total necessity. "The second time he came to me, he was more forceful, and that's when I started to realize it was only a matter of time before he…before it happened. And after that, I sensed they would kill me. The fight-or-flight response took over because I knew I had to find some way to escape."

"You fought him?"

She sent him a slight smile. "No. After he ripped the tape from my mouth, I knew what was going to occur if I didn't get away from him. I started to retch and told him I was going to throw up when he tried to kiss me, which wasn't far from the truth. I said I needed air or a bathroom or something. He dragged me out of the room by my wrists, pulled me to my feet then barked out an order to his partner. The next thing I knew I was being dragged somewhere. When I felt a breeze I realized I was outside, but I was terrified over what might transpire next."

"Clearly, you evaded them, or you would not be here," he said after a long pause in the conversation.

She drew in a ragged breath before continuing. "Luckily, my tormentor's partner untied my arms and legs, and that's when I saw my chance to kick and bolt. Before I could do that, I heard a voice whisper in my ear, 'Run.' And I did, as fast as I could. I stumbled while trying to remove the blindfold, but I recovered quickly and kept running. Then I heard the gunshot and a bullet whizzing by my head."

Rayad gritted his teeth against the force of his fury. "He gave you your freedom and then attempted to kill you?"

"It wasn't a *he*."

That temporarily shocked him into silence. "Your captor was a woman?"

"Yes, and I believe she wanted me to escape. I also believe she shot at me in an effort to convince her partner she tried to prevent me from getting away."

"After all that they did to you, you still believe in their humanity?"

"*Her* humanity. She may have been caught up in some Bonnie-and-Clyde scenario. She might have even been jealous that I was receiving her cohort's attention. I'll never know her motives or exactly why they targeted me."

"You believe these two were possibly lovers?"

"Maybe. I just remember him repeating the name Emma or maybe Erma, but it always sounded so sarcastic."

A possible clue to her abductors' nationality. "It was most likely *irmã*, Portuguese for *sister*."

"That would explain the accent and why she let him have his way with me. A sick sibling relationship for sure. Regardless, she did allow me the opportunity to escape, and for that I'm grateful."

Her attitude, though honorable, took him aback. "I

unfortunately cannot share your sense of compassion. I have no use for any person, male or female, who systematically tortures another."

She rested a palm on his forearm. "I can only imagine why you might feel that way in your line of work. But I have to continue to believe that most people are inherently good, or at least have some goodness in them. Otherwise, I might have totally withdrawn and stopped living for fear of running into bad guys around every corner. That is no way to exist."

He admired her strength. He appreciated her courage. He did have difficulty understanding her benevolence. "You're a brave woman, Sunny McAdams. Braver than many men I have known. Are you brave enough to show me your scar now?"

She came to her feet and gave him another smile. "Since you know the story behind it, I guess you should know it all. And since we're going swimming, you're going to see it all. So now I'll go change into my suit in the bunker, if you'll tell me how to open the disappearing door."

He stood and returned her smile. "Press the red button. It is unlocked."

"Okay." She turned then paused and faced him again. "I happen to love life, Rayad, and that makes me a survivor. I'm positive you're a survivor, too, and that's why we're drawn to each other."

When she walked away, he pondered her words. He had survived some of the worst scenarios, including one that had happened several years ago. Yet on that day, a part of his soul had died. He was not certain he would

ever recover what was left of it, or to halt the search for
the people who murdered his wife and child.

Sunny was surprised by how quickly she had revealed the details. Telling Rayad most of the abduction story surprisingly hadn't been that difficult, once
she'd started talking. Wearing a swimsuit in front of
him wasn't going to be quite as easy. He would then
see remnants of the one detail she hadn't bothered to
mention, though she wasn't quite sure why.

As soon as she'd put on the tasteful two-piece, her
hand automatically went to the raised welt located
right below her collarbone—and then came terrifying
memories of the knife slicing her skin, followed by the
warning issued by her terrorist in barely recognizable
English.

Do as I say or next time, I cut higher.

She shook off the recollections as she wrapped herself in the towel she'd packed, holding it closed above
the scar. Eventually, she would have to reveal it, but not
until she was safely sequestered in water.

On that thought, Sunny made her way back to Rayad,
careful to keep the towel clutched at her throat. But
when she arrived, he was nowhere to be found.

Suddenly, he emerged from the reservoir like a gorgeous, golden-skinned god, a sensual smile curling the
corners of his sexy mouth. He swam toward her until
he found his footing and stood only a few inches from
the stone bank. "I had begun to believe you had reconsidered."

She visually followed a droplet that trickled down

his sternum to where the water line circled his lower belly. She couldn't help but notice the beginnings of a thin stream of masculine hair traveling south from below his navel. She couldn't help but wonder if he was wearing swim trunks. "I haven't been gone that long."

"It seemed like an eternity."

Pretty words from a very pretty—in a macho sort of way—bad boy. "How's the water?"

"Temperate enough. Are you coming in, or do you wish to stand there and admire my aquatic skills?"

She'd been admiring a lot more than his skill a moment ago, and imagining all sorts of things. "If you're *that* good, maybe I should bow out and watch."

"If you do not swim all that well, I will assist you."

Sunny's competitive streak kicked, prompting a little temporary white lie in the form of playing the consummate helpless female. "How deep is it?"

"At the moment, I am standing on a narrow ledge that drops off into the depths behind me. I have never located the bottom, though I have tried."

She laid a dramatic hand above her breasts. "Wow. You're well over six feet, so that means it must be *really* deep."

"Do not be afraid."

She wasn't anything of the sort, and she planned to show him. With that in mind, she walked to the edge to study where Rayad was standing and to gauge the depth of the water behind him. Then in one fell swoop, she tore off the towel and executed a dive into the pool.

After Sunny surfaced several feet away from Rayad, she slicked her hair back with one hand and almost laughed when she saw the puzzled look on his face. Time to end the charade. "I happened to be on my high school swim team for four years, and I served as lifeguard during the summer. I've never been afraid of water."

Without saying a word, he shot toward her, using his long, powerful legs to consume the distance between them in a matter of seconds. "I suspected you were not being truthful," he said as he slid his arms around her.

She continued to tread water, well aware that not much separated them, both in space and in clothing, yet she wasn't the least bit afraid. In fact, her reaction had nothing to do with fear and everything to do with feminine need. At least he'd put on swim trunks so she wasn't tempted to act on those desires—yet. "I thought I'd done a pretty good acting job."

"Perhaps I know you well enough to see through your act."

That might not be up for debate since he'd demonstrated that on several occasions. "I'm sorry. I just couldn't resist raining on your macho-man parade. In case you haven't noticed, I'm rather self-sufficient."

His gaze traveled from her eyes to her chest, the scar plainly visible due to the clarity of the pool. "I have noticed your independence, and this." Keeping one arm around her, he slid his fingertips along the raised area. "He used a blade on you."

Rayad said it as a statement of fact, not a question, but he still looked as if he needed her confirmation. She saw no real reason not to explain at this point. "Yes, he did. Or that's what I assume since I couldn't see it. But

I definitely felt it. If I hadn't cooperated, he promised to be more accurate the next time."

"The scar is not as unsightly as you might think."

"It's bad enough, but I'm getting used to it. Besides, it gives me a good excuse to buy a new necklace."

His smile indicated he might actually appreciate her sarcasm. "Perhaps I will purchase that for you, although you should wear your wound proudly as a sign you had the strength to survive."

Exactly what she'd planned to do—eventually. Unfortunately, she didn't feel all that strong at the moment. Not with Rayad so close, her hands resting on his broad shoulders while her heart beat a staccato rhythm in her chest. "Are we going to just float around here like a couple of rafts, or are we going to swim?"

He pressed a soft kiss on her cheek. "How is your endurance?"

"I don't know. How's yours?"

"Excellent. I am also able to swim long distances, as well."

The sexy devil. "What do you have in mind? From a swimming standpoint?"

He looked thoroughly disappointed. "I have somewhere else to show you, but we can only see it by water."

"Sounds interesting. You lead, I'll follow."

This time he landed his lips square on her mouth, but he didn't linger very long. "When we reach the opening to the cavern, take hold of my leg."

"Is that really necessary?"

"Do you wish to be lost?"

He had her on that one. "No."

"Should you inadvertently let go, you will be in total darkness. Keep going as you will shortly return to light, and our destination. I will go slowly."

She brushed a kiss across his unshaven chin. "Don't be careful on my account."

He responded with an all-out grin. "Are you ready?"

"I'm ready."

Before she could draw another breath, Rayad took off, swimming toward the mouth of the cave they had explored earlier. She attempted to match him, stroke for stroke, but he was just too fast.

By the time she came upon the abyss, he was waiting for her, looking as fit as a fiddle and ready to take on the English Channel. She, however, was a bit out of shape. "That was exhilarating. How much farther?"

"Not very far at all."

"Apparently your ribs have sufficiently healed."

"Well enough. Now take hold of me and do not let go."

Ever the tough guy. She gave him a salute. "Aye, aye, captain."

Rather than hinder his movements by commandeering his leg, Sunny slid her hand in the back waistband of his trunks. She only caught a glimpse of the scars, but they couldn't detract from his appeal regardless of how bad they might be. Nothing could ever take away from the fact he was a compassionate, strong and extremely desirable man.

As Rayad guided them through the darkness, Sunny had a few moments of knee-jerk distress. But it didn't take long before she allowed herself to enjoy the freedom, the sounds and scents of the cavern and the man serving as her own personal escort through paradise. She soon became aware of the fact she didn't feel the least bit claustrophobic, despite the total blindness to her surroundings. Instead, she felt oddly elated, completely liberated and oh, so taken with Rayad's controlled strokes, bringing to mind some other strokes she would like to experience.

Down, Sunny—her thought as they continued on their trek. She needed to be a bit more wary, otherwise she would end up going down the wrong road with Rayad. Or maybe it could turn out to be the right road. Only time would tell.

The blackness began to fade as they rounded a bend, and a large opening revealed a gentle waterfall flowing down the stone, feeding the basin below that led to the underground aquifer.

Sunny let go of Rayad to swim forward, and when she felt sand beneath her feet, stood to admire the scene. "This is absolutely breathtaking."

"Yes, it is."

She looked back to find him staring at her. "I'm sure you've seen it so many times, you take it for granted."

He waded toward her and paused at her side. "I still appreciate its majesty, but I was not referring to the falls."

"Did you mean the sun bouncing off the water? The blue, blue skies?"

"My admiration is solely for you."

She faced him and faked a frown. "You are one charming sheikh."

"And you are one very stunning woman."

"Flattery could very well get you anywhere you want to go," she said as she draped her arms around his neck.

"Anywhere?"

Time to rephrase that. "Okay, anywhere we both mutually decide to go."

"Do you have a place in mind?"

She felt a little bit giddy and a whole lot bold. "Why don't you kiss me, and we'll find out?"

He did. A coaxing kiss, but very persuasive. He sent his palms down her sides slowly then back up again and paused precariously close to her breasts. She could tell him to stop, or she could encourage him to go. She wanted him to go, not stop.

More brazen than she'd ever been before, Sunny reached back and unfastened the clasp at her back, then loosened the tie at her neck, allowing the swimsuit top to drop and float away.

Apparently aware that she was now bare from the waist up, Rayad broke the kiss and favored her with a knowing smile. He cupped her breasts, circling his thumbs around her nipples while seemingly studying all the details. She wasn't overly endowed like her twin, but the gentle way he treated her, she couldn't care less.

Never had she let a man she'd known for such a short time go this far this fast. Did that make her more like her mother than she cared to admit? She didn't want to think about that now. She stopped thinking altogether when Rayad lowered his head and replaced one hand with his lips.

The sensations were remarkable, from the pull of

his mouth to the flick of his tongue. Waves of heat washed over her and settled between her thighs. As if Rayad sensed that, he pulled her legs up around his waist, bringing her in close contact with his very impressive erection. Then he began to move her up and down against his groin, creating a friction that brought her close to the edge of climax. If he kept it up, she would start making a few primitive sounds, or beg him to put her out of her misery. Then he had the audacity to stop moving altogether.

After Rayad set her back on her feet, Sunny bit her tongue to keep from cursing. "Nothing quite like getting turned on then immediately turned off."

He swept a hand over the back of his neck. "That was not my intention. If I had my way, I would have taken you here without formality."

That sounded like a good plan to her. "Why didn't you?"

"I am not certain this is what you want."

She crossed her arms over her bare breasts and blew out an impatient sigh. "Believe me, I'm not that good at faking it."

He retrieved her top that was floating nearby and handed it to her. "When a person has a brush with death or suffers a loss, at times they search for any means to remind themselves they are still alive."

She redressed and refastened her suit, all the while battling frustration. "Is that truly what you think I'm doing?"

"I believe it is possible."

She viewed his concerns as an affront to her character. "For your information, I'm not the kind of woman who goes searching for just anyone to meet my needs, physical or emotional. If I didn't trust you, I would never even consider crossing the intimacy line. Believe it or not, I do trust you, Rayad, and I want you more than I've wanted any man in a long time, even Cameron. If that's crazy, then I'm certifiable. But I can't help how I feel."

Some unnamed emotion reflected from his eyes. "I truly appreciate your continued faith in me, yet trust should be earned."

"You earned it when you halted our little interlude because you're worried about me. However, something tells me there's more to your worries than whether or not I'm ready. Maybe you're the one who isn't ready."

He took her hands in his and gave her a meaningful look. "It has been some time since I have been with a woman, yet my concerns lie solely with your well-being. If you decide we should enjoy each other from a carnal standpoint, you may rest assured I will grant you an experience that you will not soon forget. Although I am not averse to lovemaking in various places, our first time should be in a proper bed."

She found his self-assurance and traditional ideals oddly appealing, and believable. "Then we're agreed that when the time comes, we let nature take its course with no more second-guessing?"

His expression brightened a bit. "Agreed. You only have to ask, and I will answer your every fantasy."

Even with the sun beating down on her head, she experienced a bout of chills when she imagined him stealing into her suite tonight once they returned to the palace. And on that note… "I suppose we should think about heading back before dark. I'd like to be there in time to have dinner with Piper."

"We will dine here before we return."

Spending a few more hours in his presence in this secluded place wasn't such an awful prospect. Not in the least. Maybe she wouldn't even have to wait to fulfill her fantasies. "We can stay." She pointed at him. "And you better really have a tray from the palace, not serving me something from one of those cans on the shelf."

His grin arrived full-throttle. "You will find the fare more than adequate."

She found him utterly irresistible. "Out of curiosity, exactly where are we having dinner? Next to your bed?"

"No." He lifted her hands and brushed a soft kiss on each of them, like some chivalrous Arabian knight. "Per my original plan, we shall dine beneath the stars."

Normally, she didn't require romantic gestures, but with Rayad, she wasn't quite herself. "That sounds wonderful."

"Rest assured, it will be," he said. "And afterward, I will safely escort you back to the palace."

As far as Sunny was concerned, she didn't care if they were detained for the evening, as long as he made good on his promise to fulfill all her fantasies. In doing so, she could experience one very *hot* desert night.

Seven

They would not be returning to the palace tonight.

Rayad dreaded telling Sunny the news for fear she would not believe him. Prolonging the inevitable would not change the situation, and that truth sent him from the radio station to seek her out in the sleeping quarters where she had retired two hours ago.

When he entered, he found her on a bunk curled up on her side, her eyes closed against the dim overhead light. She looked so peaceful, he hated to wake her. Instead, he perched on the edge of the narrow bed next to hers to watch her a few moments, while she was unaware.

He had never known anyone quite like the courageous journalist. He had rarely been so quickly affected by a woman. His craving for her was both foreign and undeniable. Even now, the temptation to strip out of his clothes and join her lived strong within him. He refused to do that for many reasons. Although she had insisted she would gladly welcome him into her bed, he still had reservations. Should she ever discover the capacity in which he served his country, she would never view him the same way again. She would undoubtedly never trust him again.

Perhaps he should reconsider their evening together. Perhaps he should have returned her to the palace immediately before it had been to late to do so.

Yet when Sunny began to stir and after her eyes fluttered open, all thoughts of what should have been disappeared And when she greeted him with a soft smile., he could only consider how badly he desired her. "How long have you been sitting there?" she asked, her voice hoarse from sleep.

"Not long."

She stretched her arms above her head and sighed. "What time is it?"

"Sixteen hundred hours."

Her smile disappeared. "I'm still not fully awake. Regular time, please."

"4 p.m."

"Really?" She sat up against the metal headboard. "I didn't mean to nap that long. You should've woken me."

He had wanted to do that very thing in some very creative ways. "You were tired from the day's activities."

"True. So what's on the agenda between now and dinnertime?"

"I will be traveling to the closest village to the south

to purchase supplies. Feel free to continue your nap in my absence."

"What about the dinner you brought with you?"

The time had come to reveal the weather issue. "I received some recent news from Rafiq that prompted my decision to travel to the village."

"Are you buying souvenirs?"

"No."

Her green eyes widened. "Is the baby coming?"

"He did not mention the child or his wife, so I assume not."

She blew out a frustrated breath. "I'm not in the mood to play a guessing game, so just tell me what he said and why you have to go shopping when it's obvious you have tonight's meal."

He leaned forward, rested his arms on his legs and laced his fingers together between his parted knees. "It appears the storms are worse than first predicted. The flooding has been extensive, and it has required ground troops to evacuate the villagers to higher ground."

"Is anyone in the palace in danger?" she said, her tone hinting at alarm.

"The palace is elevated enough not to suffer any ill effects. However, the roads into the village are currently impassible."

"That means we're stuck?"

He did not care for the word *stuck*. "We will be confined here until the passage is clear."

She fell back onto the pillow and studied the stone ceiling. "How long before we can go back?"

"Three days minimum. Possibly longer."

"Great."

Her annoyance did not please him. "Do you find spending an extended period of time with me completely unpalatable?"

She sent him a sideways glance. "I didn't say that. I just feel bad that I haven't spent much time with my sister. Not to mention I only have two days' worth of clothes. Unless you have a laundry hidden somewhere, that could pose a problem since washing my stuff in the aquifer isn't exactly eco-friendly."

Her reasoning gave him some measure of relief. "I will purchase what you need in the village."

She seemed insulted by his offer. "I have my own funds, Rayad. Of course, if they don't take credit cards—"

"They do not. Therefore, you will need to allow me to assist you. Or perhaps you would like to borrow clothing from me."

"If your clothes fit me, then I seriously need to consider a diet."

She was perfect in every way that counted, in his opinion. "My shirts might be large, but they would adequately cover you."

"Yes, but there is the underwear issue."

He almost proposed she not wear any. "Again, you will find all you need in the village. I will escort you there first thing in the morning."

"Fine, but that doesn't ease my guilt over abandoning Piper when she was so kind to invite me."

Knowing Sunny would be leaving soon gave him cause for concern, though he could not say why. He had known all along that her departure was inevitable, as was his return to his duties. Still, their parting bothered him on a level he would have to examine later. "You will have ample time to visit your sister, unless you plan to immediately return to the States once we arrive back at the palace."

"I'll be staying for another couple of weeks." She pushed off the bed, rifled through the bag set on the floor and withdrew a brush. "If you're going shopping, then I might as well go with you now to pick up what I need. Besides, I don't want to stay here alone because I'm still not convinced I won't come across a bat or two."

He would like nothing better than to have her company. "Then you are not angry with me over the delay?"

She stroked the brush through her silken blond hair several times before contacting his gaze. "You have no control over the weather, Rayad. You might be a powerful guy, but you're not that powerful."

He had a powerful urge to kiss her—after he divested her of the white shirt and brown shorts. "I promise you will not have to concern yourself with my behavior during the remainder of our time together. You are still in complete control."

She paused the brush midstroke and smiled again. "I'm not sure I can promise you the same thing when it comes to my behavior. You have a way of making me lose control."

If he did not retreat soon, he would not be able to disguise his burgeoning erection, compromising his dignity. "We should travel to the village now while it is still daylight," he said as he stood.

Sunny tossed the brush back into the bag, slid her arms around his waist and pressed a kiss on his lips. "I'm ready to go shopping. And I'm really ready for our dinner beneath the stars."

So was Rayad. He only hoped he could keep his baser urges in check long enough to finish their meal. After that, he would make no promises.

The small village marketplace had been surprisingly crowded with men dressed in traditional *thawb* and women wearing *abayas*. Sunny had only seen a handful of vehicles, but a lot of livestock—from cows to camels. The smells of spices and grilling meats coming from small tents set up by vendors had made her incredibly hungry. Her darkly handsome escort had also fueled her appetites that had nothing to do with dinner.

Several times during the trip, Sunny had almost lost Rayad in the crowd. The language barrier had hindered her ability to understand his conversations with the locals, and he'd had plenty. Yet one thing she had understood— they'd called him Basil. Later this evening she would answer her curiosity and ask him why they didn't use his proper name. Why they seemed to treat him like a fellow commoner, not well-heeled royalty.

Right then, she had to haul all the supplies out of the Mercedes while Rayad opened the secret door. Cave, sweet cave. The thought made her smile.

"What do you find so humorous?" he asked when he joined her at the rear of the vehicle.

"Nothing," she said. "Just glad to be back and glad I have my own personal pack mule."

He faked a frown when she handed him two of the burlap totes. "Are you calling me an ass?"

"Not at all. But I do like your ass." She topped off the comment by patting his cargo-pant-covered bottom and heading toward the entry.

By the time they made two trips up and down the stairs, Sunny wanted nothing more than to take a bath. "Am I supposed to clean up in the reservoir?" she asked as she laid the caftans Rayad had bought her on one bunk.

"You may, or you may use one of the showers."

Clearly he'd been withholding pertinent information. "You said you didn't have a shower."

"Not adjacent to my quarters." He pointed across the room at a closed door. "You will find one in there. The pressure is adequate although the water will be cold."

She swept one arm across the perspiration beading on her forehead. "A cold shower sounds perfect. I'm still trying to recover from the heat." He wouldn't help her body temperature one bit if he kept standing there with his arms folded across his chest, the short sleeves of his black tee revealing biceps that should be registered as lethal weapons. Yep, a cold shower was definitely in order.

"I will leave you to your bathing now while I prepare our meal."

She hadn't realized how hungry she was until he'd mentioned that. "Great. I shouldn't be long since I didn't pack the hair dryer."

He smiled before he started away then paused and faced her again. "Perhaps at some point in time during our stay together, I will join you in the shower."

With that, he left the bunk room, closing the door behind him, and leaving Sunny with all sorts of questionable ideas and mental images. She couldn't wait to be alone with him under the night skies. She couldn't wait to see what might transpire after dinner. Then again, she could be disappointed if he brought out the honor card.

Fortunately, she had ways to convince him to take the next step, beginning with making herself fresh and presentable. She made quick work of the shower that was more of a stream, thankful she brought shampoo and bath gel. She then grabbed a towel from the metal locker, dried off and returned to the room to retrieve her favorite sleeveless gauze caftan.

As she held it up, she did a double take when she noticed the wide silver necklace intertwined with deep coral beads that perfectly matched the color of the dress. She had admired it, but she certainly hadn't purchased it due to her lack of cash, not to mention the rarity of the stones that carried a hefty price tag. Instead, she allowed Rayad to buy her a pair of sterling hoops that were much less expensive after he insisted.

No doubt he'd been the jewelry culprit, and she would definitely thank him, argue it was too extravagant, and then maybe show her appreciation with a big, fat kiss.

After she twisted her damp hair into a loose braid, Sunny slipped into a pair of the recently purchased sheer white muslin underwear that looked like men's boxers, only shorter. Not exactly sexy, but functional. Luckily, the dress didn't require a bra. She then applied a little mascara and lip gloss using a compact mirror, slid the earrings into her lobes, clasped the necklace around her neck and marveled over the fact she had morphed into a girly-girl. Piper would be so proud. Piper would also hate that her twin didn't have a pair of spiky heels at her disposal. Thank heavens. Barefoot seemed to be the way to go in lieu of sneakers, although she worried she might wind up with a stubbed toe, or step on a snake.

Satisfied everything was in place, Sunny walked into the corridor to find Rayad standing by the entry to the cavern. He'd changed into a plain white tee and dark blue cargo pants, and it appeared he had shaved his beard down to a shadow. One gorgeous, gorgeous man at her disposal. Lucky her.

She executed a corny curtsey. "Good evening, Your Highness. You clean up good."

He nodded slightly. "As do you. The dress fits you to perfection, yet I knew it would."

She figured he'd had a lot of experience with gauging a woman's size. He'd probably had a lot of experience with a lot of women. "Thank you," she said, her face flushed. "Since it's getting fairly late, is dinner ready?"

"It is," he said. "Now if you will follow me, I will show you to our private dining room."

Sunny wasn't too thrilled to have to climb yet another flight of stairs. But the effort was well worth it when they emerged at the top of the rock formation and stepped onto a sandy plateau. Her attention immediately turned to the host of diamond-like stars spread out as far as the eye could see, and the near-full moon hanging high overhead. An amazing panorama and the perfect start to an equally amazing night. "I'd forgotten how incredible the night sky looks in such a remote place."

Rayad slid his arms around her from behind. "I am sorry we missed the sunset, but perhaps we will see that before we return to the palace."

She didn't even want to consider leaving this place, or him. Leaning back against his chest, she caught a whiff of what must be his soap, a heady scent that reminded her of exotic incense. Not only did he look great and feel great, he smelled great. "Who needs the sun when you have all these stars?"

"We both need sustenance."

She turned into his arms and smiled. "That would probably be a good idea. Otherwise, you might have to carry me back down those steps."

He feathered a kiss on her forehead. "That would be my pleasure. Yet I would not want to stop until we reached my bed."

"Maybe I wouldn't want you to stop."

"That is good to know, as long as you are certain that is what you wish."

She couldn't quite peg why he continued to need reassurance, unless it had more to do with his reticence. Regardless, she would provide it. "Believe me, that's exactly what I wish."

He kissed her then—a long, lingering kiss that made her forget all about dinner. She focused on the feel of his tongue softly exploring her mouth and his palms roving up and down her back before coming to rest on her bottom. She remembered their sexy interval in the pool and realized if they didn't quit now, they might ignite the sand beneath their feet.

As much as she hated to do it, Sunny broke the kiss and said, "Maybe we should grab a bite to eat."

He released her and cleared his throat. "That would probably be advisable."

"Probably so."

Taking her by the hand, he led her to an area illuminated by a lone torch set into the ground. A multicolored blanket held various platters with cheeses and meats and fruit, along with a basket of bread.

Sunny's returning appetite caused her to let him go and drop down onto one of the pillows flanking the food.

After Rayad joined her on the opposing cushion, he handed her a plate. "As they would say in America, dig in."

She laughed. "Yes, that's what they would say. And yes, I gladly will."

Every bite Sunny took was pure bliss, though she couldn't say if she was driven by hunger or simply the atmosphere. They barely said two words during the meal, and before long, they'd made quite a dent in the food.

She wiped her mouth with a napkin and moved her empty plate to the middle of the blanket. "That was the best meal I've had in years."

Rayad pushed the pillow away and stretched out on his side, using his palm to support his jaw. "Do not become too accustomed to this luxury. What I have brought from the market is simple."

She briefly studied the night sky and relished the warm breeze blowing across her face. "I don't care what we eat as long as we eat it here." When she brought her attention back to him, she found him staring at her intently. "What? Do I have something on my mouth?"

"You have a beautiful mouth," he said. "And I see nothing obstructing my view of it."

She set her pillow aside and stretched out to face him, leaving little space between them. "Considering how busy our day has been, you'd think I'd be tired, even after my nap. But remarkably I'm not. And that reminds me, I have something to ask you about our trip to the village."

"I will answer to the best of my ability."

Time to play the name game. "When we were in the village, I thought I heard people calling you Basil. Did I misunderstand?"

"No, you did not. That is how they know me."

"Then they don't realize you're a prince?"

"They do not, and that is how I wish it to be."

"Why?"

"One never knows where enemies might be lurking. It is best to blend in with the masses and conceal your true identity."

Now it made sense. "Ah, it's that whole 'spy guy' thing. And by the way, you never have told me your code name."

"If I did, I would have to—"

"Kill me?"

A strange, almost wary look passed over his expression before he quickly replaced it with a smile. "I would prefer to kiss you." And he did, soft and slow and much too short, before he asked, "What do you wish to do now?"

A very loaded question. "What do you wish to do?"

"I cannot tell you what I wish to do for fear you might leave."

She scooted closer. "Try me."

"I would rather show you. Lie back."

After Sunny complied, Rayad rose above her and studied her face for a long moment. The next kiss he delivered was tempered at first, then deeper, and grew predictably hotter.

He broke away long enough to remove his shirt, then quickly divested her of the caftan. When he took her back into his arms and kissed her again, the feel of his bare chest pressed against her breasts caused her to shift restlessly against the dampness between her thighs. She wanted nothing more than to have him relieve the ache, but he'd told her she would have to ask. She could do that. Better still, she could follow his lead and point him in the right direction.

On that thought, Sunny lifted Rayad's hand from the curve of her hip, placed it on her inner thigh then held her breath while she waited for him to respond. She didn't have to wait long until he skimmed his palm higher up her leg, pausing to toy with the bottom edge of the unflattering underwear, as if determined to tease her into oblivion. A needy sound slipped out without regard for her effort to stop it, and that involuntary re-action seemed to send Rayad into action.

In one smooth move, he had her muslin pants pushed down to her knees and his hand between her legs. He continued to kiss her, his tongue mimicking the movement of the stroke of his finger, stoking a fire that threatened to sear all her control.

He took his mouth away and whispered, "You are very wet," without missing a beat with his touch.

If she could find her voice, she'd probably respond with "You think?" but she was too far gone to speak. She couldn't do anything but give in to the sensations and brace for the impending orgasm. It came swift and hard in a series of strong spasms that caused her to tremble all over.

Sunny gradually returned to reality when Rayad rained kisses on her face, but her respiration still wasn't quite steady. "Wow," she managed to say after a time.

"Did you find that satisfactory?" he asked.

"Do politicians play favorites?"

His laugh rumbled low in his chest. "That was only a sample of what I will do for you. There will be more to come, if you so desire."

You betcha she did. "I'm not sure I can handle much more."

He ran a fingertip along her jawline. "You can handle more than you realize. You will eventually see that."

At the moment, all she could see was stars, and not just the ones glimmering above her. "I'm going to take your word for that." Feeling unexpectedly bold, she rolled to her side to face him. "Take down your pants."

The demand evidently shocked him momentarily into silence. "Do you wish me to leave on my boots?"

She rose up and nudged him onto his back. "I said take down your pants, not take them off. Then you don't have to worry about your shoes."

"But—"

"No buts," she said as she wagged a finger at him. "As women say in America, do as you're told, sit back and enjoy it."

That unearthed his sexy smile. "Far be it for me to question a determined American woman."

While Rayad undid his fly, Sunny kicked out of the underpants before turning back to him to see he'd pushed his pants to his knees.

Amazing. The man had been endowed with many physical gifts, and she just discovered another one. He was mighty proud to see her. Very proud. He had every right to be.

After laying her cheek on his chest, she drew a line from his sternum down to his abdomen then lightly raked her nails up his thighs. He remained very still and silent, until she set out to explore him from shaft to tip. His indrawn breath indicated she must be doing something right, so she kept right on doing it. And when she circled her hand around him, he released a groan. That chink in his armor drove her to continue to stroke him, knowing that it wouldn't take much to send him completely over the edge. But before she could, he clasped her wrists and wrested her hand away.

"Enough," he said, his voice bordering on a growl.

She raised her head to find his eyes were closed. "Did I do something wrong?"

"On the contrary, you did everything right. That is why I stopped you."

"I think it's only fair that I return the favor."

"I prefer you not."

She felt suddenly self-conscious, and a tad miffed. "Does it bother you when a woman takes control and causes you to lose control?"

"That is not my concern."

Here we go again. "Look, if you're going to start spewing that stuff about me not knowing my own mind—"

"I was going to say that I want to be inside you."

Well, that changed everything. "I'd like that a lot."

"As long as I know you are certain you wish to proceed."

The last of her patience floated away on the warm desert breeze. "I am completely naked and still riding the pleasure train after having one of the best orgasms of my life. That pretty much speaks to my certainty."

Finally, he looked at her. "It was that good for you?"

She couldn't contain her smile. "On a scale from one to ten, I'd give it a twenty. But that doesn't mean you should puff out your chest and tell the world what a master lover you are. Not until you give me everything."

"I will give you all you need, and more."

"Then do it."

"I prefer we retire to my bed."

"I prefer we not waste that much time."

"It is not about time or convenience," he said. "It is about protection."

Aha. The condom conversation. "I'm protected against pregnancy, and I have no communicable diseases."

"Nor do I. I receive a thorough physical every six months. Therefore, you do not have to concern yourself over that. If you trust me."

Darned if she didn't on this count, too. "I trust you."

"Good. You must know I would never do anything to put you in jeopardy."

But would he understand if she couldn't go through with it? Only one way to find out. "Then what are we waiting for?"

This time he took control, nudging her onto her back and centering his dark gaze on her. "Rest assured, I am weary of waiting. Are you certain you would not rather be lying on a proper mattress?"

"I'm only sure of one thing. If you don't make love to me now, I'm going to start pouting."

He kissed her softly before presenting her with one heck of a smoldering look. "I certainly do not wish to prolong your agony."

Then he kissed her again, touched her again, bringing her to the brink of another climax and a place where the past no longer existed. But when he parted her legs and moved atop her, that past came back to roost. She couldn't breathe, couldn't divorce herself from the memories of another cruel man, no matter how hard she tried. And regardless of the consequences, she jerked from beneath him and practically shouted, "Stop!"

Shaking and ashamed, Sunny sat up and hugged her knees to her chest. She waited for a few moments of silence to pass before explaining. "The same thing happened the one and only time Cameron tried to make love to me after the abduction. He left the next morning, and I never saw him again. I wouldn't blame you if you did the same thing."

"I am not your former lover, Sunny," he said. "I would not abandon you in your time of need, nor do I expect you to do something you are not able to do."

She shifted slightly to see his forearm draped over his eyes. "But I want to make love with you, Rayad. I've thought about nothing else since you said we'd be spending time outdoors. You were answering my greatest fantasy. I can't imagine going through the rest of my life not being a whole woman again. I just don't know how to get past this."

He rolled to his side and centered his gaze on her. "With my help, if you are willing. Yet you must be aware that if we never consummate our relationship, I will always respect you and fondly remember our time together."

Her heart executed a little leap in her chest. "I really want to try, but it could take time and a whole lot of patience."

"We have nothing better to do for the next few days."

"True."

He pushed off the blanket, came to his feet and offered his hand. "Now we will retire to bed where I will expect nothing more than to hold you while you sleep. Perhaps this one night I will chase away the night-mares."

He had a knack for saying all the right things. "That sounds like a good plan. I'd suggest we sleep here, but I don't want to wake up covered in sand with a sunburn."

When she tried to gather her clothes, he said, "Leave them here, and we will retrieve them tomorrow. I want you lying next to me naked."

She smiled at his demanding tone. "All right. As long as you're naked, too."

"I have no intention of wearing clothes this evening."

Sunny followed Rayad down the dimly lit stairs and into his private quarters. After they were securely settled into bed, he brought her into his arms, where she laid her cheek on his chest and listened to the beat of his strong heart. He rubbed her arm in a steady, soothing rhythm, bringing about a welcome sense of peace.

She felt the need to express her appreciation for his patience and understanding, yet the right words escaped her. She found that odd considering her occupation revolved around proper vocabulary. But that terminology dealt with facts, not emotions. Right then her emotions were running the gamut between gratitude and much deeper feelings.

Rather than tell him exactly what was in her heart, she chose something much less heavy. "You are a wonderful man, Rayad."

He softly kissed her forehead. "You are a remarkable woman, Sunny."

He made her feel remarkable. He made her trust she could finally conquer her fears and forget the terrible ordeal. Most important, he made her believe she could finally love a man the way she should. That she could truly love him.

Eight

He had never seen any woman look quite so innocent in sleep. He could not recall feeling such a fierce need to protect someone he had known such a limited amount of time. He found the unfamiliar emotions unwelcome and inadvisable. He must show restraint and be patient. He must allow her to signal him when she was ready to proceed with their intimacy. Above all, he had to accept that she could possibly reconsider.

Needing to leave her before he forgot his vow of restraint, Rayad moved his arm from beneath Sunny to gather what he needed to bathe, and afterward, swim. He sought an activity to expend energy and allow his body to calm.

After he retrieved the soap safe enough to use in the reservoir, he set the bar on the edge then dove into the pool. The water was much colder than usual, probably due to the current mountain storms that replenished the spring. Cold would serve him well, or so he thought as he returned to the ledge to begin his morning bath. No amount of frigid water would rid him of his need, he realized, when he glanced up to see Sunny standing on the stone bank, completely nude. The shape of her breasts, the curve of her hip and the slight shading between her thighs brought about another strong erection that he suspected would not disappear in the immediate future without tending.

She removed the band securing the now-misshapen braid, shook out her hair, stepped down into the water and walked toward him. "Good morning, kind sir," she said when she reached him.

He kept his hands fisted at his sides, though he longed to touch her. Everywhere. "Did you sleep well?"

"Better than I have in a long time." She looked up at the opening in the cave's ceiling before returning her gaze to his. "It's barely light outside. You must be an early riser."

She had no idea the accuracy in her assessment, yet she would if she came any closer. "I do not wish to waste the day by sleeping too long."

"I feel the same way, but I really have to take a shower to help me wake up."

"No need. I have everything here to accommodate your bath."

She tapped her chin with a fingertip. "That's right. This is your own personal tub."

"It is."

"You use soap?"

He nodded toward the bar on the bank. "I do. It is all natural and biodegradable. A woman in the village makes it especially for me."

She raised a thin brow. "Is that all she does for you?"

"She's almost eighty years of age."

"Oh. Mind if I inspect this soap?"

He would rather she inspect him. "Be my guest."

After she retrieved the bar, she came back to him and held it to her nose. "This smells fantastic, and it explains why you smelled so good last night."

"Do you wish to try it?"

"Unless you'd like to go first."

"I will wait until you are finished."

She took a few steps back and paused on the incline to where her torso was completely exposed. While he watched, she ran the soap over her arms, then her neck and finally her breasts, where she lingered longer than necessary. He decided she was bent on enticing him, and her ploy happened to be working. By the time she moved the bar down her abdomen, then beneath the water, he perched precariously on the edge of losing control.

"Mind washing my back?" she asked as she offered him the soap.

He did not mind, but he was not certain he would want to stop there. "As you wish."

After she turned away from him, he complied with her request, taking his time lathering her silky flesh while keeping a safe berth between them. Yet carnal urges began to commandeer his common sense as he traveled down to her well-shaped buttocks. And when she moved back and positioned herself flush against him, contacting the evidence of his lack of control, all his determination to resist her floated away with the bar of soap.

Without warning, he turned her around and kissed her with all the passion he experienced at that moment. He wanted to make her yearn more than any man she had ever yearned before. He desired to make her body weep for him with the highest form of intimacy possible, and he would—if she granted him permission. "I want to bring you to climax."

"I'm almost already there," she said, her voice a breathy whisper. "But I need you to finish me."

With that goal in mind, Rayad swept Sunny into his arms, set her on the edge of the bank and took his place between her parted legs. He pressed a line of kisses on her belly, careful to watch her face for any signs of distress before moving lower. Instead of issuing a protest, she leaned back using her elbows for support, closed her eyes and spread her legs wider. That was all the permission he needed to proceed.

He began by divining her flesh with his tongue then used strokes to bring her to completion, softer yet insistent. Even when he heard the increase in her respiration and sensed her impending orgasm, he did not let up. He tried to urge every sensation from her, and give her an experience that she would not soon forget.

After a few more moments, Sunny released a low moan and then bowed over his head, her entire body trembling. "That was incredible," she muttered before straightening to level her gaze on his. "And this is totally unfair to you."

He left the water to sit beside her. "I will manage."

She sent a pointed look at his groin. "All signs to the contrary."

"I have been without relief for extended periods of time."

She rose to her feet. "That ends now. Find me a towel and meet me in bed. And please don't argue. I want this to happen."

He wanted her more than she could ever know. Yet he must remember she might not be able to see their lovemaking through. "We do not need a towel," he said as he stood. "The sheets will dry."

She climbed into bed with a smile then beckoned him with open arms. They kissed for some time before she broke the contact and straightened, hovering above him. "I've decided I need to be on top," she announced, taking him by surprise.

"That would possibly be favorable for you." And undeniable pleasure for him.

"You have to promise me something first, Rayad."

"Anything you ask."

"Keep your eyes open and look at me the whole time. I need to see your face and know it's you."

"That will be my pleasure."

And it was, he determined, the moment she straddled his thighs and guided him inside her. He gritted his teeth against the need for immediate release when she began to move her hips, slowly at first then faster, taking him deeper and deeper. All the while, he kept focused on her eyes though he found that task diffi-cult in light of his imminent climax. He mustered all his strength to hold back yet could no longer when she leaned down and whispered, "I want to feel you let go."

The orgasm arrived with the force of a grenade, bind-ing every muscle in his body. The pulsation went on for longer than he had expected, or experienced to this point in his checkered sexual history. In the time it took for him to catch his breath, Sunny eased off him and curled close to his side.

"You have to feel better."

He frowned. "Better does not appropriately describe how I feel. The question is, how do you feel?"

She rolled onto her back and laughed. "Exhilarated. Free. Like I just won a Pulitzer."

Her joy was contagious, bringing about his smile. "I am glad. I have always been convinced you have the strength of character to overcome this."

She turned her face toward him and formed her hand around his jaw. "I'm not sure I would have, had it not been for you. There is just one more thing I need from you."

He hoped it had nothing to do with his dying devo-tion or a declaration of love. He was too broken to give her that. "I am listening."

"If at all possible, I want to use the radio."

He experienced a strong sense of relief. "To confirm that I am not holding you here without good cause?"

She whisked a kiss across his chin. "I know you haven't been lying about the storms. I just need to check in with my sister."

He needed to take her features to memory for in a very short time, memories of this special woman would be all he had left. As it had been with the other remarkable woman who had once graced his life. "I will be glad to honor your request to speak with Piper. Perhaps it would be best if you do not tell her too much about our time here. I do not wish to explain to her husband."

Sunny favored him with a smile. "Don't worry. I'll pretend I'm having a terribly boring time."

"Having fun, Sunshine?"

She was speaking into a shortwave radio with a gorgeous man's-man standing behind her, running his hands up her T-shirt. She defined that as great fun. "So-so. Not much to do here."

"Where exactly is here?"

"South of Bajul."

"Adan said you were staying in a village."

"Not far from a village," she said, trying hard not to gasp as Rayad cupped her breasts. "Is it still raining there?"

"Unfortunately, yes, and it's not going to let up for at least another two days. What's the weather like there?"

"Hot." Extremely hot, and growing hotter by the minute. "How is Maysa?"

"Still pregnant, but she said she's been having some twinges, whatever that means. I hope you make it back before the big event."

She hoped her legs would hold her when Rayad unbuttoned her shorts. "Well, I just wanted to check in and see…" Her voice betrayed her when he slid the zipper down. "I just need…" To stop talking altogether.

"Sunny, are you there?"

Two more minutes and she would be. "Gotta go, sis. Bad connection. See you soon. Take care."

After she flipped the radio off, she turned into Rayad's arms and groaned. "You're determined to be a bad boy, aren't you?"

He nuzzled her neck then kissed her quick. "I know what I want, and I want you. Now."

She glanced behind her and realized the long table holding the communication equipment happened to be the only surface available. "You're not serious."

"Not here."

That gave her some relief. "Then where?"

"A place where I can finally fulfill one of your fantasies."

Her mental lightbulb snapped on. "Where we dined last night?"

"Yes."

"But it's still daylight."

He clasped her hand and brought it to his lips. "There is an erotic quality to spontaneity. Making love in the open and the possibility of detection only heightens that eroticism. However, it is highly unlikely anyone will come upon us since the perimeter is secure, if that is your concern."

She thought of one particular disconcerting scenario. "What about airplanes overhead?"

"Unless we are visited by Adan, that will not be an issue."

Great. Just what she needed—getting caught with her pants down by her brother-in-law. Time to put on the big-girl panties and get with the program. Or take them off as the case might be. "Well, no risk, no reward. Let's go."

Rayad led her back up the narrow steps and to the place where their journey to intimacy had begun. Once they arrived, Sunny discovered a different blanket spread out on the sand, and realized her new lover had planned this all along.

"Spontaneity, huh?" she said as she dropped down onto the makeshift bed.

He joined her and smiled—a sly one. "Perhaps not completely spontaneous, yet I did not know if you would agree."

He had a point. "I'll hand you that. What now?"

"Stand and take off your clothes."

"You don't want to do it?"

"I wish to watch."

His words generated more heat than the afternoon sun beating down on them. "I suppose I can do that since you've basically seen every part of me."

After returning to her feet, she crossed her arms and quickly pulled the T-shirt over her head, exposing her bare breasts. She tackled the rest of her clothing a bit slower in an effort to draw out the tension. Rayad visually followed her every move as she unfastened her shorts and let them fall to her feet, leaving her wearing the white muslin underwear.

"Satisfied?" she asked, even knowing what he would say.

"Everything, Sunny," he replied, confirming her prediction.

She shimmied out of the final garment and remained planted in the same spot, letting him look his fill. "Better?"

"Much better. Now come here."

"Not until you get naked, too."

Without hesitating, or standing, he began to strip but much faster than she had. Once he was down to his birthday suit, she reclaimed her place next to him. "You're leading this parade, so tell me what you want." And hopefully, she could deliver.

"Roll to your side away from me."

She threaded her lip between her bottom teeth. "I guess I could, but—"

"Do you trust me, Sunny?" he asked.

"Yes, I do."

"Then you must trust I will treat you with the greatest care. Now turn over and allow me to give you great pleasure."

Sunny complied and waited for what would come next, all the while thinking a month ago, she would never even consider doing this in the great outdoors. A month ago, she didn't know him. She was dizzy with anticipation. High on adrenaline and heated from head to toe.

He moved against her back, brushed her hair aside and whispered, "You will feel me better this way." Then he slid his leg between her legs, placed one hand between her thighs, and eased inside her.

Rayad had been right. The position allowed her to feel every nuance as he moved deep inside her. He began to stroke her with a fingertip, coaxing a climax that wouldn't take long at all. And it didn't.

Before she knew it—before she was ready—Sunny experienced an incredible orgasm made more powerful by Rayad's thrusts. She had truly found a paradise with him, and in turn rediscovered her natural sensuality.

Not long after, Rayad tensed against her, moved deeper inside her and released a low groan. He shuddered and when he climaxed, Sunny enjoyed every pleasant pulse of his body, knowing she'd given him as much pleasure as he had given her.

After a time, he loosened his hold on her and brought his lips to her ear. "Do you have any regrets?"

Only one. She turned into his arms and stroked his cheeks. "No regrets at all other than I hate this will all have to come to an end in the not-so-distant future. Unless you invite me to stay here indefinitely." When his expression went somber, she added, "Don't look so worried. I'm not serious, and I'm not going to start spewing sonnets and propose marriage. I know this is only temporary. When we leave here, you'll go back to your life, and I'll go back to mine."

"For that reason, I prefer we enjoy each other while we still have time."

Too little time to suit her, and that thought gave her pause. "I'm absolutely enjoying our time together now. You certainly know how to make a woman's fantasy come true."

He brushed her hair back from her face and lightly kissed her. "I vow to you I will endeavor to make each of your fantasies a reality in the days to come."

* * *

For three whole days, Rayad made good on his promise. He had touched her in every way possible and in places she didn't know existed. He had made love to her in various ways, with the exception of one due to his concern over her fear of confinement. He had been careful and considerate and extremely sexy. So sexy that he could have her with only a look, and he had several times.

Never before had she made love four times in twenty-four hours until she'd met him. Never before had she given that concept much thought. Cameron had been a once-a-week kind of guy. Her first lover had been an inexperienced jerk, but then they'd only been seventeen. Though her sexual conquests were somewhat limited, she knew enough to know that Rayad Rostam was a special breed. The kind of man who could steal a woman's heart like a thief in the night then leave with his own heart still intact.

Regardless of the possible emotional fallout, with every interesting conversation over shared meals, with every sultry kiss, every sweet nothing whispered in her ear, Sunny acknowledged she was in grave danger of losing herself to him and landing in love. Unfortunately, the danger had become her reality, and she'd already crashed and would probably burn from their inevitable parting.

She'd always been upfront to a fault, yet in this case she worried if she divulged her feelings to Rayad, he wouldn't reciprocate. She debated whether to come clean, or carry the secret the rest of her life. She despised secrets, and for that reason she decided to put it out in the open, let the chips fall and all that jazz.

On that thought, Sunny turned over in bed to find Rayad had left without her knowledge. She sat up and looked around, hoping to discover he'd gone for his morning bath and swim without her, though she would be disappointed if he had. The reservoir was undisturbed and the cavern starkly silent.

She needed to find him and confess before she lost her courage. That need drove her to search for her underwear balled up beneath the sheet at the end of the bed and put them on. Then she grabbed her discarded T-shirt and slipped it on while heading toward the bunker's entry.

When she stepped into the corridor, she heard Rayad's familiar voice, but she couldn't understand the Arabic he was speaking. She did detect a hint of anger in his tone. As soon as the conversation ended, she padded on bare feet to the radio room and peeked inside to see Rayad leaning back against the table, staring off into space.

"May I come in?" she asked.

"You may," he responded, although the stern look he gave her said she might not be welcome.

She didn't let that hinder her forward progress, or deter her from her goal. But before she started playing true confession, she would find out the reason behind his dark mood. "Were you chatting with anyone interesting?"

"Adan."

She moved to his side and hoisted herself up onto the desk. "What did he have to say?"

"Nothing that I wished to hear."

Getting information from him was like pulling hen's teeth, as her nana used to say. "I don't mean to intrude, but do you mind telling me what Adan told you that has you so cranky?"

"It does not involve you."

Cranky had become a colossal understatement. "Fine. It's probably something top secret that wouldn't interest me anyway." When he didn't respond, she determined a subject switch was in order. "I was thinking that after we bathe and have breakfast, we could go to the village a little earlier today. I saw a scarf I'd like to buy for Piper."

"That is not possible."

"I promise I'll pay you back."

He exhaled a rough sigh. "It is not possible to travel to the village, nor is it necessary."

Sunny could guess what he would say to her next question, and it made her heartsick to ask. But she had to know. "We have to leave, don't we?"

"Yes. I have been ordered to return to my duties immediately."

"What about the roads?"

"They were cleared as of yesterday."

She should be grateful he hadn't come by that information earlier, otherwise they would have missed out on several wonderful experiences. "I suppose that's good news."

"I suppose," he repeated, no clear emotion in his tone, only detachment.

Sunny felt as if he had erected a steel wall, effectively shutting her out. She refused to let him. "Look, we both knew this was going to happen, and maybe it's for the best. If we stayed together any longer, I would only…" Her determination to own up to her feelings trailed off along with her words.

Finally, he looked at her straight on. "You would only what?"

The moment had arrived to lay her heart on the line and hope it didn't get crushed. "I would only fall deeper in love with you."

He pushed off the table, laced his hands behind his neck and turned his back on her. "You cannot love me."

She wasn't at all surprised by his reaction, just the force of his demand. "I can, and I do. Believe me, this wasn't at all what I had planned, and it's ridiculous to think it happened this quickly. But I can't help the way I feel."

He faced her again, frustration reflecting in his dark eyes. "I cannot return your feelings. I will not allow it."

Allow it? "Why is that, Rayad? Because you enjoy being alone, or are you afraid of being vulnerable?"

"My fear would be for your emotional and physical safety. You are grateful for the attention I have given you, but you do not know me as well as you might think."

That made no sense whatsoever. "Unless you're some kind of ax murderer, I'm fairly sure I'm in no physical danger. And emotionally speaking, if you're intimating that I'm mistaking gratitude for love, you couldn't be more wrong. I know what it means to care that deeply for someone although I have to admit, I've never felt this strongly for anyone. Maybe you've never experienced that before, and if that's true, I feel sorry for you."

"This has nothing to do with my previous experience," he said. "If I continued an affair with you, I could be putting you in jeopardy."

Affair—that about said it all. "Is this because of your military ties?"

"That is partially true."

Just when she thought she was beginning to solve the puzzle, he introduced another piece. "What do you mean *partially*?"

"Leave it be, Sunny. There are things you do not want to know."

She hopped off the desk and moved in front of him. "I want to know everything about you, Rayad. I mistakenly believed I did. You definitely know everything about me, including details about the abduction I've never told anyone. It's only fair you return the favor by telling me what you've been hiding."

Indecision warred in his eyes before he returned to his stoic persona. "I do not dare tell you all there is to tell. I have already risked being tried for treason for breaching security by bringing you here. Rafiq would not object, but if the governing council knew, I could be hanged."

That was news to her. Distressing news. "And you're just now telling me this?"

"I felt it was worth the risk. You needed a respite in a place where you could heal."

Every moment they'd made love now somehow seemed false. "Thanks bunches for being my sheikh in shining armor, but here's a newsflash. I don't need to be rescued. I do need to know that when you made love to me, it meant something other than my consolation prize for being your bed buddy the past few days."

"You are not being reasonable. You knew this arrangement would only be short-term."

Every bitter emotion crowded in her at once, and if she didn't leave, she might actually cry. "Yes, I did know it wasn't going to be forever. I didn't know I'd be foolish enough to fall for your charms and mistake you for a decent guy capable of real emotions. And I'm really sorry I did. I'll go pack my things now."

When she started away, Rayad clasped her arm, preventing her from making a hasty exit. "I wish I could tell why it is not possible for us to be together," he said when she faced him. "But I cannot."

"Yes, you can. You owe me that much."

He hesitated as if he might have begun to waffle. "It is classified information."

She'd decided to give it another shot, and to make it a good one. "I really don't care about your government secrets, nor should you after what we've shared. You know that whatever you say will go no further than this room."

"You will never see me in the same light, and I would prefer we part while you still believe I am a man of honor."

Her belly tightened at the thought of what he could have done to make him believe she would toss him away like yesterday's trash. Her mind began to reel with the possibilities. He was a military man, and that position at times required many things, the least of which was violence. Still… "You said you're involved in intelligence. I always gathered that meant investigating insurgents and other covert activities."

"It does, but my duties go beyond that realm. They have for some time now."

Finally, she was getting somewhere. She just wasn't sure she would like where they were going. "If you're trying to protect me from the fact that you've killed someone, that's not necessary. I know the realities of warfare, and I understand that soldiers don't always have a choice. It's either kill or be killed. If that's the case with you, then I promise I won't think less of you."

A muscle ticked in his tightened jaw. "Again I implore you to leave it be, Sunny."

She couldn't leave it be, not until she had answers. Not until she quieted the warning bells in her head. "Tell me what you're hiding, or I'll walk out of here without you right this minute, even if I have to travel back to the palace on foot."

Turning his attention to some unknown focal point, Rayad remained silent for several excruciating moments. Sunny's heart began to beat faster while she waited for him to finally look her in the eye.

"I have always had a choice."

Her mind grew foggy with confusion. "I don't understand."

"If you must know everything, then I will tell you." She witnessed a flash of remorse in his eyes, then an intensity that shook her to the core as he said, "I have been trained to kill."

Nine

"You're an assassin?"

The indictment in Sunny's query had an unexpected impact on Rayad. He wanted and needed her respect, which would require details, no matter the consequences. "Trust me when I tell you my duty is necessary."

"Trust you?" She released a humorless laugh. "I'm standing in a cave with a man who intentionally shoots to kill. I slept with a killer. Forgive me if I find that a bit disturbing."

He moved forward, and when she backed away, he felt as if she had run him through with a blade. "Do you understand that if I wanted to harm you, I would have already done so?"

She seemed to mull that over for a moment. "This

isn't about me. It's about what you do. I can't begin to imagine intentionally taking someone's life."

She could not imagine the monsters he had seen. "Would you feel more comfortable if I told you my services have rarely been needed?"

"Exactly how many have there been?"

If he told her, he'd been further crossing into treacherous territory, and not because of the minimal incidents. "I pledged my loyalty and silence when I assumed my military obligation. Any admission would be a direct betrayal to my country."

"Failure to admit it will only make me worry about my judgment when it comes to men."

He despised that she would doubt herself, or his intentions. Therefore, he would supply the answers she needed. "Two men. One had been plotting to set off a bomb in the middle of the village at the behest of a radical coalition based north of Bajul. The other planned to gun down Rafiq's father during a public event. I was charged with protecting the former king."

"I see. The assassin destroyed the assassin. Makes perfect sense." The cynicism in her voice said otherwise.

"As difficult as it might be for you to believe, I was forced into this position." Now that he had revealed too much, he braced for more questions.

"Explain how someone is forced to become a killer."

He was torn between remaining silent and telling her the entire truth. To return to that part of his past would be painful, and he hated to resurrect those long-buried emotions. To refuse the woman who had boldly admitted her love for him would be unforgivable.

Rather than search for the words, he chose to show her. "If you want answers, then you must come with me to a place where you will find them."

She folded her arms beneath her breasts. "Before I agree to do this, you have to give me more information about where you are taking me."

The fact he had destroyed her trust wounded him deeply. "It is a site in the desert not far from here." He looked down at her bare feet. "Our hike will require appropriate shoes."

"I don't care if I have to don a parka and knee boots, as long as I can solve this mystery."

"As soon as you dress, I will meet you at the entry of the bunker."

"Fine. I won't be long."

After Sunny departed, Rayad questioned his wisdom, and if he would be able to provide all the information she needed to understand why he had lost his soul, and his way. Why his heart had been broken beyond repair. Why he could never be the man she needed.

The sweltering heat began to take its toll on Sunny as they trekked through several passages on rocky ground. After twenty minutes of unsuccessfully trying to keep up with her guide, she rounded one giant stone formation and entered open desert. She caught sight of Rayad standing atop a dune and headed toward him to see why he had stopped. Hopefully, they'd arrived at their destination, though she saw nothing other than desolate terrain devoid of all forms of life. But when she climbed the sand hill and came to his side, she viewed a veritable oasis in the middle of nowhere, with an olive grove on one side, along with palm trees and varied plants on the other. In the middle of all the unexpected greenery, another sight sent shockwaves coursing through her. A massive pile of stone and charred wood, soaring to at least thirty feet, if not more, marred the inviting landscape.

"What is this place?" she asked, once she'd recovered enough to speak.

"The key to my past."

When Rayad began to stride toward the ruins, adrenaline gave Sunny a burst of energy, and she matched him step for step. He stopped at a tangled metal structure that appeared to have once been a gate and took a seat on what was left of the stone support.

She claimed the spot beside him and waited for further explanation. When it didn't come, she opted to prod him. "Tell me about this place and what happened here, Rayad."

"This was once my palace," he said with surprising detachment. "It was destroyed in an explosion."

She'd predicted a fire had caused its demise. Wasn't the first time she'd been wrong today. "Was anyone hurt?"

"Two of my staff members were killed, and there were others."

As much as she hated that innocent employees had lost their lives, the *others* greatly interested her. "Who else was here?"

"My wife and our three-year-old son."

She'd mistakenly believed she wouldn't be stunned anymore today. "You told me you'd never been married."

"I told you I was not presently married."

When she thought back to their initial conversation, she realized he was right. In fact, she recalled he'd evaded the question, and she'd sensed a story behind that evasion. Time to get to the bottom of that story. "This wasn't an accident, was it?" she asked, though she knew the answer.

"It was not."

Now everything had begun to become crystal clear, except for pertinent details. "Who did this?"

He momentarily covered his face with both hands before returning his attention to the destruction. "Some vengeful person who wished to strip me of all that I held dear."

At the sound of the abject sorrow in his voice, Sunny fought to hold back her own emotions. "I am so, so sorry, Rayad. I hope the perpetrator suffered for his acts."

He fisted his hands resting on his thighs. "I have never discovered the murderer's identity, though I have spent ten years searching for the evil miscreant who destroyed my home and my life."

"And this is what led you to become an assassin."

"Yes. I used my connections in an effort to root him out, and on the day I finally confront him, I will kill him on sight."

"What if that day never comes?"

"I will not stop searching until I find them, or draw my last breath. I owe that to my wife and child."

The quest for revenge had obviously consumed him for years, and still did. "I don't know anything about your wife, but if she was like most women, she wouldn't want you wasting your life on a futile mission to avenge her death."

Rayad stood and began to pace, hands knitted together behind his neck. "Lira was not like most women. She was kind and gentle and a superior mother. She worshipped our son, Layth, as well as myself."

At least now she had names to go with his family, and a strong sense of sympathy for his plight. "I can't imagine what you've had to endure, but I do hope that someday you'll try to be happy."

He kept pacing liked a caged cougar, as if he couldn't physically stand still without succumbing to the sorrow. He also avoided looking at her. "I cannot be happy until I avenge my family's deaths by destroying their killer."

"And if that happens, will you truly be content knowing you exchanged one life for another?"

"Four lives," he said adamantly as he turned toward her. "I will achieve some semblance of atonement for my transgressions. Had it not been for my duty, they would still be alive."

She pushed off the stone pillar and stood before him. "But you still have no idea who might be responsible."

"I have followed several leads, but all have been dead ends. I still have more to investigate, including enemies of my father."

Evidently, he was into self-torture. "Then you're saying this tragedy could have resulted from your father's connections, and you might not be responsible at all?"

He dropped his arms to his sides and looked defiant. "That possibility is remote at best. Regardless, I moved Lira and Layth to this remote location to protect them. I failed in that endeavor and by virtue of the fact I should have been there that night. My covert activities prevented me from achieving that goal."

"And if you'd been there, you would be dead, too."

"In the beginning I wished that very thing. My mission aided me in moving forward."

"You're not moving forward, Rayad. You're caught in a prison comprised of guilt and hatred."

His expression went stone cold. "Have you not wished ill will on your captors?"

"As a matter of fact, I have. I've fantasized about tying my abductor up in a heavy blanket and beating him with a baseball bat. My therapist said that was healthy, as long as I didn't act on it. I thought that was kind of humorous since I can't harm a phantom."

"And you have never desired to know his identity?"

"What would be the point? It's done, and it's over. The experience has made me more cautious and maybe a little fearful. But I'm determined to get over that rather than let the experience stifle me. Believe it or not, you helped me to see the importance in regaining my life. I'm sorry you can't seem to regain yours."

He turned his attention back to the monument of destruction. "We should return to the palace now. And again I remind you not to mention this to anyone. Very few people know about my past."

"Does that include my sister?"

"Yes. Adan is bound to his promise to me not to speak of it with anyone, including his wife."

"Don't worry," she said. "Your secrets are all safe with me. Good luck carrying them to your grave."

As she walked away, Sunny realized all too well that nothing she said to Rayad would ever break through his resolve to remain static in his life. If he chose to remain immersed in his grief and his search for retaliation, so be it.

He could never be the man for her, and that made her incredibly sad. Even worse, he would never let himself love again, and she couldn't save him from that fate. She wouldn't even try.

"Well?"

After a silent drive to the palace, and an uncomfortable family dinner, Sunny had retired to her suite to unpack and get some sleep. That plan had been thwarted by her sister, who now hovered over her like a mother hen. "Well what, Piper?"

"Did you enjoy your time with Rayad?"

Until today, she could confirm that had been the case. "It was nice while it lasted."

Piper sent her a suspicious look. "Did the two of you...you know."

Unfortunately, she did know what her twin was intimating and decided to throw her a bone. "Yes, we did *you know*. Several times. Are you happy now?"

"Question is, Sunny, are you happy? I'm thinking the answer is no."

She tossed the last of her clothes onto the bureau and her tote in a nearby chair. "Look, we had a good time, it was great, but it's over. End of story."

Piper perched on the edge of the mattress and stared like a hawk scoping out its prey. "If he did something to hurt you, tell me, and I'll have Adan deal with him."

Sunny shoved the bag aside and practically collapsed into the chair. "He didn't do anything to hurt me, so I don't need you to ask your husband to beat him up. We're both adults, and we knew whatever transpired was only temporary. Now if you don't mind, it's late, and I'd like to get to bed."

Her sister put on a stellar pout and pushed up from the bed. "Okay. I know when I'm not wanted. But I want all the dirty details before you leave in two weeks, even if I have to force you to talk."

As much as she hated to drop a bad news bomb, Sunny felt she had no choice. "On that subject," she began as she stood, "I'm probably going to leave in a couple of days. I'm ready to get back to work."

"We've barely had time to talk, Sunny. Won't you reconsider staying at least a week?"

She might if she didn't have to face Rayad on a daily basis. Then again, he could be leaving shortly to return to his mission of death and destruction. "I'll think about it as soon as I get a good night's sleep."

Piper came to her feet. "Fine. I'll leave as soon as you answer one more question."

Great. Just great. "Make it quick."

"Where exactly did you stay?"

In a mystical cavern in the company of a mysterious,

tortured, gorgeous man. "Some primitive place near a small village."

"No room service?"

She'd been serviced, and often. "Definitely not. There was only one bed, but it was decent."

"I'm surprised you even noticed the bed when you had a hunk occupying it with you. If he's anything like Adan, you didn't even need a bed."

With that, Piper grinned and rushed out of the room before Sunny could launch a verbal retaliation.

Weary and worn out, Sunny took her second shower of the day, brushed her teeth and hair, dressed in her favorite blue silk sleep shirt and slipped beneath the covers. Her mind wouldn't seem to shut off and allow her to sleep, so she turned on the bedside lamp and attempted to read the mystery novel she'd brought with her. She couldn't concentrate, thanks to the mental slideshow featuring wonderful moments with Rayad. At times the recollections caused her face to flush, and other memories made her heartsick. At least an hour passed before she finally gave in to the lure of sleep.

"I need you…"

Sunny came awake with a start, at first believing she'd been dreaming. But as her vision came into focus, she saw her dream man standing next to the bed, dressed in only a pair of navy pajama bottoms. "What are you doing here?"

"I need to be next to you one last night, though I know I do not deserve it."

He looked so lost and forlorn, she scooted over and lifted the covers. "Okay, but just so you know, we're only going to sleep."

"I understand," he said as he slid into the bed beside her.

As he stacked his hands behind his head, she rolled to her side to face him. "Too much on your mind to rest?" she asked, breaking the silence.

"Yes."

"I had the same problem. I'd just drifted off right before you arrived."

"My apologies for waking you." He sent her a fast glance before going back to inspecting the ceiling. "If you wish me to leave, I will do so."

"I *wish* you would talk to me, Rayad. Let me in, and let me know what you're thinking."

He exhaled a rough sigh. "It would be too difficult."

"It would be cathartic."

When he failed to respond, Sunny assumed he was bent on ignoring her suggestion. Then suddenly he said, "My code name is Lion."

She hadn't expected that revelation. "Okay. Why are you telling me this now?"

"Layth means lion. I took it in honor of my son."

She inched closer to his side, drawn to his undeniable grief. "Did the name suit him as well as it does you?"

His ensuing smile looked so very sad. "It did. He was a very brave boy. Highly intelligent. Always in motion and into trouble at times. Yet he had a very caring side to him. He inherited that from his mother."

"He inherited some of that from you."

The comment drew his gaze. "How can you believe that when you know who I am and what I am capable of doing?"

She wanted to scream from frustration. "It's not fundamentally who you are, Rayad. It's a bitter force that drives you to try to be that man. You'll never be able to succeed because believe it or not, there's still too much good in you."

"I am beyond redemption," he said as he reached over and snapped off the light.

Against better judgment, Sunny settled her cheek on his chest. "You're so very wrong. It's obvious you loved your wife, and I suspect she loved you, too."

"You are correct. I loved her the first time I set eyes on her."

On one hand, Sunny wasn't sure she wanted to know all the details. On the other, she had the opportunity to finally glimpse the real man behind the steely exterior. "When did the two of you meet?"

"The night our fathers announced our betrothal."

Incredible. An arranged marriage that had gone right, until fate took a wrong turn. "How old were you when you married?"

"I was nineteen, and she had barely turned eighteen. Layth was born two years later. That was the most monumental day of my life." He paused and drew in a breath before continuing. "I remember how it felt the first time I held my son in my arms. I recall his first smile and the day he took his first steps when I returned from a month-long mission. For many years I have rejected those memories, but lately I cannot."

"You shouldn't deny them, Rayad. Letting yourself remember will help you finally heal."

"The loss has left a wound in my soul that will never heal."

"Have you ever cried for them?" she asked.

"No. I feared if I did, I would never stop. No man should live long enough to bury his beloved wife and child."

The slight break in his voice made Sunny want to cry for him. Instead, she moved closer and held him tighter. They stayed that way for a long time, until Rayad pulled her to him and kissed her with all the passion she had come to know in his arms. Before long, they were naked and touching each other without restraint. And when it came time to consummate their temporary, troubled union one final time, Sunny let go of her own fears and pulled him on top of her. She relished his weight, the closeness of his powerful body as he moved inside her. She welcomed her climax and loved the way he said her name when he found his own release. She loved him, period, with all her heart and soul.

In the aftermath, Rayad was so still, she thought he'd fallen asleep. But then he shifted back beside her, draped his arm across her abdomen and laid his cheek against her shoulder. That's when she felt the dampness on her flesh. That's when she knew he had finally given in to the tears that were long overdue. That's when she started to hope that maybe, just maybe, the healing had truly begun.

"Wake up, Sunshine. It's happening!"

Sunny pried her eyes open, glanced at Piper then remembered Rayad's late-night visit. She turned her head to see only an empty space beside her, and for once she appreciated his habit of sneaking off without waking her.

She sat up against the headboard and yawned. "Okay, Pookie. What's got your drawers in a wad this morning?"

"Maysa's in labor. Actually, she's been in labor all night. The doctor says it should be any time now."

"Why aren't you at the hospital?"

Piper rolled her eyes. "She's not in the hospital. She's in her suite. Apparently, tradition dictates that a future king is born at the palace, barring any emergency."

Of all the archaic practices, this had to top the list. "What if she has to have a C-section?"

Piper plopped down on the end of the bed. "According to Rafiq, they've prepared for that and have a makeshift operating room set up in the basement and an ambulance standing by. But it looks like she's going to deliver without any problems."

Sunny threw the covers aside, thankful she'd put on a T-shirt last night, and that she didn't find any obvious evidence of Rayad's presence. "I'll take a quick shower and join you."

"Meet me upstairs in the family sitting room," Piper said on her way to the door. "But hurry. I want you to be there when they bring the baby out. No one knows if it's a boy or a girl."

"I bet it's one or the other," Sunny called to her sister, but the snide comment clearly feel on deaf ears.

As much as she liked Rafiq and Maysa, she wasn't in the mood to celebrate a birth. But the prospect of seeing Rayad again drove her from the bed to complete her morning routine. Provided he actually showed up.

He did not want to be there, yet family loyalty overrode his wants and desires. He had been watching the clock for well over an hour, when he had not been thinking about his night with Sunny.

As if those memories had come to life, she appeared in the doorway, dressed in the flowing blue caftan he had purchased for her in the village and a pair of gold sandals. She looked as beautiful as she had the first time he had seen her standing beneath the palace portico. Her blond hair curled around her slender shoulders, bringing to mind the times he had kissed her there. He took a visual journey across her face, his gaze coming to rest on her lips to find her smile was absent. He was to blame for that, as well as the sadness in her eyes.

Following the lead of the rest of the men present in the room, Rayad came to his feet, battling the urge to go to her and kiss her soundly. For that reason, he thought it best to avoid her at all costs.

As unwelcome fate would have it, she crossed the room and claimed the chair next to his. "Did you finally get some sleep?" she asked with a smile.

"Some," he muttered. "And you?"

"Same here. Are you okay?"

He recognized the referral to his emotional breakdown, a subject he did not wish to broach. "I am ready to return to my duties."

"Of course you are."

The venom in her tone filled him with regret, and

the wish that he could be the man who would grant her every desire. An impossible undertaking.

When the conversation ceased, Rayad grabbed a magazine from the side table and pretended to read. The room remained abuzz with speculation over the child's gender, creating an atmosphere that hindered his concentration. Having Sunny so close did not help his predicament, either.

If only he could find an excuse to leave before the birth, yet that would be too obvious. If only the queen would get on with it.

"Ladies and gentlemen, may I have your attention please."

Rayad glanced up from the magazine to see the balding, bespectacled Deeb, the palace's executive assistant, standing in the entry. The man cleared his throat twice before he garnered everyone's attention.

"It is with great pride, and the parents' blessing, that I present to you Bajul's newest royal son, Prince Ahmed ibn Rafiq Mehdi."

A son. Rayad froze the moment Rafiq walked into the room, the infant cradled in his arms. All the memories he had tried so mightily to keep at bay came rushing in on him. The crowd gathered around the newborn thwarted any escape, and he realized Sunny was at the forefront of the celebration.

"May I hold him?" he heard her ask, and Rafiq granted her request, though Rayad found that odd since she was not a blood relative.

He also found it odd that she seemed to be approaching him, her gaze unwavering. He was completely astonished when she arrived and handed him the child. "This is what it's all about, Rayad. This new baby is a sign that life does go on even during the darkest of times."

He looked down on the sleeping child and remembered, not with bitterness and regret, but with wonder. He silently welcomed this boy into the world and prayed that no harm would ever come to him. Yet when the pain of remembrance became too great, he intended to hand him back to Sunny, and found her gone.

And there he stood, holding a child that was not his, and with little hope of ever having another.

Ten

Sunny wasn't surprised when Rayad stormed into the suite, primed for a confrontation. That had been her plan all along. A chance to implement Sunny's Last Stand.

"You had no right or cause to put me through such agony," he said, his voice teeming with fury.

She kept right on packing her toiletries, as if he'd told her he appreciated the gesture. "Like it or not, you needed a wake-up call."

He strode across the room and stood at the foot of the bed, hands fisted at his sides like he wanted to throw a punch. "That is not for you to decide."

She afforded him only a brief glance before resuming her preparation for departure. "Someone had to do it, Rayad, and it might as well be me."

"I resent your intrusion."

After zipping the carry-on, she calmly picked it up from the bench and then set it on the floor with the larger bag. Only then did she give him her full attention. "As of tomorrow, I'll be out of here and out of your life for good."

"Where are you going?"

Funny, he sounded almost disappointed. "Back to Atlanta then back to work."

"Why so soon?"

"I'd think that would be obvious. This palace isn't big enough for the both of us. As long as you're here, I can't get over you, and that is unacceptable. But before I go, I have a few things I need to say."

He took the chair in the corner, crossed his slack-covered legs like a gentleman, and said, "Please. Be my guest. That should allow me time to calm enough not to say something I will later regret."

She chose the bedpost spot that he'd recently vacated to give it her best effort before giving up. "First, I sincerely didn't mean to hurt you today by handing you the baby. I only wanted to force you to realize that life renews itself, if only you'll let it. My mistake."

He streaked a hand over his jaw. "We have been through this before."

"Secondly," she continued. "I love you, Rayad. More than you will ever know. But I won't stay another minute and watch you die inside a little more each day because you can't forgive yourself."

He uncrossed his legs and lowered his head. "I do not merit forgiveness."

She went to him, knelt down and laid her hands on

his thighs. "Yes, you do. And someday you'll wake up alone and realize you've missed out on a future full of happiness and love. Do you really want to face that, or would you rather spend your days with a woman who both loves and accepts you unconditionally?"

He took her hands, came to his feet while simultaneously pulling her into his arms. They embraced for several moments before he let her go and sought her eyes. "I do not understand what you see in me, Sunny, nor do I understand how you so readily accepted my many transgressions. I am honored to have met such a remarkable woman."

There it was—the inevitable goodbye. She refused to shed a tear, even though they threatened to make an appearance. She'd rather part on good terms and a smile, which she gave him. "I'm not so remarkable, Rayad. I'm just your average girl who hopes to one day find a guy who loves her like crazy."

"I wish that could be me. Since it cannot, I have no doubt you will find a man who better deserves you."

Hard for her to imagine that now that she'd found the best. Too bad he didn't realize it. "Thanks for the optimistic outlook on my future partner, and most important, for giving me back my confidence."

"It was always there, Sunny. You did not need my assistance, only minimal prodding. Rest assured I would not take back those moments with you, and our lovemaking meant more to me than you realize."

If she didn't get away from him now, she would have a total meltdown. In an effort to prevent that, Sunny headed to the desk in the corner, retrieved a piece of royal stationery, and jotted down her personal information. When she was done, she willed her composure to return before she went back to him and offered him the paper. "This is my temporary address until I find a new apartment, and my cell phone number. Should you happen to find yourself in Atlanta, stop by and see me. And if you change your mind and decide, miracle of all miracles, you want to give us a chance, give me a call. If you don't, call me anyway if you'd like, just so I know you're okay. That is, when you're not packing an AK-47 and searching for bad guys, of course." She attempted a smile, but she was sure it fell flat.

He stared at the page for a few moments before centering his gaze on hers. "I can make no promises."

"I know that," she said, her eyes beginning to mist. "Just promise me you'll at least try to be safe."

"I will try."

She gave in to her need to hold him again, and he thankfully accepted her embrace. He also gave her a gentle kiss that only served to shatter her heart a little more. Then he left without looking back, or saying goodbye.

After the door closed behind him, signifying the end to an unforgettable chapter in her life, Sunny stretched out across the bed and cried.

For seven long days she had been gone. For seven long nights he had missed her company.

Rayad could only think of one way to abandon all thoughts of Sunny McAdams and bring his mind back to the ever-present mission.

For that reason, he dressed in uniform and sought out his commander-in-chief. "I am respectfully requesting my immediate return to active duty, Adan."

His cousin did not bother to rise from the chair when he'd strode into the office without announcing his arrival. Nor did Adan look surprised by the request.

"The answer to that is no, Rayad. You have yet to be medically cleared."

"I am completely recovered."

"We'll see what the physician says about that."

Fortunately he had prepared for this argument. "I saw him earlier this morning and he pronounced me quite well. If you do not trust me, call him."

"I will most certainly do that," Adan said. "And then *I* will determine if I believe you are not only mentally but physically ready to return to work."

Rayad braced his hands on the desk and leaned forward. "If my memory serves me correctly, you summoned me back to the palace last week because you were in need of my services, yet you have avoided me since my return."

Adan tossed the pen he'd been gripping aside and watched it roll onto the floor. "I lied about the mission."

His blood began to boil over the deception. "Why?"

"Because of my concern for my sister-in-law's well-being."

"I did not harm her, nor would I."

"Not intentionally," Adan said. "But Piper believes you didn't help her, either. In fact, my wife is convinced you're the reason she departed earlier than planned."

He could deny that conjecture, but then he would

be telling a falsehood. "She is preparing to resume her career."

Adan inclined his head and studied him straight on. "Are you certain about that? Sunny seemed fairly down in the dumps when she left, not to mention I've been informed you took advantage of her during your respite."

One more insult, and they might come to blows, as they had a time or two in their youth. "No advantage was taken. Sunny and I are adults, and what transpired between us was consensual."

This time Adan leaned forward and glared at him. "I know you, Rayad. After your wife's death, you used your mysterious charm and machismo to pull women into your tangled web. Then you would leave them high and dry with a wounded heart."

He felt the need to defend himself, despite the truth in his cousin's acerbic comments. "What I shared with Sunny was very different. She is different. I care a great deal for her. More than I have cared for any woman in years. I would never intentionally cause her any pain, emotional or physical. Still, I am not the man for her, and that is why I was forced to let her go, although I despised every second of it."

Adan suddenly began to laugh. "Bloody hell, Rayad, you're in love with her."

He straightened from the shock of hearing his name in relationship to that word. "I did not say that."

"You didn't have to say it. It is written all over your lovesick face."

Rayad realized Adan was correct in his assumption. He had fallen in love with the beautiful journalist. He loved her still, and most likely always would love her. Yet one issue still prevented him from exploring their relationship further—he had yet to find those responsible for murdering his wife and child. "Regardless of my feelings, I cannot act on them."

Adan chose that moment to stand, sending the rolling chair backward into the bookshelf behind him. "Are you daft, Rayad? Of course you can act on them. Nothing is holding you here. You have more money than you can spend, and you no longer have a home to speak of. I will grant you an extended leave to get your head on straight and go after her, the same as I went after my wife. I have not once regretted that decision, and neither will you."

The suggestion seemed to make sense, yet he harbored several concerns. "I have not found my family's killers. She would never understand my need to complete that mission."

His cousin leaned forward and glared at him. "Perhaps it's time to move on from that mission."

Had Adan suggested that before Sunny, Rayad would have immediately rejected that notion. "If I did decide to seek her out, though I am not claiming I will, she most likely would refuse to see me."

"My bride also happened to tell me Sunny gave you her number and address," Adan said. "That is not the action of a woman who doesn't want to see you."

Another correct assessment, followed by more internal debate. "If I pursued a relationship with Sunny, I would be giving up all that I have gained in my career. I would be giving up on avenging my wife and child's deaths."

"And the gifts you would receive in return would be tenfold." Adan sighed. "Just remember, retaliation won't bring your wife and child back, Rayad. You should put the past to rest, otherwise, your futile quest will rob you of a future with Sunny. Honor your wife and son by learning to love again."

His cousin's logic only served to confuse him. "I will take your advice into consideration, but I make no promises."

"Fine, but don't wait too long to decide. And should you need to pay Sunny a visit, I will personally fly you to the States myself."

"In the meantime, I will report for duty at the base in the morning," he said as he walked away from his well-meaning cousin.

Rayad left the office in a state of turmoil. He could not go to Sunny unless he was prepared to discard his need for revenge. He could not give his all to her unless he learned to forgive himself. He could not move forward in his life unless he prepared to let go of the past.

Until he was absolutely certain he could manage all those things, he would return to his mission with only memories of a very special woman who had changed him in many ways through her unconditional acceptance. If that certainty did not come, he would face spending the rest of his days alone. And for the first time in many, many years, that concept no longer appealed to him.

He had much to decide and hoped he arrived at the correct decision. Only time would tell.

When the bell rang, Sunny was just about ready to give the pizza guy a good piece of her mind for taking two hours to deliver her dinner. Poised to do that very thing, she threw open the door, only to find not some skinny adolescent, but her erstwhile lover and favorite tough guy. She opened her mouth, closed it then opened it again. "Is this a mirage?"

He cracked a crooked smile. "No mirage. May I come in?"

"Of course. Have a seat and take a load off."

He sent her a confused look as he breezed past her then dropped down on the lounger next to the sofa. It took a minute for Sunny to move, and she was trembling so badly she thought she might shake right out of her fuzzy purple slippers.

After she sat down on the couch, she stared at him a moment, expecting him to disappear. "If I'd known you were coming, I would've baked cookies. Or at least dressed in something nicer than sweats and a hoodie."

"You look as beautiful as I remember."

So did he in his navy sport coat, matching slacks and white shirt. "Mind telling me why you're here?"

"I have been doing a lot of thinking since you left Bajul."

"About?"

"Us."

"And?"

He leaned forward, his hands clasped before his

parted knees, his usual position when he was about to get all serious. "I returned to duty for a few days, yet I could not stop remembering our time together. I could not discard that the danger I frequently face might take me away from you permanently."

I will not hope. I will not hope... "But we're not really together, Rayad."

"And that is why I am here." He hesitated a moment before he spoke again. "You have been right about many things, Sunny, the least of which involves my inability to regain my life. I want to change."

She leaned across the end table and touched his arm. "You can, Rayad. You will."

"I am still not certain that is true. I know I cannot accomplish that without your help, yet I question if it would be fair to ask that of you."

Hope crept back in despite her determination to stop it. "I can only help if you let me, and that's going to be difficult if you're determined to find your family's killer."

"I have taken a leave from the military, with Adan's blessing."

Once again she was shocked senseless. "Does Adan know about us?"

He leaned back and rubbed his chin. "He does. He was instrumental in convincing me to seek you out. He went so far as to pilot the plane that brought me to Atlanta once I decided to come here."

The next time she saw her brother-in-law, she was going to give him a big sisterly kiss. "I can only imagine that conversation."

"He told me that he regretted almost letting your sister go, but he doesn't regret seeking her out and making a life with her."

"It's obvious he doesn't."

His gaze drifted away before he leveled it on her again. "Would you be willing to return to Bajul with me?"

"Why would I do that when I just got back from there a month ago?"

"Because I wish to be with you."

"For how long?"

"Until we determine if we are suited for each other."

Not quite good enough, but close. "I can't throw away my career and run off with you on the chance that you might want to seriously pursue a relationship."

"You could still work and be based in Bajul."

Damn his logic. "That still doesn't diminish the risk I'd be taking, especially since you've never really said how you truly feel about me."

"Would you take that risk if I told you I love you?"

Exactly what she wanted to hear, but could she believe him? "How do you know you love me?"

He rose from the chair to join her on the sofa and wrapped one arm around her shoulder. "For the past few weeks, my nightmares have been replaced with dreams of you, when I happened to actually sleep. You are all I have thought about, and the ache over the loss of you has been unbearable. I know I do not deserve your forgiveness for my disregard, but I implore you—"

"Shut up and kiss me, Rayad."

He did as she asked, melding his lips to hers in a meaningful, heartfelt kiss.

Once they parted, she asked the question foremost on her mind. "If I do decide to return with you, where will we stay?"

"That is a dilemma. I would offer the cavern, but it will soon be filled with military trainees. Perhaps I should stay here for a time. I have seen little of the United States, and I have never explored Georgia."

"That sounds just peachy," she said, even knowing the Southern reference would be lost on him. "Do you honestly believe we can make this work after knowing each other such a short time?"

"Do you still love me?"

She laid her head on his shoulder. "Yes, I do."

"Will you always accept my faults and failures?"

"If you'll accept mine."

"Then I do believe we have a chance at a bright future."

"So do I." And she did.

"Someday I hope to have another child."

Only then did she know for sure he was ready to move on. "I'd like to have children, too, at some point in time."

"I am happy to hear that. And in the very near future, you should know I plan make you my bride."

She reared back and stared at him. "Hold your horses, Arabian cowboy. Let's slow down a bit. First we need to get each to know each other better before we even consider going down that road."

He pressed a kiss on her cheek. "I agree, yet I will

warn you I am not always a patient man, and I can be very persuasive."

"That might be true," she said. "But it's going to take more than pretty words and a lot of good sex to convince me we need to get married anytime soon."

He gave her a wink and a patently sexy smile. "We shall see."

She winked back. "Yes, we will."

"By the power vested in me by the great state of Georgia, I now pronounce you husband and wife."

And there, a scant three months later, while standing on the lawn of a gorgeous antebellum mansion before a few friends and family, Sunny McAdams-Rostam swallowed her pride and ate her words.

Fortunately, the kiss her new husband planted on her lips made the harried decision to jump headlong into wedded bliss seem completely worthwhile. So did the fact he looked incredible in a tuxedo. And he was rich as chocolate. So rich he'd bought her the house serving as the majestic background. Not that his money ever mattered, nor would it.

But that wealth did enable them to take an extended honeymoon in Milan following the ceremony, as suggested by Adan, who as Rayad's best man, now followed behind them as they walked back down the aisle, the matron of honor—her twin—on his arm.

When they passed the last row of chairs, Sunny leaned over to Rayad and whispered, "Do you think they have caves in Italy?"

"I am certain if they do, we will find them."

They shared a laugh as they strolled to the gazebo where the reception was being held. Once they arrived, they paused for a picture with the attendants, greeted a few guests then unfortunately parted ways when Adan took Rayad aside for an impromptu military conference.

Piper approached her then and gave her a hug. "You look fantastic in that wedding gown, Sunshine. Satin and strapless suit you well."

Sunny surveyed the bridesmaid gown from hem to neck. "You don't look so bad yourself, Pookie. And you said you couldn't wear red."

"I look like a large tomato," she said, her hand automatically going to her belly. "It's only going to get worse when I move into the second trimester."

She gave her sister a squeeze. "I can't wait to have another nephew or niece."

"I can't wait to stop throwing up morning, noon and night." Piper's features turned solemn. "Are you happy, Sunny?"

"I can't begin to tell you how happy I am. I never thought I would find anyone who is so much in sync with me, and in many ways, like me."

"So he's stubborn and bites everyone's head off in the morning?"

"Very funny, Pookie."

"Bite me, Sunshine."

"Honestly, I'd rather have something to eat. Lately I can't seem to get enough food."

Piper eyed her suspiciously. "Is there a reason for that?"

She should have known her twin would unearth her biggest secret. "Yes, there is, but I haven't told Rayad yet."

"You're going to have a baby, too?"

Sunny grabbed Piper's arm and pulled her away from the guests. "Please keep your voice down. I don't want to have to explain this to Nana and Poppa, and I sure don't want my husband to learn the news from a stranger before I have a chance to tell him."

"What news would that be?"

Sunny took her attention from her sister and gave it to said husband, who was standing to her left. "Just something I learned a couple of days ago."

Piper stepped back, a sheepish look on her face. "I believe that's my cue to give the bride and groom some alone time." She then had the nerve to give Rayad a hug and tell him, "Congratulations on the wedding, and what you're about to find out."

When Piper practically sprinted away, her low ponytail swinging in the March breeze, Rayad turned to Sunny, his face fraught with confusion. "Would you please tell me what she meant by that comment?"

She set her bouquet aside on a bench and hooked her arm through his. "Yes, I will gladly tell you, while we're taking a walk."

They took a stroll through the manicured gardens washed in gold due to the setting sun. "I still can't believe you gave me this place as a wedding gift," Sunny said after a time.

"Nothing is too good for my bride," he replied. "I personally cannot believe you continue to avoid telling me this news."

That would take a great deal of courage, and moving on to the topic slowly. "I've been thinking I'd like to put in a pool in the back of the house. It gets really hot in Atlanta during the summer, kind of like the desert."

"That is your news?"

She swallowed hard. "I'll get to that shortly. I've also been thinking the side yard would be a good place to put a play yard with swings and slides and maybe monkey bars. Of course, we'd wait until we get back from the honeymoon before we do that."

"Why would we need a play yard at this point in time?"

She lifted her bare shoulders in a shrug. "Well, Sam will be using it when Piper and Adan bring him for a visit. Zain and Madison would appreciate having a place for the twins to play when they come later this summer since they couldn't make the wedding. And of course, Rafiq and Maysa and their little boy will surely stop in at some point in time. Also, we'll need to add a baby swing for our son or daughter within the next year."

He stopped dead in his tracks and turned her toward him. "You would be willing to conceive a child within a year?"

The moment of truth had arrived. "We've already conceived a child, honey. That's my real news."

Myriad emotions passed over his face, beginning with puzzlement and ending with awareness. "You are pregnant."

"Yes, I am. About six weeks. And just so you're clear, I didn't plan this. I did forget to take my pills two days during all the wedding planning chaos." When he didn't offer a response, she grew worried. "How do you feel about this bombshell?"

"Concerned," he said. "Afraid."

Not at all what she'd wanted to hear. "What are you afraid of?"

"That I might not be able to keep you both safe at all times."

She formed her palm to his face. "Rayad, life doesn't come with guarantees, but mothers have babies every day without incident. Look at Maysa. She gave birth to a nine-pounder naturally. They're both doing fine."

"I understand that, yet I still cannot help but remember my failures."

She didn't have to ask about those presumed failures. "It's going to take time to work through this, honey, and I'll be there with you every step of the way. I only hope that when you hold our baby in your arms for the first time, you'll realize you've been given a second chance."

He clasped her hands and touched the band he had placed on her left finger less than an hour ago. "I promise you now I will not go back."

"To the military?"

"To that place where I became trapped in a hell of my own making. I will move forward with my life, as long as you are by my side. And I will endeavor to protect you to the best of my ability."

"No guns involved, I hope."

He finally smiled. "No more guns from this point forward."

"I love you, my sweet, strong husband. Always."

"As I love you, my beloved wife. For eternity."

After they sealed their commitment to each other with the second kiss of the evening, Sunny felt truly blessed to have found a really nice guy beneath that stoic exterior. Her remarkable lover. Her retired assassin. Her one true love, now and forevermore.

* * * * *

If you loved this novel, don't miss
these other sexy sheikh stories
from Kristi Gold:

ONE NIGHT WITH THE SHEIKH
THE SHEIKH'S SON
EXPECTING THE SHEIKH'S BABY
THE RETURN OF THE SHEIKH

MILLS & BOON®

Want to get more from Mills & Boon?

Here's what's available to you if you join the exclusive **Mills & Boon eBook Club** today:

✦ *Convenience – choose your books each month*
✦ *Exclusive – receive your books a month before anywhere else*
✦ *Flexibility – change your subscription at any time*
✦ *Variety – gain access to eBook-only series*
✦ *Value – subscriptions from just £1.99 a month*

So visit **www.millsandboon.co.uk/esubs** today to be a part of this exclusive eBook Club!

MILLS & BOON®

Desire™

PASSIONATE AND DRAMATIC LOVE STORIES

MILLS & BOON®

Why shop at millsandboon.co.uk?

Each year, thousands of romance readers find their perfect read at millsandboon.co.uk. That's because we're passionate about bringing you the very best romantic fiction. Here are some of the advantages of shopping at www.millsandboon.co.uk:

* **Get new books first**—you'll be able to buy your favourite books one month before they hit the shops

* **Get exclusive discounts**—you'll also be able to buy our specially created monthly collections, with up to 50% off the RRP

* **Find your favourite authors**—latest news, interviews and new releases for all your favourite authors and series on our website, plus ideas for what to try next

* **Join in**—once you've bought your favourite books, don't forget to register with us to rate, review and join in the discussions

Visit **www.millsandboon.co.uk**
for all this and more today!